DOCTOR IN THE HOUSE

DOCTOR AT SEA

Doctor in the House

Doctor at Sea

RICHARD GORDON

THE REPRINT SOCIETY
LONDON

Doctor in the House FIRST PUBLISHED 1952
Doctor at Sea FIRST PUBLISHED 1953
THIS COMBINED EDITION PUBLISHED BY THE REPRINT SOCIETY LTD.
BY ARRANGEMENT WITH MICHAEL JOSEPH LTD. 1955

PRINTED IN GREAT BRITAIN BY
HAZELL WATSON AND VINEY LTD
AYLESBURY AND LONDON

DOCTOR IN THE HOUSE

"A parcel of lazy, idle fellars, that are always smoking and drinking and lounging ... a parcel of young cutters and carvers of live people's bodies, that disgraces the lodgings."

Bob Sawyer's landlady in PICKWICK PAPERS

To
JO

NOTE

St. Swithin's Hospital does
not exist, neither do its staff,
students, nor patients

CHAPTER I

THE large and completely unused set of surgical instruments that
my father kept in his consulting-room held for the old gentleman
the melancholy fascination of a hopefully gathered layette to an
ageing childless wife. For twenty years he had not troubled to
exercise the self-deception that he might one day come to use
them. They lay in the slots of their metal trays, fitting in with
each other like the pieces of a Chinese puzzle. There was a sharp-
toothed circular trephine for boring holes in the skull; bone forceps like a pair of shiny pliers; a broad hacksaw for amputations;
scissors with long, sharp blades; probes, trocars, and bistouries;
and a row of scalpels as impotent as a line of ceremonial swords.

The instruments were in a heavy black wooden box with his
name in copperplate script on its tarnished metal label. He had
stowed it away some years ago at the bottom of a tall cupboard
in the corner, where it had become silted over with old medical
journals, out-of-date diaries, and bright advertisements from the
big drug firms that he had slung in there from time to time with
the vague belief that he might want to refer to them one day.
Occasionally, rummaging his way through the dusty papers, he
would uncover the box and light up in himself a momentary
glow of frustration: he had once been convinced he was going to
be a great surgeon, and the instruments were an expensive gift
from his admiring mother the day he qualified as a doctor.

My grandparents were, unhappily, the only ones to share his
confidence in his professional destination. The first step in becoming a surgeon of even mediocre ability is the acquisition of the
Fellowship of the Royal College, an examination he sat regularly
twice a year for six years before he faced up to the truth that his
ability was not a powerful enough propellant for his ambition.
His history after that was the not disagreeable one of a good
many other unsuccessful young surgeons: he married and went
into general practice in the provinces.

When he saw the brass plate being screwed on to his new doorpost he recognized it as the coffin-lid of his surgical aspirations. For a few months he was bitter at his abandonment of specialization, but his resentment was rapidly smoothed down by the heavy planes of domesticity, busy practice, and the momentous trivia of provincial social life. He became a prosperous, and even fairly efficient, general practitioner, and reflected on his dead ambitions only when he came across his case of instruments or thought seriously about the education of his son.

Like most doctors' children, I had from my earliest schooldays come to look upon a medical qualification like a hereditary title. Graduation seemed a future occurrence over which I had no control; indeed, neither my parents nor myself contemplated my earning a living by any other means. My father sometimes wondered timidly if I might fulfil his own surgical hopes, but experience had made him guarded in predicting his son's postgraduate attainments. I had certainly not demonstrated in adolescence any aptitude for my already settled career. Up to the age of six I had a habit of pulling to pieces birds and small mammals ingeniously trapped in the garden, and this was thought by my parents indicative of a natural inclination towards the biological sciences. The practice of medicine was to me no more than a succession of mysterious people coming twice a day through the front door, and the faint tang of antiseptic which had been in my nostrils as long as I could remember, like the scent of the sea to a fisherman's son.

Once my father stood me up on his leather examination couch, on which the most respected bodies in the district had lain in their forbidding nakedness, and showed me the framed photograph that hung above it. It was the rugby team at his old hospital, the year he had managed to scrape into the side owing to a fortunate attack of diphtheria in the regular wing three-quarter.

'Which one's you, Daddy?' I asked, running my forefinger along the double row of solemn young men in shorts.

He indicated a thin fellow at the end of the back row.

'Good old St. Swithin's!' he muttered sadly. 'You'll be there one day, my lad. And mind you get in the first fifteen like your father did.'

His love for his old hospital, like one's affection for the youthful homestead, increased steadily with the length of time he had been shot of it. As a medical student, he had felt a surge of allegiance to the place only for an hour or so a week on the football field; now it represented a glowing period in his life when he was single, irresponsible, and bouncing with ambition. I grew into the impression that St. Swithin's combined the medical efficiency of the Mayo Clinic with the teaching of Hippocrates and the recreational facilities of the Wembley Stadium. For most of my schooldays the place was an ill-defined but agreeable and definite destination, like Heaven, and it was not until I found myself on the point of going there that I troubled to crystallize my thoughts about it.

St. Swithin's was, in fact, an undistinguished general hospital which spread its grey, insanitary-looking walls across a grimy section of North London. It was not even one of the oldest hospitals in the Metropolis, and as age is esteemed in England as the first of the virtues, this alone imbued the staff and students with a faint sense of inferiority. St. Swithin's did not possess the proud antiquity of St. Bartholomew's, which for several centuries looked on to the crisp green of Smithfield and the sweet waters of the Fleet tumbling unconfinedly into the Thames; nor was it as ancient as St. Thomas's over the River, which was already old when Shakespeare came to the Globe. Its origins were obscure, but there was a tradition that it was founded to deal with the outbreak of syphilis that rolled over Europe after the discovery of America, whence it had been imported by Columbus's sailors (so setting a persistent maritime habit). St. Swithin's had, however, been in existence sufficiently long for Londoners to accept it as one of the settled institutions of their city that seemed completely reliable, like Westminster Bridge or St. Paul's. It now attended only to the pale inhabitants of the streets crammed against its walls, to whom it had been for three or four generations simply 'The Hospital,' a place you went into and either got better or died according to your luck.

I had not seen St. Swithin's until the morning I was interviewed by the Dean of the Medical School. The Dean had replied to my father's explanatory letter with the assurance that the school was always glad to see the sons of former Swithin's men, but he added that he was nevertheless obliged by the Governors to inspect each candidate and allot places solely on the strength of the aptitude they showed for the practice of medicine. As the course of study was fixed by law for a time not less than six years, this struck me as a task comparable in difficulty with determining the sex of day-old chicks. For a week I was coached earnestly by my father on every question the Dean could possibly ask; then I put on my best suit and went up to London.

St. Swithin's was heavily disappointing. It was like the time I was taken to the Zoo to see my first elephant: it was distinctive enough, but not nearly so large, clean, and dignified as I had imagined.

I walked gingerly inside the forecourt, which was separated from the main road by a long line of heavy iron railings and a gatehouse. The court contained a few plane trees and a patch of pale grass in the centre, and a pair of large black statues representing St. Swithin's most renowned sons. On the right of the gate as you went in was Lord Larrymore, the famous Victorian physician who maintained for some years that he had almost discovered the cause of tuberculosis but was cruelly forestalled by Robert Koch in Germany. On the left you saw Sir Benjamin Bone, Larrymore's celebrated surgical contemporary, who was nearly appointed to the Queen's household but was dropped at the last minute because Her Majesty objected to the expensive, but distracting, aroma of cigars and brandy exuded all day from his person.

When St. Swithin's began to find its feet as a teaching hospital at the beginning of the century the staff were as aware of their lack of presentable antecedents as a newly rich family. These two gentlemen had therefore undergone a process of medical canonization and were invested with professional abilities and intellectual qualities certainly not indicated by their true histories. Shortly after they had been elected to the staff a quarrel broke out between them, and for thirty years afterwards they refused to speak to each other. Communication was necessary on professional matters, and this was conducted by short notes in the third person carried from one to the other by the hospital porter specially employed for the purpose. In the later part of his life

Sir Benjamin refused to utter the name of his colleague at all, and gave no indication that he was conscious of the other's existence until he saw one New Year's Day that Larrymore had been given a barony and immediately died of apoplexy.

The two doctors now stared in placid, set annoyance at each other across the court, and were disturbed only by an occasional painting-up from the students and the indiscriminate droppings of the London pigeons. What they originally quarrelled about had long ago been forgotten, but it was probably too trivial to be of interest.

My attention wandered from replicas of St. Swithin's staff to their living counterparts. The personnel of the hospital seemed to be in a state of constant transition across the courtyard. The consultant physicians and surgeons could easily be picked out, for they always moved from one spot to another in public as if they were in a desperate hurry. This gave the impression that their services were urgently needed in many places at once, and was good for their professional reputations. The junior practitioners had quickly picked up the habit from their superiors. The housemen strode importantly across the courtyard, their short white coats flying behind them, their stethoscopes trailing from their necks, wearing the look of grave preoccupation seen only in the faces of very fresh doctors. This drab, hurrying band of physicians was sprinkled with nurses in long mauve dresses and starched white caps that turned up at the back like the tails of white doves. They tripped smartly from one block to another and to the Nurses' Home in the rear. Of the people in the court they were the only ones genuinely in a hurry, for they had so little time to themselves they devoured their lives with a perpetual rush to get on and go off duty.

The bulk of the pedestrians in the courtyard was made up of almost equally important-looking and hasty people whom I was unable to identify. Apart from the doctors and nurses, a hospital has to employ men and women from a good many other occupations to run it. There must be chefs to prepare the food and dieticians to tell them what to cook; girls to work the X-ray machines and wardmaids to scrub the floors; physiotherapists to prevent the patients' muscles melting away in bed, and occupa-

'tional therapists to stop their minds being similarly affected by showing them how to make mats, rugs, stuffed horses, and other unexciting articles while they are imprisoned in the wards. There must be liftmen and laundrymaids, porters and padres, stokers and statisticians; and as all these people must be paid and controlled there has to be a large number of clerks, typists, and secretaries to do so. The staff at St. Swithin's had come to outnumber the patients by four to one and now seemed to be expanding naturally, like a water-lily covering a small pond.

There were patients, too, in the courtyard. A couple of them lay on each side of the statues in their beds, tucked up firmly in red blankets and sucking convalescence from the dirty London air. A few more hobbled about on their sticks, tossed helplessly in the strong cross-currents of hospital activity; one or two fortunate ones had found quiet alcoves and stayed there, like trout backing under the bank of a rocky stream. And, as I watched, there passed through the whole lot a cheery-looking man jauntily propelling a six-foot barrow with a stiff canvas cover towards a small door in one corner labelled 'Mortuary.'

I asked for the office of the Dean, Dr. Lionel Loftus, F.R.C.P. A porter showed me into a small bare waiting-room decorated only by framed black-and-white pictures of past deans, which ran along the walls like a row of dirty tiles. As there were no chairs I sat on the edge of the dark polished table and swung my legs. The surroundings, and a week of my father's coaching, had made me depressed and nervous. My mind was filled with the awkward questions that Dr. Loftus was even then contemplating asking me, and I found to my surprise I could give no satisfactory replies to any of them. I wondered what I should say if he simply asked me why I wanted to be a doctor. The answer was, I suppose, that neither my parents nor myself had the originality to think of anything else, but this didn't seem a suggestion likely to help me into the medical school.

This disheartening introspection was interrupted by the waiting-room door opening. An old man stood on the threshold, looking at me silently. He wore a heavy black jacket buttoned high in the chest, narrow trousers, and a two-inch collar. In his hand he held a pair of gold-rimmed pince-nez, which were attached to his right lapel by a thick black silk ribbon. He was so thin, so old, so pale, and so slow he could have taken his place in the nearby post-mortem room without attracting attention.

He clipped his glasses on to his nose with a slow, shaky movement and inspected me more carefully. I leapt to my feet and faced him.

'Gordon?' croaked the old man from the doorway. 'Mr. Richard Gordon?'

'Yes, sir. That is correct, sir,' I replied with great respect.

'So you have come for entrance to St. Swithin's?' the old man asked slowly.

'Yes, sir, I have.'

He nodded, but without enthusiasm.

'Your father is a Swithin's man, I believe?'

'Oh yes, sir.'

'I am not the Dean,' he explained. 'I am the medical school secretary. I was secretary here long before you were born, my boy. Before your father, probably. I remember well enough when the Dean himself came up to be admitted.' He removed his glasses and pointed them at me. 'I've seen thousands of students pass through the school. Some of 'em have turned out good, and some of 'em bad—it's just like your own children.'

I nodded heartily, as I was anxious to please everyone.

'Now, young feller,' he went on more briskly, 'I've got some questions to ask you.'

I folded my hands submissively and braced myself mentally.

'Have you been to a public school?' he asked.

'Yes.'

'Do you play rugby football or association?'

'Rugby.'

'Do you think you can afford to pay the fees?'

'Yes.'

He grunted, and without a word withdrew. Left alone, I diverted my apprehensive mind by running my eye carefully over the line of black-and-white deans, studying each one in turn. After ten minutes or so the old man returned and led me in to see the living holder of the office.

Dr. Loftus was a short, fat, genial man with wispy white hair like pulled-out cotton-wool. He was sitting at an old-fashioned roll-topped desk that was stacked untidily with folders, copies of medical journals, letters, and reference books. On top of these he had thrown a Homburg hat, a pair of yellow gloves, and his stethoscope. He was obviously in a hurry.

'Sorry to keep you waiting, old man,' he said cheerily, 'I was held up at a post-mortem. Have a seat.'

I sat down on a hard leather chair beside the desk.

'Now,' the Dean began. 'Have you been to a public school?'

'Yes.'

'Your people can afford the fees and that sort of thing?'

'I believe so.'

'You play rugby, I suppose?'

'Yes, sir.'

The Dean began to look interested.

'What position?' he asked.

'Wing three-quarter.'

He drew a pad of paper towards him and pencilled fifteen dots on it in rugby formation.

'Three-quarter . . .' he murmured to himself. 'How old are you?' he asked sharply.

'Almost eighteen, sir.'

'Umm. First fifteen at school?'

'Oh yes, sir.'

The Dean traced lines through his dots, crossed others out, and rustled through a sheaf of typewritten papers beside him. He jerked back in his chair and inspected me closely all over.

'You're rather thin, aren't you,' he announced. 'I suppose you've got the speed?'

'I've got cups for the hundred,' I told him eagerly.

'Well, you may shape well. Lucky you're a three. The hospital's full of forwards,' he added in disgust.

He frowned at his paper pad for a few seconds. His face suddenly lightened, and I saw he had come to a decision: my hands gripped the arms of the chair as I waited to receive it. Rising, he shook me briskly by the hand and told me he had pleasure in admitting me to St. Swithin's.

I wondered for some time afterwards how he had been able to

16

discover from these questions that I had the attributes of a successful doctor, but I later found out that even this brief interview was superfluous, as the Dean always took the advice of his old secretary and told applicants this man disliked the look of that there were no vacancies.

CHAPTER II

THE medical school of St. Swithin's hospital was an offshoot of the main buildings and had its own entrance on the main road. It was a tall, gloomy structure that held three floors of laboratories, an anatomical dissection room, a lecture theatre that was clothed in perpetual dusk, and the smelliest lavatories in the district.

The school had been built by the richest brewer in London, who was happily knocked over by a hansom outside the hospital gates one slippery winter's morning in 1875. He was restored to health and normal locomotion in the wards, and to show his gratitude he purchased his peerage the following year by founding the school. The place was now far too old, dark, and small for the requirements of the students, but as the hospital could see little prospect of the accident being repeated it was impossible to tear it down.

At the beginning of October thirty new students collected there for a lecture of welcome and introduction by the Dean. Carrying a new and shiny loose-leaf folder under my arm, I walked up the stone steps for the first time and into the dingy, small entrance hall. The brewer's name was carved in stone over the doorway to indicate the hospital's enduring gratitude, and was reflected in green and gold across the face of the King George public house opposite. Below his chiselled title were the serpents entwined round the winged staff, the doctors' universal trademark, and below that Hippocrates' discouraging aphorism 'The Art is Long.'

The hall, which was painted in yellow and green, contained a small kiosk bearing the word 'Enquiries' in which a porter had firmly shut himself by pulling down the glass window, turning his back on it, and reading the *Daily Mirror* with undistractable attention. There was a short row of clothes-hooks as heavy as an orchard in August, and a long notice-board thickly covered by overlapping sheets of paper.

I glanced at the board as I passed, feeling some faint obligation to do so. The notices were an untidy jumble of typewritten official instructions about lectures, examinations, and so forth, and scraps of paper torn from notebooks scrawled with students' writing. These indicated the pathetic undercurrents of medical school life as much as the agony column of *The Times* reflects those below the existence of the middle class. The first to catch my eye was in green ink, and said angrily 'Will the *gentleman* (underlined four times heavily) who took my umbrella from the physiology lab last Thursday bring it back? How can I afford a new one?' Next to it was a faded invitation for two students to make up a party to dissect an abdomen in Edinburgh during the vacation, adding temptingly 'Digs and abdomen fixed up. Good pubs.' There were lists of text-books for sale, triumphantly set up by men who had passed their examinations and therefore had no necessity to learn anything else; several small earnest printed appeals for support of the local Student Christian Association; and a number of unfulfilled wants, from a disarticulated foot to a cheap motor-bike.

A hand on the wall pointed upwards 'To the Lecture Theatre.' The way was by a thin iron spiral staircase that ended in darkness. I mounted it, and found myself against a dull brown door attached to a spring that creaked violently as it opened.

The door led to the back of a steep tier of narrow wooden benches rising from the lecturer's desk like a football stand. Behind the desk were three large blackboards screwed to the walls, which were otherwise panelled with stained perpendicular planks. The roof was lost in a criss-cross of thin iron girders through which half a dozen electric globes were suspended to supplement the thin light that filtered through the windows under the eaves.

I sat down shyly at the extreme end of the last row of benches. Most of the new students had already arrived, and had scattered themselves here and there in the tier of seats. A few seemed to know one another and were conversing softly among themselves. The rest were isolated and silent and looked blankly at the blackboards ahead of them, like a congregation in church waiting for the service.

We were as variegated as a bunch of conscripts. Most of the students were my own age, but in the row immediately below me a middle-aged bald-headed man was scribbling some private notes with a pencil in an exercise book; every now and then he jumped, looked round him anxiously, and fidgeted like a schoolgirl. The only other occupant of my row was a pale youth with untidy ginger hair who appeared to be about fifteen, and was reading *The Origin of Species* with alarming concentration.

The clock on the wall above the lecturer's desk reached twenty past ten: the Dean was late again. We later found that this was a common occurrence as he emphasized his complete superiority over the students in his appointments by being scrupulously un-punctual. I was still staring expectantly at the blackboards when the door behind me groaned and another student entered.

'I say, do you mind if I squeeze in?' the newcomer asked. 'I hate being far from the exit.'

I shifted along the hard bench hastily. The new man seemed so much at ease in his surroundings it appeared he was senior to the rest of the waiting class. He was certainly more distinctive in his appearance. He was a tall, good-looking young man with thick black hair and a small moustache. He wore a long brown hacking jacket, narrow corduroy trousers, a green shirt, and a yellow silk square instead of a tie. He set down on the floor beside him a polished black walking-stick, and taking a monocle from his breast pocket surveyed his companions through it with blatant disgust.

'Good God,' he said.

He then opened a copy of *The Times* and began reading it.

The abashed silence in the room was maintained for another ten minutes, broken only by my new neighbour noisily turning over the pages. At ten thirty, half an hour late, a small door behind the desk opened and the Dean bounced in. He was all smiles and geniality. He stood for a moment and beamed at the class like a bishop inspecting his confirmation candidates.

The Dean was not only late but in a tearing hurry. He briefly welcomed us to St. Swithin's, made a few remarks about its his-tory and traditions, rapidly ran through the ethics of the medical profession, and explained that in future we would be bound by professional secrecy, and forbidden to make love to our patients' wives, do abortions, or walk on the grass in the hospital courtyard. He flung a few final remarks of encouragement at his listeners and shot off. His address had lasted seventeen minutes, and the only acknowledgment that the student next to me had made of his presence was folding his paper twice over and reading it under cover of the man in front.

'Oh, he's finished, has he?' said the man with the paper, as the scuffling of students getting to their feet disturbed him. He peered at the clock through his monocle. 'H'm,' he remarked. 'He's cut three minutes off his best time so far. Did he leave out that bit about the hospital traditions?'

'No,' I told him. 'He seemed to have quite a lot to say about them.'

The student raised his free eyebrow. 'Did he now? Then he's speeding up his delivery. Next year I bet the old boy gets it down to fifteen minutes dead.'

I was very afraid of this superior and critical young man, but I could not help asking a question.

"You've heard the lecture before?' I said hesitantly. 'I mean, you haven't just arrived in the hospital like the rest of us?'

'This makes the fourth time I've heard old Lofty say his little piece,' he replied, smiling faintly. 'Wouldn't have come to-day, except that I got the dates mixed. I was expecting an anatomy lecture.'

The rest of the class was filing past us through the door and clattering down the iron stairs. We rose and joined the end of the line.

'You must be a very senior student,' I said respectfully.

'Not a bit of it, old boy.' My companion absently flicked a crumpled piece of paper to one side with his stick. 'I'm not a minute senior to you and the end of the year will probably find me back here again.'

'But surely,' I said from behind him as we descended the stairs, 'if you have four years' study to your credit . . .'

He laughed.

'Ah, the ingenuousness of youth! Four years' study, or at least four years' spasmodic attendance at the medical school, is of no significance. Exams, my dear old boy, exams,' he explained forcibly. 'You'll find they control your progress through hospital like the signals on a railway line—you can't go on to the next section if they're against you. I've come down in my anatomy four times now,' he added cheerfully.

I condoled with him over this quadruple misfortune.

'Don't sympathize, old boy. I appreciate it, but it's wasted. All my failures were achieved with careful forethought. As a matter of fact, it's much more difficult to fail an examination skilfully than to pass the damn thing. To give that impression of once again just having been unfortunate in the choice of the questions, you know. . . . Come along and have a beer. The King George will be open.'

We crossed the road and the experienced examinee thrust open the door of the saloon bar with his cane. I had meanwhile decided the medical course was a far more complicated affair than I had imagined.

The King George was one of those dark, cosy, pokey little pubs that, like brewers' drays and paralytic drunks, seem to be disappearing from the London drinking scene. The small saloon bar was heavy with dark wood and thick mirrors splashed with gilt *fleurs de lis*. The dingy white ceiling was gathered into plaster rosettes, the lamps sprouted out of the walls on curly metal stems, and in the corner a pale palm drooped over a large brass pot.

The influence of the hospital on the King George was noticeable immediately. Between the mirrors the walls were covered with framed photographs of past rugby and cricket teams, from which there stared down defiantly several hundred young gentlemen who were now respectable and ageing practitioners all over the country. Above the bar, in a glass case like a stuffed pike, was the rugby ball with which the fifteen had once won the hospitals' cup for the third year running. Next to it there hung a large, old-fashioned brass fireman's helmet. Behind the beer taps a fat old man in an apron, waistcoat, and grey trilby hat stared gloomily across the empty bar.

'Good morning, Padre,' my guide called cheerily.

The old man gave a smile of welcome and stretched his hand over the counter.

'Good morning, sir!' he exclaimed. 'Well! This is a treat to see you here again! Back for the new session is it, sir?'

'Every autumn, Padre, I return faithfully to my studies. Allow me to introduce a new student—what's your name, old boy?'

'Gordon—Richard Gordon.'

'Mr. Gordon, Padre. My name's Grimsdyke, by the way,' he explained.

The landlord shook hands heartily.

'And very pleased to meet you, sir!' he said warmly. 'I expect we'll be seeing some more of you in the next five or six years, eh? What's it to be, gentlemen?'

'Bitter for me,' said Grimsdyke, settling himself on a wooden stool. 'Will you take the same?'

I nodded.

'I should explain,' Grimsdyke continued, as the landlord filled the glasses, 'that this gentleman behind the bar is really called Albert something or other, I believe. . . .'

'Mullins, sir.'

'Mullins, yes. But no one in Swithin's would have the faintest idea who you were talking about. For the memory of living man he has been known as the Padre . . . how many years have you been dishing out the booze here, Padre?'

'Thirty-five, sir, just on.'

'There you are! He remembers the present senior physicians when they were students themselves—and a pretty rowdy crowd, by all accounts. There was the incident of Loftus introducing a carthorse into the Matron's bedroom . . .'

The Padre chuckled loudly.

'That was a real night, sir! Nothing like it happens any more, worse luck.'

'Well, look at the beer you sell now,' said Grimsdyke reproachfully. 'Anyhow,' he went on to me, 'this pub is now as indispensable a part of the hospital as the main operating theatre.'

'But why the Padre?' I asked cautiously.

'Oh, it's a custom started by the housemen. One can say in front of patients "I'm popping out to Chapel at six this evening" without causing alarm, whereas a poor view might be taken by the old dears if they got the idea their doctors drank. Besides, the old boy has a not unclerical function. He's a sort of father confessor,

Dutch uncle, and Dr. Barnardo to the boys sometimes—you'll find out about it before you've been here much longer.'

I nodded acknowledgment for the information. For a minute we drank our beer in silence.

'There's just another thing,' I began.

'Speak on, my dear old boy. I am always too glad to give what help I can to new students. After all, I have been one myself now five times.'

I pointed silently at the shiny brass helmet.

'Ah, yes, the sacred helm of St. Swithin's, by God! Feared and coveted in every medical school in London. You must learn about that before you go any further. How it got there, no one knows. It's been the property of the rugger club for longer than even the Padre can remember, so I suppose one of the boys must have lifted it on a Saturday night years ago. Anyway, it has now become a totem, a fetish, a fiery cross. For the big matches against Guy's or Mary's and so on the helmet is laid on the touchline for luck and inspiration. Afterwards it is filled with beer and emptied by all members of the team in turn.'

'It would hold a lot of beer,' I observed nervously.

'It does. However, on the occasion of qualification, engagement, birthday, marriage, or death of rich relatives, the thing is taken down and the man stood a helmet of beer by his friends. Are you engaged or married?' he asked suddenly.

'Good Lord, no!' I said. I was shocked. 'I've only just left school.'

'Well . . . anyhow, it's quite a point with me at the moment. But to return to our helmet. Often the gentlemen of lesser institutions attempt to steal it—we had quite a tussle with a gang of roughs from Bart's last season. Once last year some fellows from Tommy's got it as far the River, but we won it back from them on Westminster Bridge. By Jove, that was an evening!' He smiled at the memory. 'One of the chaps got a fractured mandible. Will you have another beer?'

I shook my head.

'No, thanks. I don't drink much, you know. Hardly at all, in fact. Only if I've been out for a long walk or something and I'm thirsty.'

24

I saw Grimsdyke wince.

'Of course, one must remember . . .' he began. 'You will find that in a little while at St. Swithin's you will learn enough bad habits to make life bearable. However, there is time enough for that. Padre,' he called. 'The other half for me, if you please.'

'Could you tell me . . .?' I began, feeling I had better collect all the information I could from my companion while he was talkative.

'Yes?'

'Why—why do you fail your examinations on purpose?' Grimsdyke looked inscrutable.

'That is a little secret of my own,' he said darkly. 'Maybe I'll let you into it one day, old boy.'

I learnt about Grimsdyke's little secret earlier than he expected. It was common knowledge in the medical school and seeped down into the first-year students within a few weeks of their arrival.

Grimsdyke's reluctance to pass examinations was wholly the fault of his grandmother, a well-to-do old lady who had passed the long-drawn-out twilight of her life in Bournemouth. As she had nothing else to occupy her she developed a wide selection of complaints, which were soothed away, all in good time, by the expensive attentions of her charming physicians. Her regard for the medical profession mounted with each indisposition, and was tempered only with the regret that she had not a single medical gentleman in her own family. The only person who could have rectified the omission was young Grimsdyke, and she conceived the idea while he was still at school of enticing him into the profession by offering to pay his expenses for the course. Unfortunately, the grandmother shortly afterwards developed a malady beyond the abilities of her doctors and was carried away; but her will contained a clause bequeathing a thousand a year to the young man during the time that he was a medical student.

Grimsdyke did not immediately realize the full significance of this, and had begun his first year's study at St. Swithin's before it dawned on him that he had an excellent opportunity to spend the rest of his life in London on a comfortable allowance without the tedium of doing any work. He therefore took great pains always to fail his examinations. He came to the hospital once or twice a week, paid his fees promptly, and behaved himself, which was sufficient for St. Swithin's. He had a flat in Knightsbridge, an old two-seater car (known as The Ulcer, because it was always breaking down), a large number of friends, and plenty of spare time. 'I sometimes think,' he would admit to his cronies, 'I have discovered the secret of graceful living.'

About the time that I joined the medical school Grimsdyke's spacious days became limited. He had fallen in love with a girl and proposed to her, but she was a shrewd young woman and not only discovered the secret of his existence but refused to accept him unless he altered it.

'An embryo doctor, yes,' Grimsdyke would explain sadly, 'but a chronic hanger-on in a medical school, no. I was obliged to go out and buy some books. The power of women, my dear old boy. It is for them that men climb mountains, fight wars, go to work, and such unpleasant things.'

She must have had the personality of a Barbary slave-master, for he thenceforward applied himself to his studies as enthusiastically as anyone else in the hospital.

CHAPTER III

As there were no classes arranged for the day of the Dean's lecture I had the afternoon to myself. I slipped off quietly from the King George shortly after a bunch of senior students burst in and started a noisy drinking session with Grimsdyke. The light-hearted way in which my new companions slipped down pints of beer alarmed me. I drank very little, for I had recently left school and was under the impression that more than two glasses of beer ruined your rugger and led to equally serious moral degeneration.

'So you are going in for—um—medicine?' my housemaster had said to me during my final term.

'Yes, sir.'

'A very—er—esteemed profession, Gordon, as you should know. Unfortunately, I find the means of entry to it seems to have a bad influence on boys of even the highest character. No doubt the effect of dealing daily with the—um—fundamental things in life, as it were, is some excuse. Yet I must warn you to exercise continual restraint.'

'Oh yes, sir. I will, of course, sir.'

'I expect you will soon become as bad as the rest,' he sighed. His small opinion of medical students sprang largely from the days when he had been reading theology at Cambridge and, on his attempt to break up a noisy party of medicals in the adjoining rooms late one night, he had been forcibly administered an enema of Guinness's stout.

I had lunch alone at the A.B.C. and went down to a medical bookshop in Bloomsbury to buy some text-books. I had to get a copy of Gray's *Anatomy*, the medical student's bible, as unquestionable authority on anatomy as Hansard on a parliamentary debate. When I saw the book my heart sank under its weight. I flicked over the two thousand foolscap pages of detailed anatomical description split up by beautiful bold drawings of yellow nerves, bright red arteries, and blue veins twining their way between dissected brown muscles that opened like the petals of an

27

unfolding flower. I wondered how anyone could ever come to learn all the tiny facts packed between its covers as thickly as the grains in a sack of wheat. I also bought a set of volumes giving directions for dissections of the body, a thick tome on physiology full of graphs and pictures of vivisected rabbits, and a book of Sir William Osler's addresses to medical students.

'Is there anything else, sir?' the assistant asked politely.

'Yes,' I said. 'A skeleton. Do you happen to have a skeleton?'

'I'm sorry, sir, but we're out of skeletons at the moment. The demand on them is particularly heavy at this time of the year.'

I spent the rest of the afternoon hunting a skeleton for use in the evenings with the anatomical text-books. I found one in a shop off Wigmore Street and took it back to my digs. Most land-ladies had become accustomed to a skull to be dusted on the mantelpiece and a jumble of dried bones in the corner, but students moving into lodgings that had previously sheltered such inoffensive young men as law or divinity pupils were sometimes turned out on the grounds that their equipment precipitated in the good lady a daily attack of the creeps.

* * * * *

For the first two years of their course medical students are not allowed within striking distance of a living patient. They learn the fundamentals of their art harmlessly on dead ones. The morn-ing after the Dean's lecture the new class was ordered to gather in the anatomical dissecting room to begin the term's work.

The dissecting room was a high, narrow apartment on the ground floor of the medical school that exhaled a strong smell of phenol and formaldehyde. A row of tall frosted glass windows filled one wall, and the fluorescent lights that hung in strips from the ceiling gave the students themselves a dead, cyanotic look. The wall opposite the windows supported a length of blackboard covered with drawings of anatomical details in coloured chalks. In one corner was a stand of pickled specimens, like the bottles on a grocer's shelves, and in the other a pair of assembled skele-tons grinned at each other, suspended from gallows like the mina-tory remains of highwaymen. Down the room were a dozen high, narrow, glass-topped tables in two rows. And on the tables, in different stages of separation, were six or seven dissected men and women.

I looked at the bodies for the first time curiously. They were more like mummies than recently dead humans. All were the corpses of old people, and the preserving process to which they had been subjected had wrinkled them beyond that of ageing. Four untouched subjects lay naked and ready for the new class, but at the other tables the senior students were already at work. Some of the groups had advanced so far that the part they were dissecting was unidentifiable to an unknowing onlooker like myself; and here and there a withered, contracted hand stuck out in silent supplication from a tight group of busy dissectors.

We stood nervously just inside the door waiting for instructions from the Professor of Anatomy. Each of us wore a newly starched white coat and carried a little· canvas roll containing a pair of forceps, a freshly sharpened scalpel, and a small wire probe stuck into a pen-handle. The others, to impress their superiority on the newcomers, disregarded us completely.

The Professor had the reputation of an academic Captain Bligh. He was one of the country's most learned anatomists, and his views on the evolution of the hyoid bone in the throat were quoted to medical students in dissecting rooms from San Francisco to Sydney. His learned distinction was unappreciated by his students, however, all of whom were terrified of him.

He had several little unnerving peculiarities. For some reason the sight of a student walking into the medical school with his hands in his pockets enraged him. His private room was next to the main entrance, so it was convenient for him to shoot out and seize by the shoulders any man he saw through the window sauntering into the building in this way. He would shake him and abuse him thoroughly for some minutes before stepping back into his room to watch for the next one. This habit was thought unpleasant by the students, but nothing could be done about it because the Professor, who controlled the examinations, held the power of justice at all levels in the anatomy school.

29

The Professor appeared suddenly in the dissecting room through his private entrance. The hum of conversation at the tables immediately ceased and was replaced by serious, silent activity.

He stood for some moments looking at his new class narrowly. The sight apparently did not please him. He grunted, and drawing a sheet of paper from the pocket of his white coat called a roll of our names in a voice rough with disgust. He was a tall thin man, shaped like a bullet. His bald head rose to a pointed crown and his body sloped outwards gently to his tiny feet far below. He wore a mangy ginger beard.

He put the list of names back in his pocket.

'Now listen to me, you fellows,' he began sternly. 'You've got to *work* in this department, d'you understand? I'm not going to put up with any slacking for a moment. Anatomy's tough—you can't learn it unless you put your backs into it. Any laziness here, and . . .' He jerked his thumb over his shoulder. 'Out! See?'

We nodded nervously, like a squad of recruits listening to their first drill sergeant.

'And I don't want to see any of you men slopping round with your hands in your pockets. It's all right for errand boys and pimps, but you're supposed to be medical students. The attitude is not only unanatomical but gives you osteoarthritis of the shoulder girdle in your middle age. No wonder you all grow up into a hunchbacked crowd of deformities! I know I'm ugly, but I can stand up straight, which is more than some of you people. Do you follow me?'

We assented briskly.

'Right. Well, get on with some work. The list of parts for dissection is up on the board at the end there.'

With a final glare he disappeared through his door.

I had been allotted a leg for my first term's work. We dissected in pairs, two men to each part. My partner was a student called Benskin—a large, sandy-haired man who wore under his white coat a green check shirt and a red tie with little yellow dogs on it.

'What ho,' said Benskin.

'Good morning,' I replied politely.

30

'Are you conversant with the mysteries of anatomical dissection?' he asked.

'No. Not at all.'

'Nor I.'

We looked at each other silently for a few seconds.

'Perhaps we had better read the instructions in the dissecting manual,' I suggested.

We sat down on a pair of high wooden stools and propped the book against the dead thigh on the table in front of us. After turning over several preliminary pages we reached a drawing of a plump leg with bold red lines over it.

'That seems to be our skin incision,' I said, pointing to one of the lines. 'Will you start, or shall I?'

Benskin waved a large hand generously.

'Go ahead,' he said.

I drew a breath, and lightly touched the greasy rough skin. With my new scalpel I made a long sweeping incision.

'I think I've cut the wrong thing,' I said, glancing at the book.

'It doesn't look quite like the picture,' Benskin admitted. 'Perhaps we ought to raise some help.'

There were a pair of demonstrators in the dissecting room— young doctors passing grey years in the anatomy department for small wages in the hope of being appointed to the surgical staff of St. Swithin's in middle age. They flitted from one group of students to another like bees in a herbaceous border, pollinating each pair with knowledge. Both of them were far away from our table.

At that moment I caught sight of Grimsdyke, in a shining starched coat, strolling between the dissectors like an Englishman in a Suez bazaar. He waved languidly to me.

'How are you progressing?' he asked, crossing to our table. 'Good God, is that as far as you've got?'

'It's very difficult,' I explained. 'You see, we don't quite know how to start. Could you give us a bit of a hand?'

'But certainly, my dear old boy,' Grimsdyke said, picking up a scalpel. 'I have now dissected four legs and consider I have something of a flair for the knife. This is the gluteus maximus muscle.'

31

Grimsdyke slit his way rapidly through the muscles and in half an hour did our work for the week.

*   *   *   *   *

The routine of lectures and dissection passed the time agreeably. After a few weeks I began to distinguish more sharply the personalities of my fellow students, as an eye gradually sees the objects in a darkened room. My dissecting partner, Tony Benskin, was a cheery young man whose mental horizon was bounded by rugby football and beer drinking and clouded over only with a chronic scarcity of cash. Dissecting the fellow to our leg was the ginger-haired youth I had noticed at the Dean's lecture reading Darwin. He turned out to be a quiet and disturbingly brilliant Welshman called Evans, who started the course under the impetus of a senior scholarship. Evans dissected away conscientiously and efficiently from the start—which was fortunate, as his own companion rarely put in an appearance in the anatomy room at all. He was a handsome fellow named John Bottle, whose interests in life were ballroom dancing and the dogs. He spent most of his afternoons in the palais and his evenings at Harringay or the White City. The middle-aged man with the notebook I soon discovered to be an ex-bank clerk called Sprogget, who was left a little money after twenty years' looking at a ledger and immediately fulfilled an almost forgotten ambition of taking up medicine. Sprogget was unfortunate in being partnered by the most objectionable student in the class—a man named Harris, whom Grimsdyke named immediately the Keen Student. Harris knew everything. His greased black hair, parted precisely in the middle, and his thick-rimmed spectacles popped frequently between a pair of dissectors.

'You know, old man,' he would volunteer, 'you're not doing that bit according to the book. You ought to have exposed the nerve before you cut away the tendons. Hope you don't mind my mentioning it, but I thought it might save you a bit of trouble with the Prof later. I say, you've made a mess of the brachial artery, haven't you?'

He was incorrigible. He sat at the front of the lectures and asked grave questions to which he already knew the answers. He

32

ate a lunch of sandwiches in the locker room of the anatomy department, reading a text-book; and his conversation was limited strictly to anatomy. He regarded the barracking to which he was inevitably subjected as another instance of persecution of the intellectuals.

Grimsdyke was a useful acquaintance, for his four years' start put him on familiar terms with the senior students. One afternoon shortly after my arrival he hailed me as I was walking out of the medical school doorway.

'I say, old lad,' he called. 'Come and meet Mike Kelly. He's secretary of the rugger club.'

There was a broad young man with a red face standing beside him. He wore an old tweed jacket with leather on the elbows and a brilliant yellow pullover.

'How do you do,' I said respectfully. Kelly was not only rugby secretary but two years senior to myself.

'Pleased to meet you,' said Kelly, crushing my hand. 'You play a bit, do you?'

'A bit. Three-quarter.'

'Jolly good. The hospital's going to be short of good threes in a year or so. First fifteen at school, I take it?'

'Yes.'

'Which school?'

I told him.

'Oh,' said Kelly with disappointment. 'Well, there's no reason why they shouldn't turn out a decent player once in a while. We'll give you a run with the extra B fifteen on Saturday and see how you make out. Grimsdyke here's the captain. He'll fix you up.'

'The extra B is a bit of a joke,' Grimsdyke said as Kelly strode off. 'Actually, we are more of a social side than anything. Our boast is that we can take on any team at any game. Last summer we played a dance band at cricket, and I've arranged a shove-ha'penny match with the police for next month. I'll meet you here at lunchtime on Saturday and give you and that fat chap—what's his name . . .?'

'Benskin.'

'Benskin, that's right. I'll give you both a lift to the ground in my car. Don't worry about shirts and things.'

The St. Swithin's ground was in a North London suburb, and the extra B was the only one of the half-dozen teams run by the hospital that was playing at home that week-end. The game was not brilliant and St. Swithin's ended up with a narrow win.

'Well done,' said Grimsdyke, as I was changing. 'You and that Benskin fellow shaped pretty well. You must both be horribly healthy. With any luck you might make the third fifteen before the season's out.'

'Thank you very much.'

'Now get a move on. It's after five and we don't want to waste time.'

'What's the hurry?' I asked.

Grimsdyke looked at me with amazement.

'Why, they open at five-thirty! We'll just make the King George, if we step on it.'

'Thank you,' I said. 'But I think I ought to go back to my digs. . . .'

'On Saturday night! Good Lord, old boy, that's not done at all! Hurry up and put your trousers on.'

Afraid of social errors in this new way of living, I obeyed. We arrived outside the King George as the Padre was opening the doors. Both teams pushed into the small saloon bar while a line of glass tankards clinked temptingly on the counter. Everyone was in a good humour, pleasantly tired and bathed. We were laughing and joking and clapping each other on the shoulder.

'Here you are,' Grimsdyke said, pushing a pint into my hand. 'There'll be a five-bob kitty.'

I handed over two half-crowns, thinking it was a great deal to spend on beer in one evening.

'Drink up!' Grimsdyke said a few minutes later. 'I'm just getting another round.'

Not wishing to appear unusual, I emptied the glass. A fresh one was immediately put into my fingers, but I timidly held it untouched for a while.

'You're slow,' said Benskin jovially, bumping into me. 'There's bags more left in the kitty.'

I took a quick gulp. I suddenly made the discovery that beer tasted most agreeable. The men round me were downing it with impunity, so why shouldn't I? I swallowed a large draught with a flourish.

With the third pint a strange sensation swept over me. I felt terribly pleased with myself. Damn it! I thought. I can drink with the best of them! Someone started on the piano and Benskin began to sing. I didn't know any of the words, but I joined in the choruses with the rest.

'Your drink, Mr. Gordon,' said the Padre, handing me another tankard.

I downed the fourth glass eagerly. But I felt the party had become confused. The faces and lights blurred into one another and the voices inexplicably came sometimes from far away, sometimes right in my ear. Snatches of song floated into my brain like weed on a sluggish sea.

'*Caviar comes from the virgin sturgeon,*' Benskin chanted.
> '*Virgin sturgeon, very fine fish.*
> *Virgin sturgeon needs no urgin'*
> *That's why caviar's a very rare dish.*'

I wedged myself against the bar for support. Someone next to me was telling a funny story to two men and their laughter sounded far off and eerie, like the three witches'.

> '*That pair of red plush breeches*
> *That pair of red plush breeches,*

came from the piano corner.

> '*That pair of red plush bre-e-e-eches*
> *That kept John Thomas warm.*'

'Are you feeling all right?' a voice said in my ear.
I mumbled something.
'What's that, old man?'
'Bit sick,' I confessed briefly.
'Hold on a moment. I'll take you back to your digs. Where's

35

he live, Benskin? Help me to get him in the car someone. Oh, and bring something along in case he vomits.'

* * * * *

The next morning Grimsdyke came round to my lodgings.

'How is it?' he asked cheerily.

'I feel awfully ill.'

'Simply a case of hangover vulgaris, old boy. I assure you the prognosis is excellent. Here's half a grain of codeine.'

'What happened to me?' I asked.

Grimsdyke grinned.

'Let's say you've been blooded,' he said.

CHAPTER IV

EVEN medical students must have somewhere to live. The problem of finding suitable accommodation is difficult because they are always disinclined to spend on mere food and shelter money that would do equally well for beer and tobacco. And they are not, as a rule, popular lodgers. They always sit up late, they come in drunk on Saturdays, and they have queer things in bottles in their bedrooms. On the other hand, there are a small number of landladies who think it a privilege to entertain a prospective doctor under their roof. The connection with the profession raises their social standing in the street, and the young gentleman can always be consulted over the dinner table on the strictly private illnesses to which landladies seem distressingly liable.

I started off in lodgings in Finchley, which were clean, fairly cheap, and comfortable. The landlady had a daughter, a tall, blank-faced brunette of nineteen, an usherette at the local Odeon. One evening after I had been there about six weeks she tapped at my bedroom door.

'Are you in bed?' she asked anxiously.

'No,' I called through the door. 'I'm studying. What is it?'

'It's me foot,' she said. 'I think I've sprained it or something. Will you have a look at it for me?'

'In the kitchen,' I replied guardedly. 'Take your stocking off and I'll be down in a minute.'

The following week she developed a pain in the calf, and the one after stiffness of the knee. When she knocked on the door and complained of a bad hip I gave notice.

I moved into a top-floor room of a lodging-house near Paddington Station. Its residents represented so many nationalities the directions for working its tricky and uncertain lavatories had to be set up in four different languages, as in the Continental expresses. There was another medical student there, a man from St. Mary's who kept tropical fish in a tank in his bedroom and practised Yogi.

As I had to take all my meals out I saw little of the other lodgers except when they passed on the stairs and said 'Excuse me' in bad English. In the room next to mine was a stout young blonde, but she lived very quietly and never disturbed anyone. One morning she was found strangled in Hyde Park, and after that I thought I ought to move again.

For the following twelve months I lived in a succession of boarding-houses. They were all the same. They had a curly hat-stand in the hall, a red stair-carpet worn grey in the middle, and a suspicious landlady. By the time I reached the end of the anatomy course I was tired of the smell of floor-polish, damp umbrellas, and frying; when I was offered a share in a flat in Bayswater I was so delighted I packed up and moved without even waiting to work out the week's rent.

The share was awarded to me through the good offices of Tony Benskin, who lived there with four other students. There was John Bottle, the man who liked dancing and dogs; Mike Kelly, now captain of the first fifteen; and a youth known about the hospital as Moronic Maurice, who had surprised the teaching staff and himself by finally passing his qualifying exams, and had gone off to practise the art, to the publicly expressed horror of the Dean, as house-surgeon to a small hospital in the country.

These four were really sub-tenants. The flat was leased by a final-year student, a pleasant fellow called Archie Broome, who had lived there during most of his time at St. Swithin's and took his friends as lodgers to help out with the rent.

'We're pretty free and easy there,' he explained to me in the King George. 'I hope you're not terribly particular about the time you have your meals or go to bed and that sort of thing?'

As I had found unpunctuality for meals was taken by land-ladies as a personal outrage and sitting up to midnight regarded as sinful, I told my prospective landlord warmly I didn't give a damn for such formalities.

'That's good,' Archie said. 'We usually kick in together for the groceries and beer and so forth, if that's all right with you. Here's the key, and you can move in when you like.'

I shifted the following afternoon. The flat was in a large, old, grimy block just by the Park, up a dark flight of stairs. I dropped my suitcases on the landing outside the door and fumbled for the key. While I was doing so the door opened.

Standing in the hallway was one of the most beautiful women I had ever seen. She was a tall blonde with a figure like a model in a dress-shop window. She wore slacks and a sweater, which sharply defined her slight curves. Taking her cigarette out with a long graceful hand, she said with great friendliness, 'Hello, Richard. Come on in and make yourself at home.'

'I'm afraid . . .' I began. 'I mean, I was looking for a fellow called Broome, you know. . . .'

'That's right,' she said. She had a slight, attractive, and unplaceable accent. 'The boys are all at the hospital at the moment, but just come in anyway. Would you like a cup of tea? My name's Vera.'

'How do you do,' I said politely. I picked up my cases and entered hesitantly. After conditioning myself to living with four coarse men being greeted by a delicate girl was puzzling.

'This is the sitting-room,' Vera continued. 'How about the tea?'

'No, thanks. Very kind of you, but I've had some.'

'That's good, because I've got to go and change anyway. If you do want anything the kitchen's through there. Just look round as you please.'

The girl slipped through a door leading off the hall, leaving me in the centre of the sitting-room feeling like a participant in the opening scene of a bedroom farce. I had learnt since being at St. Swithin's that the best way to treat anything unusual was to ignore it, so I directed attention towards my new home.

The furniture in the sitting-room had an original touch which reflected the profession of the occupants. Like Axel Munthe's room in the Hôtel de l'Avenir, there were books everywhere. A row of them stood along the mantelpiece, from which the names of distinguished consultants could stare at the students in gold lettering from red-and-black bindings, rebuking their loose activities like a row of church elders. In the window an uneven line of thick volumes ran along the ledge like battlements. There were books on the floor, dropped carelessly behind chairs or lost between pieces of furniture and the wall. They were scattered over the table like litter on a beach, mixed up with jam-pots, pieces of bread, tobacco, newspapers, and beer bottles. There was Price's famous *Medicine*, four inches thick, with two thousand pages that told you about everything from measles to leprosy, from sore throat to heart failure (it was also useful for propping open windows in summer and supporting a reading lamp); there were books on diabetes, appendicitis, bacteria, and bones; books full of photographs of skin diseases, rashes, or broken limbs; heavy dull books on pathology from Scotland, with no more than a bare picture or two of a growth of an ulcer to interrupt their closely-packed print; books on obstetrics with line drawings of nonchalant babies being recovered from disquieting predicaments; and scattered among them all like their young were the thin little brown volumes of the Students' Aid series—an invaluable collection of synopses that students fall back on, like compressed emergency rations, when faced with imminent defeat by the examiners. All this knowledge—all this work, experience and advice from so many experts—all the medical instruction in the world was concentrated into a few square feet. It was ours for the taking, if only we had ever sat down and started reading.

A microscope stood in the corner, conveniently tilted to take the eye, with an open wooden box of glass slides beside it. The articulated bones of a hand lay on the table, mixed up with everything else. From the top of a cupboard in one corner a skull grinned down and provided a stand for a green hat with white cord round it that Benskin was sometimes moved to wear.

As well as this academic litter the room contained pieces of sports kit—rugger boots, woollen socks, a couple of cricket bats, and a dart-board on a splintered plywood backing. The occupants' leisure activities were also represented by a collection of signs, notices, and minor pieces of civic decoration that had from time to time been immorally carried off as trophies. It was a bad habit of St. Swithin's rugby team when playing away from home to pick up souvenirs of their visit before leaving, and in the course of seasons these had grown to a sizeable collection. There was a thirty-miles-limit sign in the corner and an orange beacon next to the skull on the cupboard. From a hook in the wall hung a policeman's helmet with the badge of the Cornwall Constabulary that had been carried off in a burst of vandalism at the end of a successful tour of the West Country. Below it a framed notice declared that the passing of betting slips was illegal, and on the opposite wall a board announcing the opening and closing times of the park. I discovered a little later that the bathroom door bore a metal notice saying 'Nurses Only,' and inside, at the appropriate place, was a small printed request not to use the adjacent apparatus while the train was standing at a station.

My inspection was interrupted by the reappearance of Vera. She was in her stockinged feet and wore only a skirt and a brassière which she was holding on with her hands.

'Richard, please do my bra up for me,' she asked. 'This damn fastener's gone wrong.'

She turned her slender shoulders.

'Thanks so much,' she said casually. She strolled back into her room and shut the door. I shrugged my shoulders and decided the only thing was to wait until the male members of the household arrived and guardedly discover Vera's precise function.

Vera, it turned out, was Archie's mistress. She was an Austrian girl, with an ensnaring personality and the ability to conduct herself towards her four sub-tenants with such graceful, impartial sisterliness that none of us would have thought of making advances towards her more than we could have contemplated committing incest. Besides, she did all the cooking and most of the little feminine odd jobs about the flat. This was appreciated as highly as her decorative qualities, for our own abilities in the kitchen did not go beyond baked beans and we were able to mend socks only by running a surgical purse-string suture round the hole and pulling it tight. Floor-scrubbing, fire-making, and the coarser domestic tasks were done by the men on a rough rota; but it was Vera who thought of buying a new shade for the lamp, ordering the coal, or telling one of us it was time to change his collar or have his hair cut.

Vera unfortunately had a bad habit of periodically upsetting

41

the smooth running of the place by having sudden fierce quarrels with Archie which always ended by her packing up and leaving. Where she went to in these absences none of us knew. She had no relatives and no money, and Archie was so horrified at his own suspicion of how she maintained herself while she was away that he never dared to ask her outright. The flat would become untidy and unscrubbed. The boiler would go out for lack of coal, and the five of us would nightly sit down to a progressively repellent supper of orange-coloured beans. In a week or so she would re-appear, as beautiful, as graceful, as sisterly as ever, throw herself into an orgy of reconciliation with Archie, and continue her house-hold duties as if nothing had happened.

I floated contentedly into the drift of life in the flat. My companions treated the time-table of domestic life with contempt. They took meals when they were hungry, and if they felt like it sat up all night. Archie lived with Vera in a bed-sitting-room, and as they were an uninhibited couple this afforded them sufficient privacy. His guests had the run of the rest of the place. We all shared the bathroom and, as we had to put shillings in the geyser, quite often the bath water as well. It was in connection with the bathroom that Vera became her most sisterly. She would walk in and start cleaning her teeth unruffled by a hairy male in the bath attempting to retain his modesty with the loofah. Although we were all far too gentlemanly knowingly to intrude while she was in the bath herself she was never worried by anyone bursting in. 'After all,' she would say flatteringly, 'you are all doctors.'

I felt I was living the true liberal life and developing my intellect, which were excuses for not settling down to the more concrete problems set by my text-books. The thought of the anatomy exam nevertheless hung over me uncomfortably, like the prospect of the eventual bill to a guest enjoying himself at a good hotel. One evening we discovered with a shock that the contest was only a month away, which gave Benskin and myself no alternative than cramming. We opened our text-books and drew a deep breath of knowledge, which we hoped we could hold until the

42

examination was over. It was the worst time we could have chosen to start work. Mike Kelly had decided to learn the clarinet. Archie's landlord was trying to raise the rent, and Vera had disappeared again. On this occasion she never returned, and by the time the exam was held I was as miserable as her lover.

WHEN I heard I had passed the anatomy examination I felt like a man who had received an unexpected legacy. I had cut down my work preparing for the test by refusing to study at all topics that had been asked in the past few papers, in the belief that examiners, like lightning, never strike twice in the same place. I scraped into the pass list in company with Tony Benskin, John Bottle, Sprogget, Evans, and Harris. Grimsdyke also succeeded, and confessed himself amazed how near he must have come on previous occasions to the disaster of getting through.

I was elated: now I was released from the dull tyranny of the study of the dead in the dissecting room to the investigation of the dying in the hospital wards. I could start to perform like a real doctor; I could buy myself a stethoscope.

I strolled into a surgical instrument-maker's in Devonshire Street to select one, like a boy buying his first pipe. With the grave and critical air of a consultant cardiologist, I chose an impressive instrument with thick rubber tubes, a chest-piece as big as a jam-pot cover, and a few gadgets I could twiddle while delivering my professional opinions.

The choice was an important one, because in hospital a stethoscope is as undisputable a sign of seniority as long trousers in a prep school. It was not thought good taste to exhibit the instrument too blatantly, but a discreet length of tubing poking out of the coat, like a well-set pocket handkerchief, explained to your colleagues you had quitted the anatomy rooms for ever. With a bit of luck you might even be taken by the public for a real doctor. To the layman the stethoscope is the doctor's magic wand; if he sees a man with one round his neck he assumes he is a physician as readily as he takes a fellow in a clerical collar for a parson. These are a pair of conditioned reflexes that have from time to time been used for extracting small sums of money from well-meaning citizens by sufficiently respectable-looking confidence tricksters.

The next morning I walked proudly through the gates of St. Swithin's itself instead of going into the narrow door of the medical school. My first call was the students' lobby, to find which consultant I was appointed to.

Teaching of the clinical subjects—medicine, surgery, gynæcology, and midwifery—is carried on by a watered-down continuation of the old apprenticeship system. The year is divided into three-monthly terms, each of which the student spends attached to a different consultant. The doctor is the Chief, who usually takes on six or seven pupils known collectively as his firm, and dignified in the physician's wards with the title of medical clerks.

Each of the clerks is given four or five beds to look after. He is obliged to examine the patients admitted to them, write their notes, and scrape up an account of the case on the consultant's weekly list. Teaching is done at the bedside either by the Chief himself, his junior consultant, the registrar, or the houseman, and the students are expected to educate themselves in the intervals by nosing round the ward for instructive signs and symptoms and doing the unending medical odd jobs.

I began clinical work on a medical firm under the instruction of Dr. Malcolm Maxworth, M.D., F.R.C.P. Dr. Maxworth was one of the hospital's oldest physicians and had charge of male and female wards—Patience and Virtue. As he appeared only once a week the new students had to start by attending a small class given by the houseman on examination of the patient. We had at the time no more idea of the correct method for this than water-divining, and a Boy Scout with a first-aid certificate would have been more use in the wards than any of us.

The wards of St. Swithin's, which were contained in two large red-brick blocks, were dull, hostile galleries made up of a succession of irritating corners in which the nurses' dusters flapped for ever in defiance. They were repeatedly being redecorated in an attempt to give them an air of modernity and cheerfulness, but the original design of the corridor-like rooms made fresh paint as ineffective as make-up on a crone. There was always a plan on foot to pull them down and rebuild, but the execution of this seemed to meet with baffling postponements. Meanwhile the staff took pride that they trod the same boards in the exercise of their art as their professional forebears, and the nurses spent a great deal of time they should have given to the patients sweeping the floors.

I walked across the court and up the dark stone stairs to Virtue ward. Tony Benskin, Grimsdyke, and Evans were already standing outside the heavy glass doors, dangling their stethoscopes and trying not to appear a little in awe of their surroundings, like Oxford freshmen or new prisoners at Dartmoor. We greeted each other in low, church tones.

The houseman came jumping down the stairs three at a time. We stiffened ourselves, like sentries coming to attention. He shot straight past and through the ward door, without appearing to notice us. A moment later his head popped out again.

'Are you relatives waiting to see someone?' he asked. He caught sight of our proud stethoscopes. 'Oh, you're the new clerks, I suppose. Damn it! I'm far too busy to show you anything.'

He scratched his curly head. He was a pleasant-looking fellow, about three years older than ourselves.

'Look,' he went on cheerfully. 'Get a sheet of instructions from Sister Virtue and see how you get on examining a few patients. I've got a lumbar puncture and a couple of aspirations to do, but I'll give you a hand when I can.'

He disappeared again. The small glow of self-importance over our promotion was dimmed. Glancing nervously at one another we went through the doors into the ward.

The houseman had already disappeared behind some screens round a bed at the far end. One or two nurses were busy attending to the patients. The four of us stood by the door for ten minutes. No one took the slightest notice.

From a small door on one side of the ward the Sister appeared. She immediately bore down on our quartet.

'Get out!' she hissed savagely.

I had never seen a Sister close to before. This unexpected proximity had the effect of being in a rowing-boat under the bows of the Queen Mary.

Sister Virtue was a fine body of a woman. She was about six feet tall, her figure was as burly as a policeman's, and she advanced on her adversaries with two belligerent breasts. Even her

46

broad bottom as she passed looked as formidable as the stern of a battleship. Her dress was speckless blue and her apron as crisp as a piece of paper. She had a face like the side of a quarry and wore a fine grey moustache.

My immediate impulse was to turn and run screaming down the stairs. Indeed, all of us jumped back anxiously, as if afraid she might bite. But we stood our ground.

'We're the new clerks,' I mumbled in a dry voice.

She looked at us as if we were four unpleasant objects some patient had just brought up.

'I won't have any nonsense here,' she said abruptly. 'None at all.'

We nodded our heads briskly, indicating that nonsense of any sort was not contemplated.

'You're not to come in the ward after twelve o'clock, in the afternoons, or after six in the evening. Understand?'

Her eyes cauterized each of us in turn.

'And you're not to interfere with the nurses.'

Grimsdyke raised an eyebrow.

'Don't be cheeky!' she snapped.

She turned quickly to her desk and came back with some foolscap sheets of typewritten notes.

'Take these,' she commanded.

We selected a sheet each. They were headed 'Instructions on Case-Taking for Students.'

'You may look at patients number five, eight, twelve, and twenty,' Sister Virtue went on sternly. 'You will replace the bed-clothes neatly. You will always ask the staff nurse for a chaperon before examining any female patient below the head and neck. Kindly remember that I do not like students in my ward at all, but we are forced to put up with you.'

Her welcome finished, she spun round and sailed off to give a probationer hell for not dusting the window-ledges the correct way.

We silently crept through the doors and leant against the wall of the corridor outside to read the instruction papers. Grimsdyke was the only one to speak.

'I wonder if she goes to lunch on a broomstick?' he said.

47

I turned my thoughts to the typewritten paper. 'A careful history must be taken before the patient is examined,' I read. There followed a list of things to ask. It started off easily enough —'Name. Address. Age. Marital state. Occupation. For how long? Does he like it?' It continued with a detailed interrogation on the efficiency with which the patient performed every noticeable physiological function from coughing to coitus.

I turned the page over. The other side was headed 'Examination.' I read half-way down, but I was burning to try my luck on a real patient. I stuffed the paper in my pocket, like a child tossing aside the instructions for working a new complicated toy. I carefully put my nose inside the door and was relieved to find Sister had returned to her lair. I thought she was probably digesting someone.

Timidly I walked down the rows of beds to patient number twelve.

'Look where you're going!' a female voice said angrily in my ear.

I spun round. Behind me was a cross-looking nurse. She was young and not bad-looking, and she wore the bows and blue belt of a qualified staff-nurse.

'Can't you see that floor has just been polished?' she demanded.

'I'm sorry,' I mumbled. She tossed her head and stalked off with a swish of starched apron.

Number twelve was a stout young blonde browning at the roots —a frequent condition in female wards. She was sitting up in bed in a green woollen jacket reading a book by Peter Cheyney.

'Good morning,' I said humbly, expecting she as well would attack me.

She immediately slipped a piece of paper in her book, set it down on her bedside locker, threw off her bedjacket, and dropped the top of her nightdress off her shoulders to reveal a large and not unpleasant bosom. Then she smiled.

'Good morning,' she said. She was obviously used to the routine.

I felt a little at a loss. I had never been in such circumstances before, anywhere.

'Er—do you mind if I examine you?' I asked diffidently.

48

'Go ahead,' she said invitingly, giving me a bigger smile. 'Thanks awfully.'

The experience was so unusual I couldn't think of anything to say. I groped for remembrance of the instructions, but the sheets in my mind's eye were as blank as the patient's counterpane. I felt like an after-dinner speaker who had risen to his feet and found he'd forgotten his notes. Then an idea rescued me unexpectedly—I would take her pulse. Seizing one wrist, I felt for the throbbing radial artery while I gazed with unseeing concentration at the face of my wrist-watch. I felt I had held her arm for five minutes or more, wondering what to do next. And all the time her gently heaving breasts kept tugging at my eyes. They fascinated me, not with any sexual appeal but alarmingly, as if they were a couple of dangerous snakes. I noticed they had fine drops of sweat on them near the nipples.

A thought exploded in my mind.

'I must fetch a nurse!' I exclaimed. I dropped her wrist as if she had smallpox. 'A chaperon, you know.'

She giggled.

'Oh, go on with you!' she said playfully.

I backed away quickly. A nurse undecorated with belts or bows was dusting a locker on the other side of the ward. She looked hearteningly junior.

'I wonder if you would kindly chaperon me with a patient for a few minutes?' I asked urgently.

'No,' she said. She paused in her dusting to glance at me. I must have looked so miserable a little pity glowed in her heart. 'Ask the junior probationer,' she suggested brusquely. 'It's her job. She's in the sluice-room cleaning the bedpans.'

I thanked her humbly and went to look for my helpmeet. She was a worried-looking girl of about eighteen who was busy polishing a pile of metal bedpans as if they were the family silver.

'Will you please be my chaperon?' I asked meekly.

She pushed a lock of straw-coloured hair out of her eyes wearily.

'I suppose so,' she said. 'If I have to.'

We went back into the ward together and gathered some screens round the stout blonde's bed. The probationer stood opposite me with a look of contempt on her face for my inexpert manipulations while I examined the blonde's tongue, her eyes, and her teeth. I stuck my stethoscope warily here and there on her chest, though the noises were as uninformative to my ears as the sound of sea on a distant shore.

Taking the earpieces out I said 'Good!' as if I had completed my diagnosis.

'Aren't you going to examine my tummy?' asked the blonde with disappointment. 'All the doctors examine my tummy. It's my tummy what's wrong.'

'To-morrow,' I said firmly. 'I have to go and operate.'

How could I tell her in front of the nurse I had not yet learned as far as the tummy?

*   *   *   *   *

Inspection, palpation, percussion, auscultation—the unalterable, ever-applicable tetrad. They were drummed into us like drill to recruits. Whatever part of the patient you examine, whatever disease you suspect, the four motions must be gone through in that order. You look first, then feel; when you have felt, you may tap, but not before; and last of all comes the stethoscope.

I began to learn how to look at a patient so that even the finger-nails might shine with a dozen diagnoses. They taught us to feel lumps, livers, and spleens; how to percuss correctly and to understand the evasive murmurs transmitted through a stethoscope. Diagnosis is simple observation and applied logic—detection, in fact. A matter of searching for clues, igniting a suspicion and knowing where to look for proof. Conan Doyle modelled Sherlock Holmes on a physician, and the reverse holds perfectly well.

Dr. Maxworth took his firm round the ward every Wednesday morning. He was a thin, desiccated little man who had never been known to appear in public dressed in anything but black coat and striped trousers. He was not really interested in students at all. For most of the round he forgot we were crowding in his footsteps, and would suddenly recall our presence by throwing a few half-audible scraps of instruction over his shoulder. He was a specialist in neurology, the diseases of the nervous system. This is the purest and most academic branch of medicine and requires for its practice a mind capable of playing three games of chess simultaneously while filling in a couple of stiff crossword puzzles between the moves. As almost all the nervous diseases we saw in the ward appeared to be fatal, it seemed to me a pretty barren speciality. But Maxworth drew exquisite pleasure from it. He was not primarily concerned with treating his patients and making them better, but if he scored a diagnosis before the proof of the post-mortem he was delighted. He was, his houseman said, a fairly typical physician.

I began to see how the ward was managed by Sister, whom I avoided like a pile of radium. Every bodily occurrence that could be measured—the pulse, the amount of urine, the quantity of vomit, the number of baths—was carefully entered against the patient's name in the treatment book, which reduced the twenty or so humans in the ward to a daily row of figures in her aggressive handwriting.

There were two functions of the physiology which Sister thought proceeded wholly in her interest. One was temperature. The temperature charts shone neatly from the foot of the beds, and each showed a precise horizontal zigzag of different amplitude. Sister wrote the dots and dashes on them herself every morning and evening. The temperatures were taken by the junior nurses, who used four or five thermometers. In spite of inaccuracies due to a different instrument being used daily on each patient and the varying impatience of the nurse to whip the glass spicule away, the figures were looked upon as indispensable. Any errors occurring through mercurial or human failings were not of great importance, however, because Sister always substituted figures of her own if the ones returned by the patient did not fit in with her notion of what the temperature in the case ought to be.

The other particular concern of the Sister was the patients' bowels. A nurse was sent round the ward every evening with a special book to ask how many times each inmate had performed during the past twenty-four hours. 'How many for the book?' she would enquire with charming coyness. The patients caught the spirit of the thing, and those returning fair scores to the nurse did so with a proud ring in their voices, but anyone making a duck confessed with shame and cowered under the bedclothes.

The number of occasions was written in a separate square at the foot of the temperature chart. A nought was regarded by Sister as unpleasant, and more than two blank days she took as a personal insult. Treatment was simple. One nought was allowed to pass without punishment, but two automatically meant cascara, three castor oil, and four the supreme penalty of an enema.

We rapidly became accustomed to our position of inferiority to everyone on the ward staff. Like all apprentices, the students were used as cheap labour by their superiors. We did all the medical chores—urine-testing, gruel meals in patients with duodenal ulcers, blood samples, and a few simple investigations. For the first few weeks everything seemed easy. It was only at the end of the three-month appointment that there crept up on me an uneasy certainty that I did not yet even know enough to realize how ignorant I was.

CHAPTER VI

THE impact of surgery on the student is likely to be more dramatic than the first gentle touch of medicine. Although surgeons have now abandoned such playful habits as hurling a freshly amputated leg at a newcomer in the theatre, the warm, humid atmosphere, the sight of blood spilt with apparent carelessness, and the first view of human intestines laid out like a string of new sausages, sometimes induces in a student a fit of the vapours—a misfortune which draws from his unaffected companions the meagre sympathy afforded a seasick midshipman.

Nevertheless, I started the surgical course with a feeling of superiority over my predecessors of ten or fifteen years ago. As I went to the pictures fairly regularly I was already as familiar with the inside of an operating theatre as with my father's consulting-room. From a seat in the local cinema not only myself but most other people in the country had achieved a thorough and painless knowledge of what went on behind the doors marked 'Sterile.' I was ready for it all: the crisp white gowns; the cool, unhurried efficiency; the tense concentrated silence broken only by the click of instruments, a curt word of command from the surgeon, or a snapped-out demand for a fresh ligature by the theatre sister. I prepared myself to face the solemnity of an operation, with the attention of everyone in the room focused on the unconscious patient like the strong beam of the operating spotlight.

I was attached to Sir Lancelot Spratt for my surgical teaching. My official title was Sir Lancelot's dresser, which meant not that I had to help him into his white operating trousers in the surgeons' changing-room, but that I was supposed to be responsible for the daily dressings of three or four patients in the ward. The name had a pleasing dignity about it and suggested the student really did something useful in the hospital instead, as it was always impressed on him by the nurses and housemen, of getting in everyone's way like a playful kitten.

The appointment to Sir Lancelot's firm was something of an honour, as he was the Senior Surgeon of the hospital and one of its best-known figures. He was a tall, bony, red-faced man with a bald head round which a ring of white fluffy hair hung like clouds at a mountain top. He was always perfectly shaved and manicured and wore suits cut with considerably more skill than many of his own incisions. He was on the point of retiring from the surgical battlefield on which he had won and lost (with equal profit) so many spectacular actions, and he was always referred to by his colleagues in after-dinner speeches and the like as 'a surgeon of the grand old school.' In private they gave him the less charming but equivalent epithet of 'that bloody old butcher.' His students were fortunate in witnessing operations in his theatre of an extent and originality never seen elsewhere. Nothing was too big for him to cut out, and no viscus, once he had formed an impression it was exercising some indefinite malign influence on the patient, would remain for longer than a week *in situ*.

Sir Lancelot represented a generation of colourful, energetic surgeons that, like fulminating cases of scarlet fever, are rarely seen in hospital wards to-day. He inherited the professional aggression of Liston, Paget, Percival Pott, and Moynihan, for he was trained in the days when the surgeon's slickness was the only hope of the patient's recovery, the days before complicated anæsthetics, penicillin, blood-transfusion, and the other paraphernalia of modern surgery had watered down the operator's skill and threatened to submerge him completely.

Sir Lancelot had made a fortune, chiefly from the distressing complaints of old gentlemen, and was charging two hundred guineas for an appendicectomy while Aneurin Bevan was still thumping a local tub in Ebbw Vale. His real success started in the 'twenties, when he earned his knighthood by performing a small but essential operation on a cabinet minister that allowed him to take his seat in the House with greater ease. The minister was delighted, and recommended him in every drawing-room of importance in London. Just at that time Sir Lancelot got it into his head that rheumatism could be cured by the removal from the body of all organs not strictly necessary for the continuance of life. As most people over the age of fifty have rheumatism and it is impossible to make it much better or much worse with any form of treatment his practice increased tenfold overnight.

The rheumatism rage lasted long enough for him to buy a house in Harley Street, a country home on the Thames, a cottage in Sussex, a small sailing yacht, and a new Rolls, in which he was still wafted round between the four of them and the hospital. By then he was ready to operate on anything—he was, he told his dressers with pride, one of the last of the general surgeons. He claimed to be capable of removing a stomach or a pair of tonsils with equal success, or to be able to cut off a leg or a lung.

Every Tuesday and Thursday afternoon he operated in his own theatre on the top floor. The list for the session was pinned up outside like a music-hall bill—the best cases were always at the top for Sir Lancelot to operate on himself, and the programme degenerated into a string of such minor surgical chores as the repair of hernias and the removal of varicose veins, to be done by his assistants when he had gone off to his club for a glass of sherry before dinner.

On the first Tuesday after my appointment to the firm I walked up the stairs to the theatre—students were not allowed to use the hospital lift—and went into the dressers' changing-room. A row of jackets and ties hung under a notice in letters three inches high: DO NOT LEAVE ANYTHING IN YOUR POCKETS. Everyone entering the theatre had to wear sterile clothing, which was packed away in three metal bins opened by foot pedals. Using a pair of long sterile forceps I took an oblong cap from one, a mask from another, and a rolled white gown from the third. Unfortunately there was no indication of the size of these coverings, and the gown fell round my feet like a bridal dress while the cap perched on my head like a cherry on a dish of ice-cream. I pushed open the theatre door and stepped inside reverently, like a tourist entering a cathedral. Standing by the door, my hands clasped tightly behind me, all I wanted was completely to escape notice. I felt that even my breathing, which sounded in my ears like the bellows of a church organ, would disturb the sterile, noiseless efficiency of the place. I was also a little uncertain of my reactions to cut flesh and wanted to keep as far away from the scene of activity as possible.

'You, boy!'

Sir Lancelot's head popped above the caps of his attendants. All I could see of him was a single brown, bushy strip that separated the top of his mask and the edge of his cap, through which there glared two unfriendly eyes like a hungry tiger inspecting a native through the undergrowth.

'Come over here,' he shouted. 'How often have I got to tell you young fellers you can't learn surgery from the door-post?'

The operating table was in the centre of the bare, tiled room, directly under the wide lamp that hung like a huge inverted saucer from the ceiling. It was completely invisible, as about twenty figures in white gowns were packed round it like Tube passengers in the rush-hour. These were mostly students. The operating team was made up of Sir Lancelot himself, who was a head higher than anyone else in the room; his theatre sister, masked and with all her hair carefully tucked into a sterile white turban, standing on a little platform beside him; his senior houseman, Mr. Stubbins, and his registrar, Mr. Crate, assisting him from the opposite side; and his anæsthetist, sitting on a small metal piano stool beside a chromium-plated barrow of apparatus at the head of the table, reading the *Daily Telegraph*. On the outskirts of this scrum two nurses in sterile clothes dashed round anxiously, dishing out hot sterilized instruments from small metal bowls like waiters serving spaghetti. A theatre porter, also gowned and masked, leant reflectively on a sort of towel rail used for counting the swabs, and another strode in with a fresh cylinder of oxygen on his shoulder. The only indication that there was a patient present at all was a pair of feet in thick, coarse-knitted bed-socks that stuck pathetically from one end of the audience.

As soon as Sir Lancelot spoke the group round the table opened, as if he were Aladdin at the mouth of his cave. I walked unhappily into the centre. My companions closed tightly behind me, and I found myself wedged against the table opposite Sir Lancelot with a man who played in the second row of the hospital forwards immediately behind me. Escape was therefore out of the question, on physical as well as moral grounds.

The operation was on the point of starting. The patient was still invisible, as the body was covered with sterile towels except

56

for a clean-shaved strip of lower abdomen on the right-hand side of which the operating light focused diagnostically. I couldn't even see if it was a young man or a woman.

Having forced me into a ringside seat, Sir Lancelot then appeared to dismiss me from his mind. He paused to adjust the cuff of the rubber glove that stretched over his bony hand. Stubbins and Crate were waiting with gauze dabs, and the theatre sister was threading needles with catgut as unconcernedly as if she was going to darn her stockings.

'Stubbins,' said Sir Lancelot chattily, making a three-inch incision over the appendix, 'remind me to look into Fortnum's on my way home, there's a good lad. My missus'll give me hell if I forget her dried ginger again. I suppose it was all right for me to start?' he asked the anæsthetist.

The *Daily Telegraph* rustled slightly in assent.

I was surprised. Dried ginger in an operating theatre? Shopping lists disturbing the sanctity of surgery? And the *Daily Telegraph*?

'I've got a damn funny story to tell you lads,' went on Sir Lancelot affably, deepening his incision. 'Make you all laugh. Happened to me last week. An old lady turned up in my rooms in Harley Street . . . Sister!' he exclaimed in a tone of sudden annoyance, 'do you expect me to operate with a jam-spreader? This knife's a disgrace.'

He threw it on the floor. Without looking at him she handed him another.

'That's better,' Sir Lancelot growled. Then, in his previous tone, as though he were two people making conversation, he went on: 'Where was I? Oh yes, the old lady. Well, she said she'd come to see me on the advice of Lord—Lord Someoneorother, I can't remember these damn titles—whom I'd operated on last year. She said she was convinced she'd got gallstones.

'Now look here, Stubbins, can't you and Crate keep out of each other's way? Your job is to use that gauze swab sensibly, not wave it around like a Salvation Army banner. How the devil do you think I can operate properly if everything's wallowing in blood? Why am I always cursed with assistants who have a couple of

57

left hands? And I want a clip, Sister. Hurry up, woman, I can't wait all night!'

Sir Lancelot had cut through the abdominal wall while he was talking, like a child impatient to see inside a Christmas parcel.

'Well,' he went on, all affability again, seemingly conducting the operation with the concentration of a gossipy woman knitting a pair of socks, 'I said to this old lady, "Gallstones, eh? Now, my dear, what makes you think you've got gallstones?" And I've never seen anyone look so embarrassed in my life!'

He returned to the operation.

'What's this structure, gentlemen?'

A reply came from under a student's mask on the edge of the crowd.

'Quite correct, whoever you are,' said Sir Lancelot, but without any congratulation in his voice. 'Glad to see you fellers remember a little fundamental anatomy from your two years in the rooms . . . so I wondered what was up. After all, patients don't get embarrassed over gallstones. It's only piles and things like that, and even then it's never the old ladies who are coy but the tough young men. Remember that bit of advice, gentlemen. . . . Come on, Stubbins, wake up! You're as useless as an udder on a bull.'

He produced the appendix from the wound like a bird pulling a worm from the ground, and laid it and the attached intestine on a little square of gauze.

'Then the old lady said to me, "As a matter of fact, Sir Lancelot, I've been passing them all month. . . ." Don't lean on the patient, Stubbins! If I'm not tired you shouldn't be, and I can give you forty or fifty years, my lad.

'So now we come to the interesting part of the story. She showed me a little box, like those things you send out pieces of wedding cake in. . . . Sister! What in the name of God are you threading your needles with? This isn't catgut, it's rope. What's that, woman?' He leant the red ear that stuck out below his cap towards her. 'Speak up, don't mutter to yourself. I'm not being rude, damn you! I'm never rude in the theatre. All right, tell your Matron, but give us a decent ligature. That's more like it. Swab, man, swab. Stubbins, did I ever tell you about the Matron when she was a junior theatre nurse? She had a terrible crush on a fellow house-surgeon of mine—chap called Bungo Ross, used to drink like a fish and a devil for the women. Became a respected G.P. in Bognor or somewhere. Died last year. I wrote a damn good obituary for him in the *British Medical Journal*. I'm tying off the appendicular artery, gentlemen. See? What's that, Stubbins? Oh, the old lady. Cherry stones.'

He tossed the appendix into a small enamel bowl held for him by Stubbins.

'Looks a bit blue this end, George,' he said in the direction of the anæsthetist. 'All right, I suppose?' The anæsthetist was at the time in the corner of the theatre talking earnestly to one of the nurses who had been serving out the instruments. Theatre kit is unfair to nurses; it makes them look like white bundles. But one could tell from the rough shape of this one, from the little black-stockinged ankles below her gown and the two wide eyes above her mask, that the parcel would be worth the unwrapping. The anæsthetist jumped back to his trolley and began to twiddle the knobs on it. Sister, who was already in a wild temper, injected the nurse with a glance like a syringeful of strychnine.

'Forceps, Sister!' bellowed Sir Lancelot. She handed him a pair which he looked at closely, snapping them together in front of his mask. For some reason they displeased him, so he threw them over the heads of the crowd at the opposite wall. This caused no surprise to anyone, and seemed to be one of his usual habits. She calmly handed him another pair.

'Swabs correct, Sister, before I close? Good. Terribly important that, gentlemen. Once you've left a swab inside a patient you're finished for life. Courts, damages, newspapers, and all that sort of thing. It's the only disaster in surgery the blasted public thinks it knows anything about. Cut their throats when they're under the anæsthetic, yes, but leave anything inside and you're in the *News of the World* in no time. Shove in the skin stitches, Stubbins. What's the next case? Tea? Excellent. Operating always makes me thirsty.'

59

CHAPTER VII

DURING the following three months I learnt a little about surgery and a lot about surgeons. I learnt more than I wanted about Sir Lancelot.

In the theatre he was God. Everything in the routine for operating sessions was arranged to suit his convenience. A white linen suit, freshly starched, was carefully warmed by the junior nurse before being laid out in his changing-room in the morning. A Thermos pitcher of iced water labelled 'Sir Lancelot Spratt ONLY' was set on a silver tray nearby. He had his own masks, his own scrubbing brush, and his own soap. When he crossed the theatre floor from the scrub-up basins to the table the onlookers scattered before him like unarmed infantry in front of a tank. If anyone got in his way he simply kicked them out of it. He rarely asked for an instrument but expected the Sister to guess which one to place in his waiting hand. If she made a mistake, he calmly dropped the wrong instrument on to the floor. Should she do no better at her second attempt he repeated his little trick. Once he silently reduced a whole trayful of instruments to an unsterile heap at his feet, and the Sister had hysterics.

Sir Lancelot had a personality like an avalanche and a down-right bedside manner that suited equally well a duchess's bedroom or the hospital out-patient department. He radiated confidence like a lighthouse through a storm. His suggestions on the removal of his patients' organs never met with their objection. The more he did to them, the greater the complications that resulted from his interference, the larger the number of supplementary operations he had to perform to retrieve his errors, the more they thanked him: there was never one but died grateful.

His teaching in the ward, like his surgery in the theatre, was full-blooded. He had a long string of aphorisms and surgical anecdotes, none of which was original or strictly accurate, but they stuck in the minds of his students long after the watery lectures of his colleagues had evaporated.

His round was held every Tuesday morning at ten o'clock, and had the same effect on the ward as an admiral's inspection of a small warship.

The preparations for his visit began about five in the morning. The night nurses started the long business of sprucing up the ward to its best pitch of speckless sterility, and when Sister and her day staff arrived at seven the energy given to preparing the long room so that nothing in the slightest way offensive should fall on the great man's eye was increased tenfold. Every article in it was scrubbed and polished thoroughly—the floor, the medicine cupboards, the windows, the instruments, the patients' faces. The bedside lockers, which usually carried a friendly jumble of newspapers, soap, jam, football coupons, and barley-water, were stripped clean and their contents buried out of sight. Even the flowers looked sterile.

The tension and activity in the ward rose together, like the temperature and pulse in a fever. At nine the senior house-surgeon, in a fresh white jacket, looked in for a worried, whispered conversation with Sister to be certain everything commanded on the Chief's last visit had been done. He didn't glance at the patients. That morning they were part of the ward furniture, or at most instruments by which the medical staff could demonstrate their abilities to Sir Lancelot.

There was one point, however, on which the patients could not be argued away from their humanity. At nine-fifteen bedpans were issued all round. The acquisition of one of these at such an hour (seven and five were the official times for their use) was usually a business comparable with catching the eye of a waiter in a busy restaurant. At nine-fifteen on Tuesdays, however, they were forced upon the patients. The nurses tripped briskly out of the sluice-room, each carrying a couple under a cloth. This was because Sister thought a request for one of these articles while Sir Lancelot was in the ward unreasonable to the highest degree —indeed, almost indecent.

The bedpans were whipped away a quarter of an hour before the Chief was due. There followed an energetic final ten minutes occupied by a process known as 'tidying' the patients. They could obviously not be allowed to disturb the general symmetry of the

61

scene by lolling about in bed anyhow, like a squad of soldiers falling in with their hands in their pockets. They had to be fitted in to the ward neatly and unobtrusively. The technique was simple. A pair of nurses descended on the patient. First he was shot into the sitting position, and retained there by one nurse while the other smoothed and squared up his pillows (the open ends of the pillow-cases always to face away from the door). He was then dropped gently on his back, so as not to ruffle the smooth surface unnecessarily with his head. The bedclothes were seized at the top by the two young women and pulled taut between them like a tug-of-war; they next applied the tension upwards from the patient's feet, which brought the top edge of the bedclothes level with the patient's nostrils. In one quick motion, without releasing the tension to which the blankets were submitted, they tucked them in firmly all round. This made it impossible for the occupant of the bed to perform any muscular movement whatever, except very shallow breathing.

The ward by ten was silent, orderly, and odourless. Sister and the nurses had changed into fresh white aprons and each of them felt like Moses immediately on his arrival at the top of the mountain. Meanwhile, another focus of consternation had formed not far away.

It was the tradition of St. Swithin's that the Chief should be greeted in the courtyard and lead his firm to the ward. Surgeons were met in front of the statue of Sir Benjamin Bone and physicians before that of Lord Larrymore. This form of reception resulted in everyone becoming cold in winter, hot in summer, and wet all the year round, and as it had apparently been going on for three or four hundred years this seemed an excellent reason for refusing to alter it.

We gathered for our first ward-round under the cold eye of Sir Benjamin. The differences that divided the firm, which were emphasized on Tuesday mornings, had already become obvious. The students stood in a little subdued group behind the statue. We wore our suits, with stethoscopes coiling out of our pockets and foolscap notebooks under our arms. We chatted quietly between ourselves, but would not have contemplated exchanging words with the two house-surgeons, who stood apart murmuring to each other with expressions of intense seriousness on their faces.

The third section of the party consisted only of Crate, the registrar. He was allowed to wear a long white coat like the Chief, but as he had no companion to talk to and was unable to converse with his housemen or students at such a solemn moment he had to content himself with looking at the sky in a reflective and earnest way, as if he were turning over in his mind the niceties of surgery or trying to forecast the weather.

At ten the Rolls drew into the courtyard and stopped opposite our group. Crate opened the door and wished Sir Lancelot good morning. The car was driven to its parking-place by the chauffeur and the Chief disappeared with his registrar towards the staff common room to leave his hat and put on his white coat. When they reappeared the rest of the party followed them to the wards.

Once Sir Lancelot burst through the ward door more people arranged themselves in his wake. Indeed, it was impossible for a man of his importance to walk about St. Swithin's at all without a procession immediately forming up behind him.

First, of course, was Sir Lancelot, the therapeutic thunderbolt. A pace behind came the registrar, and behind him the two house-surgeons, the senior one leading. After the two housemen was Sister, her long cap trailing behind her like a wind-stocking on an aerodrome. She was followed by her senior staff nurse, who carried a trayful of highly-polished instruments with which the patients could be tapped, scratched, and tickled in the aid of making a diagnosis. Sir Lancelot never used any of them and probably did not know how to, but they were produced every Tuesday nevertheless, like a ceremonial mace. Behind the staff nurse was a junior nurse bearing a thick board covered with a pad of paper, to which a pencil was attached with a piece of string. The board was marked sternly 'SIR LANCELOT SPRATT'S DRAWING PAPER.' On this he would sometimes sketch points of anatomy—not often, about once every six months, but the board had to be flashed to his hand if he asked for it. In the rear of the junior nurse, in the winter months a probationer carried a hot-water bottle in a small red blanket for Sir Lancelot to warm his hands before applying them to exposed flesh.

At the end of the party, behind even the hot-water bottle, were

63

the students: an un-uniformed, disorderly bunch of stragglers.

The Chief spent two hours examining the candidates for the afternoon's operating list, with whom he illustrated to us the principles of surgery. Sometimes he passed all morning on one case, if the patient contained a lump of sufficient interest to him; on other Tuesdays he would whip round the whole ward, diagnosing like a machine-gun. Sitting was forbidden, and towards lunchtime the students shifted heavily from one foot to the other. Sir Lancelot thought any young man incapable of standing on his own feet for a couple of hours another disagreeable product of modern life, like socialism.

On our first ward-round we were pushed easily into place by the precision with which the rest of the troupe fell in. Sir Lancelot strode across the ward, drew up sharply, and looked over the patients in the two rows of beds, sniffing the air like a dog picking up a scent. He thundered over to the bedside of a small, nervous man in the corner. The firm immediately rearranged itself, like a smart platoon at drill. The Chief towered on the right of the patient's head; Sister stood opposite, her nurses squeezed behind her; the students surrounded the foot and sides of the bed like a screen; and the registrar and housemen stood beyond them, at a distance indicating that they were no longer in need of any instruction in surgery.

Sir Lancelot pulled back the bedclothes like a conjurer revealing a successful trick.

'You just lie still, old fellow,' he boomed cheerfully at the patient. 'Don't you take any notice of what I'm going to say to these young doctors. You won't understand a word of what we're talking about, anyway. Take his pyjamas off, Sister. Now you, my boy,' he continued, gripping me tightly by the arm as I was nearest, 'take a look at that abdomen.'

I stretched out a hand to feel the patient gingerly in the region of the umbilicus. I noticed his skin was covered with goosepimples and twitched here and there nervously.

'Take your dirty little hand away!' said Sir Lancelot savagely, flicking it off the surface of the abdomen like a fly. He paused solemnly, and continued in a heavy tone, wagging his finger: 'The first rule of surgery, gentlemen—eyes first and most, hands

64

next and least, tongue not at all. Look first and don't chatter. An excellent rule for you to remember all your lives. Now look, boy, look.'

I gazed at the abdomen for a whole minute but it appeared no different from any that might be seen on Brighton beach. When I thought I had inspected it long enough to satisfy the Chief, who rose uncomfortably above me, I diffidently stretched out my arm and prodded about with my fingers in search of a lump.

'*Doucemong, doucemong,*' Sir Lancelot began again. 'Gently, boy—you're not making bread. Remember'—his finger came up again warningly—'a successful surgeon must have the eye of a hawk, the heart of a lion, and the hand of a lady.'

'And the commercial morals of a Levantine usurer,' murmured Grimsdyke under his breath.

With a glow of relief, I finally discovered the lump. It was about the size of an orange and tucked under the edge of the ribs. We lined up and felt it one after the other, while Sir Lancelot looked on closely and corrected anyone going about it the wrong way. Then he pulled a red grease-pencil from the top pocket of his coat and handed it to me.

'Where are we going to make the incision?' he asked. By now the patient was forgotten; it was the lump we were after. Sir Lancelot had an upsetting habit of treating the owners of lumps as if they were already rendered unconscious by the anæsthetic.

I drew a modest line over the lesion.

'Keyhole surgery!' said Sir Lancelot with contempt. 'Damnable! Give me the pencil!' He snatched it away. 'This, gentlemen, will be our incision.'

He drew a broad, decisive, red sweep from the patient's ribs to below his umbilicus.

'We will open the patient like *that*. Then we can have a good look inside. It's no good rummaging round an abdomen if you can't get your hand in comfortably. What do we do then? Right —take a better look at the lump we've been feeling. Do you think it's going to be easy to remove?' he asked me, gripping my arm again.

'No, sir.'

'Correct—it's going to be most difficult. And dangerous. There are at least a dozen ways in which we can make a slight error—even though we are experienced surgeons—and kill the patient like that!' He snapped his fingers frighteningly.

'Now!' He tapped the abdomen with his pencil as if knocking for admission. 'When we have cut through the skin what is the next structure we shall meet? Come on, you fellers. You've done your anatomy more recently than I have . . . what's that? Yes, subcutaneous fat. Then, gentlemen, we first encounter the surgeon's worst enemy.' He glared at us all in turn. 'What?' he demanded in general. There was no reply. 'Blood!' he thundered.

At that point the patient restored his personality to the notice of his doctors by vomiting.

* * * * *

Surgery was Sir Lancelot's life and St. Swithin's was his home. He had given more of his time for nothing to the hospital than he ever used to make his fortune. He was president or vice-president of almost every students' club and supported the rugby team from the touch-line in winter with the same roar he used on ignorant dressers in the theatre. During the war he slept every night at the hospital in the bombing, and operated on casualties in an improvised theatre in the basement as long as they came in. A team of students lived in as well and he used to play cards with them or share a pint of beer, actions which at first caused as much dismay as if he had arrived to operate in his underpants. One night St. Swithin's was hit while he was operating. The theatre rocked, the lights went out, and part of the ceiling fell in. But Sir Lancelot simply swore and went on—bombs to him were just another irritation in surgery, like fumbling assistants and blunt knives, and he treated them all the same way.

The only time Sir Lancelot became at all subdued was when he talked of his retirement. It hung over him all the time I was on his firm. The prospect of losing his two days a week at St. Swithin's depressed him, though he was cheered by remembering that the hospital would immediately acknowledge him as an emeritus consultant and perhaps call him in for cases of supreme difficulty. His connection with St. Swithin's would therefore not be completely broken; he could go on meeting the students at their clubs, and as for surgery he could continue that in private.

One day, shortly after I left his firm, he disappeared. He said good-bye to no one. He left his work to his assistant and wrote a note to the Chairman of the Governors simply stating he would not be in again. The hospital radiologist explained it later with an X-ray film. Sir Lancelot had a cancer in his stomach and had gone off to his cottage in Sussex to die. He refused to have an operation.

CHAPTER VIII

THE Nurses' Home at St. Swithin's was known, with a fair degree of accuracy, as the Virgins' Retreat. Virginity and nursing certainly seem to go together, and the Matron of St. Swithin's put her Ursulian duties first. Her regulations for the nurses' conduct suggested she was convinced they went through their waking and sleeping life at the hospital in unremitting danger of rape. It is true that a student or two occasionally entertained sinful thoughts towards one of her charges; like any other bunch of young men they were romantic souls, and the fact that young ladies took off their clothes for them in the wards did not deter them from trying for the same result in their lodgings. But, taking the nurses as a whole, their Matron's book of rules was nothing more than a blatant piece of flattery.

Intercourse between the nurses and students had to be but social to attract the Matron's displeasure. If a nurse was seen talking to a student in the hospital, apart from a brief necessary exchange of medical matters in the ward, she was dismissed unquestioned. For her to meet a student in her off-duty time—to go to the pictures or a concert, for instance—was automatically reckoned, if discovered, as the equivalent of a week-end in Brighton. And if a nurse was found in the students' quarters or a man of any sort discovered in the Nurses' Home it was an event apparently unmeasurable in terms of human horror.

In order to reduce the possibility of these alarming situations overtaking the nurse the opportunities she could present for them were heavily reduced. All first-year nurses had to be in by ten every night. The senior girls were allowed out once a week until eleven, and staff nurses were permitted in comparison a life of uninhibited lechery by being able to claim two weekly passes until twelve.

Nurses, when in the hospital, were authoritatively stripped of their sexual characteristics as far as was possible without operative interference. Make-up of any sort was looked upon by the ward sisters as the prerogative of women of the streets, and hair was supposed to be tightly tucked inside a starched uniform cap designed to be worn just over the eyebrows. The nurse's figure was de-contoured beneath uniform made out of a material similar to sailcloth, and the skirt was raised only far enough from the floor to let the poor girl walk without breaking her neck.

These regulations were naturally broken, as efficiently and as subtly as the lock on a medieval chastity belt. There were plenty of quiet corners about the hospital where a date could be arranged between student and nurse, and the couple had the whole of London to meet in. A thin, skilful brush with a lipstick could bring even from Sister Virtue nothing worse than suspicion and powder was almost invisible. As the cap had to be folded out of a linen square, with a little practice a girl could reduce it sufficiently in size so that it stuck attractively on the back of her head. As for the uniform, a nurse with any feelings of femininity in her veins immediately took her new outfit to a dressmaker to be shortened.

Shyness and the restrictions surrounding the nurses' social contacts kept me clear of my helpmeets in the ward, apart from the small amount of professional chat I dared to exchange with them. At the same time, the nurses took very little notice of me. With the senior students it was different: for them was the favour of a quick smile behind Sister's back, or a giggle in the sluice-room when no one was in earshot. The house-surgeons, who were doctors and therefore safe matrimonial investments, got cups of coffee when Sister was off duty and had their socks mended; and the registrar could quicken wildly any heart behind a starched apron bodice with a brief smile.

During my stay on Sir Lancelot's firm I began to gain a little confidence in myself in defiance of my surroundings. There was one nurse on the ward who seemed different from the rest. She was a slight little probationer downtrodden by the ward staff as heavily as I, which immediately spun a fine strand of sympathy between us. I felt sorry for her; and I thought, when I was being competently reduced to nothingness by Sister for using Sir Lancelot's special soap at the wash-basin, that she was silently commiserating with me.

She was a snub-nosed brunette with grey eyes and a small

mouth which she kept firmly closed in the ward. Her experience of St. Swithin's was even less than mine, for she had arrived at the hospital only a fortnight previously. It was axiomatic that any nurse who could stand the first six weeks would last the whole course and I was interested to watch her lips growing tighter and tighter as this critical period wore on, while she was discovering it was far less important to save a patient's life than to drop a plate of pudding, and to break a thermometer was a feminine crime just short of persistent shoplifting.

By glances, shy smiles, and putting myself in proximity to her in the ward as much as I dared, I managed to indicate my interest. One morning I was in the sluice-room half-heartedly performing the routine chemical tests on my patients' excreta when she came in and resignedly began to clean out the sink. Sister had sent her there obviously not knowing of my presence; the door shut us off from the ward; we were alone; so I took a chance.

'I say,' I said.

She looked up from the sink.

'I say,' I repeated, 'number six looks much better to-day, doesn't he? The Chief did a good job on him all right. You should have seen the way he got hold of the splenic artery when a clip came off! I've never seen so much blood in my life.'

'Please!' she said, holding her stomach. 'You're making me feel sick.'

'Oh, I'm awfully sorry,' I apologized quickly. 'I just thought you'd be interested.'

'I'm not,' she said. 'The sight of blood makes me sick. In fact, the whole damn place makes me sick. I thought I was going to put my cool hands on the fevered brows of grateful young men, and all I do is clean the floors and give out bedpans to bad-tempered old daddies who smell.'

'If you don't like it,' I suggested, shocked by her confession, 'why did you take it up at all? Why don't you leave?'

'The hell I won't! My mother was a nurse and she's been ramming it down my throat for nineteen years. If she could take it I damn well can!'

'Would you like to come out to the pictures?' I asked. I thought it best to cut out her complaints and reach my object without further skirmishing. Our privacy might be broken at any moment.

'You bet!' she said without hesitation. 'Anything to get out of this place! I'm off at six. Meet me in the tube station. I must get back to the ward or the old woman will tear me to bits.'

Feeling demurely pleased with myself, I went down to the King George to tell someone about this swift conquest. I found Tony Benskin and Grimsdyke sitting at the bar, energetically talking about racing with the Padre.

'I've just dated up that little pro on the ward,' I told them nonchalantly. 'I'm taking her out to-night.'

Benskin was horrified. He had an obsession that he might one day be trapped into matrimony by a nurse and walked round the hospital as warily as a winning punter passing the men with the three-card trick.

'It's the thin end of the wedge, my boy!' he exclaimed. 'You watch your step, or you'll end up as aisle-fodder before you know where you are. They're vixens, the lot of them.'

'And good luck to them,' Grimsdyke added emphatically. 'After all, that's what they come to the hospital for—to find a husband. They wouldn't admit it, but it's buried in the subconscious of all of them somewhere.'

'I thought nursing was supposed to be a vocation and a calling,' I said defensively.

'No more than our own job, my dear old boy. Why have we all taken up medicine? I've got a good reason, that I'm paid to do it. You've got a doctor as a father and a leaning towards medicine in your case is simply a hereditary defect. Tony here took it up because he couldn't think of anything better that would allow him to play rugger three times a week. How many of our colleagues entered the noble profession through motives of humanity?' Grimsdyke screwed his monocle hard in his eye. 'Damn few, I bet. Humanitarian feelings draw more young fellows annually into the London Fire Brigade. It's the same with the girls—nursing offers one of the few remaining respectable excuses to leave home. Let them marry the chaps, I say. They're strong, healthy girls who know how to cook. To my mind the most important function of the St. Swithin's nursing school is that it provides

71

competent wives to help in general practice anywhere in the world.'

'Three beers, please, Padre,' I said, interrupting him. 'Don't you think Grimsdyke's being unfair?'

'You've got to watch your step, sir, you can take it from me,' he said sombrely. 'I've seen more of you young gentlemen caught into marriage when you haven't a ha'penny to your name than I'd like to think about. Children soon, too, sir. Houses, gas bills, vacuum cleaners, and all the other little trappings of matrimony. It's an expensive hobby, take my word, sir, for young fellers before they're settled in practice.'

'Damn it,' I said, 'I've only asked the girl to the pictures. If I don't like her I won't see her again.'

'Easier said than done, sir. Ask Mr. Grimsdyke about that young lady last Christmas.'

Grimsdyke laughed. 'Ah, yes, Padre! I've still got it on me, I think.' He pulled out his wallet and rummaged through the papers it contained. 'Most tiresome woman—tried everything to get rid of her for a fortnight. Then I received that one morning, handed to me by a hospital porter, if you please.'

He gave me a note in angry feminine handwriting. *If you do not send an answer to this by midday,* it said curtly, *I shall hurl myself off the roof of the Nurses' Home.*

'What on earth did you say?' I asked, horrified.

'What could I say?' Grimsdyke demanded. 'Except "No reply."'

'Did she throw herself off?'

'I really don't know,' he said, replacing the letter. 'I never troubled to find out.'

I met my little nurse at six. We passed an innocuous evening and arranged a rendezvous for the next week. But the appointment was never kept. The following day she was transferred to Sister Virtue's ward, where she cracked up. One afternoon she threw a pink blancmange at Sister and went out and got a job as a bus conductress.

This incident temporarily cooled my enthusiasm for nurses. After a few weeks I attempted to kindle an affection for a fat blonde girl in the out-patient department, but after we had spent

72

a few evenings together she began to drift away from me, almost imperceptibly at first, like a big ship leaving dock. It was then that I started to worry about myself. Was it that I had no attraction for women? I never enjoyed success with my consorts while my friends apparently had no difficulty in committing fornication with theirs. I slunk into the library and looked up the psychology books: horror overcame me as I turned the pages. In my first few weeks in the wards I had been convinced that I was suffering from such complaints as tuberculosis, rheumatic heart, cancer of the throat, and pernicious anæmia, all of which successfully cleared up in a few days, but now I faced the terrible possibility of harbouring a mother fixation, oral eroticism, and a subnormal libido. I mentioned these fears to my friends that evening after supper.

'The trouble with you, my lad,' said John Bottle, without taking his eye from the microscope he was studying, 'is that you are suffering from that well-recognized clinical condition *orchitis amorosa acuta*, or lover's nuts.'

'Well,' I said sadly, 'I would willingly surrender my virginity if I could find someone to co-operate with me in the matter.'

'Can't you wait for a week?' Kelly asked testily. 'My path. exam is too near to let me go out for a night.'

His objection to my making an immediate start in my love life reflected the most serious menace to harmony in the flat.

We all agreed that it was important we should be able to ask our girl-friends to our home, and with the privacy without which the invitation would be pointless. As accommodation was limited it was equally important that the other three should not be obliged to tramp the streets angrily during the entire evening, or go to bed. Archie and Vera had been no problem because they kept to their own room, but some arrangement had to be made among the rest of us. We decided that each should have one evening a fortnight in which the sitting-room was to be his. A code was arranged: if the girl was brought in and presented to the others it required her host only to mention that it looked like rain for his friends to rise and troop out into the night like a well-drilled squad of infantry. (If he remarked that the weather was turning warmer they did an equally important service by sticking by him.) Then it was up to the man himself. But he had not the entire evening to fritter away in light amours. As the pubs shut at eleven he knew he could only count on the period until then as his own. His comrades would heartlessly return, considering they had left him time enough for a brisk seduction. If he failed to achieve his object in the time, that was his look-out. This probably had bad effects on our psychology, but it made us very persuasive.

'What about that girl from the out-patient department you were taking out?' Tony Benskin asked.

I shrugged my shoulders. 'No good.'

'Won't play?' John Bottle asked with interest. 'I thought as much . . . you want to take my tip and lay off the probationers. Altogether too young and unappreciative. They can still remember the games' mistress said it would ruin their hockey.'

Mike Kelly was sitting in an arm-chair by the fire, frowning into a yellow-covered book on fevers. He carefully put his finger on his place before speaking.

'You might try the theatre sister from number six,' he suggested faintly.

'Oh, she's no use,' John said with authority. 'Registrars only in that department. She's the sort of girl who'd hardly look at a houseman, let alone a poor bloody student.'

'There's that little blonde staff nurse just come on Loftus's ward,' Mike continued helpfully. 'She looks as if she'd be worth making advances to.'

'Hopeless!' John said. 'She suffers badly from tinnitus—ringing in the ears, and they're wedding bells.'

'How about Rigor Mortis?' Tony suggested, suddenly looking pleased with himself.

'Old Rigor . . . that's more like it!' John agreed. 'She's always ready for a tumble with anybody.'

'The nursery slopes for our friend,' remarked Mike warmly.

'Rigor Mortis?' I asked dubiously.

'Oh, that's not her real name of course,' Tony explained. 'It's Ada something or other. Haven't you come across her?'

'I don't think so.'

'She's not a great beauty,' he went on, 'so perhaps that's why

74

you haven't noticed her. But she has the kindest heart imaginable. She's the staff nurse on Loftus's male ward. I knew her well, old man. I'll introduce you. The more I think of it the more certain I am that she's what you need. She expects the minimum of entertainment and it is hardly necessary to do more than hold her hand and look plaintive. Capital! You shall meet her to-morrow.'

Tony took me to meet Rigor Mortis the following afternoon, when the ward sister was off duty. I immediately agreed that she wasn't much to look at. She had dull black hair which she pushed into her starched cap like the stuffing in a cushion, a chin like a boxer's, and eyebrows that met in the middle.

She was about six feet tall and had a bosom as shapeless as a plate of scrambled eggs. But all these blemishes melted before my eyes, which were fired with Benskin's firm recommendation that she had a kind heart.

After a minute's cheery conversation Tony explained that I had been bursting to make her acquaintance for some months. He asked her if she was doing anything on her next night off; all I had to do was mumble an invitation to the pictures, which she briskly accepted. I arranged to meet her outside Swan and Edgar's at six and we parted.

'There you are, old man,' Tony said as we left the ward. 'Meet her at six, whip her into a flick, take her back to the flat for a drink—that'll be about nine-thirty. You'll have two solid hours to do your stuff.'

I arranged for the seduction with considerable care. I stayed away from the afternoon lecture and spent the time cleaning up the sitting-room, putting the books away, straightening the cover on the divan, and arranging the reading light so the glow fell romantically in the corner. I set out a new packet of cigarettes and invested in half a bottle of gin. There were two glasses in the kitchen that happened to be the same pattern, and these I carefully washed, dried, and placed on the mantelpiece. It was only five, so I sat down and read the evening paper. I was nervous and worried, as though I was going to the dentist. I began to wish I hadn't introduced the idea at all. But I could no longer back out. I must be victorious by eleven or sink in the opinions of my friends. I took a nip of the gin and set out.

75

For a few minutes I hoped she wouldn't turn up, but she lumbered out of the Underground right enough. She looked a little better in civilian clothes, but I still thought her as unattractive as an old sofa. I suggested the New Gallery, and she agreed. She seemed fairly friendly, but I soon discovered that she was disinclined to take the initiative in conversation. If I spoke she replied; if I remained silent she appeared to be concentrating heavily on thoughts of her own. I had therefore to keep up a run of inane patter, every sentence on a different subject, until the film released us into merciful mutual silence.

About half-way through the picture I abruptly recalled the object of my expedition. Should I give just the faintest hint of what was to come, I wondered, and hold her hand? It would be the herald's call to the approaching tussle. Would she rebuff this forwardness so early, for I had hardly known her an hour? I gave a sly glance through the darkness and seized her rough palm. She gripped mine without thinking, without an indication that her mind was distracted a hairsbreadth from the screen.

The two of us stood outside in Regent Street. I asked casually if she would care to come home for a drink, and meet the boys. She assented with the same air as she accepted my hand in the cinema. We went to Oxford Circus tube station and I bought a couple of tickets. I held her arm as we walked down the road to the flat and up the steps. The stairs . . . opening the door . . . my surprise that no one was there. She sat down on the divan without a word, and I lit the gas-fire. She took a drink in an off-hand way. We sat in the glow of the gas and the dim light of my romantic bulb.

I finished a cigarette and gave her another drink. Surely, I thought, this would have some effect? She had two or three more, but sat looking absently at the fire, dully returning a sentence for each one of mine, unanimated, unresponsive, unworried.

I nervously looked at my watch and saw with alarm that it was past ten-thirty. I had to get a move on. I felt like a man going out to start an old car on a cold morning.

I held her hand tighter. She didn't object. I drew closer. She moved neither away nor nearer. I put my arm round her and started stroking her off-side ear. She remained passive, like a cow with its mind on other things.

The seconds ticked away from my wrist, faster and faster. At least, I thought, I have gone this far without rebuff. I kissed her on the cheek. She still sat pleasantly there, saying nothing. Carefully setting down my glass, I stroked her blouse firmly. I might just as well have been brushing her coat. I threw myself at her and she rolled back on the divan like a skittle. With great energy I continued her erotic stimulation. Any moment now, I thought excitedly, and the object of the evening would be achieved. She lay wholly unconcerned. Suddenly she moved. With one hand she picked up the evening paper I had left on the divan. She read the headlines.

'Oh look!' she exclaimed with sympathy, 'there's been an awful train crash at Chelmsford. Seventeen killed!'

* * * * * *

'So you had no luck?' Tony asked at midnight.

'None. None at all.'

'That's tough. Cheer up . . . other fish, you know.'

I decided to do my fishing in future in more turbulent waters, even if I had no catch.

77

CHAPTER IX

In order to teach the students midwifery St. Swithin's supervised the reproductive activities of the few thousand people who lived in the overcrowded area surrounding the hospital. In return, they co-operated by refusing to water down the demands of Nature with the less pressing requests of the Family Planning Association.

The midwifery course is of more value to the student than a piece of instruction on delivering babies. It takes him out of the hospital, where everything is clean and convenient and rolled up on sterile trollies, to the environment he will be working in when he goes into practice—a place of dirty floors, bed-bugs, no hot water, and lights in the most inconvenient places; somewhere without nurses but with bands of inquisitive children and morbid relatives; a world of broken stairs, unfindable addresses, and cups of tea in the kitchen afterwards.

It was fortunate that I was plunged into the practice of midwifery shortly after my unfruitful love life, for it is a subject which usually produces a sharp reactionary attack of misogyny in its students. Tony Benskin, Grimsdyke, and myself started 'on the district' together. We had to live in the hospital while we were midwifery clerks, in rooms the size of isolation cubicles on the top floor of the resident doctors' quarters. My predecessor, a tall, fair-haired, romantic-looking man called Lamont, had been so moved by his experiences he was on the point of breaking off his engagement.

'The frightful women!' he said heatedly, as he tried to cram a pile of text-books into his case. 'I can't understand that anyone would ever want to sleep with them. That someone obviously has done so in the near past is quite beyond me.'

'How many babies have you had?' I asked.

'Forty-nine. That includes a couple of Cæsars. I'd have made a half-century if I hadn't missed a B.B.A.'

'B.B.A.?'

'Born before arrival. Terrible disgrace for the midder clerk, of course. I reckoned I'd have time for my lunch first, and when I got there the blasted thing was in the bed. However, mother and child did well, so I suppose no real harm was done. Don't try and open the window, it's stuck. I'm going out to get drunk. Best of luck.'

Picking up his bag he left, the latest penitent for the sin of Adam.

I sat on the bed, feeling depressed. It was an unusually raw afternoon in November and the sky hung over the roof-tops in an unbroken dirty grey sheet. There was no fire in the room and the pipes emitted flatulent noises but no heat. The only decoration was a large black-and-white map of the district on which some former student had helpfully added the pubs in red ink. I looked out of the window and saw a few flakes of snow—ominous, like the first spots of a smallpox rash. I wished women would go away and bud, like the flowers.

The three of us reported to the senior resident obstetrical officer, a worried-looking young man whom we found in the ante-natal clinic. This clinic was part of the St. Swithin's service. Every Thursday afternoon the mothers came and sat on the benches outside the clinic door, looking like rows of over-ripe poppy-heads. The obstetrical officer was absently running his hands over an abdomen like the dome of St. Paul's to find which way up the baby was.

'You the new clerks?' he asked, without interest.

We each nodded modestly.

'Well, make sure you're always within call. When you go out on a case a midwife will be sent separately by the local maternity service, so you've got nothing to worry about. Don't forget to carry two pennies in your pocket.

'To 'phone, of course,' he said when I asked why. 'If you get into trouble dash for the nearest box and call me, and I'll come out in a police car. Don't wait till it's too late, either.'

He dismissed us and bent over to listen to the fœtal heart rate with a stethoscope shaped like a small flower-vase.

Our next call was on the extern sister, who controlled all the midwifery students. I found her a most interesting woman. She was so ugly she could never have had much expectation of fulfilling her normal biological function; now she had been over-taken by the sad menopause and was left no chance of doing so at all. As she had not been offered the opportunity of bearing children she had thrown herself into midwifery like a novice into religion. She knew more about it than the obstetrical officer. She could talk only about mothers and babies and thought of everyone solely as a reproductive element. In her room was a gold medal she had won in her examinations, which she proudly displayed in a small glass-covered frame between two prints of Peter Scott's ducks. She talked of the anatomy involved in the birth of a baby as other women described their favourite shopping street. She had, however, the unfortunate trick of awarding the parts of the birth canal to the listener.

'When your cervix is fully dilated,' she told us gravely, 'you must decide whether to apply your forceps to your baby. You must feel to see if your head or your breech is presenting.'

'Supposing it's your shoulder or your left ear?' asked Benskin.

'Then you put your hand in your uterus and rotate your child,' she replied without hesitation.

She gave us a rough idea of delivering babies and demonstrated the two instrument bags we had to take on our cases. They were long leather affairs, like the luggage of a dressy cricketer, containing sufficient material to restore the biggest disaster it was likely a student could pull down on himself. There were bottles of antiseptic, ether and chloroform, needles and catgut in tins of Lysol, a pair of obstetrical forceps, a peculiar folding canvas arrangement for holding up the mother's legs, enamel bowls, rubber gloves, and a number of unidentifiable packages.

'You must check your bags before you go to your mother,' Sister said.

We chalked our room-numbers on the board in the hall and went out for a drink in the King George. The snow was falling thickly, swirling round the lamp-posts and clinging to the hospital walls, giving the old building a more sinister appearance than ever.

'What a night to start stork-chasing!' Grimsdyke exclaimed.

'What happens when we get out there?' I asked.

'Getting nervous, old boy?'

'I am a bit. I haven't seen a baby born before. I might faint or something.'

'There's nothing to worry about,' Benskin told me cheerfully. 'I was talking to one of the chaps we're relieving. The midwife always gets there first and tells you what to do under her breath. They're a good crowd. They let the patient think you're the doctor, which is good for the morale of both of you.'

We went back to the hospital for dinner. Afterwards Benskin asked the duty porter if everything was still quiet.

'Not a thing, sir,' he replied. 'It's a bad sign, all right. After it's been as quiet as this for a bit they start popping out like rabbits from their warrens.'

We sat in Grimsdyke's room and played poker for matches for a couple of hours. It was difficult to concentrate on the game. Every time the 'phone bell rang in the distance we jumped up nervously together. Grimsdyke suggested bed at ten, predicting we would be roused as soon as we dropped off to sleep. We cut for who should be on first call: I lost.

It was four when the porter woke me up. He cheerily pulled off the bedclothes and handed me a slip of paper with an address scribbled on it in pencil.

'You'd better hurry, sir,' he said. 'They sounded proper worried over the 'phone.'

I rolled out of bed and dressed with the enthusiasm of a prisoner on his execution morning. The night outside was as thick and white as a rice pudding. After a glance through the curtains I pulled a green-and-yellow hooped rugby jersey over my shirt and a dirty cricket sweater over that. I tucked the ends of my trousers into football stockings, wrapped a long woollen scarf round my neck and hid the lot under a duffle coat. I looked as if I was going to take the middle watch on an Arctic fishing vessel.

The reason for this conscientious protection against the weather was the form of transport allotted to the students to reach their cases. It was obviously impossible to provide such inconsequential people with a car and we were nearly all too poor to own one ourselves. On the other hand, if the students had been forced to walk to their patients the race would have gone to the storks. A compromise had therefore been effected some ten years ago and the young obstetricians had the loan of the midwifery bicycle.

This vehicle had unfortunately not worn well in the service of the obstetrical department. It had originally been equipped with such necessaries as brakes, mudguards, lights, and rubber blocks on the pedals, but, as human beings sadly lose their hair, teeth, and firm subcutaneous fat in the degeneration of age, the machine had similarly been reduced to its bare comfortless bones. The saddle had the trick of slipping unexpectedly and throwing the rider either backwards or forwards, it was impossible to anticipate. The only way to stop the machine was by falling off. It was the most dangerous complication of midwifery in the practice of the hospital.

I searched for the address on the map. It was on the other side of the district, a short, narrow, coy street hiding between a brewery and a goods yard. It seemed as remote as Peru.

I waddled down to the out-patient hall to collect the instrument bags. The place was cold and deserted; the porter who had called me was yawning in the corner over the telephone, and the two night nurses huddled in their cloaks round their tiny electric fire, sewing their way through a stack of gauze dressings. They took no notice of the globular figure coming down the stairs: an insignificant midwifery clerk wasn't worth dropping a stitch for. For the houseman, or, if they were lucky, one of the registrars come to open an emergency appendix—to them they would give a cup of coffee and a flutter of the eyelids. But what good were the junior students?

The bicycle was kept in a small shed in the hospital courtyard, and had for its stablemate the long trolley used for moving unlucky patients to the mortuary. I saw that the first problem of the case was balancing myself and my equipment on the machine. As well as the two leather bags I had a couple of drums the size of biscuit barrels containing the sterilized dressings. There was a piece of thick string attached to the bicycle, which I felt was probably part of its structure, but I removed it and suspended the two drums round my neck like a yoke. Carefully mounting the machine, I clung to the bags and the handlebars with both hands and pedalled uncertainly towards the front gate. The snowflakes fell upon me eagerly, like a crowd of mosquitoes, leaping for my face, the back of my neck, and my ankles.

The few yards across the courtyard were far enough to indicate the back tyre was flat and the direction of the front wheel had no constant relationship to the way the handlebars were pointing. I crunched to a stop by the closed iron gates and waited for the porter to leave his cosy cabin and let me out.

'You all right, sir?' he asked with anxiety.

'Fine,' I said, 'I love it like this. It makes me feel like a real doctor.'

'Well,' he said dubiously, 'good luck, sir.'

'Thank you.'

The porter turned the key in the lock and pulled one of the gates open against the resisting snow.

'Your back light isn't working, sir,' he shouted.

I called back I thought it didn't matter and pedalled away into the thick night feeling like Captain Oates. I had done about twenty yards when the chain came off.

After replacing the chain I managed to wobble along the main road leading away from the hospital in the direction of the brewery. The buildings looked as hostile as polar ice-cliffs. Everything appeared so different from the kindly daytime, which gave life to the cold, dead streets with the brisk circulation of traffic. Fortunately, my thorough knowledge of the local public houses provided a few finger-posts, and I might have done tolerably well as a flying angel of mercy if the front wheel hadn't dropped off.

I fell into the snow in the gutter and wished I had gone in for the law. As I got to my feet I reflected that the piece of string might have been something important to do with the attachment of the front wheel; but now the lesion was inoperable. Picking up my luggage, I left the machine to be covered by the snow like a dead husky and trudged on. By now I was fighting mad. I told myself I would damn well deliver that baby. If it dared to precipitate itself into the world ungraciously without waiting for me I decided I would strangle it.

I turned off the main road towards the brewery, but after a few hundred yards I had to admit I was lost. Even the pubs were unfamiliar. I now offered no resistance to my environment and submissively felt the moisture seeping through my shoes. I leant against a sheltering doorpost, preparing to meet death in as gentlemanly a way as possible.

At that moment a police car, forced like myself into the snow, stopped in front of me. The driver swung his light on my load and on myself, and had no alternative than to decide I was a suspicious character. He asked for my identity card.

'Quick!' I said dramatically. 'I am going to a woman in childbirth.'

'Swithin's?' asked the policeman.

'Yes. It may be too late. I am the doctor.'

'Hop in the back!'

There is nothing that delights policemen more than being thrown into a midwifery case. There is a chance they might have to assist in the performance, which means a picture in the evening papers and congratulatory beer in the local. The constable who walked into St. Swithin's one afternoon with an infant born on the lower deck of a trolley bus looked as pleased as if he were the father.

The warm police car took me to the address, and the crew abandoned me with reluctance. It was a tall, dead-looking tenement for ever saturated with the smells of brewing and shunting. I banged on the knocker and waited.

A thin female child of about five opened the door.

'I'm the doctor,' I announced.

The arrival of the obstetrician in such a briskly multiplying area caused no more stir than the visit of the milkman.

'Upstairs, mate,' she said, and scuttled away into the darkness like a rat.

The house breathed the sweet stench of bed-bugs; inside it was dark, wet, and rotting. I fumbled my way to the stairs and creaked upwards. On the second floor a door opened a foot, a face peered through, and as the shaft of light caught me it was slammed shut. It was on the fifth and top floor that the accouchement seemed to be taking place, as there was noise and light coming from under one of the doors. I pushed it open and lumbered in.

'Don't worry!' I said. 'I have come.'

I took a look round the room. It wasn't small, but a lot was

84

going on in it. In the centre three or four children were fighting on the pockmarked linoleum for possession of their plaything, a piece of boxwood with a nail through it. A fat woman was unconcernedly making a cup of tea on a gas-ring in one corner, and in the other a girl of about seventeen with long yellow hair was reading last Sunday's *News of the World*. A cat, sympathetic to the excited atmosphere, leapt hysterically among the children. Behind the door was a bed, beside which was grandma—who always appears on these occasions, irrespective of the social standing of the participants. Grandma was giving encouragement tempered with warning to the mother, a thin, pale, fragile woman on the bed, and it was obvious that the affair had advanced alarmingly. A tightly-packed fire roared in the grate and above the mantelpiece Field-Marshal Montgomery, of all people, looked at the scene quizzically.

'Her time is near, doctor,' said grandma with satisfaction.

'You have no need to worry any longer, missus,' I said brightly.

I dropped the kit on the floor and removed my duffle coat, which wept dirty streams on to the lino. The first step was to get elbow-room and clear out the non-playing members of the team.

'Who are you?' I asked the woman making tea.

'From next door,' she replied. 'I thought she'd like a cup of tea, poor thing.'

'I want some hot water,' I said sternly. 'Lots of hot water. Fill basins with it. Or anything you like. Now you all go off and make me some hot water. Take the children as well. Isn't it past their bedtime?'

'They sleep in 'ere, doctor,' said grandma.

'Oh. Well—they can give you a hand. And take the cat with you. Come on—all of you. Lots of water, now.'

They left unwillingly, in disappointment. They liked their entertainment to be fundamental.

'Now, mother,' I started, when we were alone. A thought struck me—hard, in the pit of the stomach. The midwife—the cool, practised, confident midwife. Where was she? Tonight—this memorable night to the two of us in the room—what had happened to her? Snowbound, of course. I felt like an actor who

85

has forgotten his lines and finds the prompter has gone out for a drink.

'Mother,' I said earnestly. 'How many children have you?'

'Five, doctor,' she groaned.

Well, that was something. At least one of us knew a bit about it.

She began a frightening increase in activity.

'I think it's coming, doctor!' she gasped, between pains. I grasped her hand vigorously.

'You'll be right as rain in a minute,' I said, as confidently as possible. 'Leave it to me.'

'I feel sick,' she cried miserably.

'So do I,' I said.

I wondered what on earth I was going to do.

There was, however, one standby that I had thoughtfully taken the trouble to carry. I turned into the corner furthest away from the mother and looked as if I was waiting confidently for the precise time to intervene. Out of my hip pocket I drew a small but valuable volume in a limp red cover—*The Student's Friend in Obstetrical Difficulties*. It was written by a hard-headed obstetrician on the staff of a Scottish hospital who was under no illusions about what the student would find difficult. It started off with 'The Normal Delivery.' The text was written without argument, directly, in short numbered paragraphs, like a cookery book. I glanced at the first page.

'Sterility,' it said. 'The student must try to achieve sterile surroundings for the delivery, and scrub-up himself as for a surgical operation. Newspapers may be used if sterile towels are unobtainable, as they are often bacteria-free.'

Newspaper, that was it! There was a pile of them in the corner, and I scattered the sheets over the floor and the bed. This was a common practice in the district, and if he knew how many babies were born yearly straight on to the *Daily Herald* Mr. Percy Cudlipp would be most surprised.

There was a knock on the door, and grandma passed through an enamel bowl of boiling water.

'Is it come yet, doctor?' she asked.

'Almost,' I told her. 'I shall need lots more water.'

I put the bowl down on the table, took some soap and a brush from the bag, and started scrubbing.

'Oh, doctor, doctor. . . !' cried the mother.

'Don't get alarmed,' I said airily.

'It's coming, doctor!'

I scrubbed furiously. The mother groaned. Grandma shouted through the door she had more hot water. I shouted back at her to keep out. The cat, which had not been removed as ordered, jumped in the middle of the newspaper and started tearing at it with its claws.

Suddenly I became aware of a new note in the mother's cries—a higher, wailing, muffled squeal. I dropped the soap and tore back the bedclothes.

*   *   *   *   *

The baby was washed and tucked up in one of the drawers from the wardrobe, which did a turn of duty as a cot about once a year. The mother was delighted and said she had never had such a comfortable delivery. The spectators were readmitted, and cooed over the infant. There were cups of tea all round. I had the best one, with sugar in it. I felt the name of the medical profession never stood higher.

'Do you do a lot of babies, doctor?' asked the mother.

'Hundreds,' I said. 'Every day.'

'What's your name, doctor, if you don't mind?' she said.

I told her.

'I'll call 'im after you. I always call them after the doctor or the nurse, according.'

I beamed and bowed graciously. I was genuinely proud of the child. It was my first baby, born through my own skill and care. I had already forgotten in the flattering atmosphere that my single manœuvre in effecting the delivery was pulling back the eiderdown.

Packing the instruments up, I climbed into my soggy duffle-coat and, all smiles, withdrew. At the front door I found to my contentment that the snow had stopped and the roads shone attractively in the lamplight. I began to whistle as I walked away. At that moment the midwife turned the corner on her bicycle.

87

'Sorry, old chap,' she said, as she drew up. 'I was snowed under. Have you been in?'

'In! It's all over.'

'Did you have any trouble?' she asked dubiously.

'Trouble!' I said with contempt. 'Not a bit of it! It went splendidly.'

'I suppose you remembered to remove the afterbirth?'

'Of course.'

'Well, I might as well go home then. How much did it weigh?'

'Nine pounds on the kitchen scales.'

'You students are terrible liars.'

I walked back to the hospital over the slush as if it were a thick pile carpet. The time was getting on. A hot bath, I thought, then a good breakfast . . . and a day's work already behind me. I glowed in anticipation as I suddenly became aware that I was extremely hungry.

At the hospital gate the porter jumped up from his seat.

' 'Urry up, sir,' he said, 'and you'll just make it.'

'What's all this?' I asked with alarm.

'Another case, sir. Been waiting two hours. The other gentlemen are out already.'

'But what about my breakfast?'

'Sorry, sir. Not allowed to go to meals if there's a case. Orders of the Dean.'

'Oh, hell!' I said. I took the grubby slip of paper bearing another address. 'So this is midwifery,' I added gloomily.

'That's right, sir,' said the porter cheerfully. 'It gets 'em all down in the end.'

CHAPTER X

EVERYONE working in hospital is so preoccupied with the day-to-day rush of minor crises that the approach of Christmas through the long, dark, bronchitic weeks of midwinter comes as a surprise. The holiday cuts brightly into hospital routine, like an unexpected ray of sunlight in an Inner Circle tunnel. At St. Swithin's there was, however, one prodromal sign of the approaching season—a brisk increase in attendance at the children's department.

Every year at Christmas the Governors gave a tea-party in the main hall of the hospital for a thousand or so of the local boys and girls. They were men not used to stinting their hospitality, and provided richly for the tastes of their guests. It was the sort of affair that could be adequately described only by Ernest Hemingway, Negley Farson, or some other writer with a gift of extracting a forceful attractiveness from descriptions of active animals feeding in large numbers.

The children began to collect outside the locked doors of the out-patient department soon after midday; by three the front of the hospital looked like an Odeon on Saturday morning. At four sharp the doors were opened by the porters and the mob was funnelled into the building—scratching, fighting, shouting, and screaming, their incidental distractions from the fists and elbows of their neighbours overwhelmed with the urgent common desire to get at the food. They rushed through the entrance lobby, stormed the broad, wooden-floored hall, and expended their momentum in a pile of sticky, white-glazed buns.

The buns were the foundation of the party, but there was a great deal more besides—a high Christmas cake flaming with candles, churns of strawberry ice-cream, jellies the colours of traffic lights, oranges with a tenacious aroma, and sweet tea in long enamelled jugs. The non-edible attractions included paper chains, crackers, funny hats, a tree ten feet high, and Father Christmas. It was the duty of the children's house-physician to play this part. The gown, whiskers, sack, and toys were provided

89

by the Governors; all the doctor had to do was allow himself to be lowered in a fire-escape apparatus from the roof into the tight mob of children screaming below. This obligation he discharged with the feelings of a nervous martyr being dropped into the bear-pit.

It was inevitable that he should breathe heavily on his little patients a strong smell of mixed liquors, which never missed their sharp, experienced noses and gave rise to delighted comments:

'Coo! 'Ees bin boozing!'

'Smells like Dad on Saturday!'

'Give us a train, Mister!'

All this the house-physician had to endure with a set smile of determined benevolence.

The party was controlled, where possible, by the out-patient sister and a reinforced staff of nurses. Their starched caps and aprons melted in the afternoon with the ice-cream as they attempted to impose the principle of fair shares on a community demonstrating a vigorous capitalist spirit of grabbing what they could. The energy of the children diminished only if they had to retire to a corner to be sick; but the hospitality of St. Swithin's was unlimited, and it usually happened that several of the little guests were later asked to stay the night.

The reason that the annual tea-party afforded as sure an indication that Christmas was approaching as a polite postman lay in the rules for admission to the jamboree. The Governors had decided many years ago that as it was impossible to entertain every child in the district invitations should be sent only to those who had attended the hospital in the months of November and December. As all the children within several miles knew of the party and were perfectly familiar with the qualifications for entry the increase in juvenile morbidity after October 31st was always alarming. This had recently led an ingenuous new house-physician in the department to sit down and prepare for publication in the *Lancet* a scientific paper on the startling increase in stomach-ache and growing pains among London school children in the last quarter of the year.

The goings-on at Christmas-time were conducted with the excuse that the staff was obliged to entertain the patients, just as adults take themselves off to circuses and pantomimes on the pretext of amusing the children. The wards were decorated, the out-patient hall spanned with streamers, and on Christmas Day even the operating theatres were festooned. The hospital presented the grotesque appearance of a warship during Navy Week, when the guns and other sinister implements aboard are covered with happy bunting. Relatives, friends, visiting staff, old graduates, and students overran the place; it was an enormous family party.

I had dutifully returned home the first Christmas I was in the hospital, but for the second I decided to stay and join in the fun. I was then coming to the end of my second session of medical clerking, this time as a protégé of the Dean, Dr. Loftus, on Prudence ward.

A week before Christmas Eve the ward sister distributed sheets of coloured crêpe paper round the patients and set them cutting frilly shades for the bed-lamps, paper chains, cut-outs for sticking on the windows, and the other paraphernalia of Christmas. Sister Prudence was different from the majority of her colleagues at St. Swithin's. She was a fat, kindly, jovial woman with an inefficiently concealed affection for Guinness' stout. She never had a bitter word for the students, whom she regarded as pleasantly irresponsible imbeciles, and she treated the nurses as normally fallible human beings. Above all, she had the superb recommendation of hating Sister Virtue's guts.

'I'm so worried about number twelve,' she said to me quietly one afternoon. I followed her glance to a wizened, sallow old man lying flat on his back cutting out a red paper doll with no enthusiasm. 'I do hope he won't die before Christmas,' she continued. 'It would be such a pity for him to miss it all!'

On Christmas Eve the students and nurses tacked up the paper chains and fixed the Christmas tree in front of the sanitary-looking door of the sluice-room. Sister beamed at the volunteers, as she was then certain her ward would be more richly decorated than Sister Virtue's. It was a vivid jungle in paper. Red and yellow streamers hung in shallow loops across the forbidding ceiling and the dark woodwork of the walls was covered refreshingly with coloured stars, circles, and rosettes, like a dull winter flower-bed in springtime. The severely functional lights over the beds were softened by paper lanterns, which emitted so little light, however, that they transformed even a simple manœuvre like giving an injection into an uncomfortable and dangerous operation. The black iron bedrails were garlanded with crimson crêpe, the long table down the middle of the ward was banked with synthetic snow, and blatantly unsterile holly flourished unrebuked in every corner. Most important of all, a twig of mistletoe hung over the doorway. By hospital custom, to avoid interruption in the daily working of the ward the sprig was not put into use until Christmas morning; before then the nurses and the students took a new and keen appraisal of each other with sidelong glances, each deciding whom they would find themselves next to when the sport opened. As for Sister Prudence, she would have taken it as a personal insult not to be embraced by everyone from Dr. Loftus down to the most junior student. 'I *do* like Christmas!' she said enthusiastically. 'It's the only time an old body like me ever gets kissed!'

The students had a more exacting task at Christmas than simply decorating the ward. It was a tradition at St. Swithin's that each firm produced, and presented in one of the main wards, a short theatrical entertainment. This was in accordance with the established English custom of dropping the national mantle of self-consciousness at Christmas-time and revealing the horrible likeness of the charade underneath. No one at St. Swithin's would have shirked acting in, or witnessing, the Christmas shows any more than they would have contemplated refusing to operate on an acute appendix. They were part of the hospital history, and it was handed down that Sir Benjamin Bone himself when a student contributed a fine baritone to the Christmas entertainment while the young Larrymore accompanied him on a violin, deliberately out of key.

The dramatic construction of these performances was as rigidly conventional as classical Greek drama or provincial pantomime. There were certain things that had to be included, or the audience was left wondering and cheated. It was essential at one point for a large student to appear dressed as a nurse with two pairs of rugger socks as falsies. There had to be a song containing broad references to the little professional and personal idiosyncrasies of the consultant staff—oddities that they had previously been under the impression passed unnoticed. Equally important were unsubtle jests about bedpans and similar pieces of hospital furniture. One scene had to represent a patient suffering under the attentions of a scrum of doctors and students, and there was always a burst of jolly community singing at the end.

The players had their conventions as well. No troupe would have contemplated for a moment taking the boards sober, and the most important member of the cast was the supernumerary who wheeled round the firkin of beer on a stretcher. It was also essential to carry a spare actor or two in the company, as on most occasions some of the active performers were overcome before the last scenes and had to be carried to the wings.

Two days before Christmas Grimsdyke took the initiative by ordering our firm to assemble in the King George at opening time that evening. There were seven of us: Grimsdyke and Tony Benskin, John Bottle, the middle-aged student Sprogget, Evans the brilliant Welshman, the keen student Harris, and myself. We collected round the piano in a corner of the bar.

'Now, look here, you fellows,' Grimsdyke began with authority. 'We must scratch up a bit of talent between us. Time's getting short. We've only got a day and a half to write, produce, and rehearse what will be the most magnificent of performances that ever hit St. Swithin's. Can any of you chaps play the piano?'

'I can play a bit,' I said. 'But mostly hymns.'

'That doesn't matter. Those hymn tunes can be turned into anything you like with a bit of ingenuity. There's one thing settled at any rate. What sort of piece shall we do? A panto, or a sort of pierrot show?'

'I think I ought to tell you,' said Harris aggressively, 'that I am considered pretty hot stuff at singing "Little Polly Perkins from Paddington Green". I gave it at the church concert at home last year, and it made quite a sensation.'

'Please!' said Grimsdyke. 'Can anyone else do anything? You can conjure, can't you, Tony?'

'One does the odd trick,' Benskin admitted modestly. 'Nothing spectacular like sawing a nurse in half, though—just rabbits out of hats and suchlike.'

'It'll amuse the kids, so we'll put you in. You can also dress up as a nurse somewhere in the show. John, you'd better take the romantic lead. What can you do, Sprogget?'

'Me? Oh, well, I don't do anything . . . that is, well, you know . . .' He gave an embarrassed giggle. 'I do child imitations.'

'Good for you. Child imitations it shall be. Evans, my dear old boy, you shall be general understudy, stage manager, wardrobe mistress, and ale carrier. You haven't got one of those lilting Welsh voices, I suppose?'

'My voice is only any good when diluted with forty thousand others at Twickenham.'

'Oh well, Harris will have to sing, I suppose. It's unavoidable. That seems to have settled the casting difficulties.'

'What about you? What are you going to do?' I asked him.

'I shall write, produce, and compère the piece, as well as reciting a short poem of my own composition in honour of St. Swithin's. I think it should go over very well. I suppose nobody has any objections to that?'

We shook our heads submissively.

'Good. Now what we want is a title. It must be short, snappy, brilliantly funny, and with a medical flavour the patients can understand. Any suggestions?'

The seven of us thought for a few minutes in silence.

'How about "Laughing Gas"?' I suggested.

Grimsdyke shook his head. 'Too trite.'

' "Babies in the Ward"?' said Benskin eagerly. 'Or "The Ninety-niners"?'

'They were both used last year.'

'I've got it!' Harris jumped up from behind the piano. ' "Enema for the Skylark"! How's that?'

'Horrible.'

We thought again. Grimsdyke suddenly snapped his fingers. 'Just the thing!' he announced. 'The very thing! What's wrong with "Jest Trouble"?'

His cast looked at him blankly.

' "Jest Trouble," you see,' he explained. 'Pun on "Chest Trouble." All the patients know what that means. Get it? Exactly the right touch, I think. Now let's get on and write a script.'

94

The production was born with—in relation to its small size and immaturity—intense labour pains. As the cast had to continue their routine hospital work the producer found it difficult to assemble them on one spot at the same time; and when they did arrive, each one insisted on rewriting the script as he went along. I drooped over the piano trying hard to transform the melody of 'Onward Christian Soldiers' into a suitable accompaniment for a cautionary duet Benskin and Grimsdyke insisted on singing, beginning:

> *'If the ill that troubles you is a tendency to lues,*
> *And you're positive your Wasserman is too.'*

And ending:

> *'My poor little baby, he's deaf and he's dumb,*
> *My poor little baby's insane:*
> *He's nasty big blisters all over his tum,*
> *What a shame, what a shame, what a shame!'*

When the King George closed we moved to the deserted students' common room; when we were hoarse and exhausted we flopped to sleep on the springless sofas. We rehearsed grimly all the next day. Late on Christmas Eve Grimsdyke rubbed his hands and announced, 'This would bring a smile to the lips of a chronic melancholic.'

CHAPTER XI

THE patients saw plenty of Christmas Day. They were woken up by the night nurses at five a.m. as usual, given a bowl of cold water and wished a Merry Christmas. After breakfast the nurses took off their uniform caps and put on funny hats, and shifted into hidden side-wards any patients who seemed likely to spoil the fun by inconsiderately passing away. Sister Virtue was particularly successful in the rôle of Valkyrie: her long experience of diseases and doctors enabled her to spot a declining case several days before the medical staff. She had only to fix her glare on an apparently convalescent patient and give her bleak opinion that 'He won't *do*, sir,' and the houseman confidently made arrangements for the post-mortem.

When I arrived on the ward in the middle of the morning I found a wonderful end-of-term spirit abroad. People were allowed to do things they felt forbidden even to contemplate at any other time of the year. Smoking was permitted all day, not only in the regulation hour after meals, the radio was turned on before noon, and, as if this wasn't enough, the patients were issued with a bottle of beer apiece.

Sister was visiting each of the beds distributing presents from the tree, and two up-patients, dressing-gowned old gentlemen with a brace of alarming blood pressures, were dancing the high-land fling in nurses' caps and aprons. Three or four of the students were steadfastly pursuing nurses with sprigs of mistletoe: the chase was not exacting.

As I entered the ward a giggling nurse ran out of the sluice-room followed by Tony Benskin, who had a look of intense eagerness on his face.

'That's enough, Mr. Benskin!' she cried. 'You've had enough!'

Benskin pulled up as he caught sight of me.

'I thought you said you were coming early to test urine,' I remarked.

'One meets one's friends,' he explained simply. 'One must be

96

social. After all, it's Christmas. Come in the sluice-room. I've got a bottle.'

I followed him in.

'And I thought you were scared of nurses.'

'Delightful creatures,' said Benskin, beaming. 'So refreshingly sex-starved.'

I noticed the gin bottle he had invited me to.

'Good God, Tony,' I said. 'Have you got through all that so early in the day?'

'It's Christmas, old boy.'

'Tony, you're sloshed already.'

'What of it? There's plenty more gin in the instrument cupboard. Grimsdyke hid it there yesterday. After all, it's Christmas. Have a drink.'

'All right. I suppose it's my party as much as yours.'

The gin in the instrument cupboard was finished by midday, when Dr. Lionel Loftus appeared with his wife, and his two ugly daughters that were produced every Christmas-time like the decorations but without success. He got a hilarious reception.

'Here's the old Dean!' cried Benskin, leaping up on a bed. 'Three cheers for the Dean, boys! Three cheers for old Lofty! Three cheers for the jolly old Dean!'

The Dean stood, all smiles, in the doorway, while three cheers were given and the ward broke into 'For He's a Jolly Good Fellow.' He kissed Sister under the mistletoe, presented his houseman with a bottle of sherry, and shook hands with the patients. His own part in the programme was fairly simple: all he had to do was put on a chef's hat and carve the turkey in the middle of the ward. He was not good at carving and the last patients had a cold meal, which was the disadvantage of eating Christmas dinner on the medical side of the hospital. The surgeons were naturally more skilful, and Sir Lancelot Spratt had been known to slit a bird to ribbons in a couple of minutes.

During dinner Grimsdyke appeared. I was sitting on a bed with my arm round a nurse. Both of us were blowing squeakers.

'Hello, old boy,' Grimsdyke said in a worried tone. 'Merry Christmas and all that sort of thing. How are you feeling?'

'Fine! Have a drink.'

'All the boys are pretty high, I suppose?'

'Of course. Benskin's as stiff as a plank.'

'Oh God! I hope he'll be all right to go on this afternoon.'

I put my squeaker down contritely.

'I'd clean forgotten about that! Perhaps we'd better go and see how he is.'

'Where's he got to?' Grimsdyke asked nervously.

The nurse told him. 'I saw him going into the sluice-room. He said he felt tired and wanted a rest.'

Benskin was resting when we found him. He was lying on the stone floor with his head against the base of the sink.

'Wake up! Wake up!' Grimsdyke commanded with an anxious note in his voice. 'The show, man! We're due to start in half an hour!'

Benskin grunted.

'Oh Lord!' Grimsdyke said in despair. 'We'll never get him on the stage. . . . Tony! Benskin! Pull yourself together!'

Benskin opened his eyes fleetingly.

'Merry Christmas,' he muttered.

'Why not try an ice-pack on his head?' I suggested. 'Or an intravenous injection of vitamin C? It's supposed to oxidize the alcohol.'

'We'll try throwing water over him. It might be some use. Give me that measuring glass.'

We poured a pint of cold water over the ineffective actor; he lay dripping like a cherub on a fountain, but equally inactive.

'Let's hold him by the arms and legs and shake him,' I said.

'Do you think it would do any good?'

'It may do. Shock therapy is sometimes effective.'

Grimsdyke held Benskin's arms, and I took his feet. He was a heavy man, and we strained as we lifted him.

'Ready?' Grimsdyke asked. 'Right—one, two, three, shake.'

We were still shaking when the sluice-room door opened and Sister Prudence walked in.

'Hello!' she said. 'What's up?'

'Mr. Benskin fainted,' Grimsdyke said quickly. 'I think the excitement was too much for him.'

Sister Prudence shot a diagnostic look at the patient. Her professional training enabled her to act swiftly and decisively when faced with an emergency.

'Nurse!' she called, starting to roll up her sleeves. 'Run down to the accident department and bring up the suicide box. Take your jacket off, Mr. Grimsdyke. You can help me with the stomach pump.'

* * * * *

Benskin's stomach was washed out with bicarbonate solution, which was always kept handy to frustrate local suicides. He was given a cup of black coffee and a benzedrine tablet. By that time he maintained that he was ready to face his audience.

'It will be a pallid performance,' he admitted thickly. 'But at least I shall be on my feet.'

The show was due to open in Fortitude ward, on the male surgical side.

'Always test on men's surgical,' Grimsdyke said. 'Surgical patients are either well or dead. They don't hang about in the miserable twilight like medical ones. Besides, half the medical patients have got gastric ulcers, and who can feel jolly on Christmas Day after a poached egg and a glass of milk?'

Our troupe arrived made-up and in the costume of white flannels and shirts with green bow ties that Grimsdyke had ordered. The stage was improvised on the floor at one end of the ward out of the screens otherwise used to hide patients from their companions. Grimsdyke, who succeeded in looking smart in his flannels, worried his way round his indifferent actors like the headmistress at a kindergarten play.

'Are we ready to start?' he asked anxiously. 'Where's the piano?'

'It looks as if we've lost it somewhere,' I told him.

'It doesn't matter about the bloody piano,' John Bottle cut in. 'We've lost the beer as well.'

Grimsdyke and Bottle disappeared to find these two essential articles of stage furniture, while Harris muttered the words of 'Polly Perkins' over to himself repeatedly, Sprogget stood in the corner with a look of painful concentration on his face talking like

99

a three-year-old girl, and I rubbed red grease-paint into Benskin's white cheeks.

'What are you feeling like now?' I asked him.

'I often wondered what it was like to be dead,' he said. 'Now I know. Still, the show must go on. One cannot disappoint one's public.'

The piano, the actors, and the beer were collected on the same spot; the audience, who had been waiting uncomfortably on the floor, on the edge of the beds, or leaning against the wall, began a burst of impatient clapping.

'For God's sake!' said Grimsdyke frantically. 'Let's get going. Are you ready, Richard? What the hell are you doing underneath the piano?'

'I seem to have lost the music for the opening chorus,' I explained.

'Play any damn thing you like. Play the closing chorus. Play God Save the King.'

'I'll vamp.'

The screen representing the proscenium curtain was pushed aside, and the only presentation of 'Jest Trouble' took the boards.

The performance was not a great success. It happened that Mr. Hubert Cambridge, the surgeon in charge of Fortitude ward, had a desire to remove two hundred stomachs during the year and had approached Christmas in a flurry of gastrectomies. As the patients had not a whole stomach between them and each had suffered a high abdominal incision that made even breathing painful they were not a responsive and easy-laughing audience. The nurses, students, and doctors who made up the bulk of the house were already unsympathetic to the actors because of the long wait for the curtain to be pulled aside when they could have spent longer over their dinner. Only the cast, who (with the exception of Benskin) had been going strongly at the beer, thought themselves devilishly funny.

The opening chorus successfully defied the audience to make out a word of it, then Grimsdyke told a joke about a student and two nurses that extracted a languid round of clapping. The next item was Benskin's conjuring act. He appeared in a black cape and a tall magician's hat, and scored instant applause when, during his preliminary patter, John Bottle was seized with the idea of setting a match to its peak over the top of the backcloth. The hat blazed away for some seconds before Benskin realized what had happened and angrily put it out in a bowl of goldfish.

His proudest trick was pouring water from one jug to another and changing its colour in the transference; but his aim was not good that afternoon and at his first attempt most of the liquid slopped on to the ward floor.

'Nurse!' came an easily audible hiss from the back. It was Sister Fortitude. 'Go and clear up the mess that young man's making!'

A nurse with a mop picked her way through the audience and started swabbing round the performer's feet while he pretended that he, out of everybody else in the room, did not notice her. After that he angrily produced a string of flags out of a top hat and left the stage in a huff.

The rest of the performance was received by the audience with good-natured apathy. Harris made his appearance to sing 'Little Polly Perkins' in a Harry Tate moustache, standing in front of Bottle, Sprogget, and Benskin, who joined in the choruses. Towards the end of the third verse a roar of laughter swept the audience. Harris felt the glow of success in his heart, and sang on lustily. When the laughter rose to a second peak a few seconds later he hesitated and glanced behind him. The cause of his reception was obvious at once. Benskin, finally overcome, had been suffering a sharp attack of hiccoughs before being sick in the corner of the stage. At that moment the lights fused, and no one thought it worth finishing the performance.

* * * * *

At Christmas-time came the few hours of every year that the official barrier between students and nurses was gingerly raised: there was a dance in the nurses' dining-hall which the young men were allowed to attend.

The dance disorganized life in the Virgins' Retreat for some weeks before the French chalk went down on the floor. Each nurse's escort was discussed in detail that would have been justified only if the young lady expected to remain in his arms for the rest of her life. Dresses were cleaned, repaired, and borrowed, and the probationers wept in front of their mirrors at the devastation already done to their figures by the carbohydrates in the hospital diet and the muscular exercise of nursing. On the evening of the dance the girls flew off duty eagerly, bathed, powdered, dressed, and scented themselves, and went down to meet their men under the marble eye of Florence Nightingale in the hall.

As I had no particular attachments in the hospital at the time I approached a gawky nurse on the ward called Footte and asked, with a smirk, if she would be my consort. She gave her gracious acceptance. Shortly afterwards I met Benskin in the courtyard.

'Are you going to the nurses' hop?' I asked him. 'I've just let myself in for taking the junior staff on Prudence.'

'You bet I am, old boy! Having recovered from the excesses of Christmas Day I shall be taking old Rigor Mortis along. It's the biggest party of the year.'

I was surprised.

'Is it? I thought it was a strictly teetotal affair.'

'And so it is. You don't imagine the Matron would allow liquor to befoul the chaste floors of the Virgins' Retreat, do you? It's as dry as a bishop's birthday. This has the effect of making everybody get a big enough glow on beforehand to last them the night, and results in some interesting spectacles.'

On the evening of the dance Benskin and I spent an hour of determined drinking with the Padre before crossing over to the Nurses' Home to meet our partners. Benskin immediately suggested a few scoops. 'Bad form to arrive too early, you know,' he explained to the girls. 'People think you want to hog all the sausage rolls.' The four of us went back to the King George, which was now full of young men and young women in evening dress taking prophylaxis against a dull evening. We settled ourselves at a corner of the bar. After some time Miss Footte started looking mistily at me and stroking the back of my neck; I noticed that even Rigor Mortis, who had an apparent amnesia about the incident in the flat, was becoming mildly animated.

The first time I looked at my watch it was after ten.

'It's getting on,' I said. 'Hadn't we better go?'

'Perhaps we'd better. Where's the Padre?' Benskin leaned over the bar counter. 'Padre! I say, how about a little this-and-that for the hip?' He handed a silver flask across the bar. 'There's a long way to go yet.'

'Certainly, sir! How about you, Mr. Gordon? If I might advise you, sir, from my experience . . .'

'I'll have a bottle of gin,' I said. 'Can you put it on the slate until the New Year?'

'Of course, Mr. Gordon. You get your allowance quarterly, don't you? Anything you like, sir.'

Arm in arm, all four, we went singing to the Nurses' Home.

The gaunt dining-hall was dripping with paper-chains, and a five-piece band was stuck up on a tinsel-ringed dais in one corner. There was a Christmas tree, a running buffet on trestles, streamers, paper hats, Chinese lanterns, and all the standardized trappings of respectable jollity. On a stage at one end, opposite the band, there sat throughout the evening the Matron, in full uniform. Next to her, also uniformed, were the three sister tutors. Behind them were five or six of the senior sisters in a row, and the lot were separated by sandwiches and sausage rolls on small tables. They were a jury that was constantly forming unspoken verdicts. Very little escaped them. If a girl danced with too many men or too few it was remembered until the end of her training, and if she turned up in an off-the-shoulder gown she might as well have had 'Hussy' tattooed across her clavicles.

There was an interval between dances when we arrived. We pushed our way up to the buffet.

'Look at that!' Benskin said in disgust, pointing to a row of glass jugs. 'Lemonade!'

He reached across the table and picked up a half-full pitcher.

'I think we might stiffen this a little,' he continued, with a shifty glance over his shoulder towards the stage. 'Hold the jug, old boy, while I get my flask out.'

He tipped his flask of whisky into the drink and I added half my bottle of gin.

'That should be more like it,' Benskin said with satisfaction, stirring the mixture with a jelly spoon. 'Guaranteed to bring the roses to the cheeks. One sip, and never a dull moment afterwards.'

He was still stirring when Mike Kelly appeared at the table with one of the operating theatre nurses.

'Mind if we join the party, Tony?' he asked. 'I've got some rum in my pocket.'

'Put it in, old boy!' Benskin invited him. 'Nothing like a lemonade cocktail to get the party going. That's right, pour the lot in. You didn't have much left, anyway.'

'The best part of half a bottle!' Kelly said indignantly. 'It's all I've got, too.'

'Fear nothing,' Benskin said, stirring rapidly. 'I know of secret caches. Now! Let us taste the devil's brew.'

He poured a little in six glasses and we sipped it with some foreboding.

'It's strong,' Benskin admitted, gulping. 'Odd sort of taste. I suppose that rum was all right, Mike? You hadn't been palmed off with a bottle of hooch, had you?'

'Of course it was all right. I got it off the Padre.'

'Oh well, it must be the lemonade. Cheers, everyone.'

We had almost finished the jug when Harris pushed his way into the group.

'You dirty dogs!' he exclaimed angrily. 'You've pinched my blasted jug of lemonade! I had half a bottle of sherry and some crème de menthe in that, too!'

*   *   *   *

I did not remember much about the dance. Isolated incidents came back to me in flashes the next day, like fragments of a dream. I recalled two gentlemen doing the old-fashioned waltz with their partners, catching the tails of their coats together, and covering the floor with broken glass and the best part of two bottles of gin; other gentlemen overcome with the heat and having to be assisted to the fresh air; Nurse Footte laughing so loudly in my arms I noticed her uvula waggling in the back of her throat, and my thinking how horrible it was. All the students were drunk, and the Matron, being unaware of such things, beamed and thought she was giving these high-spirited young men a great evening. The next morning, however, she democratically joined in cleaning the hall herself and was horrified to find a hundred and thirty empty spirit bottles tucked away in the potted palms, behind the curtains, in the seats of the sofas, and on top of the framed portraits of her predecessors in office.

The nurses' dance marked the end of the Christmas holiday at St. Swithin's. Everyone knew that the next morning the operating theatres would start work again, new patients would be admitted, lectures would begin, and the students would troop round the bare and gloomy wards with their Chiefs. But that night it was still Christmas, and the hospital was alive with marauding students who leaped on the night nurses while they made cocoa in the ward kitchens. And they, dear girls, screamed softly (so as not to wake the patients) before surrendering themselves to their students' arms. After all, there had to be some compensations for being a nurse.

CHAPTER XII

IN the New Year I began work in the out-patient department. It was my first contact with the hard routine of the general practitioner's surgery. In the wards the patients are scrubbed, combed, and undressed, and presented to the doctors in crisp sheets; but in out-patients' they come straight off the streets and examination is complicated by clothes, embarrassment, and sometimes the advisability of the medical attendant keeping his distance.

The department was the busiest part of the hospital. It was centred round a wide, high, green-painted hall decorated only by coloured Ministry of Health posters warning the populace against the danger of spitting, refusing to have their babies inoculated, cooking greens in too much water, and indiscriminate love-making. There led off from the hall, on all sides, the assortment of clinics that it had been found necessary to establish to treat the wide variety of illnesses carried in through the doors every day. There were the big medical and surgical rooms, the gynæcological department and the ante-natal clinic, the ear, nose, and throat clinic, the fracture clinic, and a dozen others. The V.D. department was approached through discreet and unmarked entrances from the street; in one corner the infertility clinic and the birth control clinic stood next to one another; and at the other end of the hall were the shady confessionals of the psychiatrists.

On one side was a long counter, behind which four or five girls in white smocks sorted the case notes from their filing cabinets and passed them across to the patients with the carefully cultivated air of distaste mixed with suspicion employed by Customs men handing back passports. There were telephones in the middle of the hall for emergency calls, and, outside every clinic door, rows of wooden benches that looked as inviting to sit on as a line of tank-traps.

The department was run chiefly by the hospital porters. These were an invaluable body of men, without whom the work of the hospital would immediately have come to a standstill. They were experts at such common tasks beyond the ability of the doctors as directing patients to the correct department, holding down drunks, putting on strait-jackets, dealing tactfully with the police, getting rid of unwanted relatives, and finding cups of tea at impossible hours. They stood, in their red-and-blue livery, inspecting with experienced Cockney shrewdness the humanity that daily passed in large numbers under their noses.

As soon as a patient entered the building he came up against a porter—a fat one sitting on a stool behind a high desk, like a sergeant in the charge-room of a police station.

'What's up, chum?' the porter demanded.

The patient would begin to mumble out his leading symptoms, but he would be cut short with 'Surgical, you,' or 'Throat department,' or the name of the appropriate clinic. The porters were the best diagnosticians in the hospital. They unerringly divided the cases into medical and surgical so that the patients arrived in front of the correct specialist. If a porter had made a mistake and consigned, for instance, a case of bronchitis to the surgical side, the complications that would have arisen and the disaster that might have overtaken the patient were beyond speculation.

After passing the porter the patient visited the counter to collect his case notes. St. Swithin's kept faithful records of its visitors, and several residents of the district had been neatly represented by a green folder containing the obstetrical notes of his birth, an account of the removal of his tonsils, the surgical description of the repair of his hernias, a record of his mounting blood pressure, and details of the post-mortem following the final complaint that carried him off. Clutching his folder in one hand, he took his place at the end of the queue seated outside the door of his clinic. The queue shifted up the wooden seat as each patient was called inside by the stern-faced nurse at the door: the movement was slow and spasmodic, like the stirrings of a sleepy snake.

For the first half-hour the patient amused himself by reading carefully through his folder of confidential notes, comparing in his mind what the doctors had written about him with what they told him to his face. After a while this became boring, so he read the morning paper. When he had exhausted the paper, he passed the remainder of the time in clinical discussion with his neighbours. This was the most attractive part of the visit, and a pleasure he had been storing up for himself.

Discussion of one's illness with neighbours on the bench was done with pride: the patients wore their symptoms like a row of campaign medals.

'Wot you in for, cock?' he began to the man next to him.

" 'Art trouble,' was the reply, delivered with gloomy zest.

'Anyfink else?'

'That's enough, ain't it?' replied the neighbour sharply. ' 'Ow about you?'

'The doctor says I am a walking pathological museum.' The patient rolled the syllables off his tongue deliberately.

'Go on!'

'I've got diabetes mellitus, 'emeroids, normocytic anæmia, chronic bronchitis and emphysema, 'ammer toe, cholecystitis, and an over-active thyroid.'

'That's a packet, all right,' his neighbour admitted grudgingly.

'And I 'eard 'im say I've got a positive Wasserman, too!' he added in triumph.

' 'Ave you 'ad any operations?' inquired a thin woman on the other side of him in a voice rich with misery.

'Not to date, touch wood, I 'aven't.'

The woman gave a loud sigh.

'I wish as I could say the same,' she remarked, shaking her head sadly.

' 'Ow many 'ave you 'ad, missus?' asked the patient, anxious over his own record.

'Fifteen,' she told him, in tones of exquisite martyrdom.

'Coo! I'm glad I 'aven't got your complaint.'

'That's the trouble. They don't know wot's wrong with me. The last time they took out my colon. The doctor said it was the worst they'd ever 'ad in the 'ospital. Took them four and a 'arf hours, it did. Then they 'ad to leave some of it behind. I'm lucky to be 'ere now, if you ask me.'

'Must have been a bad do,' the patient said, respectful of such exuberant pathology.

'Bad do! I was left to die four times!'

' 'Oo's your doctor, missus?'

'Mr. Cambridge. Wot a lovely man! 'E's got such soft 'ands.'

I soon discovered another peculiarity of out-patient work. In the wards the patients are all ill: in out-patients' they are nearly all healthy. Men and women with organic disease formed a small fraction of the hundreds who came past the fat porter at the door every day. Most of them complained of vague aches and pains that they had been trotting up to the surgeries of their own doctors for several months, and they, poor men, had got rid of them temporarily by handing them a note to St. Swithin's. This was an example of an established medical practice known as snag-shifting, which went on just as actively in St. Swithin's itself.

The most usual condition in out-patients' was headache, which was slightly more common than troubles of the poor feet, giddy spells, the rheumatics, and insomnia ('Not a wink for forty years, doctor'). Most of the symptoms were manifestly incompatible with life if they had existed, but every patient had to be investigated in case something sinister lay beneath. This provided an excellent opportunity for snag-shifting. A persistent patient with headaches could, with a few strokes of the pen, be transferred to the eye department. It simply needed the houseman to scribble 'Headaches. Any eye signs?' on the notes and the patient moved to another queue outside another doctor's door. After the eye department had found nothing and were tired of the fellow appearing in front of them week after week they sent him to the throat clinic. The throat surgeons usually operated on all their patients and would probably remove his tonsils or the inside of his sinuses; when he continued to attend with his headaches afterwards, they would pack him off to the general surgeons with the suggestion his complaint was the result of sepsis lurking in his gall-bladder, kidney, or some other organ comfortably outside their province. The surgeons might operate or not, according to the length of their waiting-list at the time; whatever happened, after a few more visits to out-patients' he would find himself having all his teeth out in the dental section, who packed him off afterwards to the physiotherapy department in case the headaches—which continued—were due to disfunction of the neck muscles. From the physiotherapy department the patient went as a last resort to the psychiatrists, and as they were then unable to transfer him to anyone he probably continued to visit them and talk about his headaches once a week for the remainder of his life.

While I was working in out-patients' the hospital authorities installed a bar for tea and buns in the hall to break the tedium of the long wait. The regular patients were delighted, and showed their appreciation by spending as many of their afternoons as they could enjoying a medical tea-party with their fellow sufferers.

'Times have changed,' one of the old porters said gloomily, looking at the girl distributing cups of tea from the new counter. 'None of this 'ere nonsense in the old days. Mollycoddling, I call it.'

He wistfully described the routine of forty years ago. The patients had to be inside the building and seated at the benches by eight o'clock every morning. Then the doors were locked and anyone coming late had no alternative than to wait until the next day. The consultant arrived at nine, and strode to his room accompanied by a senior porter. When the doctor had settled himself in his chair the porter went to the door and shouted: 'Nah then! All them with coughs, stand up!' A handful of patients came to their feet and shuffled into the room. When they had been seen the porter returned and commanded: 'Stomach pains, diarrhœa, and flatulence!' The possessors of these alimentary disorders filed before the doctor while the porter marshalled the chronic cases who had come simply for a new bottle of medicine. The patients found the system convenient, and it was abolished only when the senior physician left for Harley Street after a remarkably heavy morning treating chest symptoms and found a stall outside the hospital from which was being sold 'Genuine St. Swithin's Cough Mixture.' This was bought off the patients for twopence and retailed to the public by the stallkeeper at sixpence a bottle.

We each spent two days a week in the accident room, where I began to feel I was at last learning a little medicine by discovering how to put a bandage on without dropping it on the floor, to sew up cuts, to remove foreign bodies from eyes, and to apply a kaolin poultice. A pair of us were obliged to sleep once a week in a couple of bunks in a small room by the accident entrance, to attend the minor injuries that trickled in unendingly during the night. This system was nearly the end of Tony Benskin. In his wanderings round the sleeping hospital he had met, and taken a fancy to, one of the night nurses, and turned himself into a red-eyed wreck all day by sitting most of the night in her company.

The conditions in a ward at night are admittedly lightly aphrodisiac. The nurse sits alone at one end of the long room, which melts away on each side into shadows and is illuminated only by a single red-shaded lamp on the desk in front of her. The soft warm light makes her as desirable as a ripe peach. There is not much room at the desk, so the student and nurse sit close together. To avoid disturbing the patients they must whisper, which turns every remark into an intimacy. They are the only two awake in a sleeping world and they draw together with a tingling sense of isolation.

The nurse mixes the student a milk drink from the patients' night rations. It is surprising what can occur in such conditions over a couple of cups of Horlicks. Their knees touch under the desk; their hands brush together in a determined accident; their fingers entwine and they sweat into one another's palms until the night sister is due on her round. The student pours soft endearments over the girl like treacle on a pudding, though his technique is sometimes ruined by his being interrupted in a delicate submission to her charms by a rough voice from the nearest bed demanding 'Can I 'ave the bedpan please, nurse?'

Benskin's romance might have ended harmlessly if it had not been for a lapse on the last night of our appointment. We were on duty together, and to celebrate the end of the session we persuaded the casualty nurse to do our work and spent the evening in the King George. At closing time Benskin rushed to see his night nurse, while I flopped into bed.

Just after three I was shaken awake. Automatically I reached for my trousers, thinking it was the porter demanding my attendance in the accident room: but it was Benskin. He was in a pitiful state.

'Old man!' he said urgently. 'You've got to help me! Something terrible's happened!'

I tried to concentrate on the disaster.

'What's up?' I asked sleepily.

'You know that girl up in the ward—Molly. Remember, the one I've been popping up to see?'

'Umm.'

'Well—listen, old man, don't go to sleep for God's sake! To-night I nipped up to see her as usual, and I was brimming over a bit with the old joys of spring and so forth owing to being full of beer. . . .'

'Disgusting.'

'. . . and Christ Almighty, before I knew where I was I'd proposed to the bloody woman!'

I tried to clear sleep and alcohol out of my eyes, like soapsuds.

'Did she accept?' I asked, yawning.

'Accept! She said "Yes, please," as far as I remember. Don't you realize what's happened? Can't you see the gravity of the situation?'

'Perhaps she'll have forgotten by the morning,' I suggested hopefully.

'Not on your life! You know what these women are—at night nurses' breakfast it'll be a case of "Guess what, girls! Tony Benskin proposed to me at last and we're going to be married in May!" Oh God, oh God!' He clasped his head. 'It'll be all round the hospital by nine o'clock.'

'I gather you're not keen on the idea of marrying her?'

'Me! Married! Can you see it?' he exclaimed.

I nodded my head understandingly and propped myself up on an elbow.

'This needs some thought.'

'How right you are!'

'Surely there must be something you can do . . . can't you go back and explain it was all in fun?'

Benskin gave a contemptuous laugh.

'You go,' he said.

'I see your point. It's tricky. Let's think in silence.'

After about twenty minutes I had an idea. I criticized it to myself carefully and it seemed sound.

'I think I've got the answer,' I said, and explained it to him.

He leapt to his feet, shook me warmly by the hand, and hurried back to the ward.

The solution was a simple one. I sent Benskin round to propose to every night nurse in the hospital.

CHAPTER XIII

THE clock on the lecture-room wall crept towards ten past four: the Professor of Pathology had overrun his time again.

It was a gloomy, overcast afternoon at the beginning of April. The lights were reflected from the brown varnish on the walls in dull yellow pools. The windows just below the ceiling were, as usual, shut tight, and the air was narcotic. The students packing the tiers of uncomfortable benches were sleepy, annoyed at being kept late, and waiting for their tea.

The Professor was unconscious of the passage of time, the atmosphere in the room, or the necessity for food and drink. He was a thin little white-haired man with large spectacles who was standing behind his desk talking enthusiastically about a little-known variety of louse. Lice were the Professor's life. For thirty years they had filled his thoughts during the day and spilled into his dreams at night. He had, at points during that time, married and raised five children, but he was only faintly aware of these occurrences. The foreground of his mind was filled by lice. He spent his time in his own small laboratory on the top floor of the hospital wholly occupied in studying their habits. He rarely came near his students. He left the teaching to his assistants and considered he had done his share by occasionally wandering round the students' laboratory, which he did with the bemused air of a man whose wife has invited a lot of people he doesn't know to a party. He insisted, however, on giving to each class a series of lectures on his speciality. He was the greatest authority on lice in the world, and when he lectured to other pathologists in Melbourne, Chicago, Oslo, or Bombay, men would eagerly cross half a continent to hear him. But the students of his own hospital, who had only the effort of shifting themselves out of the sofas in the common room, came ungracefully and ungratefully, and found it all rather boring.

As the lecturer droned on, describing the disproportionately complicated sexual habits of an obscure species of louse, the

114

students glanced sullenly at the clock, shuffled their feet, yawned, folded up their notebooks, put away their pens, and lolled in their seats. Some of the class started chatting to their neighbours or lit their pipes and read the evening paper as comfortably as if they were sitting in their own lodgings. From the back row came a subdued stamping of feet on the wooden floor—the students' only means of retaliation on their lecturers. But the Professor had by now forgotten the presence of his audience and if we had all marched out into the fresh air or set the lecture theatre on fire he would have noticed it only dimly.

I was sitting at the back with Tony Benskin and Sprogget. Benskin always took a place as far back as he could, for some lecturers had the unpleasant habit of asking questions of students who were dreamily inspecting the ceiling and at a distance it was possible to give the impression of overpowering concentration even if asleep. It was also convenient for making an exit unobtrusively when the lecturer became insupportably boring. Attendance at lectures was compulsory at St. Swithin's, and a board was passed round the benches for each student to record his presence by signing it. This led to everyone in the medical school rapidly becoming competent in forgery, so that the absence of a friend could easily be rectified. This unselfish practice diminished after the Dean counted the students at his own lecture and found not only that thirty-odd men were represented by ninety signatures but that some of the absentees had in their enthusiasm forgetfully signed the board in different places four times.

The Professor had left me behind some time ago. I was cleaning my nails, letting my thoughts wander pleasantly to the comfortable drone of the lecturer's voice. Unfortunately, in their wanderings they stumbled across a topic I wished they could have avoided.

'I say, Tony,' I asked softly. 'I suppose you couldn't lend me three or four quid, could you?'

Benskin laughed—so loudly that men in the three rows in front of him turned round.

'I thought not,' I said. 'All the same, it's damned difficult. Now we've started the path. course I've got to have my microscope back. While we were in the wards it was perfectly all right for it to lodge in Goldstein's window, but if I don't get it soon I shan't be able to do the practical classes at all.'

'I sympathize,' Benskin said. 'Have no doubts about that. My own instrument is at present locked in the coffers of Mr. Goldstein's rival down the road, and I see no prospect of recovering it from the clutches of said gentleman at all. The old moneybags are empty. For weeks now I've had to wait outside the bank until the manager goes to lunch before cashing a cheque.'

My microscope was an easy way of raising ready money; I could pawn it without inconvenience when broke and reclaim it the moment my allowance came in. But I had recently piled up so many other commitments that this simple system had broken down. My tastes had altered expensively since I first arrived at St. Swithin's, though my allowance had stayed much the same. Then I smoked a little, drank hardly at all, and never went out with girls; now I did all three together.

'The funny thing is, old man,' said Benskin when the Professor had exhausted the educational qualities of lice, 'that I was just thinking of putting the leeches on you for a quid or so. The cost of living is extremely high with me at the moment. I suppose there really is no possibility of a small loan?'

'None at all.'

'I must raise a little crinkly from somewhere. Surely one of the students has a couple of bob he can jingle in his pocket?'

'You can try Grimsdyke,' I suggested. 'He usually has a bit left over for his friends.'

Benskin frowned. 'Not since he got married, old boy. The little woman takes a dim view of the stuff being diverted from the housekeeping to the pockets of old soaks. No, there's nothing for it—it's a case of bashing the old dishes again.'

All of us had recurrent bouts of insolvency, and each had his favourite way of raising enough money to pay his debts. Dishwashing by the night was the most popular way of earning small sums, as it did not interfere with classes, it could be taken up without notice, and the big hotels and restaurants in London paid comparatively well for a few hours spent in the stillroom. Babysitting was Sprogget's speciality, and John Bottle occasionally brought home a few pounds from the tote or by winning the waltz competition at an Oxford Street palais. But Benskin sometimes overspent himself so much that more settled employment had to be found. One afternoon during a time when he was suffering a severe attack of poverty he appeared in the students' common room in his best blue serge suit, with his shoes brightly polished, his hair neat, a white handkerchief smartly in his pocket, and a plain peaked cap in his hand.

'What on earth are you doing?' Grimsdyke asked. 'Playing bus conductors?'

Benskin beamed at him.

'Not a bit, old boy. I've got a job for a couple of weeks. A damn smart move on my part it was.'

'A job? What sort of a job? More dishwashing, I suppose?'

'Private chauffeur,' Benskin told him proudly. 'In a Rolls, too. I'll tell you what happened. I was up at out-patients' this morning when a fellow came in with the most horrible gastric ulcer I've seen. He had to leave off work at once, of course, and when he told me his job was chauffeur to an old bird with bags of oof who makes jam or something I saw ways of relieving the old exchequer. Do you follow me? I nipped smartly round to the old boy's house in Hampstead and told him the bad news in person—very impressively, too. I then explained the situation in a few words, and offered humble self to fill the gap in his household.

'It so happened that the old chum and his missus are due to start a fortnight's holiday touring Scotland to-morrow, which would have been squashed by the chauffeur's ulcers if I hadn't presented myself as a worthy alternative. I got all this from the patient of course, but I didn't let on and gave the impression that I could tear myself away from valuable studies just so the old folk wouldn't miss their nice restful holiday. He seemed a decent old cove and was very upset about his old chauffeur, but he has no more idea of driving a car himself than working a railway engine. So my offer was gratefully accepted.'

'Have you got a licence?' I asked.

'Of course,' he replied in a hurt tone. 'For almost a month now.'

Benskin disappeared the following morning. After four days he reappeared in the hospital. He had lost his cap, his best suit was torn and covered with oil, one of his shoes was ripped, and he was still broke.

'Well?' I said.

'One meets snags,' Benskin replied in a subdued voice. 'All was well to begin with. The old jam merchant was a great believer in the quiet life, and we trundled gently out of Town to Doncaster. They put me up in the servants' quarters of the local hostelry, where I met a hell of a nice little piece among the chambermaids —however, that will do for later. The next day I drove in an exemplary fashion to Newcastle, by which time I could see that the old couple had invested plenty of confidence in Benskin, whom they looked upon as a clean and careful driver.'

'What happened after Newcastle?' Grimsdyke asked resignedly.

'That's where the rot set in. I'd driven all that bloody way without a drink, as I left London flat broke. At Newcastle I touched the old boy for a quid, and when we stopped for lunch at some old-world boozer on the road I sneaked round the back and downed a few scoops. This would have been all right, but the old chum decided he wanted a stroll to look at the local countryside and left me among the lackeys in the servants' hall or whatever it is. I met a most amusing type there—an Irish porter who had started off life studying divinity at Trinity. We had a lot to talk about—bobbing back scoops all the time, of course. I set off with my customers about four o'clock, but regret to say I only made about a hundred yards. After that I piled the crate up in a ditch. I didn't hurt myself, luckily, but now the old couple are languishing in the local cottage hospital with a fractured femur apiece.'

He added that he did not see much chance of the engagement being renewed.

*　　*　　*　　*

To retrieve my microscope I washed dishes with Tony Benskin in a West End hotel for a couple of nights and sold some of my text-books. I was then content to return to academic life, but Benskin was aflame to increase his savings by trying his hand at another trade.

'Do you see that notice?' he asked eagerly as we left the staff

118

entrance of the hotel in the early morning. ' "Extra waiters wanted. Apply Head Waiter." That's an idea, isn't it?'

'No,' I said. 'I'm going to spend a few nights in bed. Besides, I don't know anything about waiting. And neither do you.'

Benskin lightly brushed these objections aside.

'There's nothing to it, old man. Anyone can dish up a bit of fish. It's money for nothing, if you ask me. And the tips! Think of the tips. At a swep-up joint like this the customers don't slip threepenny bits under the plate when they swig down the remains of their brandy and wipe the caviar off their lips. I've been waited on quite long enough to grasp the technique—if you want a fat tip it's only a matter of handing out the soup with a look of haughty distaste on your face.'

'You think you could look haughty, do you?'

'One is a gentleman,' Benskin replied stiffly. 'I'm going to stay behind and have a word with this head waiter chap.'

'I'm going home to bed. We've got to appear at a lecture in five hours' time.'

'All right. See you later.'

I was dropping off to sleep when Benskin got back to Bayswater. He was jubilant.

'A push-over, old boy!' he said. 'I saw the head waiter—a nasty piece of work he was, too. However, he took one look at me and said to himself "Benskin's the man! He'll raise the tone in the dining-room all right." '

'So you got the job?'

'Starting to-night. I'll just have time to nip away from the hospital, get my evening clothes out, and appear as the Jeeves of the chafing dish.'

'I suppose they know at the hotel that you have had no experience of waiting at all?'

'Well, no, not exactly. I saw no reason for putting obstacles in my own way, so I gave the impression I had dished it out at some of the larger doss-houses around Town, with summer sessions on the coast. They seem pretty hard-up for fish-flingers at the moment, as they took me at my word.'

'Well,' I said, turning over. 'Don't forget to wear a black tie.'

When I reached the flat after work that evening Benskin was in a high state of excitement.

'Must get the old soup and fish out,' he said, hauling his battered tin trunk from the top of the wardrobe. 'I pinched a bottle of ether from the theatre this afternoon to get the stains out.'

Benskin's tail suit had been bought for him by his father when he was sixteen. Since then he had greatly increased in size in all directions. We all worked hard to straighten out the creases with John Bottle's travelling iron, while Benskin rubbed hard at the lapels to remove the grease.

'I must have been a dirty little devil at table,' he reflected.

'Some moths have been having a go at it down here,' I said, pointing to the trousers.

'That doesn't matter,' Benskin replied testily. 'I'm only the bloody waiter, anyway.'

He put the clothes on. By lowering the braces as far as he dared the trousers could be made to cover the upper part of his ankles; the braces themselves, which were red and yellow, only remained invisible behind the lapels of the coat when he remembered not to breathe too deeply. The sleeves came as far as the mid-forearm, and the top buttons of the trousers had to be reinforced with safety-pins. But it was the shirt that presented an apparently insoluble difficulty. It was tight, and the button-holes were worn: even the shallowest of respirations caused the studs to pop out and expose a broad strip of hairy, pink, sweaty chest.

'Quite enough to put the people off their meal,' John Bottle remarked.

We tried using bigger studs and brass paper-fasteners, but, if Benskin wished to continue to breathe, the shirt was unwearable. Even strips of sticking-plaster inside the stiff front were not strong enough to withstand the pressure of his inhalations. For half an hour we worked hard at the infuriating gap while the shirt-front became limp under our fingers.

'For God's sake!' Benskin exclaimed angrily. 'Isn't there anything we can do about it? Look at the time! If I'm not there in twenty minutes I've had it. Surely one of you fellows has got a stiff shirt to lend me?'

'What! Your size?' Bottle asked.

'Why the devil didn't I think of buying a dickey!'

I had an idea.

'Let us apply the first principles of surgery,' I said.

'What the hell are you getting at now?'

'Supposing you have tension on a surgical incision. What do you do? Why, make a counter-incision, of course, in a site where it doesn't matter. Take your jacket off, Tony.'

A quick rip with the scissors up the length of the shirt-back from the tail to the collar and Benskin was once again the perfect English gentleman. He left the flat in high spirits, convinced that he would make enough in the evening to keep him in drinks for a fortnight. Unhappily, he was no better at serving hot soup than driving a car and was dismissed by the furious maître d'hôtel between the fish and the entrée.

CHAPTER XIV

'B.I.D.,' I said. 'Brought in dead. What an epitaph!'

I was standing in the cold, bright post-mortem room on the top floor of the hospital. It was a large room with a glass roof, tiles round the walls, three heavy porcelain tables, and one side made up of a bank of numbered metal drawers like the front of a large filing cabinet. The unfortunate patients were brought by the cheery-looking fellow on his trolley to a special lift, taken to the roof, and packed away neatly in the refrigerated drawers. Each corpse bore a label giving the name, religion, and diagnosis, but the man on the table in front of me had only the three letters on his tab. He had been picked up in the street by the police a few hours before and brought futilely to the accident room.

I pulled the heavy rubber gloves tight and began my incision with the big post-mortem knife. I never liked doing post-mortems. They made me feel sick. However, under the medical school regulations I was required to perform three of them, so I had to get on with it.

Every morning at twelve the physicians and surgeons came up to the room to see their unsuccessful cases demonstrated by the heartless pathologist. Often they had been right in life, and had the satisfaction of feeling with their fingers the lesion they had built up in their imagination from examination of the body surface, deduction, and studying the black and grey shadows on X-ray films. Occasionally they were humbled.

'So there *was* a tumour of the cerebellum after all!' I once heard Dr. Malcolm Maxworth exclaim, going red in the face. 'Damn it, damn it, damn it!'

Maxworth was not angry on the dead patient's behalf: it was simply that in the daily contest between his mind and the tricks of the body the body had for once won a game.

Our afternoons were spent wandering round the dusty pathology museum inspecting the grotesque specimens in the big glass jars of spirit. They had everything in the St. Swithin's museum, from two-headed babies to tattoo marks. Each specimen was neatly labelled and numbered, and a clinical history of the case was set out on a card attached to the bottle. 'How much better than a tombstone!' Grimsdyke said as he read the last dramatic illness of John O'Hara in 1927 and held the remains of his ruptured aneurism in his hand. 'I suppose everyone wants to be remembered somehow. What could be better than giving a bit of yourself to the pathologists? Nobody knows or cares where this fellow's grave is, but his memory is kept fresh in here almost daily. A whopping aneurism! I bet it caused a panic in the ward when it burst.'

Twice a week during the three-month pathology course we had classes in forensic medicine. This was a subject that fascinated me, because I was a conscientious reader of detective stories and took delight in the realization that I too now knew how to distinguish human blood from animal's, compare bullet wounds, and differentiate murder from suicide. The lecturer was a portly, genial man whose picture appeared fairly regularly in the Sunday papers inspecting the scene of all the more attractive crimes. We learnt from him the favourite ways of committing suicide, abortion, homicide, and rape: the lecture on the last subject, which was illustrated with lantern slides, was the only one I can remember when I couldn't find a seat.

After the pathology course we began a round of the special departments, spending a few weeks in each. I was sent to learn a little about eyes and then to the throat surgeons, where I learned how to look into ears, up noses, and down throats. The E.N.T. clinic was busy from early morning until long after the others had finished at night, for the London atmosphere silted up patients' sinuses and roughened their lungs. 'That stuff's really irrespirable,' said the surgeon, flinging his arm in the direction of the window. 'Thank God I live in the country.' He was a big, brusque, overworked man who had nevertheless extracted a fortune from the respiratory damage caused by London air. He was supposed to be the fastest remover of tonsils and adenoids in the country, which he did every Thursday afternoon in out-patients', passing the anæsthetized children through his hands with the efficiency of a Chicago pig-killer.

After the throat department I was glad to sink into the restful atmosphere of the skin clinic. This was run by two very old and very gentlemanly specialists who conversed with each other, the students, the nurses, and the patients in whispers. They were both formally dressed in expensive suits, and each arrived at the hospital with a Rolls and a chauffeur. I had not expected such opulence and satisfied tranquillity from dermatologists, but on reflection it struck me that diseases of the skin were the most agreeable of all to specialize in. They are quiet, undramatic affairs which never get you up in the middle of the night nor interrupt your meals. The patients never die, but on the other hand they never seem to get better. A private patient, once diagnosed, is therefore a regular source of income to his doctor for the rest of his long life.

*   *   *   *   *

I still lived in the flat in Bayswater with Benskin and Bottle. Archie Broome and Mike Kelly had qualified and left, and we had been joined by Sprogget and Evans.

One evening after supper Bottle leant back in his chair and said, 'What shall we do to-night? Could you take a flick, anyone?'

'There's nothing on much,' said Tony in a bored voice. 'We might pop out for a pint a bit later.'

'I've got a novel to finish,' Evans said. 'It's got to go back to the library by the sixteenth. What's the date to-day, John?'

Bottle picked up the calendar from the mantelpiece. 'The fourteenth,' he said. He frowned. 'I say, do you chaps realize it is exactly five weeks to-day to our finals?'

'What!' Benskin jumped up in his chair. 'It can't be. They're not till the end of October.'

'Well, this is the middle of September.'

'Good God!' said Sprogget nervously. 'We shall have to start doing some work.'

Bottle put the calendar back.

'I'm afraid you're right. I've hardly looked at a book since we came out of the anatomy rooms. We've had a bloody good holiday, and now we've got to pay for it.'

Benskin, who believed in making his unpleasant decisions

swiftly, immediately picked up a copy of Price's *Practice of Medicine* from the bookshelf and wiped the dust off the cover with his sleeve.

'At least that settles our evening for us,' he said. 'From now on it's a case of burning the old midnight oil. Good heavens! Is there all this on tuberculosis?'

Our evenings afterwards were swiftly blown away in a gale of industry. We collected up our dusty books from the floor, the chairs, and the back of the cupboards, and left them in heaps, open, on the table. As soon as we returned from our work in the hospital we started reading. We ate bread and cheese when we felt like it and took caffeine and benzedrine tablets to keep awake. We worked past midnight, sometimes until four in the morning, cramming three years' study into thirty-five nights.

Each of us developed a favourite attitude for concentration. I found I could learn best sitting on a hard chair with my elbows on the table; Benskin was apparently able to absorb knowledge comfortably only if he removed his collar, tie, shoes, belt, and socks and stuck his large pink feet on the mantelpiece. Bottle preferred to take his text-book and sit alone in the lavatory, and Sprogget would pace nervously up and down the narrow hallway repeating under his breath the signs and symptoms of innumerable diseases and giggling grotesquely when he couldn't remember them. Only Evans passed the pre-examination stage in tranquillity. His mind was so efficient he found it necessary to do no more than loll in an arm-chair and read gently through his text-books as though they were the Sunday papers.

For an hour or so we would work without speaking, filling the room with tobacco smoke. But it was a thin, taut silence, like the skin of an inflated balloon. Benskin was usually the first to break it.

'What the hell's the dose of digitalis?' he asked angrily one night.

'Six grains eight-hourly for three doses, followed by three grains three times a day for two days, and half that dose four times daily for two days,' I replied brightly.

'I'm sure that's not right,' he said. 'It's somewhere round two grains a day.'

'Of course it's right!' I barked at him. 'I've only just learnt it.'

'Richard's right,' said Evans quietly from his chair.

'All right, all right! Don't fly off about it. I haven't got as far as digitalis yet, anyway.'

Sprogget's head appeared at the door.

'Is a presystolic murmur at the apex diagnostic of mitral stenosis?' he asked anxiously.

'Yes,' Evans said.

'Oh damn! I didn't think it was.' He looked as if he was going to burst into tears. 'I'm bound to fail, I know I am!' he exclaimed.

'You'll be all right,' Benskin told him gruffly. 'It's nervous types like me who'll come down. Do you get cyanosis in pneumonia?'

We took one night a week off: on Saturday we all went out and got drunk. The rest of the time we were irritable with each other, uncommunicative, and jumpy. Benskin's usual sunny good humour seemed to have left him for ever. He scowled at his companions, complained about everything in the flat, and developed the symptoms of a gastric ulcer.

The grim period of study and Benskin's bad temper were relieved by only one incident before the examination. One Sunday night the famous helmet disappeared from the King George. No one knew who had taken it and no one had seen it go: it had simply vanished from its hook some time during the evening. The theft made Benskin furious, particularly as he had reasons to suspect the students from Bart's, whom St. Swithin's had beaten soundly earlier on in the year in the inter-hospitals' rugby cup. The next night he took himself off to Smithfield and climbed over the venerable walls of that ancient institution. He didn't find the helmet, but he put his foot through a window and was asked to leave by a porter. His foray came to the ears of the Dean of St. Swithin's, who called him to his office, abused him soundly for ten minutes, and fined him three guineas. The Dean could not appreciate at all Benskin's plea that the loss of the helmet justified such strong action. Whether this had any connection with an event that occurred shortly afterwards and established itself for ever in the hospital tradition with the title of the Dean's Tea Party was never known. Benskin was suspected, and there was a rumour that he had been spotted coming out of a small printer's in the City: but there was never any proof.

A few days after his interview with Benskin the Dean entered his office to find his personal secretary rummaging through his desk.

'Hello!' he said. 'Lost something?'

'Not exactly, sir,' she said, giving him a worried look. 'I was just wondering why I hadn't seen the invitations?'

'Invitations? What invitations?'

'To your At Home to-morrow,' she replied simply. 'The 'phone's been ringing all morning. The Deans of all the other hospitals in London have been through to say that the notice is a little short but they will be glad to come for cocktails in the library. There have been some people from the Medical Research Council, too, and a professor from Birmingham.' She looked at a pencilled list in her hand. 'About thirty have accepted so far, and there looks like a good many more have arrived by the second post.'

The Dean hurled his hat on the floor.

'It's an outrage!' he shouted in fury. 'It's a disgrace! It's a . . .! By God, these bloody students! By God, I'll punish them for this! You just wait and see!' He poked a quivering finger at her so forcefully she leapt back with a little squeal.

'You mean—it's a hoax?' she asked timidly.

'Of course it's a hoax! It's these damn hooligans we've been giving the best years of our lives trying to educate! Send me the School Secretary! And the Professor of Medicine! Get me the Head Porter! Ring up all those people and tell them the thing's a damnable practical joke!'

'What, all of them?'

'Of course, woman! You don't think I'm going to be made a fool of by my own students, do you? Get on to them at once!'

At that moment the 'phone rang again. She picked it up.

'Hello . . .' she said. 'Yes, he's here now. Certainly. One moment, please.'

She turned to the Dean. 'The Lord Mayor's Secretary,' she exclaimed. 'He says the Lord Mayor would be delighted.'

The Dean fell into his arm-chair like a knocked-out boxer.

'Very well,' he groaned. 'Very well, I know when I'm beaten. Get me those catering people, what's-is-names, instead.'

The party was a great success. Although the Dean entered the library black with anger he found himself in the middle of so many of his distinguished contemporaries that he mellowed rapidly. Didn't the leading heart specialist in the country grip him by the arm and tell him how much he appreciated his latest paper? Didn't the Lord Mayor himself hint of a donation towards the new library, and, more important, ask for an appointment in Harley Street? Besides, he had quickly seen to it that the expenses would be borne by the Governors. He said a genial good-bye to his last guests as they climbed into their cars in the courtyard. Suddenly he saw Benskin, with his hands in his pockets, grinning at him from the shadow of Lord Larrymore's statue. The Dean's face twisted malignantly.

'Do you know anything about this, damn you?' he demanded.

'Me, sir?' Benskin asked innocently. 'Not at all, sir. I think it may have been someone from Bart's.'

CHAPTER XV

To a medical student the final examinations are something like death: an unpleasant inevitability to be faced sooner or later, one's state after which is determined by the care spent in preparing for the event.

The examinations of the United Hospitals Committee are held twice a year in a large dingy building near Harley Street. It shares a hidden Marylebone square with two pubs, a sooty caged garden, an antique shop, and the offices of a society for retrieving fallen women. During most of the year the square is a quiet and unsought thoroughfare, its traffic made up by patrons of the pubs, reclaimed women, and an unhappy-looking man in sandals who since 1931 has passed through at nine each morning carrying a red banner saying 'REPENT FOR YE DIE TO-MORROW.' Every six months this orderly quiet is broken up like a road under a pneumatic drill. Three or four hundred students arrive from every hospital in London and from every medical school in the United Kingdom. Any country that accepts a British qualification is represented. There are brown, bespectacled Indians, invariably swotting until the last minute from Sir Leatherby Tidy's fat and invaluable *Synopsis of Medicine*; jet-black gentlemen from West Africa standing in nervous groups and testing their new fountainpens; fat, coffee-coloured Egyptians discussing earnestly in their own language fine points of erudite medicine; hearty Australians, New Zealanders, and South Africans showing no more anxiety than if they were waiting for a pub to open; the whole diluted thoroughly by a mob of pale, fairly indifferent, untidy-looking British students conversing in accents from the Welsh valleys to Stirlingshire.

An examination is nothing more than an investigation of a man's knowledge, conducted in a way that the authorities have found to be the most fair and convenient to both sides. But the medical student cannot see it in this light. Examinations touch off his fighting spirit; they are a straight contest between himself and the examiners, conducted on well-established rules for both, and he goes at them like a prize-fighter.

There is rarely any frank cheating in medical examinations, but the candidates spend almost as much time over the technical details of the contest as they do learning general medicine from their text-books. We found the papers set for the past ten years in the hospital library, and the five of us carefully went through the questions.

'It's no good wasting time on pneumonia, infant diarrhœa, or appendicitis,' Benskin said. 'They were asked last time. I shouldn't think it's worth learning about T.B. either, it's come up twice in the past three years.'

We all agreed that it was unnecessary to equip ourselves with any knowledge of the most frequent serious illnesses we would come across in practice.

'I tell you what we *ought* to look up,' said Evans. 'Torulosis.'

'Never heard of it,' Benskin said.

'It's pretty rare. But I see that old Macready-Jones is examining this time, and it's his speciality. He has written a lot of stuff about it in the *B.M.J.* and the *Lancet.* He might quite easily pop a question in.'

'All right,' I said. 'I'll look it up in the library to-morrow.'

My chances of meeting a case of torulosis after qualification were remote, and I wouldn't have recognized it if I had. But to be well informed about torulosis in the next fortnight might make the difference between passing and failure.

Benskin discovered that Malcolm Maxworth was the St. Swithin's representative on the Examining Committee and thenceforward we attended all his ward-rounds, standing at the front and gazing at him like impressionable music enthusiasts at the solo violinist. The slightest hint he was believed to have dropped was passed round, magnified, and acted upon. Meanwhile, we despondently ticked the days off the calendar, swotted up the spot questions, and ran a final breathless sprint down the well-trodden paths of medicine, snatching handfuls of knowledge from the sides where we could.

*　　*　　*　　*　　*

The examination is split into three sections, each one of which must be passed on its own. First there are the written papers, then *viva voce* examinations, and finally the clinical, when the student is presented with a patient and required to turn in a competent diagnosis in half an hour.

On the morning the examination began the five of us left the Bayswater flat early, took a bus along Oxford Street, and walked towards the examination building in a silent, sickly row. I always found the papers the most disturbing part of the contest. They begin at nine o'clock, an hour when I am never at my best, and the sight of other candidates *en masse* is most depressing. They all look so intelligent. They wear spectacles and use heavy fountain pens whose barrels reflect their own mental capacity; once inside they write steadily and sternly, as though they were preparing leaders for the next week's *Lancet*; and the women students present such an aspect of concentration and industry it seems useless for men to continue the examination at all.

I went with a hundred other students into one of three large, square halls used for the examination. The polished wooden floor was covered with rows of desks set at a distance apart that made one's neighbour's writing completely indecipherable if he had not, as was usually the case, already done so himself. Each desk was furnished with a card stamped with a black examination number, a clean square of pink blotting-paper, and a pen apparently bought second-hand from the Post Office. The place smelt of floor-polish and freshly-sharpened pencils.

A single invigilator sat in his gown and hood on a raised platform to keep an eye open for flagrant cheating. He was helped by two or three uniformed porters who stood by the doors and looked impassionately down at the poor victims, like the policemen that flank the dock at the Old Bailey. The students scraped into their chairs, shot a hostile glance at the clock, and turned apprehensively to the buff question paper already laid out on each desk.

The first paper was on general medicine. The upper half of the sheet was taken up with instructions in bold print telling the candidate to write on one side of the paper only, answer all the questions, and to refrain from cribbing at peril of being thrown out. I brought my eyes painfully to the four questions beneath. At a glance I saw they were all short and pungent.

Give an account of the sign, symptoms, and treatment of heart failure was the first. 'Hell of a lot in that!' I thought. I read the second and cursed. *Discuss the changes in the treatment of pneumonia since 1930.* I felt the examiners had played a dirty trick by asking the same disease two papers in succession. The next simply demanded *How would you investigate an outbreak of typhoid fever?* and the last was a request for an essay on worms which I felt I could bluff my way through.

Three hours were allowed for the paper. About half-way through the anonymous examinees began to differentiate themselves. Some of them strode up for an extra answer book, with an awkward expression of self-consciousness and superiority in their faces. Others rose to their feet, handed in their papers, and left. Whether these people were so brilliant they were able to complete the examination in an hour and a half or whether this was the time required for them to set down unhurriedly their entire knowledge of medicine was never apparent from the nonchalant air with which they left the room. The invigilator tapped his bell half an hour before time; the last question was rushed through, then the porters began tearing papers away from gentlemen dissatisfied with the period allowed for them to express themselves and hoping by an incomplete sentence to give the examiner the impression of frustrated brilliance.

I walked down the stairs feeling as if I had just finished an eight-round fight. I reached desperately for my packet of cigarettes. The other candidates jostled round, chattering like children just out of school. In the square outside the first person I recognized was Grimsdyke.

'How did you get on?' I asked.

'So-so,' he replied. 'However, I am not worried. They never read the papers, anyway. I'm perfectly certain of that. Haven't you heard how they mark the tripos at Cambridge, my dear old boy? The night before the results come out the old don totters back from hall and chucks the lot down his staircase. The ones that stick on the top flight are given firsts, most of them end up on the landing and get seconds, thirds go to the lower flight, and any reaching the ground floor are failed. This system has been working admirably for years without arousing any comment. I heard all about it from a senior wrangler.'

Benskin's broad figure appeared among the crowd in the doorway. He was grinning widely and waved cheerily at us.

'You look pretty pleased with yourself,' I said.

'I am, old boy. To-day I tried out Benskin's infallible system for passing exams, and it worked beautifully. What number are you?'

'Three hundred and six.'

'I'm a hundred and ten. All I had to do was walk into the room labelled "Two to Three Hundred," wander round a bit while people got settled, and tell the invigilator chap they hadn't given me a place. He apologized at first, then he looked at my card and turfed me out pretty sharply to find the right room. I was pretty humble, of course, and murmured a lot of stuff about my nerves —however, in my wandering round the desks I'd taken damn good care to read all the questions. Now, if you look up the regulations you'll see candidates are admitted up to twenty minutes after the start of the examination, so I had plenty of time to dodge down to the lavatory and look it all up before presenting myself, breathless and distraught, at the correct room. Pretty smart, eh?'

'I hope they can't read your writing,' I said bitterly.

* * * * *

The oral examination was held a week after the papers. I got a white card, like an invitation to a cocktail party, requesting my presence at the examination building by eleven-thirty. I got up late, shaved with a new blade, and carefully brushed my suit. Should I wear a hospital tie? It was a tricky point. Examiners were well known for harbouring an allergy towards certain hospitals, and although my neckwear might convince them I was not from St. Mary's, for instance, or Guy's, my interrogators were quite as likely to be opposed to men from St. Swithin's.

I put on a quiet nondescript tie and a white stiff collar. The dressing-up was important, for the candidate was expected to look like a doctor even if he gave no indication of ever becoming one; one fellow who had once unhappily appeared in his usual outfit of sports coat and flannels was turned over to a porter by the outraged examiner with instructions to 'Show this gentleman to the nearest golf-course.'

It is the physical contact with the examiners that makes oral examinations so unpopular with the students. The written answers have a certain remoteness about them, and mistakes and omissions, like those of life, can be made without the threat of immediate punishment. But the viva is judgment day. A false answer, an inadequate account of oneself, and the god's brow threatens like an imminent thunderstorm. If the candidate loses his nerve in front of this terrible displeasure he is finished: confusion breeds confusion and he will come to the end of his interrogation struggling like a cow in a bog. This sort of mental attitude had already led to the disgrace of Harris, who had been reduced to a state just short of speechlessness by a terrible succession of *faux pas*. The examiner finally decided to try the poor fellow with something simple and handed him a breast-bone that had been partly worn away with the life-long pressure of an enlarged artery underneath. 'Now, my boy,' said the examiner. 'What do you think caused that hollow?' All he wanted for a reply was the single word 'Pressure,' but Harris looked at the specimen in blank silence. With a sigh, the kindly examiner removed his pince-nez and indicated the two indentations they left on each side of his nose. 'Well,' he continued helpfully, 'what do you think caused that?' Something clicked in Harris's panicky brain. The depressed nasal bridge . . . a picture flashed up that he had seen so often in the opening pages of his surgery book. 'Congenital syphilis, sir,' he replied without hesitation.

I was shown to a tiny waiting-room furnished with hard chairs, a wooden table, and windows that wouldn't open, like the condemned cell. There were six candidates from other hospitals waiting to go in with me, all of them in their best clothes. They illustrated the types fairly commonly seen in viva waiting-rooms. There was the Nonchalant, lolling back on the rear legs of his chair with his feet on the table, showing the bright yellow socks under his blue trouser-legs. He was reading the sporting page of the *Express* with undeceptive thoroughness. Next to him, a man

134

of the Frankly Worried class sat on the edge of his chair tearing little bits off his invitation card and jumping irritatingly every time the door opened. There was the Crammer, fondling the pages of his battered text-book in a desperate farewell embrace, and his opposite, the Old Stager, who treated the whole thing with the familiarity of a photographer at a wedding. He had obviously failed the examination so often he looked upon the viva simply as another engagement to be fitted into his day. He stood looking out of the window and yawning, only cheering up when he saw the porter, with whom he was now on the same warm terms as an undergraduate and his college servant.

'How are you getting on this time, sir?' the porter asked him cheerily.

'Not so dusty, William, not so dusty at all. The second question in the paper was the same one they asked four years ago. What are they like in there?'

'Pretty mild this morning, sir. I'm just taking them their coffee.'

'Excellent! Put plenty of sugar in it. A low blood-sugar is conducive to bad temper.'

'I will, sir. Best of luck.'

'Thank you, William.'

The other occupant of the room was a woman. A trim little piece, I noticed, probably from the Royal Free. She sat pertly on her chair with her hands folded on her lap. Women students— the attractive ones, not those who are feminine only through ines- capable anatomical arrangements—are under a disadvantage in oral examinations. The male examiners are so afraid of being prejudiced favourably by their sex they usually adopt towards them an undeserved sternness. But this girl had given care to her preparations for the examination. Her suit was neat but not smart; her hair tidy but not striking; she wore enough make-up to look attractive, and she was obviously practising, with some effort, a look of admiring submission to the male sex. I felt sure she would get through.

I sat alone in the corner and fingered my tie. They always made the candidates arrive too early, and the coffee would delay them further. There was nothing to do except wait patiently and think about something well removed from the unpleasant quarter of an hour ahead, such as rugby or the lady student's legs. Suddenly the door was flung open and a wild-eyed youth strode in.

'It's not too bad!' he exclaimed breathlessly to the nonchalant fellow. The two apparently came from the same hospital.

'I had Sir Rollo Doggert and Stanley Smith,' he said with a touch of pride. This brought a nod of appreciation from all of us, as they were known as two of the toughest examiners in London.

'Doggert started off by asking me the signs and symptoms of pink disease,' he continued. 'Luckily I knew that as I had happened to look it up last night . . .'

'Pink disease!' cried the worried man. 'My God, I forgot about that!'

'So I saw at once the way to handle him was to talk man-to-man, you know—none of this servile business, he much prefers to be stood up to. I reeled off pink disease and he said very good, my lad, very good.'

'Did he ask you anything else?' his friend said anxiously.

'Oh yes. He said, supposing I was out golfing with a diabetic who collapsed at the third tee, what would I do? Well, I said . . .'

The visitor gave a description of his examination in detail, like the man who comes out of the dentist's surgery and insists on telling the occupants of the waiting-room his experiences on the excuse that none of the frightful things that can happen really hurt.

The raconteur was stopped short by the porter. He marshalled us into line outside the heavy door of the examination room. There was a faint ting of a bell inside. The door opened and he admitted us one at a time, directing each to a different table.

CHAPTER XVI

'YOU go to table four,' the porter told me.

The room was the one we had written the papers in, but it was now empty except for a double row of baize-covered tables separated by screens. At each of these sat two examiners and a student who carried on a low earnest conversation with them, like a confessional.

I stood before table four. I didn't recognize the examiners. One was a burly, elderly man like a retired prize-fighter who smoked a pipe and was writing busily with a pencil in a notebook; the other was invisible, as he was occupied in reading the morning's *Times*.

'Good morning, sir,' I said.

Neither of them took any notice. After a minute the burly fellow looked up from his writing and silently indicated the chair in front of him. I sat down. He growled.

'I beg your pardon, sir?' I said politely.

'I said, you're number 306?' he said testily. 'That's correct, I suppose?'

'Yes, sir.'

'Well, why didn't you say so? How would you treat a case of tetanus?'

My heart leapt hopefully. This was something I knew, as there had recently been a case in St. Swithin's. I started off confidently, reeling out the lines of treatment and feeling much better.

The examiner suddenly cut me short.

'All right, all right,' he said impatiently, 'you seem to know that. A girl of twenty comes to you complaining of gaining weight. What do you do?'

This was the sort of question I disliked. There were so many things one could do my thoughts jostled into each other like a rugger scrum and became confused and unidentifiable.

'I—I would ask if she was pregnant,' I said.

'Good God, man! Do you go about asking all the girls you

know if they're pregnant? What hospital d'you come from?'

'St. Swithin's, sir,' I said, as though admitting an illegitimate parentage.

'I should have thought so! Now try again.'

I rallied my thoughts and stumbled through the answer. The examiner sat looking past me at the opposite wall, acknowledging my presence only by grunting at intervals.

The bell rang and I moved into the adjoining chair, facing *The Times*. The newspaper rustled and was set down, revealing a mild, youngish-looking man in large spectacles with a perpetual look of faint surprise on his face. He looked at me as if he was surprised to see me there, and every answer I made was received with the same expression. I found this most disheartening.

The examiner pushed across the green baize a small sealed glass pot from a pathology museum, in which a piece of meat like the remains of a Sunday joint floated in spirit.

'What's that?' he asked.

I picked up the bottle and examined it carefully. By now I knew the technique for pathological specimens of this kind. The first thing to do was turn them upside down, as their identity was often to be found on a label on the bottom. If one was still flummoxed one might sneeze or let it drop from nervous fingers to smash on the floor.

I upturned it and was disappointed to find the label had prudently been removed. Unfortunately there was so much sediment in the jar that it behaved like one of those little globes containing an Eiffel Tower that on reversal cover the model with a thick snowstorm. I could therefore not even see the specimen when I turned it back again.

'Liver,' I tried.

'What!' exclaimed the surprised man. The other examiner, who had returned to his writing, slammed down his pencil in disgust and glared at me.

'I mean lung,' I corrected.

'That's better. What's wrong with it?'

I could get no help from the specimen, which was still tossing in swirling white particles, so I took another guess.

'Pneumonia. Stage of white hepatization.'

The surprised man nodded. 'How do you test diphtheria serum?' he demanded.

'You inject it into a guinea-pig, sir.'

'Yes, but you've got to have an animal of a standard weight, haven't you?'

'Oh yes . . . a hundred kilogrammes.'

The two men collapsed into roars of laughter.

'It would be as big as a policeman, you fool!' shouted the first examiner.

'Oh, I'm so sorry,' I stammered miserably. 'I mean a hundred milligrammes.'

The laughter was renewed. One or two of the examiners at nearby tables looked up with interest. The other candidates felt like prisoners in the condemned block when they hear the bolt go in the execution shed.

'You could hardly see it then, boy,' said the surprised man, wiping his eyes. 'The creature weighs a hundred grammes. However, we will leave the subject. How would you treat a case of simple sore throat?'

'I would give a course of sulphonamide, sir.'

'Yes, that's right.'

'I disagree with you, Charles,' the other interrupted forcibly. 'It's like taking a hammer at a nut. I have an excellent gargle I have been prescribing for years which does very well.'

'Oh, I don't know,' said the surprised fellow warmly. 'One must make use of these drugs. I've always had excellent results with sulphonamides.'

'Did you read that paper by McHugh in the *Clinical Record* last winter?' demanded the first examiner, banging the table again.

'Certainly I read it, George. And the correspondence which followed. Nevertheless, I feel it is still open to doubt——'

'I really cannot agree with you——'

They continued arguing briskly, and were still doing so when a second tinkle of the bell allowed me to slide out and rush miserably into the street.

*   *   *   *

The days after the viva were black ones. It was like having a severe accident. For the first few hours I was numbed, unable to realize what had hit me. Then I began to wonder if I would ever make a recovery and win through. One or two of my friends heartened me by describing equally depressing experiences that had overtaken them previously and still allowed them to pass. I began to hope. Little shreds of success collected together and weaved themselves into a triumphal garland. After all, I thought, I got the bottle right, and I knew about tetanus . . . then I forgot about it in my anxiety over the last section of the examination, the clinical.

The clinical is probably the most chancy of the three parts. The student may be allotted a straightforward case with sounds in the chest that come through his stethoscope like the noise of an iron foundry; or he may get something devilish tricky.

The cases for clinical examinations were collected from the out-patient departments of hospitals all over London, and were in the class referred to by physicians informally as 'old chronics.' They had their lesions healed as far as possible; now they walked round in fairly good health but with a collection of clicks, whistles, or rumbles inside them set up by the irreversible process of their diseases. These are just the sort of things examiners like present-ing to students. A case of vague ill-health or an indefinite lump are too arguable, but a good hearty slapping in the chest gives a right to fail a man forthrightly if he misses it.

For this service the patients were given seven-and-six and free tea and buns. But most of them would happily have performed with a strictly amateur status and provided their own sandwiches. The six-monthly visits to the examination were their principal outings of the year. They attended their own hospitals monthly to show off the signs they proudly possessed to a single doctor and discuss their ailment with fellow-patients on the benches out-side, but in the exam they were inspected by hundreds of doctors —or as good as—and chatted to the élite of fellow-sufferers. It is much the same as winning an international rugby cap.

I arrived at the examination building in plenty of time, to find out what I could of the cases from men who had already been examined. I knew Benskin had been in early and looked for him in the hall to ask what there was upstairs.

'There's an asthma in a red scarf, old boy,' he said helpfully. 'And an old man with emphysema just behind the door as you go in—if you get him be sure to examine his abdomen, he's got a couple of hernias thrown in.'

I made a mental note of it.

'Then there's a little girl with a patent ductus—you can't miss her, she's the only child in the room. Oh, and a woman with burnt-out tabes. He'll ask you what treatment you'd give her, and he expects the answer "None".'

I nodded, thanked him, and made my way to the examination room.

My first impression of the clinical examination was of a doctor's surgery gone into mass-production. Patients were scattered across the room on couches, beds, and wheel-chairs, the men divided from the women by screens across the centre. They were in all stages of undress and examination. Circulating busily between them were a dozen or so nurses, examiners in white coats, and unhappy students dangling their stethoscopes behind them like the tails of whipped puppies.

I was directed to a pleasant, tubby little examiner.

'Hello, my lad,' he began genially. 'Where are you from? Swithin's, eh? When are you chaps going to win the rugger cup? Go and amuse yourself with that nice young lady in the corner and I'll be back in twenty minutes.'

She was indeed a nice young lady. A redhead with a figure out of *Esquire*.

'Good morning,' I said with a professional smile.

'Good morning,' she returned brightly.

'Would you mind telling me your name?' I asked politely.

'Certainly. Molly Ditton. I'm unmarried, aged twenty-two, and my work is shorthand-typing, which I have been doing for four years. I live in Ilford and have never been abroad.'

My heart glowed: she knew the form.

'How long have you been coming up here?' I asked. 'You seem to know all the answers.'

She laughed.

'Oh, years and years. I bet I know more about myself than you do.'

Just the thing! There is a golden rule for clinical examinations —ask the patient. They attend the examination for so many years and hear themselves discussed so often with the candidates they have the medical terms off pat. All I had to do was play my cards correctly. I talked to her about Ilford, and the wonderful advantages of living there; of shorthand-typing and its effects on the fingernails; of her boy friends and her prospects of matrimony (this produced a few giggles); of the weather and where she went for her holidays.

'By the way,' I said with careful casualness, 'what's wrong with you?'

'Oh, I've mitral stenosis due to rheumatic fever, but I'm perfectly well compensated and I've a favourable prognosis. There's a presystolic murmur at the apex, but the aortic area is clear and there are no creps at the bases. By the way, my thyroid is slightly enlarged, they like you to notice that. I'm not fibrilating and I'm having no treatment.'

'Thank you very much,' I said.

The tubby man was delighted when I passed on to him the patient's accurate diagnosis as my own.

'Capital, capital!' he beamed. 'Spotted the thyroid, too . . . glad some of you young fellers use your powers of observation. Been telling my own students for years—observe, observe, observe. They never do, though. Right you are, my lad. Now just take this ophthalmoscope and tell me what you can see in that old woman's eye.'

My heart, which had been soaring like a swallow, took a sharp dive to earth. The examiner handed me the little black instrument with lenses for looking into the eye. I had often seen it used in the wards but I never seemed to find time to learn how to employ it myself. There was a knack to it, which I did not possess; and I knew plainly enough that the defect was sufficient to fail me out of hand. I imagined the examiner's sunny friendliness turning into a storm of irritation; my hand shook as I took the instrument. Slowly I placed it closely between my eye and the patient. All I could see was something that looked like a dirty tank in an aquarium with a large, dim fish in it. The time had come for quick thinking. Looking intently through the instrument I let out a long whistle of amazement.

'Yes, it is a big retinal detachment, isn't it?' the examiner said happily, taking away the ophthalmoscope and patting me on the back. I saw myself marked over the pass number, and with a grateful smile at the redhead tripped downstairs in elation.

In the hall I met Benskin again. He was looking profoundly miserable. 'What's up?' I asked anxiously.

Benskin shook his head and explained in a choked voice what had happened. While I was examining medical cases he had been questioned in practical midwifery. One of the tests for prospective obstetricians was provided by a life-size papier mâché model of half the female trunk, into which a straw-stuffed baby was slipped through a trapdoor. The candidate was then provided with a pair of obstetrical forceps and required to deliver it *per via naturalis*. This was demanded of Benskin. He solemnly applied the two blades to the head, taking care to put the correct one on first. He locked the handle, took it in the approved grip, and gave a strong pull. Nothing happened. He pulled harder, but the straw fœtus refused to be born. He felt sweat on his brow and his mouth went dry; he saw his chances of passing fading like a spent match. He gave a desperate heave. His feet slipped on the polished floor and over his head flew mother, baby, forceps, and all.

The examiner looked at him lying on the floor for a second in silence. Then he picked up one blade of the forceps and handed it to him.

'Now hit the father with that,' he said sourly, 'and you'll have killed the whole bloody family.'

CHAPTER XVII

'ONE doesn't fail exams,' said Grimsdyke firmly. 'One comes down, one muffs, one is ploughed, plucked, or pipped. These infer a misfortune that is not one's own fault. To speak of failing is bad taste. It's the same idea as talking about passing away and going above instead of plain dying.'

We were sitting with Benskin in the King George. It was immediately after opening time in the morning and we were alone in the bar. We sat on stools, resting our elbows on the counter and our heads on our hands. All three of us looked pitifully dejected. The examination results were to be published at noon.

'It's the heartless way they do it,' I said. 'Picking you out one at a time in front of everybody. I wish they'd show a little decent discretion about the business. I'd much prefer it if they sent you a letter. You can at least slink away and open it in the lavatory or somewhere.'

'In Tibet, I believe,' Grimsdyke went on, 'they simply execute the unsuccessful candidates on the spot.'

'Well, they probably welcome it.'

'They failed Harris pretty decently,' Benskin said reverently, as though speaking of the dead. 'He's so sure he'll have to take it again in six months he's not even bothering to hear the results. When he floundered badly in his viva the old boy simply looked dreamily out of the window and said, "Young man, how mysterious and wonderful is Nature! Now we see the leaf turning gold on the branch and falling to the ground. The flowers and plants have lost their summer beauty and withered, and the earth looks dead beyond hope of resurrection. But in the month of April the spring will come, the trees will burst into green flames, the shoots will leap up through the black soil, and petals will cover the bare flowerbeds. And you and I, my boy, will be here to see it, won't we?" '

'I think that was very bad form,' said Grimsdyke.

The Padre put three small glasses in front of us.

'Whisky?' Grimsdyke said. 'I thought we ordered beer.'

'If you will permit me, Mr. Grimsdyke, I would like to suggest, on the basis of my experience, something a little more nourishing. I know what a difficult time this is for you young gentlemen. Will you please accept these with the compliments of the house?'

'Here, I say, Padre . . . !'

He held up his hand.

'Not a bit of it, sir. The money I have been obliged to take off you in our long acquaintance more than justifies it. Here's jolly good luck, gentlemen!'

'Bottoms up,' said Benskin.

'I'm sure I've failed, all the same,' I said, putting my glass down. 'How could I get through after that terrible viva?''

Benskin snorted.

'It's all very well for you to talk. What about my midwifery clinical? That came under the heading of ugly incidents.'

'You never know, my dear old boy,' Grimsdyke said hopefully. 'You may have done brilliantly in the papers.'

'Let's not talk about it,' I said. 'Let's discuss rugger instead.'

*   *   *   *   *

At noon we arrived in the examination building. The same number of candidates were there, but they were a subdued, muttering crowd, like the supporters of a home team who had just been beaten in a cup tie.

We pushed our way into the large hall on the ground floor. It was packed full with anxious students. On the side of the hall facing us was the foot of a marble staircase. To the left of the staircase was a plain, open door, over which had been recently pinned a large black and white card saying 'EXIT.' To the right was a clock, which stood at a few minutes before twelve.

We had heard exactly what would happen. At midday precisely the Secretary of the Committee would descend the stairs and take his place, flanked by two uniformed porters, on the lowermost step. Under his arm would be a thick, leather-covered book containing the results. One of the porters would carry a list of the candidates' numbers and call them out, one after the other. The candidate would step up closely to the Secretary, who would say simply 'Pass' or 'Failed.' Successful men would go upstairs to receive the congratulations and handshakes of the examiners and failures would slink miserably out of the exit to seek the opiate of oblivion.

'One thing, it's quick,' Benskin muttered nervously.

'Like the drop,' said Grimsdyke.

One minute to twelve. The room had suddenly come to a frightening, unexpected silence and stillness, like an unexploded bomb. A clock tinged twelve in the distance. My palms were as wet as sponges. Someone coughed, and I expected the windows to rattle. With slow scraping feet that could be heard before they appeared the Secretary and porters came solemnly down the stairs.

They took up their positions; the leather book was opened. The elder porter raised his voice.

'Number two hundred and nine,' he began. 'Number thirty-seven. Number one hundred and fifty.'

The tension in the room broke as the students shuffled to the front and lined up before the staircase. The numbers were not called in order, and the candidates strained to hear their own over the low rumble of conversation and scraping of feet that rose from the assembly.

'Number one hundred and sixty-one,' continued the porter. 'Number three hundred and two. Number three hundred and six.'

Grimsdyke punched me hard in the ribs.

'Go on,' he hissed. 'It's you!'

I jumped, and struggled my way to the front of the restless crowd. My pulse shot high in my ears. My face was burning hot and I felt my stomach had been suddenly plucked from my body.

I lined up in the short queue by the stairs. My mind was empty and numb. I stared at the red neck of the man in front of me, with its rim of blue collar above his coat, and studied it with foolish intensity. Suddenly I found myself on top of the Secretary.

'Number three oh six?' the Secretary whispered, without looking up from the book. 'R. Gordon?'

'Yes,' I croaked.

The world stood still. The traffic stopped, the plants ceased growing, men were paralysed, the clouds hung in the air, the winds dropped, the tides disappeared, the sun halted in the sky.

'Pass,' the man muttered.

Blindly, like a man just hit by blackjack, I stumbled upstairs.

*   *   *   *   *

The bar of the King George was full. I crashed through the door like a hot wind.

'I've passed!' I screamed.

The bar rose in turmoil. I couldn't see any of it. It was a pink jumble of faces, a numb sensation of handshakes, a dim perception of backslapping.

'Congratulations, sir!' shouted the Padre, thrusting his hand through the mob. 'Congratulations, doctor! Here you are, sir. A quart tankard, sir. With my every best wish.'

Someone pushed the deep pewter mug into my hands.

'Down the hatch!'

'One gulp, old man!'

I was too breathless to drink. I wanted to laugh, cry, dance, and run all at the same time.

'I can't believe it!' I exclaimed. 'It isn't true! The first thing I knew I was shaking hands with the old boys and signing my diploma.'

'How about the other two gentlemen?' the Padre called.

'Oh Lord!' I felt suddenly guilty. 'I'd quite forgotten to wait for them!'

At that moment the door flew open. There entered Benskin and Grimsdyke wearing each other's jackets, attempting to pull in with them a violently neighing carthorse.

'I think it's all right,' the Padre said.

The party went on until closing time. Every student in the school seemed to be inside the tiny bar. I emptied and re-emptied my tankard. Everyone was shouting and singing, leaning on each other, jostling their neighbours, slapping their friends on the back. The angry owner of the horse had been asked inside and was now singing 'The Lily of Laguna' to a co-operative audience. The room filled tighter as the news of more successes was brought in, like victories to a triumphant headquarters.

'Bottle's through,' I heard Evans bawling over the hubbub. 'So's Sprogget.'

'How about you?' I shouted back.

Evans delightedly stuck his thumb in the air.

I suddenly found myself jammed between Benskin and Grimsdyke.

'Hooray!' shouted Benskin, ruffling my hair.

'It's bloody funny!' Grimsdyke shouted. 'Bloody funny!'

'What is?' I bawled at him.

'We're three bloody doctors,' he hollered.

We burst into roars of laughter.

*　　*　　*　　*　　*

My feelings in the next few days were those of a private unexpectedly promoted to general overnight. In a minute or two I had been transformed from an unearning and potentially dishonest ragamuffin to a respectable and solvent member of a learned profession. Now banks would trust me with their money, hire firms with their cars, and mothers with their daughters. I could sign prescriptions, death certificates, and orders for extra milk, and no one could contradict me. It was wonderful.

As soon as the exam results were out the Chiefs made appointments to the resident staff of St. Swithin's. I became housephysician to Dr. Malcolm Maxworth, and had to begin work the next week. I saw from the list that Evans had been awarded the plum position of house-surgeon to the Professor, and Grimsdyke became a junior obstetrical officer. Sprogget had not bothered to apply for a job at St. Swithin's and Benskin was not given one. The Dean had vetoed the appointment.

I packed up and left the Bayswater flat. The landlord had been wanting to get rid of us for some time and took the opportunity of taking possession himself. We had a row about damages, but Sprogget settled it by threatening officially to report the plumbing to the local Medical Officer of Health unless the estimate was reduced considerably.

In the hospital I was given a small, bleak room with an iron bedstead, a desk, a chair, and a telephone. But I unpacked with delight—I was living there free of charge, and at last, at the age of twenty-three, I was earning some money.

There was a letter waiting for me, addressed ostentatiously to Dr. Gordon in Benskin's handwriting. I opened it.

'Dear old boy,' it began. 'I expect you will be surprised to hear that I have got married. As a matter of fact, I have for a long time been bloody keen on Molly (the nurse I proposed to that night), and we decided to do the old ring stuff as soon as I got through. I didn't say anything to you coarse fellows, because you have such warped ideas on such things. I have a job waiting for me in general practice at home, and we are now having the old honeymoon in Cornwall. Let me warn you against the swank of calling yourself doctor, old lad. I signed myself in the visitors' book as Dr. Benskin, and we had only just got into bed when the porter came banging on the door shouting at me that the cook had scalded herself. The marriage was consummated, but only just. Your old chum, Tony.'

'I'm damned!' I said. 'The old stoat!'

I was still staring at the letter when the 'phone rang. It was Sister Virtue, whom I now had to work with as a colleague. Her tone was only a little less severe than the one she used on students —to her, new housemen were hardly less reprehensible.

'Dr. Gordon,' she rasped. 'When are you going to appear in the ward? I have a stack of notes for you to sign and three new patients have been admitted. You can't expect the nursing staff to run the hospital on their own.'

I looked at my watch. It was six in the evening. I had to tell the Padre about Benskin.

'Half-past six, Sister,' I said. 'I've only just arrived. Will that be all right?'

'Not a minute later,' she snapped, discontinuing the conversation.

I walked across to the King George with Benskin's letter.

'I knew it all along, sir, if I may say so,' the Padre said calmly. 'It's always the same with the ones that run a mile if they see a nurse and talk big about staying single. I've seen it a good many times now, sir. And you watch out, Dr. Gordon—I bet you're next.'

'Well, I don't know about that, Padre. There's no one on the cards at the moment.'

'Ah yes, sir, but wait till you've been about the hospital a bit as a doctor instead of a student. Why, the nurses are all over you. You get proper spoilt, you lads do.'

'I must confess noting a certain sweet co-operation among the girls I hadn't found before. Perhaps you're right. Anyway, I'll watch my step.'

I took a few sips of my beer.

'It's quiet in here, Padre, to-night.'

'Early in the evening yet, sir.'

'I know . . . but it seems oppressively quiet, if you know what I mean. I suppose it's because there's been so much fun and games going on the last few days. It's . . . well, lonely. This qualification business is all very well, but it soon wears off. For about three days the world is at your feet, then you realize it's the beginning, not the end. You've got to fight a damn sight harder than you did in your exams to do your job decently and make a living.'

'That's right, sir. They all say the same. You've got to face it, them carefree student days is over for good. Life is hard, sir. It's bad enough for a publican, but a damn sight worse for a doctor.'

'Well, let's not get miserable about it,' I said. 'Still, these last few days I've begun to wish I'd got a bit more out of my education.'

'Come off it, sir,' said the Padre genially. 'You've made a lot of friends, which mark my words you'll hang on to till your dying day. And that's valuable, sir. A lot of people can get an education, but not many of 'em can collect as sound a bunch of good friends as you young gentlemen do. Wherever you go, sir, no matter how many years to come, you'll still remember Mr. Benskin and the rest and the good times you've had in these four walls.'

'You know, Padre,' I said, 'that's exactly what I think myself. I was just too frightened to say so.'

The door opened. A porter stood there.

'Dr. Gordon,' he said. 'I've been looking for you all over. Wanted at once in the ward, sir. Emergency just come in.'

I looked at the half-full glass of beer. I picked it up, hesitated, and left it.

'All right,' I said, pulling my stethoscope out of my pocket. 'I'm coming.'

Times have changed, I thought as I walked over to the hospital. I suddenly realized that from now on it was always going to be like this.

DOCTOR AT SEA

To

THE MERCHANT NAVY

*They have a
lot to put up with*

NOTE

The *Lotus* and her crew are as fictitious as the *Flying Dutchman* and her insubstantial company.

CHAPTER I

IT would be unfair to describe the *Lotus* as an unlucky ship. It was just that she was accident prone, like a big, awkward schoolgirl.

Even her period of gestation in the shipyard was full of mishaps. She was laid down in Wallsend in 1929, and had advanced to the shape of a huge picked chicken when the depression blew down bitterly on Tyneside. For the next four years she rusted untouched behind locked gates, and when they started work again her design was changed on the drawing-board from a North Atlantic ship to a Far East trader. Shortly afterwards the company ordering her went bankrupt and she was bought on the stocks by another, who began to turn her into a whaler. They too rapidly slid into insolvency and abandoned her to a fourth, the Fathom Steamship Company of St. Mary Axe. It was this concern that succeeded in launching her, after she had been through as many fruitless changes in construction as a human embryo.

At her launch she holed and almost sunk a small tug, and on her maiden voyage as a cargo-passenger ship she lost a propeller during a gale in the Australian Bight. At the beginning of the war she came home from New Zealand, painted grey, and was one of the first vessels to reveal to the Admiralty the effectiveness of the magnetic mine. She lost most of her bows in the Thames Estuary, but stayed afloat long enough to be dragged into dock for repairs. After several months she set off again to join a convoy, and had her stern blown away by a bomb twenty-five minutes after leaving port.

The stern was patched up, and she managed to pass the rest of the hostilities without getting herself involved in any dangerous action, apart from shooting down an American Mustang in error with her Oerlikons in 1945. At the end of the war she refitted and returned to peaceful trading, disturbed only by an explosion in the engine-room in the Caribbean and the cook going abruptly insane one insupportably hot afternoon in the Red Sea and passing among his shipmates with the meat hatchet.

Much of the damage from both these accidents was repaired, but the repeated structural changes had induced in the *Lotus* a premature senility, a state of chronic invalidism. She was too cold in the higher latitudes, too hot in the Tropics, and she groaned pitifully in bad weather. But the Fathom Steamship Company unmercifully sent her anywhere in the world where she could find the shareholders a profit. She carried lead and lemons, boiler-tubes and barley, copra and cows. She took steel from Baltimore to Brisbane, wool from Auckland to Archangel, coal from Swansea to Singapore. She was one of the world's shopping baskets.

There was enough room on board for thirty passengers, though she rarely carried more than a dozen and often none at all. They were people going to unusual places, or too poor to afford a big ship, or experienced travellers who cringed before the bonhomie of the boatdeck and the deadly gin-and-sin routine of a sophisticated liner. The Company was indifferent to them: passengers earned little more than complaints, but freight meant money.

In the opinion of the crew, one of the severest disasters to overtake the *Lotus* since the war was her Commander, Captain Vincent Hogg, who was officially required to act at various times once his ship was at sea as the sole representative on board of the Fathom Steamship Company, the King, and God, for all three of them he substituted himself with impartial grandeur. His officers accepted him as farmers tolerate a prolonged drought, giving daily prayers for Divine removal of the affliction. The weight of his personality fell most heavily on the Mate, Mr. Hornbeam, who had passed his Master's examination twenty years before and was waiting for a command with the pitiful patience of an impoverished expectant relative. Promotion in the Company was simply a matter of dead men's shoes. He had in a drawer in his cabin an alphabetical list of the Fathom Line's Captains, with their exact ages and notes on their partiality for drink, loose women, and other items reputed to shorten life, but all of them retained irritatingly good health. He enjoyed the unstinted sympathy of the Chief Engineer, Mr. McDougall, who hated the Captain like a red-hot bearing; and the Captain disliked the Chief Engineer like fog round the Goodwins. McDougall looked upon the ship as a shell for the transportation of his engines, and complained daily when the navigational position from the bridge was some miles astern of the one he calculated from his revolutions. Indeed, according to the Chief Engineer, the machinery and boilers of the *Lotus* should have arrived in any port several days in advance of the rest of the vessel.

There were two other Mates, a gang of engineers, a wireless operator, and—as the *Lotus* carried more than ninety-nine souls when she was full—a doctor.

The doctor was by order of the Ministry of Transport, the uncompromising power who prescribes on every item of a sailor's life from the number of lifeboats to be available in emergency to the number of times he shall have eggs for his breakfast. Ninety-eight souls can sail the seas until they are carried away with obscure nautical illnesses, like the shipmates of the Ancient Mariner: their health is preserved with a bottle of black draught, the *Ship Captain's Medical Guide,* and a scalpel also used for sharpening the chart-room pencil. The Second Mate or the Chief Steward holds the keys of the drug chest and practises daily, after breakfast. All pains below the umbilicus are treated with strong purgative, all disturbances above with Ministry cough mixture, and lesions on the remainder of the body with turpentine liniment. Obviously there occur from time to time more alarming complaints, and these are submitted to surgery under wireless instructions by the Captain on the saloon table, after the patient and the surgeon have taken sufficient brandy to instil in each other confidence that both will survive the operation.

But one more soul on board brings to all the benefits of medical science—or as much of it as the doctor can remember, because ship surgeons are notoriously forgetful of these things. The sea induces an attitude of pleasant detachment towards problems that strain thought ashore, including those of the diagnosis and progress of disease, and the doctor has few professional obligations to distract him from his pastimes or enrich him with experience. For these reasons the companies naturally dislike the expense of carrying him—but then, the Fathom Steamship Company would have objected to the expense of lifeboats.

When I met the *Lotus* she was lying in Liverpool, due to sail with a cargo of machinery and motor-cars to Santos, in Brazil. It had then been raining on Merseyside for four days. The damp November wind channelled itself down the river, broke against the waterfront buildings, and ran up the cold streets behind. The birds on the Liver building, that are unfairly supposed by Liverpool seafarers to flap their wings when passed by a woman of untarnished virtue, wept ceaselessly on to the bleak pierhead. The Birkenhead ferry forced its way miserably across the choppy harbour, the landing-stage looked as forlorn as a bandstand in midwinter, and even the stonework of the St. George's Hall appeared in danger of showing through its crust of soot.

It was about eight in the evening, the hour when the shipowners are fed in the Adelphi. As they glumly finished their Martinis in the little American bar they calculated among themselves the rain's cost in delayed cargo working. Outside in Lime Street the adolescent tarts already clung hopefully to their damp doorways. The dripping buses took home the last pale shipping clerks, the overhead railway rattled along its grotesque track, and the dock police steamed themselves warm in front of the stoves in their cabins. The *Lotus* herself lay lifeless at her quay with tarpaulins tented over her hatches, creaking gently at her mooring ropes like an old bed in a bad dream.

I stood in the rain on the quayside reading a large sheet of printed instructions for resuscitating the apparently drowned. This was the only information of any sort available to passers-by. The wharf was deserted. The cranes huddled together in a row, a few railway trucks crouched between their legs; the warehouses were shut, locked, and abandoned even by the cats; the *Lotus*, lit with a few dim lights, looked as uninviting as a shut pub.

I was a young doctor with a bad diploma passing through the difficult stage of professional adolescence when you discover the medical schools teach as little about medicine as the public schools do about life. My knowledge of seafaring was based only on *Treasure Island*, pictures in the windows of Cook's, and a walking-on part I had been allowed to play in a students' production of *The Middle Watch*. I was nevertheless a recognized sailor. I had in my pocket a new seaman's identity card with my fingerprints on it, a document that made me the professional descendant of Drake and Cabot, subject to and protected by a batch of Parliamentary Acts, the target of missionaries' good intentions and girls' bad ones, and entitled, if I felt like it and there was enough room, to doss down in the Sailors' Home.

The first problem presented by nautical life was how to get aboard the ship. A slippery gangway reached up from the wharf to the *Lotus*'s afterdeck, but there was no one to welcome me at the top. After a few damp minutes I climbed the gangway nervously and looked around me. I was on a dirty iron deck littered with pieces of timber, scraps of rope, and coils of wire, like the junk room in a ship chandler's. A heavy wooden door led into the upper works, and as the rain was coming down my neck persistently I opened it and stepped inside.

Hostile darkness surrounded me; I smelt the faint bitter-almonds tang of cyanide. Uneasy tales of the sea blew through my mind, like a sudden cold draught in an old house. It occurred to me that the *Lotus*, like the *Marie Celeste*, had been freshly abandoned by her terrified crew, or was manned with lost souls from the *Flying Dutchman*. I shivered.

A light, an oil lantern, sprung into mid-air in front of me. A voice behind it snapped: ' 'Op it!'

I jumped back, hitting the door with my head.

'Get the 'ell out of it, Charlie,' the voice continued, coming nearer.

'I—I'm a member of the crew,' I managed to say.

The light advanced on me. Behind it two eyes stared with concentrated suspicion.

'The new Doctor,' I explained humbly.

The voice at once took on a friendly inflection.

'Sorry, Doc! I thought you was trying to pinch something.'

'No . . . I just came aboard. There didn't seem to be anyone about. I hope it was all right?'

'Sure, it's all right. Liberty Hall, this hooker. Make yourself at home. Spit on the deck and call the cat a bastard.'

'Thank you.'

'Glad you've come, Doc,' he continued affably. 'I've got a bit of a cold, like.' He sneezed to add point to the remark. 'Could you give us something for it?'

'Yes, certainly . . . But wouldn't a bit later do? I'm extremely wet. I'd like to find my cabin and so forth.'

'Sure, Doc. Follow me. I'll take you to see the Mate.'

He walked off, the lamp swinging high in his hand. I stepped timidly behind him, along narrow alleyways, round sharp corners, up unidentifiable ladders.

'Sorry there ain't many lights,' he apologized over his shoulder. 'But the engineers has got the jennies stripped to-night.'

'Oh, really?'

That sounded more alarming than ever.

He came to a cabin door and opened it.

'The new Doctor,' he announced, as if he had just materialized me out of a hat.

There were three men in the cabin—the Mate, Archer the Second, and Trail the Third. Hornbeam was sitting in the only chair with his reefer unbuttoned and his stockinged feet on the washbasin. It was a small cabin, designed like a crossword puzzle, and the visitors had to adapt themselves to the interlocking pieces. Archer, who was a tall, pale man with an expression like a curate just beginning to have doubts, had wedged himself between the bunk and the bookcase above it with his legs dangling on to the deck, like a human question mark. Trail, squatting between the locker and the desk, was a fat youth going through a florid attack of *acne vulgaris*.

'Talk of the devil!' Hornbeam said immediately.

'We wondered when you were going to turn up,' Archer said. 'Have a bottle of beer.'

'Move over, Second, and let the Doctor park his fanny,' Hornbeam said. He introduced himself and the others. 'Give us another bottle, Third. Do you mind drinking out of a tooth-glass?'

'No, not at all.'

The welcome was cordial enough, but it disturbed me. It is a habit among seafarers to accept every newcomer on terms of intimacy, but I was a fairly new doctor and stood on my professional dignity like a girl with her first pair of high heels.

'I hope I'm not butting in,' I said stiffly.

'Not a bit of it! Throw your coat on the hook there. We were only having a quick peg.'

I climbed up on the bunk next to Archer without enthusiasm. It seemed as comfortable as trying to drink on a bus in the rush hour.

'You just passed out of medical school?' Archer asked.

'Certainly not! I've been in practice for . . . some years.'

'Oh, sorry. Been to sea before?'

'I'm afraid not.'

'You'll soon pick up the routine. I hope you're hot stuff on the diseases sailors get.'

This brought a roar of laughter from the other two.

'We doctors have to be "hot stuff" on very many things,' I said.

I gave a superior smile. Since I qualified I had fed on professional respect and I found the conversation irritating.

'By George, we find some queer doctors at sea,' Trail said, handing me a glass of beer. 'Don't we, Mr. Hornbeam? Usually they're getting away from their wives or the police, or both sometimes. Or else it's drink. That's the commonest. Sometimes it's drugs, though.'

'I drink very little.'

Trail took no notice. 'I remember old Doc Parsons I sailed with when I was doing my time,' he went on cheerfully. 'He was a real scream. As tight as a tick from morning to night. We reckoned he got through a couple of bottles of gin a day, easy. Started before breakfast, every morning. Said the world was so bloody awful he couldn't face it at the best of times, but especially with his last night's hangover. Then one day in the Red Sea the Mate ripped his arm open, and old Parsons said he'd operate. Laugh! The lot of us went down to the hospital to watch. I was doubled up. He'd been at the bottle extra strong and he was as blind as a bat. Kept dropping the knife on the deck and falling over the table. In the end the Mate clocked him one and got the Chief Steward to do it.'

Archer leant forward.

'Do you remember old Doc Hamilton in the *Mariesta*?' he asked.

The other two began to laugh again.

'He was a real queer 'un,' he explained to me. 'Started on the grog before we sailed—had to be carried up the gangway. By the time we reached Gib. the Old Man stopped his tap—no more booze, you understand. So he went down to the dispensary and drank all the surgical spirit. When he finished that he scrounged meths from the engineers. They tumbled to it, of course, and wouldn't let him have any more. In the end he drank the acid from the wireless batteries.'

'The police came for him when we got home,' Hornbeam added. 'I don't know what it was for. Something about abortions, I think.'

'I remember we buried an old doctor off Teneriffe,' Archer said thoughtfully. 'He hanged himself. He did it with his belt,' he continued in my direction.

I began to understand that the medical profession was not held in the highest esteem at sea.

'I assure you I shall not commit any of those things,' I said.

'The voyage hasn't started yet,' Archer observed. 'Why, look what happened to old Doc Flowerday.'

'Yes, that was a shame,' Trail said, nodding his head sadly. 'He was as mad as you make 'em. But I was sorry about it, for one.'

Hornbeam agreed.

'He was a nice old boy. You heard all about it, I suppose, Doc?'

'No, I haven't. Why? Should I?'

He suddenly looked uncomfortable.

'I thought they might have told you something about it in the office,' he said vaguely. 'He was the last doctor before you.'

He sighed gently into his beer.

'It was a pity,' he continued. 'In a way.'

I shifted myself nervously on the bunk.

'What was a pity?'

Hornbeam drained his glass.

'His . . . well, his end, as you might say.'

They sat in silence for a while. The reference to Dr. Flowerday had saddened them, and no one seemed to wish to reopen the conversation. I sat and anxiously speculated on his possible fate, for which I had now a good number of workable theories.

CHAPTER II

I WENT to bed that night feeling like my first day at school when someone pinched my tuck-box. But in the morning the rain had stopped and the sun threw a bloodshot early glance on Merseyside. The ship had come to life overnight. She rattled with the noise of steam winches loading cargo, and the ghosts of the evening were replaced by persons who shouted, coughed, and used bad language on each other with comforting humanity.

I had breakfast in the saloon with Hornbeam and the Mates. Their conversation was as mysterious to me as the chat at the hospital lunch-table would have been to them: it was about 'tween decks and stowage, dunnage and ullage, tank tops and cofferdams. The only fact I could grasp was that the *Lotus's* sailing date was as unpredictable as Judgment Day.

After breakfast I went to my cabin, sat on the narrow strip of settee, and opened the first page of *War and Peace*. This I had bought in three volumes from a bookseller's near Euston Station before catching the train for Liverpool. I thought the voyage would allow me to achieve a ten-years' ambition of finishing the thing; besides, I was determined to make use of the time I was obliged to spend inactively at sea improving my mind. And its long, restful paragraphs might begin to soothe my headaches.

A fortnight ago I had been an assistant in general practice—the medical equivalent of the poor curate, the unbriefed barrister, the new subaltern—living in an atmosphere of Dettol and damp overcoats and dispensing the loot of the National Health Service like a maniacal Lady Bountiful. My principal had a bedside manner and two stock remedies with which he had built up a local reputation of infallibility, and we divided the work between us. He saw the private patients, who diminished in number each Budget day, and took the morning surgery; I had the night calls and the evening clinic. As my clinic came conveniently after work, school, and high tea, it was popular with everyone who wanted a certificate, new teeth, hair, or spectacles, or simply to pass the time.

The patients brought their troubles and left them on my doorstep like unwanted babies. They wedged themselves into the uncomfortable and unhygienic-looking sofas in our waiting-room, mirthlessly turning the pages of *Punch*, and glancing shiftily at their neighbours wondering what they had got and if it was catching. There were so many of them they could idle the drab hours of their evening away contentedly. It was cheaper than the pub, and more interesting.

For this I was paid the same wages as an engine-driver; in ten or fifteen years, however, if I behaved myself, I would become a partner and take a share in the spoils. But my life at the time was illuminated with a more pressing excitement: I was going to get married.

Marriage is as much of an obligation for a young doctor as celibacy for a Roman Catholic priest. A medical bachelor is unpopular with the patients, except for visits to eligible daughters, and as even these are now obtainable on the National Health he is a frank financial liability to the practice. My principal had no intention of losing his patients through marital hesitation on the part of his young assistant, and after he had made this as plain as possible he asked his wife to apply a woman's practical mind to the problem and set about finding me a bride.

She procured the daughter of a town councillor. She was a girl called Wendy, a blonde, but of the arid sort, like the stubble in a wheatfield after a hot harvest. Her position in local society made it impossible for me to escape: once the town saw what my principal's wife was up to, Wendy and I were mated as firmly as two rats put in the same cage in the biological laboratory.

We became engaged. The wedding approached with the speed of an early winter.

I suppose, looking back on it, there was good reason for my subconscious to slip into disorder, like a wrecked gear-box in an overdriven car. Wendy was a nice girl. She was well educated, and could talk about things like trigonometry and economics. But she had her defects. Her voice was as dull and authoritative as a Salvation Army drum, she walked like an overloaded wheelbarrow, and she had a figure like a stook of corn. I began to suffer an attack of *terror celibans*, or bachelor's panic.

More robust personalities than mine would have stood up to it: it is a common premarital complaint. But I did not. I developed headaches. I immediately diagnosed a cerebral tumour and hurried to London to see a brain specialist, savouring everything on the way with exquisite farewell tenderness, even the fish served for lunch by British Railways.

The brain specialist listened to me for five minutes and packed me off to a psychiatrist. The psychiatrist was an important and busy man and I arrived at the end of the day, but he let me talk for a quarter of an hour while he signed a few letters and looked for his car key.

'A long holiday,' he said sternly, putting on his overcoat. 'Why don't you take a ship? You won't have any work to do. I did it when I was your age. Signed on a cattle boat going to Murmansk. Half the deckhands were washed overboard one night and I had to turn-to with the rest of them to work the ship. Great fun.'

'I don't think I'd be much good as a deckhand.'

'Anyway, you've got to have a holiday. Put on your best suit and walk down Leadenhall Street. You never know your luck.'

'All right, sir,' I said doubtfully. 'If you advise.'

Thus my honour was saved by modern psychiatry.

The next afternoon I tramped Leadenhall Street, trying to get a berth out of every big shipping office and, by mistake, a branch of Barclays Bank. It was one of those unfriendly November days when dawn and dusk meet each other in a dim conspiracy over the lunch-table. The rain drizzled on to the grimy pavements, soaking through my mackintosh and the seams of my shoes, and my depression deepened with the twilight. It looked as if the sea had rejected me.

When the offices began to close and the important shipping men were already hurrying westwards I walked up the creaking stairs of the Fathom Line building, prepared to sail with Captain Bligh if necessary. There I was introduced to a Mr. Cozens, a little bald man crouched in a high leather chair. He was suspiciously pleased to see me.

'Our *Lotus*, Doctor,' he said, 'is in need of a surgeon. We should be delighted to have you. Forty pounds a month, no need for uniform, just the Company's regulation cap. Can you leave for Santos on Monday?'

But a seafaring friend had once warned me to treat a new ship like a prospective bride and discover her exact age and precise tonnage before committing myself. And I was touchy on such points.

Cozens rapidly sketched for me a description of the *Lotus*. 'She isn't a *big* ship,' he concluded. 'Nor a *fast* ship, exactly.' He smiled like a house agent. 'But she's a very *nice* ship.'

I wondered what to do. I was being asked to sail in a ship I had never seen, to a place I had never heard of, in the employ of a business I knew nothing about. I looked anxiously through the dark window running with comforting English rain. The wisest course was obviously to go back to Wendy and settle for a fortnight in Sidmouth instead.

'Very well,' I said. 'I accept.'

'Excellent!' said Mr. Cozens, with relief. 'I'm sure you'll find yourself well suited, Doctor. She's a very nice ship indeed. Quite a lady.'

I nodded. 'Where do I go now?'

'There are a few formalities to be gone through, I'm afraid, Doctor. Regulations and such things, you understand. First of all, I must supply you with a letter of appointment. If you'll just wait one minute I'll get one of the girls to type it.'

Running away to sea has become more elaborate since the un-hedged days when the errant son slipped down to the docks at nightfall, mated up with a bos'n at a wharfside tavern, and sailed with an Indiaman on the dawn tide. Now there are forms to be filled in, documents to be issued, permits to be warily exchanged for a string of personal data. The next day I was sent down to the Merchant Navy Office, an establishment which was a cross between a railway booking-hall and the charge-room of a police station on a Saturday night. There I poked my letter of appointment nervously through a small window at a clerk, who glanced through it with the unconcealed disgust of a post office employee reading one's private thoughts in a telegram.

'Got your lifeboat ticket?' he asked gloomily, his steel nib arrested in mid-air.

'My what?' I saw for a second the picture of myself shivering on a sinking deck, refused permission to enter the lifeboat because I had not purchased my ticket at the proper counter. 'Where do I buy it?' I asked wildly.

The man looked at me with pity. 'They send us some mugs these days,' he observed wearily. 'Lifeboat ticket,' he repeated, mouthing the words as if addressing a deaf idiot. 'Ministry certificate. Savvy?'

'No,' I admitted. 'I haven't.'

'Got any distinguishing marks?' he asked, giving me a chance to redeem myself. 'Or blemishes? Tattoos?'

'No. None at all. As far as I know.'

He nodded and gave me a chit entitling me to a free photograph at a shop across the street. I queued between a tall negro in a jacket that half covered his thighs and a man in a strong-smelling roll-necked sweater who picked his teeth with a safety-pin. When my turn came I had to face the camera holding my number in a wooden frame under my chin, and I felt the next step would be in handcuffs.

Now, sitting in my cabin with *War and Peace*, my Company's regulation cap hanging from a hook above me, I saw that Mr. Cozens was wrong. The *Lotus* wasn't a nice ship at all. She was a floating warehouse, with some accommodation for humans stuck on top like a watchman's attic. All the cabins were small, and mine was like a railway compartment quarter-filled with large pipes. I wondered where they went to, and later discovered I was situated immediately below the Captain's lavatory.

My appraisal of the *Lotus* was interrupted by a knock on the jalousie door. It was Easter, the Doctor's steward. He was a little globular man, who felt his position was not that of a mere servant but of a slightly professional gentleman. As an indication of his superiority to his mess-mates a throat torch and a thermometer poked out of the top pocket of his jacket, and he frequently talked to me about 'We of the medical fraternity.' He was always ready to give advice to his companions on problems of a medical or social nature that they felt disinclined to pour into the ears of the Doctor, and had an annoying habit of counselling them, for the

168

good of their health, to hurl into the sea the bottles of physic just handed to them by their medical attendant.

'Good morning, Doctor,' he said. 'I have a message from Father.'

'Father?'

'The Captain.'

'Oh.'

'He said he wants a bottle of his usual stomach mixture, pronto.'

'His usual stomach mixture?' I took off my spectacles and frowned. 'How do I know what that is? Has he got a prescription, or anything?'

'Dr. Flowerday used to make him up a bottle special.'

'I see.'

The problem grew in importance the more I thought of it.

'The Captain suffers from his stomach quite frequently, does he?'

'Ho, yes, sir. Something chronic.'

'H'm.'

'When he has one of his spasms he gets a cob on, worse than usual. Life ain't worth living for all hands. The only stuff what squares up his innards is the special mixture he got from Dr. Flowerday. Makes him bring up the wind, Doctor. Or belch, as we say in the medical profession.'

'Quite. You don't know what's in this medicine, I suppose?'

'Not the foggiest, Doctor.'

'Well, can't you remember? You were with Dr. Flowerday some time, weren't you?'

'Several voyages, Doctor. And he was very satisfied, if I may make so bold.'

It occurred to me that this might be the point to clear up the Flowerday mystery for good.

'Tell me, Easter,' I said sharply, 'what exactly happened to Dr. Flowerday?'

He scratched his nose with a sad gesture.

'If you wouldn't mind, sir,' he replied with dignity, 'I'd rather not talk about it.'

I got up. It was useless sounding Easter on the fate of my

169

predecessor or on his balm for the Captain's gastric disorders.

Down aft there was a cabin with a notice stencilled above the door saying CERTIFIED HOSPITAL. It was a fairly large apartment which smelt like an underground cell that hadn't been used for some time. There were four cots in it, in a couple of tiers. One bulkhead was taken up with a large locker labelled in red POISONS, one door of which was lying adrift of its hinges on the deck.

Inside the locker were half a dozen rows of square, squat bottles containing the supply of medicines for the ship. These— like the Doctor—were prescribed by the Ministry of Transport. Unfortunately the Ministry, in the manner of the elderly, elegant physicians who come monthly out of retirement to grace the meetings of the Royal Society of Medicine, holds trustingly to the old-established remedies and the comely prescriptions of earlier decades. There were drugs in the cupboard that I had seen only in out-of-date books on pharmacology. I picked up a bottle: *Amylum*. What on earth did one do with amylum? There was a pound of Dover's powder and a drum of castor-oil big enough to move the bowels of the earth. At the back I found an empty gin bottle, some Worcester sauce, a tennis racket with broken strings, a dirty pair of black uniform socks, two eggs, a copy of the *Brisbane Telegraph*, and a notice saying NO FUMARE.

I dropped these through the porthole, taking care with the eggs. Below the shelves of bottles was another compartment. I looked into it. It held a heavy mahogany case labelled INSTRUMENT CHEST, which contained the left component of a pair of obstetrical forceps, a saw, a bottle-opener, and a bunch of tooth-picks; but there were five gross of grey cardboard eyeshades, over seven apiece for all hands.

I saw that prescribing was going to be more difficult than in general practice, where I scribbled a prescription on my pad, and the patient took it to the chemist, who deciphered my writing and slickly made up the medicine. We had been obliged to attend a course of lectures on pharmacy and dispensing in medical school, but these were always held on a Saturday morning, when most of the students were already on their way to the rugger field. For this reason there was an informal roster among the class to forge the signatures of their companions on the attendance sheet, before slipping softly away themselves when the lecturer turned to clarify some obscure pharmacological point on the blackboard. As I had attended the greater number of my pharmacy lectures by proxy in this way, I now felt like a new wife in her first kitchen.

I picked up one or two bottles hopefully, and I was delighted to find that my predecessor, Dr. Flowerday, had his pharmacy lectures on Saturday mornings also. On the back of each bottle was a small label bearing in shaky handwriting guidance such as 'Good for diarrhœa,' or 'This mixed with Tinct. Ipecac. seems all right for colds,' or 'Apparently inert.' There was also a sheet of cardboard on which Dr. Flowerday had written in Portuguese, Spanish, French, and Hindustani translations of three questions which he seemed to find adequate for investigating his patients: 'Have you a cough?' 'Where is the pain?' and 'Have you been with any dirty women recently?'

I found an old pair of pharmacist's scales and a glass graduated in drachms, and started to make up the Captain's medicine. The first one turned into a pink putty, and was abandoned (it later came in useful for minor infections of the crew's feet). The second tasted strongly of peppermint but seemed adequate. I corked it and carried it up to the Captain's cabin.

I had not met Captain Hogg before. He had been ashore the previous night and he never came down for breakfast. When I had asked Hornbeam about him he replied unconvincingly, 'He has his good points.'

'What are they?' Trail asked gloomily.

I enquired what form Captain Hogg's malignity took.

'Oh, he thinks the sun shines out of his bottom,' Trail said. 'They all get like that. It's living alone too much that does it. They ought to be made to carry their wives with them to keep them under control.'

'The Old Man isn't married,' Hornbeam told him.

'Neither was his father,' Trail said.

I knocked on the cabin door.

'Enter!'

I went in.

Captain Hogg was of a curious shape. He was like a huge pear.

From the sharp top of his bald head he came out gradually until the region of the umbilicus, from which point he spread abruptly in all directions. He was sitting in an arm-chair in his shirt-sleeves, his face obscured by the book he was reading. It was a periodical called *True Horrors*, on the front of which a vivid blonde with an alarming bosom was struggling unsuccessfully with a gorilla, a man in a black mask, and her underclothes.

The book didn't move. I stood just inside the door, holding the medicine bottle in front of me like a talisman. He spoke:

'Well?'

I rubbed my right shoe slowly up my left calf.

'Doctor, sir,' I said.

The magazine came down. For a moment we stared at each other with interest. I thought he looked as friendly as a firing-squad.

'Ah!' he said.

I proffered the bottle.

'Your stomach mixture, sir.'

Either my prescribing or Dr. Flowerday's directions were at fault; perhaps the ship's drugs had degenerated with time. Some unplanned reaction occurred within the bottle. With a sharp pop the cork flew into the air.

'You may find this a little strong,' I said, picking up the cork quickly. 'I recommend taking it well diluted.'

He took the bottle silently and stood it on the desk beside him.

'Your cap,' he said. 'You have a cap?'

'Yes, sir. Company's regulation pattern.'

'Why aren't you wearing it?'

'I'm sorry, sir, I——'

'The cap is worn on all official visits to the Captain. If I were asking you up here for a peg, that would be different. But I'm not. It's a matter of etiquette. There's no tramp ship stuff about this vessel. This is my ship, you understand, Doctor? *My* ship. If we get that straight we shall rub along splendidly together.'

'Yes, sir.'

I was a medical student again, before the Dean for filling the senior surgeon's rubber operating boots with iced water.

'Good. You haven't been to sea before?'

'No, sir.'

'You'll find the routine fairly simple, as far as you're concerned. You take your surgery at nine every morning, and at ten you bring me up a list of the sick on board and what's wrong with 'em. There's none of this damn medical secrecy nonsense at sea. I want to know all about them. I have to carry the can in the end. Understand?'

'Yes, sir.'

'Good. Then at eleven o'clock we inspect the ship—you wear your cap again. Dinner is at twelve-thirty and supper at six. Do you play cribbage?'

'No, sir.'

He looked disappointed.

'Pity. The last doctor played a good hand. Passes the tedium of the evenings at sea.' He indicated the magazine. 'I'm a great reading man myself, but I like a game of crib now and then.'

On a sudden thought he leant over and rummaged in the desk.

'I've got a book on it here. Read that through, then we might be able to have a few games.'

'Thank you, sir.'

He hesitated a moment, staring at the square toes of his shoes.

'Did you know Dr. Flowerday?' he asked.

'No, sir.'

'He was the last doctor. Very good man. We all liked him very much. Unfortunately, he didn't know when to stop. I shouldn't like to see you go the same way. The Company might think there was something wrong with my ship.'

My mouth went dry.

'What—er, what happened to him, sir?'

Captain Hogg glanced at me, then returned to inspecting his toes.

'Of course, a man's entitled to think what he likes,' he said forcefully. 'I'm a respecter of anyone's opinions. But there are limits, Doctor. Limits.'

'Yes, sir.'

'You've never thought you were somebody else, for instance? Have you, Doctor?'

'No, sir. I—I can't recall doing so.'

173

'Well, there you are. It happens sometimes at sea. I've seen some of the best of fellows get taken that way. I remember when I first went Mate, the Third thought he was Cleopatra. Very awkward it was for all hands.'

'I can see it would be, sir.'

'But Dr. Flowerday had a weakness. I tell you in strict confidence, Doctor.'

'Of course, sir.'

It appeared that my predecessor, after having drunk two bottles of gin a day for several years in the service of the *Lotus*, got religion shortly after leaving Singapore, and extinguished himself one night in the Indian Ocean through the mistaken impression that he had the rightful ability to walk upon the water.

CHAPTER III

THE *Lotus* sailed, to the surprise of her crew, three days later. We spent the time tethered to the quay, loading heavy packing-cases from railway trucks. It was an interesting performance. The cases were raised to the level of the ship's deck, drawn horizontally inwards, and lowered into the holds. This was done with the derricks and steam winches, each set manned by a gang of Liverpool dockers, who went about their work with the leisurely decorum of the House of Lords considering an unimportant Bill on a hot afternoon.

There was a docker at each winch, and the rest of them worked either down the hold or on the quay. Each gang was controlled by a man in a long overcoat and a bowler hat, who directed their activities with the economy of gesture of an experienced bidder at an auction. The twitch of a little finger, an inclination of the head, the drop of an eyelid, and four tons of crated machinery went spinning through the air and down the hatch as cleanly as a holed-out golf ball.

The stowage of the cargo was supervised by the mates, under the directions of Archer. He had his bunk covered with cargo manifests, bills of lading, and plans of the ship with the different merchandise coloured in with crayon.

'The Second gets the thin end of it,' he said. 'He's always cargo officer. Too much work in it for me.'

'But it looks fairly simple. Don't you just go on putting the stuff in until the ship's full?'

'Haven't you ever packed a case for a holiday? The things you want first always seem to be at the bottom. If that happened in the ship there'd be trouble. You can't tip everything out.'

'I see what you mean.'

'Besides, there's the trim of the ship to think about. There's more in cargo than meets the eye.'

He looked at his plan. 'Numbers one and four are full, but

175

there's plenty of room in two and three. We'll be here a week yet, you can bet on that.'

But orders, based on some deep calculation in the Fathom Line offices, came for us to sail. Twenty-four hours later, in the morning, the *Lotus* left.

An air of excitement spread through the ship before sailing, as everyone began to go about their jobs more briskly. I was greatly stimulated by the promising departure, for I had become thoroughly used to living alongside the wharf in the past few days and occasionally doubted that we would ever sail at all. The dockers who had made free with our decks were turned down the gangway, leaving behind them a litter of newspapers, cigarette packets, and matches trampled into the rusty steel. The wide hatches were covered with heavy slabs of wood, and square tarpaulins lashed over them. At the head of the gangway the quartermaster fixed a blackboard announcing confidently THE S.S. *LOTUS* WILL SAIL AT TEN O'CLOCK FOR SANTOS NO SHORE LEAVE, and a thin black stream of smoke shot powerfully upwards from the funnel. Our bleak masts were enlivened with flags: the red ensign trailed over our stern, the Company's house-flag—a red F topped by an anchor on a white square—was hoisted at the mainmast, and from the foremast the blue-and-white P announced our intentions to the waterside.

'That at least is a flag I recognize,' I said to Trail. 'The Blue Peter.'

'Yes, we'll soon be on our way, Doc. It's a bloody nuisance. I was just getting a nice little piece lined up last night. It's always the same.'

'I shall be glad to get to sea, I must say. I've seen enough of Liverpool.'

'You'll get your bellyful of sea all right, don't you worry. Shouldn't get too excited, though. They may change their minds and send us into Cardiff when we get out in the Irish Sea. Not a bad place, Cardiff, though I prefer Middlesbrough myself. The pubs are better.'

Shortly afterwards Trail reappeared on deck with his cap on, looking very determined and ten years older.

176

'Got to do the testing,' he explained brusquely. 'Tugs'll be here any minute now.'

I heard him ring the bridge telegraphs and sound the whistle, which blew a long silent plume of steam into the air for some seconds before it struck its note. The Customs officers gave us a final suspicious look and made for the shore, their threatening bags of rummage tools over their shoulders. Men in yellow rain-coats and misshapen trilbys hurried aboard with desperate last letters addressed to Captain Hogg, and rushed away again anxiously looking at their watches. A Mr. Swithinbank, a pale youth with steel spectacles from the Liverpool office, came breathlessly down the deck after me, with a paper in his hand.

'Here's the Bill of Health, Doctor,' he said. 'Cripes! For a moment I thought I'd lost you! You can't sail without it.'

'Thank you very much,' I said, taking the document reverently.

'Are you all right?' he asked quickly, making for the gangway. 'Medical stores O.K.? Too late now, anyway. Have a good voyage. Cheery-bye!'

'Good-bye,' I shouted after him helplessly. 'We seem a bit short of sulphonamides.'

'Bring us a ham from Brazil if you remember it,' he called over his shoulder. 'Don't forget the poor starving English.'

He hurried away between the railway wagons and lorries on the quay. It was almost ten. Two sailors, who had somehow managed to drink themselves to a standstill at that hour, staggered up the gangway and collapsed on the deck.

'Take 'em below,' Hornbeam shouted to the Bos'n, with the air of a man handling a familiar situation. 'They'll be logged to-morrow morning. Has Smiley turned up yet?'

'No sign, Mr. Hornbeam.'

'I dunno,' Hornbeam said resignedly. 'If you docked a ship in Hell you'd still get deserters. Get my watch turned-to, Bos'n. I'm going to stations.'

'Aye aye, sir.'

Two tugs nuzzled under our bow and stern, their skippers standing impassively at the wheel in their oilskins like waiting taxi-drivers. The pilot came aboard—an alarmingly unnautical figure in a tweed overcoat and bowler hat, carrying an umbrella and a black Gladstone bag. I watched Trail knock on the Captain's door, salute, and announce 'Tugs alongside and pilot aboard, sir.' He stepped aside as Captain Hogg appeared, resplendent in gold braid, and mounted solemnly to the bridge. The gangway came up, the two tugs plucked the ship away from the quay, and the ropes fell into the water with long splashes. The *Lotus* became suddenly changed into an entity, a being in her own right, instead of a rusty appendage of a dirty Liverpool wharf.

I leant over the rail with Easter, watching the steadily widening gap of water between us and the shore. I had never been on a moving ship before, apart from a brief passage from Margate to Southend in a paddle steamer, and I felt excited and apprehensive. I found the belief that we should now all be transported by the *Lotus* from Liverpool to the Tropics too outlandish to take seriously.

'Well, we're off,' was all I could think to say.

'Yes, sir. In an hour or so we'll be well out in the River.'

'You know, Easter, to me it seems almost impossible for this little ship to take us all the way to South America.'

'Sometimes, sir,' he answered gloomily, 'I think it's a bloody miracle she moves at all.'

We shook with a gentle ague as the engines picked up speed, slipped down the channel of thick Mersey water, passed the tolling buoys and the Bar Light, out into the Irish Sea; in the afternoon a sharp sea-wind blew down the deck and the Welsh mountains were huddling on the horizon. I pranced delightedly round the ship, which was now musical with the wind, looking at everything like a schoolboy in the Science Museum.

I had a letter in my pocket from Wendy, which I purposely kept unopened until we were under way. It was a short prim note, wishing me a good voyage, hoping my headaches were better, and mentioning that I was not to think of ourselves as betrothed any longer. It appeared she had become enamoured of the son of the local draper. I tore the letter up and scattered it over the side: the pieces spread on the sea and were left behind. I laughed. I felt a cad, a devilish cad. But now, surely, I was allowed to be: I was a sailor. A wife in every port for me! I thought. Watch out, my girls, watch out! A rollicking sailor lad, indeed! With a snatch of sea-shanty on my lips I went below for a cup of tea, aware that I was perhaps not quite myself.

* * * * *

My elation lasted less than a day. The next morning I was sick.

The *Lotus* creaked and groaned her way through the water like an old lady in a bargain sale. She climbed to the top of a wave, paused for breath, shook herself, and slid helplessly into the trough of the next. I lay on my bunk and watched the sprightly horizon jumping round the porthole, trying to think about eminently terrestrial objects, such as the Albert Hall.

Easter put his head round the door. In his hands he had a cup of tea and a small roseless watering-can, of the type reserved for the conveyance of tepid water in English country hotels.

'Good morning, Doctor,' he said briefly. 'Will you be in for breakfast?'

I rolled my head on the pillow.

'Not feeling too good, Doctor?'

'I think I am going to die.'

He nodded, gravely assessing the clinical findings.

'Throwing up much?' he asked pleasantly.

'Everything.'

'If I may take the liberty, a good meal is what you want. Plate of fried eggs and bacon and you'll be right as rain. Works like a charm. Hold it a moment, Doctor, I'll fetch a bowl."

I held the bowl like a mother with a newborn infant.

'Feeling better now you've got all that up?' he asked solicitously.

'A bit.'

A thought struck him.

'Wouldn't like a bit of cold beef and a few pickles, would you? They'd do just as well.'

'No, no, no! I don't want anything. Nothing at all. I just want to be left alone.'

'Very good, Doctor. Just as you say. Perhaps you might feel like a bit of lunch?'

'I doubt it very much.'

He left me in ecstatic solitude. I lay rigidly on the bunk, concentrating on the words stencilled, by order of the Ministry of Transport, immediately above me: CERTIFIED TO ACCOMMODATE 1 SEAMAN. Seaman, indeed! All I wanted to see was a tree.

It was essential to keep my mind fixed on something beyond the clouds of nausea spiralling round me, so I started to count the rivets in the deckhead. I had reached ninety-eight when Hornbeam came in. He was smoking a pipe.

'Hello, Doc! I hear you're off colour. What's the trouble?'

'I'm seasick.'

He looked surprised.

'Yes, I suppose she is pitching a bit,' he admitted, glancing through the porthole. 'Do you mind if I use one of your matches?'

He blew mouthfuls of smoke into the cabin.

'Better out than in,' he said, as I put the bowl down again.

'I suppose so.'

'You know what, Doc? I'm going to give you a genuine cure for seasickness. I can't often treat a doctor, but this is just the thing. Do you want to try it?'

'What is it?'

'A pint of sea-water. It's an old sailors' cure. When I was an apprentice it was the only thing that stopped me on my first voyage. If we were sick we got kicked down the bridge ladder and given a pint glass just out of the sea-bucket by the Mate. Shall I get you some?'

I raised my hand.

'I think I'd rather not have anything at all at the moment, thank you.'

'As you like, Doc. I'm only making a suggestion. Have you tried covering one eye?'

'It wasn't much good.'

'No, I don't believe it is. Damn! Can I have another match? My pipe's gone out again.'

'Would you mind lighting it outside? It's a bit—a bit strong at the moment.'

'Oh, sorry! I didn't think of that.'

I called weakly after him at the door.

'How long is this likely to go on for?'

He calculated for a few seconds.

'Not very long. I should say we'd be in pretty calm water in five or six days.'

'Five or six days!'

I groaned.

I lay and tried to analyse my condition, like the dying surgeon, John Hunter. It was, of course, a ridiculously simple malady when one looked at it with scientific detachment. The endolymph in my semi-circular canals was stimulating the endings of my cochlear nerve, which transmitted influences to the brain and initiated the reflex arc of vomiting. It should be easy for a little will-power to inhibit the reflex. After all, the brain was the master. . . . I exercised the will-power.

'Morning!' Trail said from the doorway. 'When you've got your head out of that bowl I'll tell you a sure-fire cure for sea-sickness.'

I fell back on the pillow. I had given up. When the angel of death arrived I would shake him cordially by the hand.

Trail came over to the bunk. He put his hands in his trouser pockets and pulled out two bottles of stout.

'Guinness,' he said proudly. 'Drink these and you'll be fine by lunch-time. Works like magic.'

'Oh God!' I said. 'Oh God, oh God!'

Trail looked puzzled.

'What's the matter? Don't you like stout? Here, take it easy! That one nearly went over my uniform.'

He left me wondering submissively how long it would be before Easter came back and started talking about lunch. And it was bound to be Irish stew.

*   *   *   *   *

After three days the sea and I achieved a compromise. The sun came out, the wind dropped and lost its malice, the water was tidied up like a room after a wild party. For myself I learned to lean against the sway of the ship, and I felt well enough to risk lunch in the saloon.

It was my first meal at sea. I sat with the Captain, the Chief Engineer, Hornbeam and Archer, and the Chief Steward, a thin little mouse-faced man called Whimble. As soon as the bell rang we converged on the dining saloon with the briskness of seaside boarders: Captain Hogg disliked anyone to be late.

I was on the Captain's right hand, the Mate on his left. The Chief Engineer faced the Captain, and the other two sat themselves between.

'Ah, Doctor!' Captain Hogg said, jovially enough. 'Decided to join us at last, have you?'

'Yes, sir.'

He unfolded his napkin and tucked it under his chin with deliberation.

'Seasickness,' he said slowly, 'is entirely mental. You imagine it.'

I shrugged my shoulders.

'Well,' I said, in my professional tone, 'there are more complicated reasons than that. I admit there may be a psychological element. But there is obviously some fault with the balancing apparatus in the ears, and probably with the gastric nerves.'

The Captain broke a roll.

'No.' He said it decisively. 'It is entirely mental.'

He started drinking soup loudly.

No one spoke until he had finished.

'Mr. McDougall,' he said, slipping half a roll into his mouth, 'have you got that book you were going to lend me at supper last night?'

The Chief looked up. He was a thin, wrinkled Scot with a face dominated by a thick strip of sandy eyebrow, from which his eyes looked out like a couple of Highland gamekeepers inspecting poachers through the undergrowth.

'Aye,' he said. 'You mean *The Squeaker*?'

The Captain nodded.

'That's it. I like a bit of Peter Cheyney.'

'But surely,' I said immediately, '*The Squeaker* was by Edgar Wallace? It was written over twenty years ago.'

'No,' the Captain said. 'It was Peter Cheyney.'

'You know, sir, I'm perfectly . . .'

'Peter Cheyney,' he said, with the emphasis of a full stop. He then fell upon a plate of mutton chops, which disappeared into his mouth like a rush-hour crowd going down an escalator.

We continued eating in silence.

Captain Hogg finished his chops and brought his knife and fork together with a flourish.

'Mr. Whimble,' he said.

'Sir!'

The Chief Steward jumped, and choked over a chop bone.

'I have, I suppose, tasted worse chops than these. In a fifth-rate café on the Mexican coast possibly. Why don't you throw the cook over the side? If he'd served filth like this to the Captain when I was an apprentice the fellow would have had his bottom kicked round the deck.'

'I'm sorry, Captain,' Whimble mumbled. 'I'll see to it.'

'I should think so. You never get cooking like you used to. All they think about these days are vitamins and calories, and such stuff. What good's that to a man? Fad, that's all it is. You don't need vitamins or calories,' he said with disgust. 'Eh, Doctor?'

'Well, they are really two quite different factors. And vitamins are terribly important.'

'Bosh! I'm not a doctor—I don't pretend to be. But if you get a good bellyful of meat and spuds every day you'll be all right.'

'You must have vitamins,' I insisted, but feebly.

'Vitamins are bosh, Doctor. Bosh!'

I began to see that opinions were forbidden, even professional ones. Our mealtimes were going to be rollicking.

CHAPTER IV

THE next morning after breakfast I went to my cabin, wedged myself on the settee, and again opened *War and Peace* at page one. I had not felt well enough to start the book since we sailed, but now I looked forward to a leisurely stroll through its pages during the rest of the voyage. I had almost reached the end of the first paragraph when a conversation started in the alleyway outside my cabin door.

The door was on a hook for ventilation, so I was able to overhear it clearly. There were two speakers, who used the adenoidal grunts with which the citizens of Liverpool communicate with each other.

'Ullo,' said one. 'Whatcher doin', la'?'

'Come to see ——ing quack.'

'Ar. What's ——ing trouble, la'?'

'Dunno. Reckon I must've picked up a ——ing dose, or something.'

'Where, in Liverpeule?'

' 'Sright. Nice bit of skirt she was too.'

'You can never tell, la'.'

'——ing right there.'

A short silence.

'What's quack like?'

'Oh, he's a young ——er.'

'Reckon he's much good?'

'——ing medical student, most likely.'

'If we was homeward bound reckon I'd wait and see a proper doctor,' the sufferer said. I opened the door. 'Good morning, Doc,' he added brightly. 'Can you see us a second, in private like?'

'Go down to the hospital,' I said coldly. 'I'll be along in a few minutes.'

'Very good, Doctor.'

When I arrived at the hospital I found that Easter had diagnosed and prescribed for the condition with an efficiency founded on wide experience of it.

'Take these, chum,' he said, handing over a bottle of sulphathiazole tablets, 'and in a couple of days you'll be feeling like a box of birds, as they say in New Zealand.'

The patient stuffed the bottle in his waistband and jauntily walked out.

'Don't you think I ought to give him a short lecture?' I suggested.

Easter seemed to find this amusing.

'We all has our thoughtless moments, Doctor, don't we? Take a card,' he said, abruptly drawing a pack from his pocket. 'Any one. Don't let me see it.'

I took one automatically.

'Right,' he said. 'I will now shuffle them, see? No deception. You could have taken any card in the pack. Let me concentrate.' He screwed up his fat face in a spasm of thought. 'Four of diamonds,' he said.

'That is perfectly correct. Though I hardly think we should be doing this sort of thing when we are supposed to be treating patients.'

Easter slipped the cards back into the top pocket of his jacket with a subdued air of triumph.

'Dr. Flowerday always liked me to show him a few tricks. Used to have him in fits, sometimes. Didn't half get narked when he couldn't find how they was done.'

'And how was that one done, if I may ask?'

'Them's all four of diamonds, actual,' Easter said carelessly, tapping his pocket.

'You seem to be quite a specialist in this sort of thing.'

'For three years ashore I was Pin Hung, the Famous Chinese Magician. Round the halls. Mostly the North—Barrow, Carlisle, Sunderland. Grimsby was my favourite. Always hit the jackpot in Grimsby. I've a book of cuttings down below . . .'

'All right. Later on in the voyage, possibly.'

He flicked three cards from his sleeve and manipulated them on the top of a tin of bandages.

'Now then, Doctor. Try your luck. Bet you a dollar that you can't spot the lady.'

'Easter,' I said with interest, 'how is it that you have come to land up in your present position? A man of your peculiar talents would be far more at home on the racecourse than in a ship's hospital.'

'That's the trouble, Doctor. I worked the race trains for years. But I got fed up with it. You can get put inside too many times.'

I stared at him.

'Do you mean—are you trying to say that you have been in prison?'

I was alarmed. In shore practice this was not a condition usually found in one's colleagues.

'Ho, yes,' he replied, with the air of a man admitting he knew Brighton or Scarborough fairly well. 'Didn't like it much, though. Too bloody cold in winter.'

'So you came to sea instead?'

'That's right, Doctor. Used to be on the Western Ocean run for donkeys' years in the big passenger boats. When I was a lad, that is, and could run about a bit more. So I came back to it. Signed on as a steward. It's a good life, and you gets your grub regular. I took this job on when a mate of mine jumped ship in Sydney and I helped out in the surgery homeward bound. I like it better than waiting in the saloon. More dignified. And Dr. Flowerday used to let me dispose of surplus equipment and stores on the coast, if I could. Penicillin and such like, that ain't got long to go before it's U.S. That be all right with you, Doctor? Dr. Flowerday and I used to have an understanding about the proceeds.'

'I think we shall have to consider that later.'

'Very good, Doctor. There's one of the crew sick in his cabin.'

'Then why the devil didn't you tell me before? Instead of fooling around with all these damn card tricks.'

'There ain't no hurry, Doctor. It's only Chippy. The Carpenter.'

'What's the matter with him?'

'He's having one of his turns.'

I was suspicious. A diagnosis of the turns, to which over half of the middle-aged population of the country seems liable, can represent any condition from attacks of flatulence to full-blown epileptic fits.

'We'd better go and see him at once.'

'Very good, Doctor.'

I followed Easter aft, to the crew's accommodation in the poop. We went up an iron ladder to a door with CARPENTER AND LAMPTRIMMER stencilled over it. It was a bleak little cabin, with green-painted steel bulkheads and a couple of metal bunks one above the other. The only decoration was a photograph of an oblong tombstone with 'Mother's Grave' written underneath it.

On the top bunk was the patient, huddled under a grey ship's blanket. I gave him a shake. A head poked out at me, and I recognized the man with the lamp I had met at the top of the gangway. He needed a shave, there was dried saliva at the corners of his mouth, and his eyes looked like a couple of cherries on a blancmange.

'Aghurrr!' he said.

'Now what's the trouble, my man?' I started briskly.

He disregarded me. His eyes were on something else in the cabin, behind me. He pointed shakily to the corner.

'Get away, you bastards!' he yelled.

I jumped.

'Now don't get excited . . .' I said nervously.

He crouched into a corner of the bunk, pulling the blanket tightly round him.

'Get away!' he screamed. 'Get away from me!'

He brushed something from the bunk rail.

'What is it?' I asked. 'What's the trouble?'

The man started muttering, so that I had to lean closely over him to hear.

'It's them dogs,' he said. 'Bloody great Alsatians. Bloody great green ones. Look! Five of the bastards!'

I turned sharply round to Easter.

'This man has got D.T.s,' I announced.

'Ho, yes,' Easter said casually, not shifting from the doorway. 'Been having them for years. Long as I can remember, anyway.'

187

'But we must do something about it! I hope you realize this is a serious condition? You seem to treat it very lightly.'

'He always gets 'em about this part of the trip. He'll be as right as rain for weeks now. Been on the booze since we sailed. Says it makes him sad leaving Liverpool.'

The patient rattled the bunk.

'Get your paws orf my face!' he yelled.

'If I might make so bold, Doctor,' Easter said, still leaning on the door, 'I would say this was an occasion for the medical comforts.'

'Medical comforts? What on earth are you talking about?'

'Bottle of brandy,' he explained. 'It's issued buckshee, like, for the hospital. You can get another from the Chief Steward if you indent for it.'

'But I haven't seen anything of this brandy.'

'I usually keeps it in my cabin, Doctor. Dr. Flowerday and I had an understanding about it.'

'Is there any left?'

'Almost half, Doctor,' he said proudly. 'Dr. Flowerday used to give him a glassful and talk to him, gentle like, as if he was a baby. Worked like a charm. Shall I fetch the bottle?'

'Here they come again!' the patient shouted.

'Perhaps you'd better,' I said.

I gave him a tumbler of brandy and explained that the five green Alsatians were not really present, like a nurse soothing a night-scared child. After a couple of glasses and half an hour's persuasion I had reduced the intruders to three in number, and to terriers of normal colour. I felt entitled to be satisfied with this. I left the patient sleeping in his bunk with the empty glass in his hand and went back to my cabin.

'Seen many cases like him ashore?' Easter asked with interest, collecting the remains of the brandy.

'No. I have not. There seems a great difference, Easter, between the practice of medicine on shore and at sea.'

'Funny you should say that. Same thing always struck me about the doctors.'

CHAPTER V

It is remarkable what spiritual contentment can be obtained from washing your own socks. I soaped a pair in the basin and hung them to dry on a line Easter had stretched across my cabin. I glowed with a modest sense of achievement. This was the first time I had been obliged to do any washing, which I had previously looked upon as an esoteric feminine function comparable with giving birth.

The crew of the *Lotus* did their own laundering—even Captain Hogg, who appeared in the early afternoon on the strip of deck round his cabin with a bundle of white uniforms under his arm and a basket of clothes-pegs. The other officers hung their shirts over their bunks and smartened them afterwards in the bathroom with the Third Mate's travelling iron. Down aft, the crew set aside Sunday afternoon for the laundry, when it was usual to see large firemen and deckhands dressed only in underpants and tattoos scrubbing their singlets with bar soap in the fire-buckets. The clothes were then strung thickly round the winches and ventilators and flapped round the stern of the ship like some fantastic signal.

Drying was simple, for we had reached the Tropics and the ship's company was in white uniforms. I had only to fix a white cover on my Company's regulation cap, but the officers appeared unexpectedly one morning in white shorts and shirts, like a crop of snowdrops. The other hands were less affected by the order. Easter changed his blue serge jacket for a white one, but the rest were permitted the informality of uniform usual in the Merchant Service and did no more than roll their dungaree trousers half-way up their calves and remove their shirts.

'We should have been in whites two days ago,' Hornbeam grumbled. 'It's the Old Man's fault.'

'Why? What's he done now?'

'The old bastard sunbathes every afternoon and keeps us in blues until his knees are brown.'

I felt I was becoming quite a sailor. I let my days pass uncaringly, carried away in the drift of the sea routine. In a ship everybody seems constantly to be getting up or going to bed. The watch changes every fourth hour, which brings one of the mates, warm from his bunk, to the bridge, and sends a couple of engineers scuttling down the complicated ladders into the engine-room and stokehold. As well as the officers, two A.B.s go on the bridge to take turns at the wheel, and a gang of greasers and firemen troop below. All this movement is set off by the ship's bell on the bridge, which rings through each watch an arithmetical progression of half-hourly strokes.

Members of the ship's company who had no watches to keep—people like Whimble, Easter, and myself—all arranged their days round the after-dinner siesta. In the afternoon the whole ship died. All hands, apart from those essential for the running of the vessel, tottered away from the saloon table, and, encouraged by a weighty meal and the noon session of gin, crashed gratefully into their bunks. This was a habit I found condemnable, but irresistible. In medical school and practice the afternoon had been my busiest time, and I was determined to pass the hours between one and four studying *War and Peace*. At first I never drank before the meal and avoided the cook's suet roll, of which Captain Hogg must have eaten several fathoms every voyage. But—whether I was the subject of mass-suggestion or sea air contains some subtle narcotic—I was unconscious before I got the taste of the ship's cheese out of my mouth, and I stayed asleep until Easter shook me at four with a cup of tea and a small piece of confectionery known in the Merchant Service as a tabnab. This habit I regarded nervously as the first indication of moral degeneration.

At five-thirty every evening my bath was run by Boswell, the bath steward. Boswell, like Easter, had seen better days, and the courtly manners he had learned in big P. & O.s and Cunarders had not deserted him. Whatever the temperature, he wore a shining white jacket, a stiff wing collar, and a black bow tie. He would arrive at my cabin door at half-past five precisely, a clean blue-and-white towel folded over his arm, and announce 'Your bath awaits, Doctor,' as if it were an important delegation. He fol-

lowed me to the officers' bathroom, which smelled like a seaside
cave at low tide, spread the towel over the chair, and mixed the
water with his skinny hand. He dipped in a foot-long thermometer with a little metal bucket at the end, anxiously inspected
the temperature, and made a careful adjustment to the taps (later
I found the thermometer had not worked for several years). He
then poured some fresh hot water from a large shining copper
can into a small bowl for the feet, and laid on the white wooden
rack across the bath my flannel, a long-handled scrubbing brush,
a loofah, and a bar of sea-water soap.

'Would there be anything else you require, sir?' he asked every
evening. I found it difficult to complicate such a simple act as
taking a bath any farther, and he would bow deeply and retire
backwards through the steam. I knew he did so with disappointment, for a bath suggested to him as many variations as soup to a
French chef. Every few days he would press me to take a few
spoonfuls of mustard in it, or some washing soda, or a tumbler of
rose-water. 'Might I recommend a little Sloane's?' he asked once.
'I used to put it in regularly for one doctor I looked after in the
Cunard. Very good for the joints, I believe.'

Boswell's manners were unfortunately not sufficient to overcome the discomforts of the *Lotus*'s bathroom. There were no
portholes or ventilators, so water collected on the deckhead as
efficiently as in the main condenser in the engine-room, and thence
fell thickly in rusty brown drops. The deck was covered with
some crumbling material that left potholes to trip the bather and
make him catch his head or his shins against sharp projecting
pieces of steel. The bath itself was shaped like a coffin, and was
furnished with a pair of fearsome taps that gave between them hot
and cold sea water and a disproportionate amount of steam.
There was an alternative—the fresh-water shower outside Hornbeam's cabin, but owing to some subtle mechanical fault many feet
below in the engine-room this emitted only ice-cold water or
superheated steam, and after escaping a third-degree burn I decided to stick to the safer tepid waters under Boswell's supervision.

Boswell did not stop at baths: far greater was his pride in the
officers' lavatories. These were not much more efficient than the

bath, and in rough weather became alarmingly unreliable. But to Boswell they were a porcelain monument to his own calling. He spent the morning cleaning and polishing them, and on our arrival for inspection would bow low and flush each as we passed with the jaunty pride of the satisfied artist.

'There's more in lavatories than meets the eye, sir,' he explained to me one day, with a sigh. 'You've got to *understand* lavatories to do this job.' I gathered from Easter that as he contentedly did his morning task Boswell dreamed of his retirement in charge of a small underground nest of them at one of the quieter corners of Liverpool.

My professional duties were not exacting. I saw a couple of patients in the morning, perhaps half a dozen at five. The most common trouble was the constipation, Doctor. This I first treated with pharmacopœial doses of the usual remedies, but I soon found it was necessary to multiply the amount by three for most of the patients and by five for the Bos'n and firemen. There were boils and warts, a few burns from the engine-room, and several vague illnesses whose leading symptom was a disinclination to work. We had a few more cases resulting from careless choice of friends during our last nights in Liverpool. The approach to the medical attendant by sufferers from this embarrassing condition varied from the shifty request—with a sidelong glance at Easter—to ' 'Ave a word wiv you a minute, Doctor,' to the full-blooded storming of the surgery by the experienced invalid with his 'Say, Doc, can you fix this for us by Friday?'

At eleven we inspected the ship. Hornbeam, Whimble, Mc-Dougall, and myself gathered outside the saloon door and saluted when Captain Hogg's boots appeared on the companion-way from his cabin. This homage he returned with the grace of a publican handing back a counterfeit half-crown.

We lined up behind him and set off touring the decks, each of us trying to look as disagreeable as possible. We filed in and out of Boswell's lavatories with dignity, and zealously searched for dust under the coconut matting. The progress was broken only when Captain Hogg's eye was jarred by something that gave him displeasure, when he would turn his fury not only on the man responsible but on his parents as well. At first I shivered at the onslaught: then I grew to appreciate the range and power of the Captain's imagination and the felicity with which he turned his sentences, until I listened to him with fascination. As for the victims, they shrugged their shoulders and took no notice. Raving Captains were just like storms at sea: you had to put up with them until they blew themselves out, and not become unreasonably excited.

After inspection the Captain went on the bridge to supervise the daily ceremony of finding the noon position of the ship. I went up there only once, because Captain Hogg looked on visitors like a sour landowner spotting picnickers on his front lawn. It was a shady, restful place, lined with dark wood and brass, like an old-fashioned saloon bar. The sea was surprisingly far below, and the only sound was the irregular loud clicking of the gyro repeater, like the ticking of an arrhythmic clock. Abaft the bridge was the chartroom, where rulers, set-squares, and neatly sharpened pencils were arranged like a tidy school desk, and the chronometers nestled under thick glass like a pair of premature infants in an incubator. Hornbeam once offered me his sextant and let me work out our position, but I disgusted him by putting the *Lotus* within a few miles of Cleveland, Ohio.

I spent most of my time chatting to the officers off watch, leaning on the rail, playing quoits, or nosing round the deck. I was beginning to learn what everything was called. Ships have a distinct anatomy of their own, and our daily rounds were as confusing to me as my first demonstrations in the dissecting room. I recognized fairly early on the difference between port and starboard, fore and aft, and a binnacle and a barnacle; but I was still uncertain where to find such obscure pieces of marine furnishing as the jumper stays, the monkey island, and the shrouds.

*　　　*　　　*　　　*

The tenth morning of the voyage I sat down resolutely in my cabin and took *War and Peace* from the locker. Somehow I had not yet found time to pass the first page. I opened it, smoothed down the paper, and began again the first paragraph. Hornbeam rattled the jalousie door and came in.

'Morning, Doc! Everything bearing an even strain?'

'Good morning, Chief,' I said. 'I think so, thanks very much.'

'Good.'

Picking up the first volume of *War and Peace* he neatly squashed a cockroach that was scuttling across the bulkhead.

'These damn roaches,' he said. 'Come out in families once it turns hot. Had any in bed with you?'

'No, not yet.'

He pulled a tobacco tin from his pocket.

'Would you like the makings?' he asked, offering it.

'No, thank you. I'm afraid it's a nautical knack I haven't picked up.'

'It's easy enough. Can't stand tailor-mades.'

He neatly rolled a cigarette between his fingers and thumbs. Whenever I tried the same manœuvre I squeezed the tobacco out like the cream from an éclair.

'Wish you'd have a look at the Sparks, Doc,' Hornbeam continued affably.

'Why, what's the trouble?'

'I just saw him shake hands with a lifeboat.'

'Ah, yes. I was rather afraid something like that might happen.'

Our Wireless Operator was probably the luckiest man on the ship. He was one of those blithe people who live in a world of their own. He had been at sea for forty years, crouched over a telegraph key with the staccato song of Morse in his ears. This seemed to have induced psychological changes in him. For the rest of us, our universe was bounded by the steel and wooden limits of the *Lotus*—but not the Sparks. He passed his day in the company of soft-skinned maidens and amiable philosophers, with whom he could often be seen laughing, conversing, and singing while he walked round the deck or sat in the corner of his cabin. Sometimes he did a coy little dance with some of his companions, or played a simple game; and occasionally they would have a restrained tiff, which always ended happily in the way just observed by the Mate. The Sparks was by far the happiest person under Captain Hogg's command.

'I suppose he's quite harmless?' I asked. 'I mean, he doesn't send out dangerous messages or anything?'

'Oh, he's not in that stage yet,' Hornbeam assured me tolerantly. 'I've seen a good many worse than him. The Morse gets 'em in the end. I just thought you ought to know. I saw him kissing a ventilator yesterday,' he added darkly.

'We are all entitled to our little aberrations, I suppose.'

'You're right there, Doc. Life at sea wouldn't be possible without a bit of give and take. Old Sparks is all right. Just a bit dippy. Like some of these tanker types.'

'Tanker types?'

He nodded, lighting the cigarette and filling the cabin with smoke.

'Men in tankers. It's a dog's life. They run to places like the Persian Gulf and they can unload in a couple of days. That means the boys don't get much of a run ashore when they're home. Besides, you can't live on top of a few thousand tons of petrol all your life without getting a bit queer. Of course, they get the money. . . . But is it worth it? Friend of mine went Mate in a tanker to make a bit and ended up by cutting his throat. Made a hell of a mess in the chartroom, so they told me.'

From Hornbeam's conversation I gathered that suicide at sea had a panache not seen ashore.

'I think I'll stick to dry cargo,' I said. 'That seems dangerous enough for doctors.'

'Are you coming to the Third's do to-night?' Hornbeam asked. 'That's the reason I looked in.'

'I didn't know he was having one.'

'It's his birthday—twenty-first—and he's having a few beers. You're invited.'

'I don't drink much, you know.'

'Oh, don't be scared, Doc. None of us drinks while we're at sea. I'll say you're coming.'

The party was after supper, in the Third Mate's cabin. As I

was anxious not to appear at all anti-social I was the first to arrive.

I had not been in his cabin before. It was smaller than mine, with just enough room for a man to stand between the bunk and the strip of settee on the opposite bulkhead. There was a port-hole over the settee and a forced-draught vent in the deckhead that stabbed a narrow stream of cold air across the bunk. Opposite the door was a small desk covered completely with bottles of gin. The rest of the cabin was covered with girls.

They were everywhere—in frames over the bunk, pasted to the bulkhead, suspended from the pipes crossing the deckhead. There were plain photographs of ordinary girls, shadowy nudes from *Men Only,* taut scissor-legged girls in impossible brassières from *Esquire,* a few bright beer advertisements from Australia of sur-prised but unresisting girls with their skirts caught in mangles, car doors, stiles, and dog leads, girls with no clothes playing on the beach, girls with all their clothes caught in a highly selective gale, even pictures of Chinese girls covered from neck to ankle.

'Come in, Doc!' the Third said. 'Have a peg.'

He pushed a glass into my hand and half-filled it with gin in one motion.

'Happy birthday,' I said faintly. 'You seem to have an eye for art.'

'Got to brighten the old cart up a bit. Here's to you.'

He pointed above the bunk to the photograph of a sharp-chinned young lady trying earnestly to look like Dorothy Lamour.

'That's a nice bit of crumpet. Met her in Hull last voyage. She's an intelligent bit, mind you,' he added seriously. 'Works in Boots' library.'

He indicated her rival next to her.

'Now there's a girl for you. Came across her in Adelaide. Last time we were there her brother came and socked me on the nose. She still writes to me, though.'

'I hope he didn't hurt you.'

'He did a bit. He's one of the wharfies. That one's from St. John. But this Sheila here's the best of the bunch. Lives in Durban. Father's got pots of cash.'

'You seem to scatter your affections pretty widely.'

'They all love sailors. When a girl knows a fellow's going half-way round the world in a week's time she takes the brakes off a bit. Have a seat on the bunk.'

I sat down and rested my head uncomfortably on the paper bosom of a blonde.

The other guests arrived together. There was Hornbeam, the crazy Sparks, Whimble, the Second Steward, and the Chief, Second, Third, and Fourth Engineers. Archer was absent, keeping Hornbeam's watch on the bridge. The ten of us crammed ourselves into the tiny cabin. Hornbeam had his elbow in my face and his shoes on the Chief Engineer's knees. Whimble wedged himself behind the door and stuck his feet against the end of the bunk. The host struggled between everyone's legs, handing out drinks. I felt that something would shortly give way and project the lot of us into the sea.

The Third's health was drunk by all hands.

'Have another, Doc,' he said.

'No, really . . .'

'Come off it! It's only five bob a bottle.' He half-filled my tumbler again. 'How do you like the sea?' he asked.

'It is a very interesting form of existence.'

'Of course, you realize this is only part of it,' Hornbeam explained. 'It varies a good bit. As you know, British ships are in three classes.'

'Tankers . . . ?'

'No. First of all there's the P. & O. Then there's the Merchant Navy, which is the set-up we're in. After that there's the Old Grey Funnel line.'

'Also known as the Royal Navy,' McDougall explained. 'It was nationalized years ago.'

'The P. & O. must not be confused with ordinary hookers,' Hornbeam continued. 'It's a sort of—well, a floating Horse Guards, if you get me. They hate to be called Merchantmen. If you make a noise drinking your soup . . .'

'They wear swords and spurs,' Trail said.

'I don't believe it.'

'Well, they ought to. Oh, very posh, very posh. Good

shower of bastards on the whole, though. Have some more gin.'

'Not for . . . Oh, all right, as you've poured it out. It tastes better than the stuff you get ashore.'

'Everything does. By the way, you know the Second Engineer, Doc? Mr. Macpherson.'

'Pleased to meet you.'

'Mr. MacPhail the Third and Mr. Macintosh the Fourth.'

'What, are you all Scots in the engine-room?'

'We've a Taffy and a couple of Geordies,' Macpherson said. 'Had to have them in to do the dirty work.'

'You know what they say,' McDougall added proudly. 'If you open the engine-room hatch of any British ship and shout "Jock" someone'll be bound to come up.'

MacPhail started singing 'I belong to Glasgow,' but petered out for lack of support.

'Coming ashore with us in Santos, Doc?' Hornbeam asked.

'Certainly. I intend to take advantage of the voyage to broaden my education.'

'Santos will broaden it all right. Plenty of nice girls there.'

'I'm sure I should be pleased if you'd introduce me to them.'

This remark started everyone laughing.

'You don't need any introductions. It's keeping them away that's the trouble.'

'Well, I shall not be interested in meeting any of that sort.'

'Oh, you'll have to come with us to Madame Mimi's,' Hornbeam said reproachfully. 'It would be like going to London and missing the Houses of Parliament.'

'Are you suggesting,' I said coldly, 'that I should visit a brothel?'

'Where the hell else do you think there is to go in Santos?' Trail said testily. 'Anyway, Madame Mimi's is as respectable as the Liverpool Museum.'

'I wouldn't put that past suspicion,' Hornbeam said.

Trail cut the conversation short by pouring out gin all round and beginning a complicated story about two sailors losing their way in Lime Street station.

After an hour everyone was pretty cheerful.

'Don't make such a row,' Trail said. 'Father'll hear.'

'To hell with Father,' I heard myself say.

'Spoken like a sailor, Doc!' Hornbeam slapped me on the chest. 'Good old Doc! Best one I've ever sailed with.'

'I say, really . . .'

'You're the only one that's sane!'

This brought a round of applause.

'You're all mad at sea,' I said defiantly. 'The lot of you.'

The company immediately indicated their disbelief with the usual word.

'You are,' I said. 'Or you wouldn't be here.'

'Have some more gin,' Trail said.

'Thank you.' I swallowed another mouthful. 'As I was saying. I have made a diagnosis. From careful—not to say exacting— study of you in the past ten days I conclude that you're all suffering from the death wish.'

'What the hell's that?' McDougall asked angrily.

I held up a hand.

'Silence. As a disciple of Hippocrates I demand respect and silence. The death wish. When you are born all you want to do is die.'

This again filled the cabin with derision.

'Shut up, you blokes. Let the poor blighter speak,' Trail said.

I continued. 'That is what the psychologists say. Some people hang themselves. Others go into monasteries and . . . and things. Some climb mountains and live in caves. Others write poetry. Look at English poetry,' I demanded hotly of Hornbeam. 'Look at it! Redolent with the death wish!' I screwed up my eyes and struck an attitude of recitation.

> '. . . for many a time
> I have been half in love with easeful Death,'

I declaimed stumblingly.

> 'Call'd him soft names in many a musèd rhyme,
> To take into the air my quiet . . .'

I slipped off the bunk, but Hornbeam caught me.

'Death wish to the eyebrows, the lot of you! You withdraw— to sea. To sea! That's what it is!'

'You're full of prune-juice, Doc,' someone said.

'I will not have insults,' I cried. 'If you would care to defend yourself like a gentleman, I shall take you up on it. You have the death wish, by God! You've all got it. So had Nelson. I've got it as well.'

I fell over McDougall's feet and no one bothered to pick me up.

CHAPTER VI

THE next morning I was suffering from a sharp attack of the
death wish. But my performance had raised me surprisingly in the
eyes of my shipmates. My earnest years as a medical student, my
dignified excursion into practice, my prim approach to seafaring
had built a scaffold underneath me: the Third Mate's gin had
slipped the bolt.

My companions were relieved to find that I was not only sane
but human: for my part, I began to realize that the sea, which
washes away terrestrial affectations and inhibitions, had a great
deal to recommend it. Sailors are of the few remaining people
who make their way in companies across the unsignposted face of
the world with the help of the sun and the stars, and spend most
of their lives lying at the unhindered fancy of the weather. Their
sense of values in human and elemental behaviour is therefore
unblunted; they look on their existence as a long uproarious joke
relieved by not unentertaining interludes of necessary tragedy. I
thought them the last of the Elizabethans.

I believe there is no process so restful as moving at bicycle pace
through the sunshine of the South Atlantic. We were steaming at
ten knots, which meant we should be about three weeks reaching
Santos. The metallic fragment of England in which we all existed—except the Wireless Operator—creaked easily onwards
with a faint haze of smoke rolling from the funnel, scattering the
nimble flying fish with her bow. Even crossing the Line caused no
more disturbance than my having to stand drinks all round. The
hot sun welded the days together so that they became indistin-
guishable. It was impossible to tell whether it was Tuesday or
Thursday, and it didn't matter.

Only twice a week were we reminded of the calendar—Friday
and Sunday. At four-thirty on Friday afternoons we had boat
drill. Captain Hogg stood on the bridge and pulled the cord of
the whistle, which sent us scurrying up the ladders in our blue-
and-orange life-jackets to the boatdeck. I was in boat number

four, in charge of the Third Mate, who ticked our names off with a roll-call. I was alarmed to find that among my companions in an emergency would be the Carpenter with a tendency to D.T.s and a pleasant-faced greaser who, I heard from Easter, had just returned from a ten-year stretch for armed robbery.

'Swing out!' Captain Hogg shouted through the loud hailer.

The canvas covers were stripped off the boats, and three men set to the handle of each davit to lean it out from the ship's side. When this had been done to Captain Hogg's satisfaction the boats were swung in again and everyone dispersed.

'Board of Trade sports,' Trail said with disgust. 'Waste of time.'

'Why do we do it then?' I asked.

'Oh, it has to go in the log-book. There'd be hell in Liverpool if we didn't. Some skippers cook the log, but not this baby. Anything to give him a chance of bawling through a loud hailer.'

Sunday was recognizable, as it was the only occasion when we flew the flag at sea. From eight to midday the red ensign waved from the gaff on the mainmast, to convince the Almighty that we had not forgotten him—for there was no one else but ourselves to see it. The appearance of the flag that symbolized the Sabbath was greeted warmly by all hands, not through reverence but because, under Ministry of Transport regulations, we all got an extra half-day's pay.

Sunday was also marked by the ceremony of full inspection. This was ordered by Captain Hogg's copy of *Instructions for Masters*, the manual through which the Fathom Steamship Company directed and advised their commanders, which contained in its yellow pages regulations designed to right such nautical disasters as mutiny, epidemics of smallpox, lost anchor, and imminent shipwreck. At eleven o'clock the four of us fell in behind the Captain, who indicated the exceptional occasion by carrying a torch and a walking-stick. On the poop the ship's company was lined up ready for us—deckhands under the charge of the Bos'n on the port side, firemen and greasers to starboard, and catering staff, in fresh white jackets, standing nervously athwartships. Captain Hogg passed down the ranks scowling into each face like a vengeful but short-sighted victim at an identification parade, then we marched in and out of the little, green-painted crews' cabins that each smelt of feet and hair-oil. They had been cleaned and tidied so that nothing in the slightest degree disturbing could fall into the Captain's visual fields. The decks were scrubbed, the blankets folded ostentatiously, and the owners' possessions—varying from a guitar to a caged canary—were set in unnaturally tidy piles. Captain Hogg shone his torch beneath the bunks, inspected the undersurfaces of tables and chairs, and thrust the crook of his walking-stick into every inviting orifice. Usually his rummaging produced nothing more than a cloud of dust and an empty beer-tin, but occasionally he would drag out a saloon plate, a silver coffee-pot, a mildewed loaf, a pair of underpants, or the crumpled photograph of an inconstant girl friend.

'Mr. Hornbeam!' he would shout, waving the find under the Mate's nose. 'What's the meaning of this? Eh? We'll find the chronometers in here next!'

The last call was my hospital. Sunday was the only occasion when it was inspected, and Easter spent the morning polishing the brasswork and tipping all the small movable objects and surgical debris into a large white bin labelled 'Sterile Dressings.' As we arrived he stood smartly to attention beside the door, hiding a large black patch on the bulkhead.

'All correct, Doctor?' the Captain growled every Sunday.

'Yes, sir. All correct.'

He fixed Easter with his eye.

'Any complaints?'

'I am very happy, Captain,' Easter replied unctuously.

'All right. Pipe down, Bos'n.'

The crew were scattered to their Sunday indolence and we went up to the Captain's cabin, where we stood in a line in front of him, our caps under our arms, and he emphasized the points that had incurred his disapproval. Then we all sat down and had a gin.

There were no religious observances on board the *Lotus*—an omission that was deplored only by Easter. This surprised me. 'I didn't know you were a churchgoer,' I told him.

'Ho, yes, Doctor. I likes a nice service of a Sunday. Breaks the monotony a bit. Not much good in an old tub like this, but in the big passenger boats I used to sing hymns at the back. I've got a bit of a voice,' he added modestly.

'I'm very pleased to hear it.'

'Used to take the plate round as well. Real nice job that is. Must be the sea air what makes them generous. You see them old skin-flints what wouldn't give a tanner to a blind baby at home sticking in quids and suchlike. Made quite a bit out of that in my time.'

'You mean you actually helped yourself from the collection?'

'Sort of commission, as you might say,' he explained amiably. 'Nothing much, mind you. No one knows what there is in the kitty, but you've got to be pretty nifty slipping it out before the Purser spots you. Charity begins at home, don't it, Doctor?'

* * * * *

My clinical practice continued its easy routine, and was centred round preservation of the health of the Captain's stomach. I had never known an organ to produce such widespread clinical effects. If it functioned painlessly life was tolerable, even at mealtimes; but the first twinges of dyspepsia immediately communicated themselves to everyone on board. Fortunately I was able to dena-ture my mixture of its explosive properties, and it combated spiritually with the Captain's diet. My morning visit to him with the sick-list gave me an opportunity to see how the battle was going by judging the state of the old gentleman's temper—a matter of importance on the ship beyond the belief of any lands-man. If he was in a good mood he took the chit without question, and sometimes even demonstrated extreme geniality by offering me a gin (he saw nothing unusual in drinking after breakfast). If my mixture was not up to strength, or if he had eaten too many platefuls of Madras curry the night before, he would seize the paper and scowl at it like a Tudor monarch affirming a list of executions.

'What's wrong with that man?' he would demand, stabbing the sheet with his blunt finger. 'McKlusky, J., Ordinary Seaman. Why's he off duty? What's this—P.U.O.?'

'Pyrexia of unknown origin, sir,' I explained timidly. 'He has a temperature.'

'Well, why has he?'

'I'm afraid I don't know, sir.'

'Why don't you? You're the Doctor, aren't you? What the devil do you think would happen to us all if I didn't know a lighthouse when I saw one? Eh? What have you got to say to that?'

He slammed the paper down on his desk. I said nothing to it.

'Now, look here, Doctor,' he went on. 'I'm not in your line, and I don't pretend to be. But I can tell you what's wrong with this man—he's constipated. I haven't been to sea for forty years for nothing. Give the bastard a double dose of black draught and kick him back on duty. If he still shirks I'll put him in the log-book. That's an order!'

'Yes, sir.'

This put me in a state of professional agitation. But Captain Hogg would have agitated the whole General Medical Council.

The Captain was at his most terrifying when conducting the ceremony of placing an offender's name in the log-book. This was the only disciplinary action left in his hands: flogging at the mainmast, keel-hauling, and hanging from the yardarm at sunset have been abolished by Parliament, and Captain Hogg made it plain that he thought the world all the worse for it.

One night shortly after we reached the Tropics I was pulled from my bunk by Hornbeam to see a couple of firemen who had been fighting in the foc's'le. Both of them were drunk. They were in the hospital, blood-spattered and muttering surly threats at each other, separated by Easter with the heavy pestle from the drug locker.

'Now keep quiet for the Doctor,' he said cheerfully, 'or I'll bash your ruddy brains in with this. These two have filled each other in something proper,' he added to me as a clinical explanation.

During the two hours needed to sew them up I gathered that the pair of them, Kelly and Crosby, came from the opposite sides of a Liverpool street; and a feud had smouldered between them since they first threw stones at each other from the shelter of their mothers' skirts. Too late they had found themselves both aboard the *Lotus*, and had been living in grudging amicability since we sailed. But that evening Kelly had been unable to repress any longer his opinion that Crosby's mother was not only a harlot, but the oldest and most ugly in all Liverpool, and Crosby cracked the end of a bottle and went for him.

The next morning at ten I was summoned to the Captain's cabin, which had the ceremonially grim air of a Portsmouth court-martial. Sitting at the desk was Captain Hogg, an expression on his face of uninhibited malevolence. Set before him were his gold-braided cap, *Instructions for Masters*, the log-book open at the correct page, a sheet of yellow blotting-paper, and a large silver ink-pot with a pen in it, so that everything was at hand for making the damning entry. Hornbeam was in a chair beside the Captain, looking seriously at his own feet. The Bos'n and the Donkeyman were positioned on each side of the door, and I was ordered curtly to the corner. In the middle of the circle were the two delinquents, twisting their caps in their hands and throwing nervous glances round the cabin from the gaps in their bandages.

'Right,' Captain Hogg began briskly. 'Now we are all assembled we can begin. First of all I want to make something perfectly plain to you two. You are going to get a completely fair hearing this morning. Understand? You are quite at liberty to put questions to me or any other of the officers. You may call any witness you like in your defence. As far as I'm concerned a man is innocent until he's proved guilty, whether it's murder or pinching a ha'penny stamp. You'll never find me giving a man a bad character till it's proved. I'm a fair captain, I am. Get me?'

The two firemen nodded hesitantly.

'Very well. Now, tell me your version of the affair.'

He folded his arms judicially.

The feud that had burned so brightly a few hours before was now outshone by the peril that faced the two opponents. They had composed a story during breakfast, which was begun by Kelly in the tone of bitter repentance that had occasionally swayed sympathetic members of a magistrate's bench.

'Well, sir, it was like this 'ere, sir. Me and me mate was 'avin' a cupper tea . . .'

'You bloody liar!' Captain Hogg shouted. 'You were rotten drunk, both of you bastards! Oh yes, you were! Don't answer me back or I'll kick you round the deck. You were drunk in the foc's'le and you started fighting like the pair of goddam cut-

206

throats you are. My God, you're a crowd of loafers up forrard! You oughtn't to be at sea, you ought to be in jail, the lot of you! Stand up straight when I'm talking to you, blast you!' He thrust a finger under Kelly's nose. 'You turn my ship into a Liverpool rough-house and you come up here with some cock-and-bull story you think I'm going to swallow. What do you take me for, eh? I was at sea when you were playing marbles in the filth of a Liverpool gutter. Mr. Hornbeam!'

'Sir?'

'You found these men fighting?'

Hornbeam nodded.

'Doctor!'

'Sir?'

'Did you or did you not find these men were drunk?'

'Well, sir, the scientific tests . . .'

'There you are! The Doctor agrees with me! You were soused, the pair of you!' He banged the desk with his fist, making the pen leap out of the ink-pot. 'Do you know what I'd like to do to you?' he demanded. 'I'd like to give you every holystone on board and make you scrub the boatdeck till the plates showed through. Then I'd put you in irons in the chain-locker and keep you on bread and water till we got back to Liverpool. That's the sort of treatment scum like you need! I'd like to put you in an open boat here and now, and get rid of the pair of you for good. Do you understand, you couple of lazy sons of bitches?'

But fortunately the Captain's justice was obligatorily tempered with mercy. 'Fined five shillings,' he muttered. 'Good morning.'

It was fortunate that Captain Hogg was, through reason of his being a captain, confined most of the day to his own quarters. He passed his time sitting in an arm-chair reading magazines similar to the one hiding his face on the first occasion I met him. In the corner of his cabin was a pile three feet high of these periodicals, from all parts of the English-speaking world. He consumed them earnestly and steadily, like a man with plenty of time looking up a train in Bradshaw. 'There's one thing I do like,' he announced at dinner one day, a forkful of beef and vegetables at his mouth, 'and that's a good book.'

For the rest of the voyage I bowed to his opinions like a Victorian schoolboy and took the greatest pains possible to avoid him.

The Leader of the Opposition in the *Lotus* was the Chief Engineer, McDougall. He alone of the engineers had unresented entry into the saloon and our company; the mates looked upon them instinctively as intruders, a relic of the days when thin funnels first poked their way through the proud canvas. The engineers lived away from the rest of us in tiny hot cabins clustered amidships, and ate in a pokey messroom ventilated by the oily breath of the engines. We saw them only when they leant over the rail in their black and sweaty boiler suits, or lay on their backs dissembling one of the pieces of ugly machinery that sprung from *Lotus's* deck.

McDougall had a noisy cabin by the engine-room hatchway, in which he received visitors with a half-tumbler of neat whisky (he maintained that gin was a drink fit only for harlots). His surroundings were as untidy as a nursery. Scraps of steel and paint-pots littered the deck, the bunk sagged under pieces of dismantled machinery, and the bulkheads supported charts, graphs, a row of sombre engineering books, and an incongruous nude leaving her bath on a boilermaker's calendar. Scattered everywhere, like thistledown blown by a breeze, were scraps of half-used cotton waste.

'Where would ye all be without my engines?' he demanded. 'Do ye know what you've got to thank us for? Everything from the propeller revolutions to your shaving water and the ice in your gin.'

He thought of his engines, as Boswell did of his lavatories, as living beings possessed of souls.

'Ye'll be no damn good as an engineer till you make friends with your engines,' he told me. 'Talk to 'em, that's what you've got to do. Give 'em hell if they play you up. It pays in the end, lad. Many a time I've had a row with me mates or the wife, and it's been a comfort to know I've got a real pal down below. If ye cut my veins, Doc, ye'll find fuel oil there, not blood.'

McDougall believed that the best engineers came from Scotland, the best Scots from Glasgow, and the only effect of modern innovations like oil furnaces, engine-room ventilation, and refrigerators was a glaring deterioration in the standard of young men coming to sea. When he showed me round his engine-room, he exhibited the reverence of an old dean in his cathedral. We stood on the quivering control platform in the centre of the *Lotus*'s clamorous viscera and he waved his arm proudly and shouted, 'This is where we do a man's job, Doc.'

I nodded, looking nervously at the pipes straining with the pressure of superheated steam.

'That's the main steam gauge,' McDougall explained, pointing to a dial on the panel in front of us.

'What's the red line for?' I shouted back.

'That? Och, that's the safety mark.'

'But, I say, isn't the needle well past it?'

'That doesn't matter, lad. We've got to get the old tub moving somehow.'

He took me down greasy ladders, along a narrow cat-walk between pieces of spinning machinery, through the boiler-room where Turnbull, the Geordie Seventh Engineer, sweated eight hours of his twenty-four watching the oil fires. We crouched along the tunnel that carried the propeller shaft to the stern, and stood at the end in a little triangular humid space where the thick revolving metal pierced the plates and disappeared into the sea.

'There ye are, Doc. All us lads and all that machinery to keep this turning. If it wasn't for us that old windbag on the bridge would be out of a job.'

'He doesn't seem to be very appreciative, Chief.'

'Och, we've got better than him conducting the trams in Glasgow,' McDougall said with disgust. 'You watch, Doc, I'll run him off this ship before he's much older. You wait and see.'

McDougall's threat was wholly serious. He had in a locked drawer in his cabin a foolscap book labelled shamelessly HOGG, in which he entered immediately every derogatory fact he discovered about the Captain. When he was particularly annoyed he took the book out and read it, underlining in red ink wherever he thought a passage was not sufficiently condemnatory standing on its own. This book he sent to the Marine Superintendent of the Fathom Line by registered post every time the ship returned to Britain, but its effect was largely cancelled by a similar volume about McDougall put in the Superintendent's hands by the Captain. The two passed their lives in a running fight on oil consumption, engine revolutions, and repair bills, and the daily ceremony by which McDougall handed Captain Hogg a chit on his speed and fuel supplies was always conducted in bitter silence. About once a week the Captain became too much for him, and the Chief Engineer then shut himself in his cabin, took out a fresh bottle of whisky, and determinedly threw the cap through the porthole.

As the ship's company became used to me they paid me the compliment of sharing their troubles with me. I soon discovered all of them were hypochondriacs. In small ships where they had no doctor they worried in case they caught anything; in bigger ships, where there was a doctor living down the alleyway, they brought along their symptoms like bruised children running to their mother. The Second Mate was the severest sufferer from hypochondriasis. The locker in his cabin was a therapeutic bar: he had five different brands of antiseptic, all the popular stomach powders, lotions for rubbing under the arms and between the toes, drops for sticking in his eyes or up his nose, gargles and liniments, hair food and skin-balm, and a frightening collection of purgatives.

I found him gargling lustily in his cabin one afternoon.

'Hello, Second,' I said. 'What's up? Got a cold?'

He spat guiltily into the basin, as though I had caught him at some wickedness.

'No,' he explained. 'I always gargle three times a day. I was reading an article in *Happy Health* that said every cubic inch of air is loaded with millions of microbes.'

'Well, so's every inch of your throat.'

'Listen, Doc,' he went on, sounding worried. 'There's something I've been wanting to ask you for a long time. Where could I get my blood cholesterol measured?'

'Your what!'

'Yes, you see there was an article in—either the *Reader's Digest* or one of the Sunday papers at home—that said some doctors in California had discovered if your blood cholesterol was above 245 milligrams per cent you were bound to get arteriosclerosis. I've all the symptoms. I . . .'

'You're far more likely to fall down a hatch and break your neck.'

'Do you think so?' he asked eagerly. 'Still, it's got me worried. I'm sure I've got an intervertebral disk as well. There's a pain I get round here in my back every time I sit down.'

'Rubbish! You're healthier than I am.'

He looked dolefully at his medicine chest for a few moments. 'Of course,' he continued, 'what I really need is a woman.'

'I'm inclined to agree with you,' I said.

I sat down reflectively on his bunk. I had become aware in the past few days of feeling—not blatantly sex-starved but unquestionably peckish. I put it down to the sea air. My life ashore had passed undisturbed except for Wendy and occasional vague thoughts that it would be nice to take a girl to the pictures. But now I began to think even the girls in the Third Mate's cabin were delightful. Wendy herself became frighteningly glamorized as my mind's eye behaved like a magazine photographer's lens, and substituted curves for angularity and an inviting expression for the usual one that indicated she thought her nose was running.

'Now, if this was a real passenger ship,' the Second continued, 'everything would be squared up by now. Have you been in one?'

'This is my first ship.'

'I forgot. I was Third in one for a bit. It was like a floating Ball of Kirriemuir. I don't know what it is. As soon as these females get aboard a ship they're all after you. Not a moment's peace. Then there's dances and race meetings and all the fun and games. Not to mention the moonlight and the phosphorescence on the water. I haven't seen any phosphorescence yet. But they fall for it, every time. The places they get to! We found one couple on the steering engine. I used to go under the lifeboats.'

'What about the Captain?'

'He was at it like everyone else. He jacked himself up a nice bit of snicket first day out of Southampton. What a trip that was!'

'I take it you're not married,' I said.

'I've been married. Got hitched during the war when I was a Third. It didn't work out. We've split it up now.' He took a cigarette out of the tin thoughtfully. 'It's no good being married at sea. Oh yes, every leave's a honeymoon, I know what they say.

But long voyages and young wives don't mix. You leave the allotment of your pay and if you don't get a letter at every port you wonder what's up. Anyhow, I reckon you can't ask a girl to sit by the fireside for six months, or a year, or two years maybe. It isn't fair. It isn't human.'

'What about you?' I asked.

'Oh, I always hold you're entitled to count yourself as single at sea,' he said.

Our reflections were interrupted by the engine-room telegraph ringing faintly on the bridge above.

'What's that?' I asked. 'I thought they tested them at noon.'

'I expect she's stopped,' Archer said calmly.

'Stopped! But isn't that important?'

'She often stops. It's the first time she's done it this trip. Something's blown up down below, I suppose. Come on deck. From now on it's usually pretty funny.'

We stepped on to the sunny deck, just below the wing of the bridge. The *Lotus* had stopped sure enough. She wallowed in the swell like a dead whale.

'Now watch,' the Second said.

Captain Hogg appeared on the bridge. He had been disturbed in his siesta, and was dressed only in a tartan dressing-gown. He looked like Macbeth the day the wood moved.

'Mr. McDougall!' he shouted. 'Mr. McDougall!'

He banged the rail with his fist.

'Quartermaster! Present my compliments to the Chief Engineer and ask him to come to the bridge!'

'Aye aye, sir.'

Captain Hogg clasped his hands behind him and strode fiercely across the deck. After five minutes McDougall appeared. He was in a boiler-suit and held in his hand a scrap of cotton waste, material that appears as indispensable to engineers as stethoscopes to doctors. They glared across the bridge, playing havoc with each other's blood pressure.

'The ship's stopped,' Captain Hogg announced.

'Aye,' said McDougall. 'I know.'

'Well . . . why the devil has she stopped?'

McDougall lit his pipe.

'You tell me, Cap'n, and then we'll both know.'

'Damn it, Mr. McDougall! Can't you keep the ship going between ports?'

'Not this ship.'

'When I first came to sea engineers took their orders from the bridge. Their job was to raise steam and keep it.'

'When I first came to sea Cap'ns behaved like gentlemen.'

'I will not be spoken to like that!'

'I will speak to ye how I like.'

'I'll have you put in the log-book, Mr. McDougall!'

'I'll report ye to the Company, Cap'n.'

'I will not be obstructed by a pigheaded Scot!'

'An' I will not be told my job by an ignorant Sassenach!'

'Damn you, sir!'

'And damn you, too!'

At that moment the argument was annulled by the telegraph ringing again and the *Lotus* slowly getting under way.

'It's always like that,' the Second said. 'You know how it is. Oil and water won't mix.'

CHAPTER VII

THE voyage extended. The ship ran deeply into the Tropics and
Captain Hogg started work on his Master's Letter from Santos.
We stayed fairly peaceful until the afternoon he threw the Chief
Steward down the bridge ladder.

Whimble was the most introverted and anxious member of the
Lotus's company; and he had a strict rule on board—he never
drank. When he came to my cabin early in the voyage and I
recalled that the social formulæ of my new life demanded I
offered him a peg, he grasped his abdomen with a sigh of horror.

'Not a drop, Doctor!' he declared. 'Never touch a dram of it!'

'What, not at all?' Finding a teetotaller in the *Lotus* was like
running into a sober Scot on Burns night.

'Not for twenty years! It's my liver, Doctor.' He warily indicated the region of his umbilicus. 'I had a real bad turn in
Cardiff. Five operations and left to die three times. I need say no
more to you, need I, Doctor?'

'No, no more at all.'

'So I said to myself, "Walter," I said, "be a man! Not another
drink you're going to have till your dying day!" And not a drop's
soiled my lips since. Will-power, Doctor, that's what it is. I used
to do Pelmanism a bit when I was younger.'

When I passed this information to Hornbeam, illuminated with
admiration, he pushed his cap back on his head and roared with
laughter.

'He's right in a way, Doc,' he said. 'You'll never see him with
a glass in his hand. He keeps it in his locker, mostly. Or his hot-
water can, or under the bunk. He gets a bottle a day easy—
buckshee, of course. Pinches it from the bond-room and fiddles
the bar accounts so it's poor beggars like you and me that have to
pay for it in the end.'

'He cooks the books, does he?' I said in surprise. 'I'd have
thought he was too timid to be dishonest.'

'Don't you believe it. There isn't a chief steward afloat who wouldn't flog the funnel if he thought he could get away with it.'

I observed Whimble fairly closely after that. Once Hornbeam had given me the diagnosis it was simple to pick out the symptoms. In the early morning, when he did his round of the galley and the stores, he was a pale and nervous man who flattened himself against the bulkhead when he glimpsed Captain Hogg's threatening silhouette at the other end of the alleyway. At nine he paid his daily visit to the little bond-room below the water-line, and came up with the ship's supply of liquor. After that he went to his cabin to clean his teeth. He reappeared slightly flushed, and took his place in the inspection procession with confidence. Then he cleaned his teeth again. He found it necessary to clean his teeth before dinner, at tea-time, and on several occasions during the evening. By ten at night, when he prepared the Captain's sandwiches in the pantry, his spectacles were awry and he sang snatches of bawdy songs as he slapped on the mustard with a flourish. The end of his day was marked shortly afterwards by the flash of a bottle sailing out of his porthole, and the light splash as it hit the water and joined the others that marked, at neatly regular intervals, the progress of the Chief Steward round the world.

To restore this and other profitable discrepancies, Whimble was forced to spend several hours a day sitting in his tiny office with the store-books and a ready-reckoner, biting his pen and working out worried sums on a scrap of paper.

'Father's very hard, very hard!' he explained to me one day. 'Always chasing me up over the catering. And the Company looks at every grain of rice they give you. What d'you think they'd do if I was a pound of butter out at the end of the voyage?' He indicated the sea with his thumb. 'It would be "Out, Walter, me boy," and no mistake. I don't know how I make ends meet sometimes, really I don't.'

His problem was not so much making ends meet but arranging them to do so with a worthwhile overlap. The drawers under his bunk were filled with tins of ham, peaches, lard, tongue, and pineapple, which were ready to be slipped over the side to a furtive rowing-boat our first night in port. Tins of cigarettes were stacked behind his books in the office, and two or three bottles of whisky were locked in the glass locker with the ostentatious label FOR

ENTERTAINMENT OF CUSTOMS. 'If you're wanting any medical stores on the coast, Doc,' he confided in me when I dressed a cut on his hand one evening, 'let me have the list and we'll split the comish fifty-fifty.'

'Very kind of you, I'm sure.'

'Of course, there won't be much in it. There isn't much of anything in this hooker. In a big passenger job that's different. The Purser gets his comish on everything down to the bell-boys' tips. Why, the barman in one of those makes more than the Old Man.' He looked gratefully at his fresh bandage. 'If you want a few bottles of Scotch to flog the other end it might be arranged,' he added generously. 'I can get it ashore for you. Trust Walter. Never touch a drop of it myself, mind you.'

Whimble had justification enough for secret drinking at our expense in the Captain's table manners alone. Captain Hogg made a point of complaining at least once a meal about the menu or cooking. 'Beef!' he would exclaim, contemptuously spitting out a half-chewed morsel as big as a golf ball. 'Flea-ridden cow, more likely! Where the devil did you dig this up from, Mr. Whimble?'

'Fresh on board this trip, sir. Saw it loaded with my own eyes, if I may respectfully say so, sir.'

'I don't believe you, Mr. Whimble. You've had this in the freezer since last voyage, or I'm a Dutchman. What do you say, eh, Doctor?'

As there was no point in disagreeing with the Captain about anything I nodded sympathetically.

When he was especially enraged with a dish, Captain Hogg would lift his plate shoulder high, bellow 'Steward!' and demand, 'Throw that muck over the side and bring us a decent piece of bread and cheese.' This he would eat glaring at Whimble, in a silence broken only by the rhythmical snapping of his jaws. On other occasions he would suddenly be overcome with longings, like a pregnant woman. 'Mr. Whimble,' he would demand in the middle of a plate of liver and bacon, 'why don't we ever have any avocado pears?' Or, 'Steward! Are there any pikelets on board?'

After the meagre nourishment of my student's lodgings and the G.P.'s table the portions served in the *Lotus*'s saloon looked heavy with the threat of dyspepsia; but the sea air and the prospect of sleeping all afternoon soon led to my eating as much as anyone else, apart from Captain Hogg. The menu was conservative, like a good commercial hotel's, and ran mostly to joints and puddings. All of them were prepared with care by the First Cook, a large, soft-eyed, likeable man, who sweated among his spitting roasts in the galley whistling and basting the meat with the delight of an esteemed craftsman.

'A contented cook, Doc,' he said, 'and you gets a contented crew.' He whistled a few bars. 'Nice leg of pork cold for supper. Fond of crackling?'

'I'm glad you're contented,' I told him. 'Most of the cooks I meet ashore seem to have duodenal ulcers.'

He wiped his hands on his trousers and felt in his hip pocket.

'That's why I'm contented,' he said. He flourished a photograph of a thin simpering young woman in an off-the-shoulder dance frock. 'Sweetest little girl in the world. That's the wife.'

'You're a very lucky man.'

'Yes, Doc, I reckon I am. One of the luckiest of the lot. How'd you like a bit of dressed crab as well?' he added, glowing with bonhomie. 'I could always open a tin.'

But already, three thousand miles away, disaster was being prepared for the *Lotus's* cooking. The next afternoon Easter came to my cabin and said, 'Beg pardon, Doctor, but the Cook reckons he wants to do himself in.'

'What! You mean commit suicide?'

'That's right, Doctor. He's been on the booze since dinner, and the lads spotted him rigging up a bit of rope in his cabin.'

'Good heavens, man! Haven't you done something about it?'

'Ho, it's all right now,' Easter said calmly. 'The Bos'n slugged him and he's out cold. He'll be tame enough when he comes to. It's always the same. They never string themselves up in the end.'

'But what's the trouble?' I asked. It seemed barely credible. 'He struck me as a happy enough sort of fellow.'

'Sheilas,' Easter said with contempt. 'Drive a man to it some of them, don't they, Doctor? His wife's vamoosed with a bus-driver. Just got a cable from his pal to say so.'

'That's a bit of tough luck. He seemed to be pretty fond of her.'

'It ain't the first time it's happened by a long chalk. Cor, I've seen these bits waving good-bye to their husbands at the docks, then going home to collect the allotment, a quid a week regular, and ending up with black babies and suchlike. There ain't no depths, Doctor, what women won't stoop to. And the worse they treat the blokes the more they seem to like 'em. Mugs, ain't we?'

'Well, I think you'd better keep an eye on the Cook,' I told him. 'Perhaps I should have a chat with him—psychology, you know. I hope he won't let it interfere with his cooking.'

The next morning was Sunday. The Cook was back at work— but a sad, lonely, tuneless man. He pottered miserably round the galley, pausing every now and then to break into unexpected tears over the carrots or the boiling duff. Suddenly he would cry out startlingly, 'Rosie! Rosie! I love you!' then he would fall silent and look grimly along the edge of his carving-knife, under the terrified glance of the galley-boy who crouched over the potato-bucket.

The Sunday dinner, nevertheless, appeared on the saloon table. Rosie could not have chosen a worse day for her defection, for the menu was the longest of the week: there was always Scotch broth, boiled turbot, steak-and-kidney pie, beef, carrots, boiled and roast potatoes, and plum duff, all of which the Captain consumed steadily and usually without complaint. But that day the Cook's grief had intruded into the meal. The soup was cold, and Captain Hogg flung his spoon into the plate after the first mouthful with the command: 'Steward! Chuck this dishwater into the scupper!' The turbot was underdone, and it was barely touched by anyone. Only the steak-and-kidney pie seemed up to the usual standard. 'Give us a big helping,' the Captain growled. 'If the rest's as filthy as the soup it won't be worth eating. Call yourself a Chief Steward, Mr. Whimble? You're not fit to be in charge of an ice-cream barrow.'

He began eating his pie in silence. We were all a little bad-tempered, for Sunday dinner was pleasantly anticipated and we had prepared ourselves with extra morning gin. I watched the Captain sorting out the portions of kidney and felt thankful for the sake of our digestions that peace had fallen on the table.

Captain Hogg suddenly jumped to his feet. He held his

napkin to his mouth and his face was the colour of the port light.

'Look!' he hissed. 'Look at that!'

His finger quivered in the direction of his food. Whimble nervously stretched across the table and removed from a pile of piecrust a dental plate with three teeth attached to it.

'Oh dear!' Whimble said.

'Is it yours?' the Captain thundered.

'Oh no, sir! I've never seen it before, sir.'

Captain Hogg thrust his napkin forward.

'Put it in that!' he commanded. The teeth, in a pool of gravy, were wrapped up. 'I am taking this up to my cabin and stowing it in the safe. I am then showing it to the general manager the minute we arrive in Liverpool. By God, I'll see you pay for this, Mr. Whimble!'

Shaking his fist he left the saloon, pausing to shout an order for cold ham and pickles in his cabin. We sat in silence, the pie going cold in front of us. Whimble tried to take a drink of water, but he was shaking so much he spilled it over the cloth.

'I don't think I want any more,' Hornbeam said, pushing his plate away. 'Whose are they, Doc? Yours?'

'They're probably the Cook's. He's been a bit forgetful this morning.'

'Har!' Whimble croaked. 'The Cook!' He jumped from the table, eager to pass on his castigation. The gentle, easy-going Cook, who filched tins of ham and corned beef through Whimble's good graces, was the only person on board whom he could bully. Pausing only to clean his teeth on the way, he confidently made for the galley.

But it was a changed Cook whom he found sitting on the potato locker with a gin-bottle, crooning to himself. He saw the accident in a different light. Before Whimble could say anything he was gripped by the shirt, a chopping-knife pointed at his throat, and the Cook demanded, 'Give me my bloody teeth back!'

Whimble broke away with a shout that brought us all from the saloon. We found him running down the deck chased by the Cook, who had his knife in his hand and was wearing a frightening toothless snarl.

'Murder!' Whimble shouted.

The Cook was not steady on his feet, fell over a stay, and burst into tears. But Whimble had no time to see this. His only thoughts were of self-protection, and he decided the unpleasantness represented by Captain Hogg was less than that embodied in the Cook. He jumped up the ladder leading to the bridge and hammered on the door of the Captain's cabin.

'Help!' he cried. 'Save me!'

The door was flung open.

'What the blazes is the matter with you?'

'Look,' said Whimble, pointing behind him.

'Are you mad?'

'The Cook's after me with a knife!' he whimpered, calming at the sight of Captain Hogg. 'He wants his teeth back.'

'Teeth! Teeth! Did you say teeth? Get off my bridge!'

'He'll murder me!'

'Get off my bridge, damn you!'

'Give me the Cook's teeth first!'

Captain Hogg picked Whimble up by his shirt collar and gave him a push. He uttered a little squeal as he lost his balance at the top of the ladder and came sliding down feet first. At that moment the steward was mounting it with the Captain's tray of ham and pickles.

'There goes our supper,' Hornbeam said gloomily. After that no one thought it worth while finishing the meal.

CHAPTER VIII

THE next morning my professional tranquillity was split like an old sail in a storm.

I had settled down in my cabin after breakfast to read *War and Peace*, with which I first killed three or four cockroaches, when Easter came in. He showed me a new card trick and described the occasion when he was steward on a Greek tramp and had won from the skipper, an incorrigible but luckless gambler, as a final stake one night in the Mediterranean the exclusive services of his stout but agreeable wife until Gibraltar.

'There's something, Doctor,' Easter went on. 'One of the crew took queer in the night.'

'What's wrong with him?'

'Vomiting and suchlike. Shall I chase him up here?'

'I think we'd better pay a domiciliary visit.'

The patient was a young deckhand. He was lying on his bunk, holding his abdomen and groaning.

'Good morning,' I said briskly, taking his pulse. 'What's the trouble?'

'Aw, cripes! I got the bellyache something horrid.'

'Just let me have a look at the—er, stomach.'

He stretched himself on his back. I reached out a hand and felt the right-hand quadrant of his abdomen. Immediately I felt as if I had eaten a bunch of safety-pins and they had all opened inside at once.

I dragged Easter outside the door and shut it.

'Easter,' I said hoarsely. 'This man has acute appendicitis.'

'Cor!'

'This is urgent. How far are we out of Santos?'

'About two days, the Mate reckons.'

'Well, we must make land before then and put the poor chap in hospital. I'll go up and see the Captain.'

Captain Hogg had just got out of his bath. He stood in his slippers with a towel round him, looking at me like Bligh offering

Christian the cheese. I could appreciate that it was one of his gastric mornings.

'Well?'

'Er—good morning, sir.'

'Good morning!'

'Could you do twice the speed you are, sir?'

'What!'

He jumped so violently he shook drops of water from his chest on to the carpet.

'I mean—you see, sir, one of the crew has developed acute appendicitis. He will have to be operated on as soon as possible. I understand from the engineers that it is possible for the vessel to make a few more knots, and I thought . . .'

Captain Hogg sat down on the edge of his desk. He gave a sharp tug to his left ear, as though pulling the pin out of a Mills bomb.

'For every knot above the cruising speed of my ship,' he began quietly, 'the bill for fuel oil practically doubles itself. What do you think the Company would have to say? Eh?' He banged the desk. 'Operate, Doctor, operate!' he shouted. 'What do you think I pay you for?'

'Yes, sir,' I said.

I recognized at once that the Captain's advice on therapy had obvious drawbacks. In the first place, I had a meagre idea of how to remove an appendix. A medical qualification is like a marriage licence—it gives you official permission to go ahead, but it doesn't guarantee you know enough to tackle all the difficulties after the honeymoon. I had diligently attended the operating theatre in my hospital, but there were always so many students present whenever the surgeons removed an appendix that all I usually saw of the operation were the boils on the neck of the man in front of me.

The second difficulty was equipment. Although appendices have reportedly been removed by second mates with bent spoons and a bos'n's knife, I felt that my academic inhibitions made it impossible for me to operate skilfully with the products of an ironmonger's shop. Thirdly, there was professional assistance. Easter was an admirable character for whom I had a sincere admiration as a man of the world, but when it came to dabbling in clinical medicine he was as dangerous as an unlabelled bottle of strychnine.

I called him into my cabin.

'Easter,' I said earnestly, 'have you seen a case of acute appendicitis before?'

'Ho, yes, Doctor. Every time I eats pickles I'm reminded of it.'

'Pickles?'

'That's right, Doctor. I was on the Western Ocean run at the time. The old Doc was scared to operate, so he puts the patient in the ship's hospital and tells me to keep him on a light diet, see. That night I goes along and asks if there's anything he wants, like, before I turn in, and the patient says to me "Yes," he says, "I should like just a few pickles." "Pickles!" I says. "You can't have no pickles! Don't be barmy! The doctor would have me over the side if I was to give you pickles. We of the medical fraternity don't reckon pickles is a light diet. Not for 'arf a minute we don't," I says.'

'Well, the next morning I brings him 'is breakfast—two poached eggs done special—and when I goes to shake him—Cor! He was cold to the touch. Them pickles was his last wish, Doctor, and I refused him. Sad, ain't it?'

'Quite so, Easter,' I said. 'Let's have a little less of your reminiscences and a little more action. We must operate on this man before sundown. Do you realize what that means? We must strip the hospital, scrub it out with antiseptic, rig up some lights and an operating table, and find some instruments from somewhere. Savvy?'

'Very good, Doctor. We of the fraternity always rises to the occasion, as they say.'

'Well, start rising.'

He hesitated.

'If I might be so bold, Doctor . . .'

'Yes?'

'Perhaps it might make things go a little easier if you and me was to have a bit of the medical comforts to start with.'

I clapped him gratefully on the shoulder.

'Capital idea, Easter. Reach down the bottle from my locker.'

'How's it going?' I asked.

'It's bloody 'ot.'

'What's the temperature?'

He got up and inspected the thermometer in the corner.

'Hundred and six,' he said.

'Can't you put the forced draught on?'

'Blows soot in.'

'Oh, all right. We'll have to put up with it, I suppose. How have you got on with the operating table?'

He had a wooden trestle table along one bulkhead, which he set up proudly. It left just enough room on either side for the pair of us.

'I got it off Chippy,' he said. 'He uses it for mixing the paints on.'

'It's better than nothing. If you scrub it hard enough it'll be reasonably sterile.'

As I spoke, two large, rusty drops fell from a pipe crossing the deckhead on the spot where the operation wound would be.

'Damnation! Can't you do anything to stop that?'

Easter shook his head.

'Been like it for years. It's a job for the shore engineers, that is.'

'Well, you'll have to fix up some sort of screen. Have we got any dressings and gloves, and so forth?'

'There was some in the locker. Seem to have been there since the war.'

'Get them sterilized in the galley. How about instruments? What have you found?'

Easter pulled two handfuls of metal objects from his trouser pockets.

'I've been on the scrounge,' he explained. 'I thought these would come in handy, like.'

I looked at his booty, which he spread on the table. There was a pair of pliers, two saloon forks, a packet of darning needles labelled 'A Sailor's Friend,' some paper-clips, a stiletto, a potato knife, a pair of tweezers, a surgical scalpel, and a uterine curette.

'You'd better sterilize the lot,' I said gloomily. 'Except the pliers. Shouldn't there be a set of surgical instruments on board?'

226

'They seem to have disappeared, Doctor.'

'You mean you flogged them?' He scratched his nose guiltily. 'There's nothing for it but to use what we've got,' I told him crossly. 'I damn well hope you get an appendix, too!'

I went out on deck. I needed some fresh air. The day was already becoming too much for me.

Outside the hospital I found Chippy. He was sitting on the deck with a hatch cover—a thick piece of wood about six feet by two used in rows to cover the hatches. He was polishing it carefully with emery paper.

'Hello, Chips,' I said. 'Getting everything shipshape for Santos?'

He looked up at me gloomily.

'He'll slide off this lovely,' he said.

'Who will?'

'Why—'im down there.' He pointed aft with his thumb. 'The poor bloke what's for the knife. Slide off it like a wet fish, he will,' he added with relish.

I was perplexed.

'What's he want to slide off a hatch cover for?' I asked.

'Why, when they buries 'im, of course.' He gave it another rub. 'Lot of work I've put in on this 'ere 'atch cover.'

'Now, look here, Chippy. What gives you the idea my patient's going to die?'

'Oh, they always does. I've seen five appendicitises at sea. 'Ad their time, every one of 'em. Over the wall they went on a 'atch cover.'

I stamped off in disgust. I felt I had been professionally insulted. I climbed the bridge ladder angrily to report the Carpenter's pessimism to one of the Mates. There I found the Second moodily sorting out flags.

'What ho, Doc,' he said. 'When's the carve-up?'

'In about an hour.'

'Think that ensign'll do?'

'Do? What for?'

'Why, in case—in case of accidents. To cover the body.'

'There isn't going to be any body, damn you!'

'Well, Father told us to take precautions. Means a lot of work

227

for all hands, Doc. It'll be a shame if they're all disappointed now.'

I admit that they do give one an excellent funeral at sea. The properties are traditionally adapted from the ship's gear and the routine is prescribed as firmly as that for entering and leaving port. As soon as the body is available it is turned over to the bos'n, who sews it up in canvas with half a dozen firebars from the galley. For this he receives a bottle of whisky. Meanwhile, the Carpenter has been polishing and attaching rope handles to a hatch cover, and the quartermasters have been pressing their best uniforms. The ceremony is held at sunset or sunrise on the same day, because ships spend most of their time in tropical waters and the performance might be marred by the corpse if it became aggressively high. The vessel stops, a rail is taken away from the side, and the ship's officers, including the abashed Doctor, line up with the Captain. Caps are removed, and at the appropriate moment the body is marched to the rails on the hatch cover by the quartermasters—who receive a bottle of whisky between them for their services—and smartly tipped overboard. The Mate, who has charge of all deck stores including flags, at the same time edges himself down to the rail and grabs the ensign—which costs the Company money—before it slips into the sea with its bundle. The ship then starts again and everyone goes off for an obituary peg.

'I should hate to spoil your fun,' I said coldly, 'but this patient is going to walk off the ship in Liverpool.'

I returned into the hospital, where Easter was boiling the instruments over a Primus stove.

'Everyone thinks there's going to be a funeral,' I said. 'I never heard such nonsense.'

'Ho, yes,' Easter remarked calmly. 'That's why I couldn't fit a screen under that there pipe as you said. Bos'n says he's got to keep all his spare canvas for the shroud.'

'But it's monstrous!'

Easter chuckled over the steaming instruments.

'Cor, I've seen some funny funerals at sea! Remember one we had in the Indian Ocean. Chinaman it was. Got knifed. Blimey, we pushed him overboard all right, but he wouldn't sink. Bobbed about like a buoy. The Old Man wasn't 'arf flummoxed. In the end we had to leave him to it. Couldn't pull him out again, could we? Probably still bobbing about somewhere, if the sharks ain't got him.'

'I'm going to see the patient,' I said sternly. 'Get everything ready in an hour's time.'

The patient was sitting in his cabin eating fish and chips and drinking a bottle of beer.

'What the devil's this!' I shouted. 'I thought I told you to have nothing by mouth?'

'Oh, sorry, Doc,' he said awkwardly. 'But seeing I was feeling so much better like, I thought I could do with a bit of grub.'

'Better, man! How dare you say you're better! That's for me to decide. You only think you're better. You've got an acute appendix inside you.'

He pulled a fish bone out of his mouth repentantly.

'There's just one thing, Doc,' he said respectfully. 'Do people often get this appendix taken out twice.'

'Twice? What do you mean?'

'Well, I had it taken out the first time in Birkenhead when I was six . . .'

I sprang at him and pulled up his shirt. A faint, white two-inch scar. I started to laugh.

*   *   *   *   *

'Not operating, Doctor? Why?' Captain Hogg demanded.

'I've charmed it away, sir,' I explained. 'A trick I learnt in infancy from a gypsy.'

CHAPTER IX

WE arrived at Santos in the early afternoon. As we slowed down to approach the river mouth between the deep green hills the shore heat hit us like the blast from the engine-room hatchway.

'It'll be nice and cosy alongside,' Easter said gloomily.

We sailed up the greasy river between the rows of ships tied thickly along each bank, the ensign of the United States of Brazil flying in courtesy from our foremast. Hornbeam went to his station forrard, and Archer took the Lamptrimmer and his gang of deckhands aft. The tugs came up, the mooring ropes flew out, and we were pushed into place as neatly as a well-parked car. The gangway rattled down and a section of the rail was pulled away: we had arrived.

But we were still flying the yellow Q flag, indicating we were in quarantine. A troop of stout Brazilian customs and health officials immediately tramped aboard, headed by an important-looking man in a white suit whom I took to be the Doctor.

I saluted.

'Boa dia, senhor,' I said in carefully incubated Portuguese.

He held out his hand.

'Afternoon, old boy,' he replied. 'How's tricks?'

'Very well, thank you.'

'Nothing infectious?'

'No.'

'Haul down the yellow peril, then. Can you let me have a few hundred English cigarettes?'

Once the quarantine flag was down people came aboard like Navy Week visitors on a Bank Holiday. There were policemen, stevedores, money-changers, ship chandlers, water purveyors, fruit sellers, harbourmasters, launderers—and the agents. The agents were the men in charge of the Fathom Line's business in Santos, and could get any commodity at short notice from five thousand tons of oil to a new bell for the ship's cat. They were a pair of tall genial Englishmen with minds like efficiently arranged shopping lists.

'Hello, Doc,' one said. 'Want any medical stores?'

'Chief Steward's got the list.'

'Good. You've taken over from Flowerday, have you? He was a rum bird. Coming to have a peg?'

'Not just now.'

'Fair enough. By the way, there's some mail for you somewhere.'

I had forgotten that the agents look after the ship's mail. I went out on deck and found most of it had been distributed. All over the ship men were leaning on uncomfortable steel corners reading their letters. I passed the Carpenter, who had several closely written sheets in his hand and kept saying 'No! It can't be! It can't be!' to himself. I hoped it was nothing serious.

'Coo!' one man shouted. 'I've 'ad a baby!'

'I've 'ad six,' his companion said morosely, not looking up. This nonplussed the new father.

'Wot, all at once?' he asked.

I ran into Whimble.

'Letter for you, Doc,' he said. 'I gave it to Easter.'

I suddenly felt excited. I had forgotten England and home in the past three weeks as efficiently as a patient with amnesia. My past seemed a disconnected existence. All at once I felt a letter would be like a familiar face in a big crowd.

I saw Easter leaning on the rail and hurried towards him. I wondered who it was from. Wendy, perhaps? Telling me she was crying over my picture and reading Conrad? From my principal, genially wishing me a good voyage? Or my parents, asking where I'd put the keys of the garage? From old classmates envious of my double release? I didn't care. It was a letter, a letter. Whoever sent it proved the most important thing in the world—I was not forgotten.

I took the envelope from Easter. I couldn't recognize the handwriting. I tried to open it with dignity, but excitedly tore the flap. It said: '*The —— Laundry. Dear Sir, If you do not collect your washing within seven days of this date it will be sold to defray charges.*'

I tossed it into the dock. I leant on the rail and looked at the unfamiliar colours, the dirty yellow sheds, the strange un-English mountains in the background with the white road wriggling up them to São Paulo, the dusky lounging men and slim graceful women on the wharfside, the signs in Portuguese, the odd open tramcar behind, the surprising uniforms of the police, the glare of the unaccustomed sun . . . I realized tardily I was on another side of the world.

* * * * *

After conditioning myself to the exclusive company of my ship-mates for three weeks I found the rush of locals on board un-settling. The silence of the sea passage was broken by the noise of the winches, and the bare decks became littered with hatch covers, wires, tarpaulins, pieces of dropped cargo, and resting Brazilians. The Brazilians have a great capacity for rest. When they have nothing to do for a few minutes they see no point in continuing to support the burden of keeping awake and fling themselves into the nearest piece of shade. Whether they are lying on a stone wharf, the top of a couple of packing-cases, or some pieces of scrap metal does not appear to detract from the enjoyment.

The cargo came out by the exact reverse of the technique that put it in at Liverpool. As I had nothing else to do I joined Easter, who was watching crates of machinery being drawn out of number five hatch with the pleasantly indolent air of a Londoner observing road excavations.

'Hope you've locked your cabin, Doctor,' he said. 'And screwed up the port. These boys would pinch the soles off your shoes if you wasn't careful.'

I pointed towards the policemen on the gangway.

'But don't they keep an eye on it?'

'What, them vigilantes? Them's the worst of the lot.'

As the winches paused I heard feminine giggles and zestful screams coming from the crew's quarters in the poop. A plump dark girl with a basket of washing under her arm appeared on the deck, struggling formally with a large sailor.

'That's Maria,' Easter explained. 'She does your laundry for

232

you. Three blokes got something off her last trip.'

'What!'

'Wouldn't mind having a go at her myself,' he continued solemnly. 'They don't seem to think much of things like that out here. All the girls is tender-hearted. I reckon it's the climate.'

'It all seems very unhygienic to me, to say the least.'

'Mind you, some of 'em's real smashers. Ho, I've had some fun here, I have. You going ashore to-night, Doctor?'

'I might stretch my legs. Though I fear I shall do nothing more exciting than go to the pictures.'

'Ah, you can get some queer pictures out here too,' Easter went on. 'Pal of mine went ashore one night to have his pleasure, as you might say, and the next day he went off with a crowd of the lads to one of them odd picture houses. Blimey, he was the big feature. Didn't 'arf get his leg pulled about it.'

'I think I will go and see Mr. Hornbeam,' I said. Santos sounded a place that would have provided Easter with extensive reminiscences.

Hornbeam's cabin was as full as a compartment in a suburban train in the rush-hour. There were the agents, the chief stevedores, the customs, the immigration officers, and a few unidentifiable officials. Hornbeam was sitting with his white shirt undone to the waist, looking pleased with himself. His table was filled with bottles of gin, whisky, and beer, and half a dozen open tins of Player's. Everyone was helping themselves.

'Come in, Doc!' he called. 'Have a peg. This is our Doctor, gentlemen.'

'How do you do,' I said, taking a glass.

'It's always open house in the Mate's cabin in port,' Hornbeam explained, pouring himself another gin. 'Everyone wants the poor bloody Mate. Now what about this trouble in number three?' he said to the head stevedore. 'Can you get another gang on there to-night?'

'To-morrow morning, Mister Mate. To-night, no good.'

'We'll have to put up with it, I suppose.'

He took a sheaf of papers from a ragged Brazilian who appeared in the doorway.

'Cargo plans? All right. Have a peg, chum. Coming ashore to-night, Doc?' he added to me.

'I thought of it. Are you?'

'Certainly I am. Never been ashore in Santos yet. To-night I am. We'll collect here about midnight. . . .'

'Midnight?'

'There's no point in going anywhere before eleven in this part of the world. Nothing livens up before twelve.'

'If that's the case I think I'd better turn in for a bit.'

'That's the idea, Doc. You're in the land of siesta now, don't forget. God, it's hot, isn't it?'

* * * * *

I screwed the closely meshed wire-netting in the porthole to keep the flies out and went to sleep. The Second woke me up about nine.

'Coming ashore,' he asked. 'We're going up to the Mate's cabin. They sting you for drinks in Brazil so we reckoned we'd get a glow on us before we went off.'

I sat up and rubbed the sweat off me with a sheet.

'I'll be up when I've had a shower. The Mate's coming with us, isn't he?'

Archer laughed.

'I wouldn't know about that. I've never seen him get ashore anywhere yet.'

When I reached the Mate's cabin I saw at once that he had not been taking a siesta himself. His visitors had gone and the bottles were empty. He sat behind a jumble of dirty glasses and cigarette-ends, humming absently to himself.

' 'Lo, Doc,' he said languidly. 'Fetch a bottle out of the locker there. I'm coming ashore with you young lads to-night. Keep you out of trouble, eh? Muy bien. Cheerio.'

Archer and Trail were in the cabin, dressed in their shore-going rig. The scattered places in which they bought their clothes and their over-compensation for wearing uniform most of their lives gave them a startling appearance. Trail was particularly arresting. He wore a pair of green cotton trousers he had bought

234

in Rio, a yellow shirt from Calcutta, the sort of sports coat that is, fortunately, popular only on the Australian beaches, suède shoes from Ceylon, and a tie with a luminous girl on it from New York.

We all sat down and drank determinedly.

'Have to drink beer ashore,' Trail said. 'A gin costs about twelve bob. I got some cruzeiros for you, Doc.' He handed me a bundle of dirty notes. 'That's the sub you put in for. How about you, Mr. Hornbeam?'

'Got some in the kitty,' he said thickly.

He pulled a tin out of his locker and spilt the contents on the table. There was currency from all over the world—Australian florins, South African sixpences, nickels and quarters, escudos and francs, Canadian dollars, Japanese yen, New Zealand pounds, rupees, pesos, pesetas, and guilders, a few marks, and a couple of Pitcairn Island postage stamps.

'Always like to have a bit of ready cash,' he explained, rummaging through the pile. 'No cruzeiros, though. What's this?' He held up a coin and squinted at it. 'Springbok ha'penny. No good. I'll take the dollars ashore and flog 'em. Don't you blokes go without me,' he added threateningly. 'I'll get a cob on if you don't wait. Where are we bound for, anyway? Have another peg.'

The Third drew a small book from his pocket and turned over to the letter S.

'Santos . . .' he said. 'Oh, that's fixed. We'll take the Doc to the Whores' Ball.'

'The what did you say?' I asked.

'The Whores' Ball. Funniest thing this side of the Line. It doesn't start till midnight. We'll look into the Ritz Bar first.'

'I want to see the Bidu Bar,' Archer added. 'I met a hot bit of blonde in there last time.'

'You game, Doc?'

By this time my critical faculties were mildly blunted with gin.

'Game? Of course I'm game. I'm a sailor, aren't I?'

'That's the spirit!' Trail said. 'Down the hatch, lads, and let's get moving. It's after eleven.'

'What about the Mate?' I asked. I turned to look at him. He was lying with his head in a pool of currency, asleep.

'It's always the same with the Mate,' Archer explained. 'He never makes it. Hasn't been ashore for years. It's best to leave him there until he wakes up. Now for the bright lights!' Trail put down his glass. 'Come on, Doc!'

Singing softly we filed down the gangway and, slightly intoxicated, for the first time in my life I put foot on foreign soil.

CHAPTER X

THERE are few attractive cities in Brazil, and Santos is not one of them. In the centre is a fairly pleasant square with gardens in it, a new post office, and the Town Hall. It would pass for a little bastion of bourgeoisie in the South of France on a hot day. But the waterfront caters, efficiently, for different tastes. It is a tall line of buildings on a cobbled street that looks like the slums in Glasgow draped with neon.

The Third led us jauntily towards a lighted doorway with RITZ BAR—DRINKS AND GIRLS shining over it.

'Here we go, lads!' he said. 'If our mothers could see us now!'

The three of us piled inside and took a table by the door. It was a long room, brightly lit, with a bar down one side, a small dance floor, and a band. The walls were lined with foreign flags and signs such as WELCOMES TO OUR BRITISH FRIENDS, HAVE A SWELL TIME BABY, and WE TAKE POUNDS AND DOLLARS. The room was full, but not with Brazilians. There seemed to be sailors there from every country with a seaboard. There were stiff blond Swedes and Norwegians, a crowd of drunk Greeks in the corner, some Dutchmen, a pack of Frenchmen arguing with Spaniards, blank-faced masticating Americans, and a good many small dark-eyed dangerous-looking men of unplaceable nationality. By the door, stroking his long moustache, stood a nervous Brazilian policeman.

'I say!' I exclaimed. I stared at the place like a child brought up to Town to see the lights. 'It looks a bit tough, doesn't it?'

'The Santos waterfront is the toughest in the world,' Archer said lightly. 'That's why we're sitting near the door. If anything starts don't wait to see what it's all about, but hop it. They have a habit of arresting everyone in sight down here. Ever been in jail?'

'Not yet.'

'This isn't the place to start. I got pinched two years ago for being drunk. They let me go next morning, luckily. Had to rub shoulders with some pretty queer birds. None of this single cell and bath business you get in Britain.'

A Brazilian girl, dark and rounded, in a black dress and a decorative lace apron, came upon us.

'Três cerveja,' Trail said.

'Sure, baby.'

She strolled off, giving us the benefit of her hips.

'She brings the beer,' Trail explained. 'If you like you can dance with her. Look over there.'

There were about twenty of the girl's colleagues in the room, all similarly dressed. I watched one at the table next to ours being asked for a dance by an American, who used the technique of slapping her on the bottom and grabbing her arm as she passed. The girl smiled acquiescence, and they took the floor.

The band played only sambas and rumbas. The polite versions of these dances produced in London restaurants have the same relationship to Santos sambas as vintage Burgundy to raw apple-jack. Similarly with the dancing. The Brazilian girls, though languid in daytime, come to life like flashing electric signs at nightfall. Not only do they dance lustily, but they do so without any inhibitions whatever. If any couple in London were seen performing in the manner accepted as normally sociable in Brazil, they would be immediately asked to leave.

The girl brought our beers and opened them. Trail handed her a hundred-cruzeiro note and pinched her bottom. She grinned at him. I wondered what would have happened if he had tried the same technique in a Lyons' teashop.

'Don't reckon we'll stay here long,' Trail said. 'It's getting on. How do you like Brazilian beer?'

'It tastes like soapy water to me.'

'It carries a kick in it somewhere. Finish it up, we've got to look in at the Bidu.'

'Saw a chap get killed outside there last trip,' Archer said to me.

The Bidu Bar was exactly the same as the Ritz except that the signs round the walls were in Portuguese and the girls were fatter.

We didn't stay long. We had a couple more beers and left. Trail rubbed his hands. 'And now,' he said, 'for the Whores' Ball.'

The function to which Trail was so attracted was held on the top floor of an old building on one of the side streets. We could hear the music, the inescapable samba, blaring down the street from the open windows before we turned the corner. The way in was through a narrow door with TAXI DANCING painted over the top of it and up a long, narrow, unbroken flight of stairs. At the foot of the stairs was a ticket office, inside which a fat man in his vest was barred up like the Crown jewels.

We paid, and mounted the staircase. At the top were two solemn policemen, who immediately advanced on us. Archer's remarks about the carelessness of the police in arresting people flashed into my mind. I jumped nervously and began to walk backwards down the stairs.

'Don't be alarmed,' Archer said. 'In England you leave your hat and coat, don't you?'

By that time a policeman had grabbed hold of me, pulled aside my arms, and searched me for weapons. I caught sight of a table behind him that explained Archer's remarks. On it was neatly arranged a collection of revolvers, knives, blackjacks, knuckle-dusters, and razors.

'The Brazilian likes going around with a bit of cutlery in his belt,' Trail explained. 'Makes him feel big. Unfortunately he tends to be a bit on the excited side. These cops sometimes miss a knife or two, so we'd better keep near the windows. Don't mind a jump, do you?'

We went inside. Three girls immediately came up to us and told us they loved us. Trail waved them aside. 'We came to hear the music,' he told them affably.

We strode across the floor and sat down. It was bigger than the American Bar and had more space for dancing. The walls were bare of any decoration and the floor was rough boards polished only by the customers' feet. There were tables scattered round the floor, and girls scattered round the tables. The atmosphere was like a laundry with a breakdown in the ventilating system.

At one end was the band—on a platform six feet above the floor, and surrounded by barbed wire.

'What's the barricade for?' I asked.

'If they dislike the music here they don't hide their feelings,' Trail explained.

'What about all these girls? What do they do?'

'If you pay fifty cruzeiros you'll find out.'

'Oh, I see. Let's have some beer.'

We sat and drank and watched the dancing. It was the sort that Trail described as 'the bumps and grinds.' I looked nervously at men sitting at the other tables, with an expectant sensation between my shoulder-blades. When they saw a girl they fancied they grabbed her and joined the jactitating couples on the floor. After the dance they either went off with her, dragged her back to their own tables, or left her, according to the strength of their inclination. I saw a party of our Liverpool greasers in the corner, their shirts unbuttoned and outside their trousers, throwing Merseyside witticisms at their neighbours. Everyone seemed to be having a good time.

A warm brunette descended on my knee.

'Hallo, darling!' she said. 'You come wit' me?'

'No!'

She laughed and ruffled my hair.

'You dance wit' me, no?'

'Go on, Doc,' Archer called. 'Give the girls a treat.'

'But I can't dance.'

'Come on, darling,' said the girl. She snatched hold of me and pulled me out of my chair. Then she clapped me to her bosom like a belladonna plaster and pushed me on the dance floor.

We jostled with the rest of the dancers. It was like being lashed to an upholstered pneumatic drill. I struggled round in her clammy embrace, trying to keep my feet, wriggling out of other men's way, and reflecting that I was a long way from home.

When the music stopped I disengaged myself and looked for our table. By this time the Third was talking earnestly to a thin, brown girl who had taken my chair.

'Thirty cruzeiros,' he said forcefully. 'Trinta. See?' He held up three fingers.

She shook her head. 'No!' she insisted. 'Cincoenta. Fifty, fifty, fifty!'

'Oh hell,' the Third said. 'Let's get out of here.'

We trooped down the stairs. 'Where now?' Archer asked when we were in the street.

'Madame Mimi's,' Trail said with finality. 'It's the only place where you can get a decent bottle of beer in town.'

'I think I'm going back to the ship,' I said.

'Come on, Doc! You don't have to sample the goods. Besides you'd get knifed walking back alone. Where is it, Second? Somewhere near the Rua Bittencourt, I think . . .'

He led us along threatening unlighted streets, where the pedestrians shuffled guiltily in the shadows like large rats.

'I think this is the number,' he said, stopping by the heavy door of an unlighted house. 'You fellows stay here and I'll go and see.'

He jumped up the steps and rang the bell. After a minute or so I saw him jab it again. The door opened. An old woman with her hair tied in a handkerchief stood against the inside light.

'Boa noite, senhora,' Trail began. He held a conversation in Portuguese with her, and I saw that he spoke the language rapidly and with great force, but unintelligibly. After he had delivered a string of sentences embellished heavily with gestures she held up a finger and disappeared to fetch help. A tall man in a dressing-gown came back with her. After a few words he pushed the Third abruptly down the steps, delivered a few hostile sentences, and slammed the door.

'Wrong place,' Trail explained, picking himself up. 'That seems to be the dentist's. It must be the house on the other corner.'

At the next door we were received with pleasure and shown immediately into the parlour.

Madame Mimi's was a sedate establishment. The parlour was furnished in the austere, grubby style popular with the Continental middle-class; it was a large apartment with big shuttered windows, containing several small tables and a larger one in the corner where Madame sat with three or four of her charges. On a dark, broken sideboard down one side were two unlighted candelabras, a sickly-looking plant, and a radio. Round the walls were pictures of the saints. Business was poor, and the room was quiet and inactive. One felt one had called on the vicar's daughters for tea.

Madame immediately recognized my companions and greeted them warmly.

'Ah, hello, my little boys! Back so soon, eh? How goes it in cold England?'

She embraced the two of them. She was a big, over-powdered woman in a black dress, with a figure like a thawing snowman.

'Not so dusty,' Archer said. 'Meet one of our shipmates.'

We embraced.

'Madame is a wonderful character,' Trail explained. 'Hails from France originally. She built up her own team here like a football manager.'

'Now, boys,' Madame said. 'You would like some beer, no?'

'Lay it on, Madame,' Archer said, sitting down and slapping his knee. 'Lay on everything.'

Madame clapped her hands.

'Is that little girl Dina still here?' Trail asked.

Our hostess shrugged her shoulders powerfully.

'She is gone. She married a gentleman from São Paulo.'

'Well, he hasn't done badly,' Trail observed. 'Let's have a look at the latest talent.'

Madame's assistant brought the tall green beer bottles and glasses, and three girls came over to sit with us. They were pretty girls—slim, dainty, smiling, glowing with co-operation.

'Americano?' asked the one next to me eagerly.

'No. Ingles.'

'Cigarette?' she asked, as winsomely as a schoolgirl appealing for pocket money. I gave her one, which she put carefully in her handbag. She began to stroke the back of my neck. I clasped my hands in front of me and stared defensively at the opposite wall.

'I lof you,' she said.

We sat like that for some time. Meanwhile, Trail and Archer had their girls on their knees and were conducting a conversation in a mixture of English, Portuguese, and giggles.

'You come with me?' the girl asked, playfully pulling a hair from my neck.

'No,' I said. 'I—I não gostar, or whatever it is. Nothing doing. Go and talk to my amigos. . . .'

I looked round and saw Trail and Archer disappearing up the stairs leading to the operational portion of the building.

'Hey!' I called, jumping up. 'Don't you fellows leave me!'

'It's all right, Doc. We won't be long,' Trail called over his shoulder. 'Finish the beer for us.'

I sat down gloomily and bit my lip, feeling like a warning to young men. The girl, discouraged, got up and left me. I took my handkerchief out and wiped my forehead.

But Madame, ever solicitous, assumed immediately that my companion had for some reason not pleased me. She directed a large grinning blonde to take her place.

'No, no!' I said in alarm. 'No! Please . . . go away, there's a good girl.'

'Não?'

'No. Sorry and all that.'

I looked uncomfortably round me. I wanted to get out. But I didn't know the way back to the ship, and I was scared to walk out of the place on my own. I took a gulp of beer and sat biting my thumbnail.

I was hardly aware that another had joined me. She sat quietly beside me without speaking. I looked up. She was sitting demurely with her hands clasped in her lap, as pathetic as a wallflower at a village dance.

'Hop it! Vamos! Pronto!' I told her.

'Please . . . please!' she said.

'My dear young lady, I have no intention . . .'

Two tears rolled compellingly down her thin cheeks.

'Please come,' she urged softly. 'No one come with me this week. If you no come I get fired.'

I licked my lips. This was the sort of dilemma even Big White Carstairs would have had difficulty sorting out.

She laid a hand on my arm, as softly as an alighting butterfly.

'Please come,' she whispered.

243

I coughed, and ran my finger round my collar. My conscience strained to suppress my sense of gallantry. Just then two large tears followed the first.

'How much?' I heard. It was me.

'Hun'red cruzeiro.'

'Oh . . . ah . . . very well then . . .'

I pulled the note from my pocket. Seizing it, she pulled me by the hand towards the staircase of sin.

We went into a bare room that contained only a bed, a basin, and several more pictures of the saints. She locked the door. I stood and scratched my left ear.

Deftly, as though peeling a banana, she stripped off her clothes. She jumped on the bed and gave me an inviting smile. Suddenly she held her right side and groaned.

'Hello,' I said, immediately interested. 'What's the trouble?'

She bit her lip for a moment, then said, 'Nada . . . nada.'

'Have you got a pain? Er—dor?'

She nodded.

'Where?'

She pointed under her right ribs.

'That's curious,' I said. 'Just let me have a look a minute, will you? By Jove, this is unusual . . . Deep breath, now.'

After five minutes' careful examination of her abdomen I concluded that the young lady was suffering from inflammation of the gall-bladder.

'Look here,' I said, 'you ought to go to hospital.'

She smiled up at me from the pillow.

'Hospital . . . operaçao, or whatever it is.'

I indicated with signs.

'Oh, não,' she said.

'Oh, yes,' I said firmly. 'Here'—I took a pencil and paper from my pocket and wrote on it—'you take that to the chemist—farmacêutico—and they'll give you something to make it better. Then you must go to hospital, see? O.K.?'

She took the prescription and grinned.

'Very well,' I said automatically, 'call me if you have any severe pain during the night. Good evening.'

I let myself out. Trail and Archer were waiting downstairs.

'Come on, you dirty old man,' Trail said, grabbing my arm. 'Time to get back to the ship.'

It occurred to me that was the only consultation I had ever paid for.

CHAPTER XI

THE next morning I woke, sweating and penitent, in my un-ventilated cabin. Jumbled harbour sounds replaced our usual noiseless morning at sea, and the steam winches were already working in frantic bursts on the deck outside. There were foot-steps and shouting all over the ship, and when I turned over for my watch I saw an unknown, half-naked Brazilian picking his teeth and solemnly inspecting me from the open cabin door. As I shaved I reflected sharply on the change in my recreations in the last four weeks.

At breakfast I found Archer and Trail as unruffled as if they had spent the evening in a suburban cinema.

'I hear you had a bit of a lash-up last night,' Hornbeam said. 'Have a good time in Mimi's?'

'One must see how the other half lives,' I murmured.

'She was a nice little piece you got hold of,' Trail said, in a complimentary tone. 'Wouldn't have minded her myself.'

Hornbeam, who had an unphysiological resilience to alcohol, nodded as he ate his way with relish through a dish of bacon, chops, eggs, and liver.

'Sorry I couldn't come with you blokes,' he said cheerfully. 'I reckon I was tired. The quartermaster put me in my bunk about three.'

'This is not much of a place, anyway,' Trail said. 'Not a patch on B.A.'

'They've cleaned up B.A. a lot now,' Archer added, with dis-appointment. 'Do you remember Underneath the Arches, Mr. Hornbeam? A string of them running down behind a sort of colonnade affair from the Boca practically to the Plaza de Majo. They had a purity campaign down there after the war.'

'They needed it,' Hornbeam said, reaching for the tomato sauce. 'Any more bacon going, Steward? I get peckish in port.'

'What are you doing to-day, Doc?' Archer asked. 'Going ashore?'

'I was thinking of it.'

'What, going back for an encore?' Trail said.

'No, I assure you I was only thinking of a hair-cut.'

'You're right there, Doc,' Hornbeam said. 'You look like an old rope fender.'

My hair had last been cut in the wintery twilight of a London afternoon, more than a month ago: now it overhung my newly sunburned ears, and its length reflected our distance from home. But I was reluctant to step ashore alone, for the only Portuguese I was confident of saying was 'Good morning,' and I was not in the position to refuse a shampoo, singeing, scalp massage, hot towels, and any unusual luxuries that might be provided by Brazilian barbers' shops. I explained this to Easter during surgery, and he immediately relieved my difficulties.

'I should be very glad to oblige, Doctor,' he said with dignity. 'If requested.'

'You cut hair, too, do you?'

'Done quite a few hair-cutting jobs ashore. Worked six months steady at it once, helping out a pal what had a little barber's shop in Doncaster. He ran a book really, but the shop kept the coppers away. Got pinched last year, so I heard.'

'Very well, Easter. You may try your skill on me.'

He set up his saloon on the strip of deck outside my cabin. He first spread out several sheets of the *Liverpool Echo*, then brought from his quarters a camp stool and a length of cloth striped like a butcher's apron. He tied the cloth tightly round my neck and drew a pair of scissors and a comb from his hip pocket.

'How do you like it?' he demanded.

'Oh, sort of short round the back.'

'Wouldn't like a crew cut, would you? Suit your sort of head, if I may be so bold, Doctor.'

'No, thank you.'

He began snipping round the nape of the neck.

'Bit of fun and games about noon,' he continued. 'The *Violet's* coming in astern of us where that Royal Mail boat was yesterday.'

'The *Violet*? What's she?'

'Another one of the Fathom hookers. Does the run from the River Plate to Pernambuco and New York. Captain Beamish in

247

command. Cor! He ain't 'arf a queer 'un. Needs his head examined, I reckon.'

'That's what they're cleaning up the wheelhouse for, is it?'

'Ho, yes, got to have her looking posh when we has company. Sorry, Doctor, was that your ear?'

'If I get a septic wound from this,' I said sternly, 'I shall order your kit to be burned as a sanitary measure.'

He blew hard through the comb and bit deeply into my hair with it.

'I likes hair-cutting,' he continued, unruffled. 'Bit of an art, like knocking up a sculpture. You never know how it's going to turn out when you start.'

I sat in the sunshine, unresisting, while my hair fell in small bundles across the *Liverpool Echo*. The increasing warmth and Easter's conversation behind the regular sharp snip of his scissors encouraged a pleasant feeling of euphoria. I was looking forrard, towards the mouth of the river; the long quay, with the tall German cranes grouped eagerly round open hatchways, was lined with ships as far as I could see. In the water on our port side a clean, grey-and-white, neat Swedish tanker was being turned slowly by a pair of tugs, like a birch log between two water-rats. Immediately ahead of us the Stars and Stripes dropped over the stern of the *Omar C. Ingersoll* of Baltimore, a cargo ship the same size as the *Lotus*, designed with the American combination of stark lines and grotesque, mysterious appendages. Just below me, on the foredeck, a dozen Brazilians clutched a swaying crate labelled AUSTIN that hovered from the sling over No. 2 hatch.

'I reckon you was right not to trust the barbers ashore,' Easter said. 'They ain't up to much, and they'll rook you as soon as look at you. Not as bad as the ones in Port Said, though—for a dollar they'll give you a shampoo and introduce you to their sister.' He wiped the comb on the leg of his trousers thoughtfully. 'Mind you,' he went on, 'you can have some fun in Port Said if you're up to the tricks. Very rude in places, it is, very rude.' He swept away the cloth and stood back proudly. 'Lovely,' he said. 'Care for me to read your bumps while I'm at it? Used to be Phreno the Bump Man at fairs for a bit.'

'That will be enough, thank you. How much do I owe you?'

'Fifty Woods, Doctor, seeing it's you.'

I went to my cabin to fetch the cigarettes, and found I looked like a caricature of a Prussian general; I suspected that Easter had learned the elements of barbering while serving one of his terms in jail. The advent of the *Violet* seemed to justify the Company's regulation cap, so I fitted a new white cover and stepped back on deck with Easter's art hidden underneath.

By now there was an atmosphere of serious preparation on board. Captain Hogg was shouting at a pair of deckhands painting the large red F on the funnel, Hornbeam was supervising the desperate removal of a potful of black paint just spilled over the white bridge, and the Bos'n was trying to rig a line of electric bulbs along the gangway without disturbing the fat policeman who slept in a deck-chair by the rail. As noon approached, the crew began leaning over the port rail and Captain Hogg climbed on the monkey island over the wheelhouse and impatiently trained his glasses towards the bow. I went to the boatdeck and squeezed between two davits, trying to catch the familiar Fathom Line houseflag moving slowly through the forest of strange masts.

'Mind you don't fall in,' Hornbeam said, coming up the ladder. 'A mouthful of this water would kill you. Any sign of her yet?'

'Can't see anything from here.'

'The Old Man and Beamish are great pals,' he told me contentedly. 'They'd ram each other's ships if they thought they could get away with it. Not that I have any time for Beamish,' he added. 'In fact, I'm not certain I wouldn't rather sail with the one we've got.'

This struck me as severely damning to Captain Beamish.

'What's the matter with him?'

'Thinks he's one of the big ship boys—you know, everything frightfully pukka, wipe your feet at the top of the gangway, kiss me hand and call me Charlie. They say he was a cadet in the P. & O., but got chucked out. I can't say I blame them.'

'But surely,' I said despairingly, 'there must be some good captains in the world?'

'There's one or two. Old Morris on the *Daisy* isn't bad. He did me a good turn once in Belfast when I got mixed up with the cops. But as soon as they get their fourth ring most of 'em get bloody-minded. You wait and see—I'll go the same way.'

We stood chatting between the lifeboats for a while until Captain Hogg bellowed from above us: 'Ahoy there, Mr. Trail! Stand by to dip ensign!'

'There she is,' Hornbeam said, pointing down the river. 'See?'

'What, that?'

His account of Captain Beamish made me imagine his ship as equally superior; but the *Violet,* as she swung round the bend in the river, turned out to be a vessel smaller than the *Lotus,* narrow, as angular as a piano, with patches on her plates and two tall, mournful ventilators drooping over her bridge. She was high in the water, with a wide streak of red showing at the bottom of her rusty hull, and the tips of her propeller blades cut the surface below her overhanging stern.

'Makes us look like the *Queen Lizzie,* doesn't it?' Hornbeam said as she drew nearer. 'Watch for the fun when we start saluting.'

It was clear that Captain Hogg was going to pay his respects grudgingly. He stood on top of the wheelhouse glaring across the water to the *Violet,* and on the wing of the *Violet's* bridge a thin, tall figure in a shining white uniform glared back at him. As the mainmasts of the two ships drew level Captain Hogg shouted, 'Lower away!' and the *Violet's* ensign fluttered down a foot in curt acknowledgment. The two Captains scowled at each other as they passed, and no one in either crew would have been surprised if they had stuck out their tongues.

'The brotherhood of the sea,' Hornbeam said. 'I bet Father's just waiting for her to foul our ropes as she comes alongside.'

Captain Beamish nevertheless arrived for lunch on board the *Lotus* as soon as his gangway was down. He turned out to be a thin, brown, wrinkled man with a face like a tortoise. He compensated for his own shabby ship by turning himself out sprucely; his long neck stretched from the high starched collar of his uniform, two rows of glossy medal ribbons shone on his bosom, his trousers were unsullied with sitting, and his feet stood in white buckskin shoes. He sat down at the table, placed a monocle in his right eye, and crumbled a roll in his bony hand with an expression on his face as if he expected it to release an unpleasant smell.

Captain Hogg was coldly polite, and introduced us all. 'This is my Chief Officer, Mr. Hornbeam . . . my Doctor . . . my Chief Engineer . . . my Chief Steward.' Captain Beamish received these presentations in silence. Before we had finished the soup it appeared that he was a man sparing of words, for the only conversation he permitted himself was to interrupt his host's remarks every few minutes with the expression ''Strordinary!'

When we reached the treacle roll he cut into Captain Hogg's description of how he once docked in Liverpool without tugs, by glaring at me and snapping, 'Doctor!'

'Sir?'

'Which hospital d'y' come from?'

'St. Swithin's, sir.'

'Strordinary! Must know Dr. Jenkins.'

'Jenkins? No, I'm afraid I don't, sir.'

'Jenkins was a very well-known man in the Line.'

I shook my head solemnly, without making any comment. I had gathered that doctors became well known in seafaring life only through the originality with which they left it.

'You look very young, Doctor,' he continued. 'Fully qualified, I suppose?'

'Of course I am,' I said angrily.

''Strordinary. Looks very young indeed,' he added in a slightly softer voice to Captain Hogg, who immediately began looking at me with suspicion.

'Lost my damned Bos'n this trip,' Captain Beamish went on. 'Blast him.'

'What was up?' Captain Hogg asked, piling the last fragments of suet roll on to his spoon.

'Had to put him over the wall off Pernam. Dead, y'know.'

'Go on! What of?'

''Strordinary thing altogether. Meant to ask your Doctor. Had a turn of the shakes and died before sunset.'

'Very likely smallpox,' I said firmly. 'Your ship will have to be fumigated for three weeks and all hands isolated in the fever hospital. The one in Santos is extremely unpleasant, but they will probably take you up to São Paulo as you're certain to get it, anyway.'

I sat and sulked over the cheese-dish.

'Bad about the Bos'n,' Captain Beamish said. 'Don't get his type any more. Respectful. Knew my ways. I may not be in command of a big ship, but I'll have her run decently. Eh, Captain?'

Captain Hogg had his mouth full of cheese, but he nodded violently enough to spill pieces on to the tablecloth.

'Don't know what things are coming to. The Third wore the same uniform three days running last week. D'y'know what happened yesterday? Steward brought me a glass of water without a tray. Communism, that's what it is.'

Captain Beamish then said nothing else for the rest of the meal.

The *Violet's* officers came aboard before supper and noisily packed themselves into Hornbeam's cabin. I found it startling to see the familiar Fathom Line uniforms and badges with different faces over them. They sat and drank gin, enjoying the fragmentary friendship of the sea that had been established by a few hours or a day or two in a dozen years at ports all over the world.

'Here's our Doc,' Hornbeam said, as I squeezed through the door. 'Meet Mr. Molony, Chief Officer from that old barge down aft.'

'Hello, Doc,' he said, shaking hands. 'Enjoying the sea?'

'I am, rather, thank you.'

'How did you get on with our Old Man at dinner?'

'I must say he was pretty rude.'

Molony laughed loudly, while Hornbeam filled up his glass.

'He takes some getting used to. Do you know what?' he asked Hornbeam. 'He chased me up for eating peas off a knife the other day. Can you imagine it? Now there's bugling, too. We signed on a Yankee galley-boy in New York who brought a trumpet with him, so we get bugle calls to meals. Anyone would think we were a ruddy battleship.'

'All skippers are the same,' Hornbeam said wearily. 'Do you remember old Jack Andrews in the *Buttercup*? What happened to him?'

'Didn't you hear? He got put ashore in Cape Town last year.'

They began to talk earnestly of men and ships I had never heard of, and their conversation took on an odd parochialism extending across the face of the earth.

As the *Violet* was due to sail again at midnight our guests left early. I leant on the rail and watched her float slowly into the river, her portholes drawing yellow streaks across the greasy water. She blew three hoots of farewell to us and followed her tug towards the sea. Captain Hogg stood outside his cabin staring after her, and no doubt Captain Beamish was on the bridge glaring astern at us. I wondered if I should meet any more Fathom Line captains, and if they would be any less unnerving.

A man in a pair of khaki trousers and a loose orange shirt was waiting in my cabin. He grinned as I came in.

'Hi'ya, Doc,' he said. 'I'm off the *Omar C. Ingersoll*. Pleased to meet ya.'

We shook hands.

'I guess I shouldn't have bust in, but your Chief Mate said it was O.K.'

'Perfectly all right,' I said. 'What can I do for you?'

'I just want a bottle of aspirin. We're right out, and we ain't carrying a medic. I don't want to put you to no bother, though.'

'No trouble at all, my good man,' I said. 'I'll fetch you some from the hospital.'

'That's mighty swell of you, Doc,' he said, grinning at me again. 'Mighty swell.'

In return for the bottle of aspirins he presented me with two hundred Chesterfields, *The Case of the Luckless Legs,* three bars of chocolate, *Life,* and a photograph of the *Omar C. Ingersoll*. At the gangway he slapped me on the back and said, 'Come aboard and have a cup of coffee sometime, Doc. Just go up the gangway and ask for me.'

'Very kind of you,' I said. 'And you are . . . the Bos'n? Er, Mate, possibly . . . ?'

'Aw, hell no, Doc! I'm the Captain. So long!'

I went to my bunk reflecting that the feudal system at least had the advantage of leaving you in no doubt whom you were talking to.

CHAPTER XII

WE spent a week in Santos, all baking in our cabins like a big dish of *escargots*. Our next port was to be Buenos Aires, to load grain and hides for home.

'Shan't be sorry to get away,' said Trail the morning we sailed. 'Stinking place, this. Fancy living here!'

'When are we off?'

'About midday. They've finished cargo in all hatches except number five. It's hot, isn't it? I'll be like a fried egg when I come off the bridge.'

We left the city of tolerance behind us and turned south towards the River Plate.

Our voyage down the coast was enlivened by Christmas, which fell upon us half-way between Santos and Montevideo. The festival is celebrated most warmly by Englishmen when away from their own country, just as London Scots afford the fiercest welcome to the New Year. As I had now a fair insight into the behaviour of the *Lotus* and her crew I expected the day would pass with a flourish.

On Christmas morning Easter awoke me with my tea at seven.

'Good morning, Doctor. And a Merry Christmas to you, Doctor, with my best respects.'

'Thank you, Easter. And the same to you.'

'Bloody 'ot again, ain't it?'

'What's on the thermometer?'

He looked at it closely.

'Hundred and two. Won't be nearly so chilly by midday, neither.'

'It seems very strange to me to have Christmas in this climate.'

'Cor,' Easter continued, 'I remember one Christmas we had in the Timor Sea. I was in a Yankee ship then—one of them all-metal jobs inside. She was hot enough to melt a bos'n's heart. Early on Christmas morning the Chief Engineer goes and dies, see . . .'

'Really, Easter . . .'

'. . . so I reckons we got to chuck the poor bastard over the wall pronto, because in that heat you wouldn't be able to get near him after dinner-time, let alone dress him up in a canvas suit. I tells the Mate—nasty bit of work he was—but he won't have none of it. You know what these Yanks are. Crazy for embalming. "He's got to be embalmed," he says, "then we'll pop him in the galley freezer and he can have a decent burial in the soil of God's Own Country. Besides," he says, "we ain't going to have no funerals on Christmas Day." "Yes," I says, "but who's going to do the embalming?" "You are," he says, "there's instructions in the Pharmacist's Mate's Handbook, and you can get on with it. If you do him nice I'll give you a bottle of Scotch, and if you makes a pig's bottom of him I'll kick you round the deck."

'What could I do? I tells the Skipper, but he gets a cob on and says it's orders. So I reckon instead of arguing it's best to get on with it while he's still pretty fresh. The Butcher and me goes in there and gets to work, me promising the Butch half of the Scotch —used to be in the meat works at Chicago, the Butch, and reckoned something like that was right up his alley.

'Oh, we made a lovely job of him,' Easter continued with pride. 'It would have brought tears to his mother's eyes. When we'd finished the Butch and I gets the hospital stretcher to carry him down to the freezer, while the Skipper and all hands gathers round the cabin door to have a dekko. I goes in first holding one end of the stretcher, the Butch holding the other, and the Mate comes in after us to see what sort of a job we've made of him. Well, I dunno. Either we'd made the poor bloke so lifelike, or it was that hot, or he was starting to pong a bit, but the Mate gets inside and passes out like a light. So what could we do? The Butch and I puts him on the stretcher and carries him on deck for some air. When the Skipper sees us coming out with the Mate lying there instead of the corpse he takes one look and bloody well faints as well. Cor, what a lash-up! Stiffs all over the deck. Wasn't 'arf a funny Christmas, that wasn't.'

'Thank you, Easter,' I said. 'You have cheered my Christmas morn.'

'The Bos'n's got toothache,' he added.

'Has he? How badly?'

'Something cruel, he reckons.'

'Send him to the hospital. I'll be along in half an hour.'

The Bos'n was a big man with a complexion like an old football and a face as threatening as a battleship's gun-turret. I found him sitting in the hospital chair, holding his jaw and moaning.

'Merry Christmas,' I said.

I shone a torch in his mouth and announced 'It'll have to come out.'

'O.K., Doc,' he said, squaring his shoulders. 'I can take it.'

We had fortunately found a pair of dental forceps on board, and I hoped they would fit the tooth. I had never extracted one before, but from the ranks of dentists I had seen in action in the hospital out-patient department it looked pretty simple. One simply pulled hard, as though extracting a nail from a plank, and the tooth appeared in a flurry of saliva and blood.

'Easter,' I said. 'What have we in the way of anæsthetics?'

'If I may be so bold, sir, and especially seeing it's Christmas, how about the medical comforts?'

'Capital idea. Are there any left?'

'I took the liberty of telling the Chief Steward last night that you was wanting some special for the season.'

'Very well. Go and fetch them, Easter.'

The three of us sat in a circle and purposefully drank brandy.

'Have another glass,' I told the Bos'n. 'After all, you're the patient.'

He said the pain was beginning to wear off.

'Nevertheless,' I said firmly, 'we must proceed with the operation. I don't want you messing up my Christmas Day with toothache. Open wide,' I commanded. I applied the forceps. 'Is that the one?'

He nodded vigorously.

I gripped the forceps hard and pulled. It was like trying to crack a fresh Brazil nut. I gave another tug. The Bos'n grunted and screwed his eyes up.

'This may hurt a little,' I remembered to say.

I threw all my weight against the tooth. Sweat was running

down my face and into my eyes and I was breathing like a middle-aged wrestler.

'It's no good!' I grunted. 'I'm just not tough enough. Easter, apply counter-pressure to his shoulders, will you? That's right. Now—one, two, three, together heave!'

The patient slipped down the chair.

'Oh Lord!' I said.

'If I might suggest,' Easter said. 'Dr. Flowerday used to find it very useful to put his knee in the bloke's chest.'

'Like that?'

'That's right, Doctor. Now shove your elbows against his shoulders.'

There was a crash, and the patient landed on the deck with me on top of him.

'Hold on, Doctor!' Easter shouted. 'It's coming!'

I set my jaw and threw myself into a final effort; but the tooth was as firm as a rivet in a ship's plate. I was about to roll off the patient in exhaustion when he decided it was time to intervene himself. Two large, powerful hands came up and enveloped mine. The Bos'n gave a sharp heave and the tooth came out like a pip from an orange.

He stood up, spat a mouthful of blood in the sink, and looked at me anxiously.

'Are you all right, Doctor?' he asked. 'Didn't hurt you, did I?'

'No, I think I'm all right,' I panted.

'Gawd, that's better! Merry Christmas, Doctor.'

The Bos'n walked contentedly aft, and I went to join my shipmates. There was an air of geniality on board, fostered not only by the season but the fact that Christmas was technically Sunday and therefore everyone had another half-day's pay.

After midday the officers were invited to Captain Hogg's cabin for drinks. Everyone came—even the Chief Engineer, who allowed his aversion for both the Captain and the foolish Sassenach custom of celebrating on December 25th to be overcome by his satisfaction of getting a free drink out of his enemy.

The Captain had already been setting himself in the mood for Christmas, and welcomed us with guarded geniality. We were all cleanly dressed and sober, except the Wireless Operator, who had already been having a party in his cabin with his own friends.

'Good morning, gentlemen, good morning!' Captain Hogg said, giving us a cold smile. 'Compliments of the season, gentlemen, on behalf of myself and the Company.'

'It was Christmas Day in the workhouse . . .' the Sparks began. Hornbeam clapped a hand over his mouth.

'Help me with the drinks, Mr. Whimble, will you? That's right. Pink gins all round, I suppose? Help yourselves to iced water, gentlemen. Here's to a Merry Christmas.'

'Same to you, sir!' everyone said, respectfully raising their glasses.

'. . . the Master called down the halls,' the Sparks continued. 'Did you like your Christmas dinner? And the inmates answered . . .'

Hornbeam shut him up again.

'I propose,' Captain Hogg said, glancing sternly round the company, 'on this solemn day in our year to make a short speech.'

There were murmurs of assent all round: he had as much risk of objection as Hitler ever had.

'This is *my* ship,' Captain Hogg went on. 'My ship. She is in my care, and so are the lives of all of you in her.' He took a swallow of gin. 'My ambition,' he continued, 'is to have a happy ship. Do you understand? That means that every damn one of you's got to knuckle under. This ship—my ship'—he waved his glass expansively—'is a floating village. We have our butcher, our baker, and our lamptrimmer. We have our own storekeeper—even our own doctor.' This brought a roar of laughter and a round of applause. 'But I'—he hit his chest—'I am the squire of the village. Get that straight. Give me another gin, Mr. Whimble.'

'On this occasion,' he resumed, 'I look upon you all with a fatherly eye. All of you. I am proud of you. You are the best crew I've ever sailed with. You are——'

He stopped. He glared out of the porthole. His face twisted alarmingly. The *Lotus* had stopped.

'Mr. McDougall,' he hissed, 'the ship's stopped.'

McDougall didn't move.

'Aye,' he said.

'What is it?' Captain Hogg asked heavily. 'Are you celebrating

258

Christmas so much down below that you have let the boilers go out?'

McDougall carefully drained his gin.

'We no celebrate these cissy festivals in my department. We save it up for Hogmanay.'

'So! You come up here and take my liquor——'

'And listen to an old windbag like you——'

'How dare you, sir! I have never been insulted like that in all my years at sea!'

'All your years! I was on watch below when you were flying yellow at the mizzen.'

Captain Hogg shook a fist at him.

'I was in sail, sir!'

'You ought to have stayed there. You'd make a good barge skipper.'

'We didn't need engineers in those days,' Captain Hogg shouted.

'And in ten years' time we won't need captains.'

'Damn you, sir! I won't be talked to like this! I'll have you logged. I will. I mean it. I——'

'It was Christmas Day in the workhouse——' the Sparks began.

'Aw, go to hell!' McDougall said.

'Please, please!' cried Whimble.

'I've had enough of this, Mr. McDougall——!'

'And I've had more than enough——!'

'Steady the Buffs!' said Hornbeam jovially.

At that moment the Second Steward arrived and announced that dinner was served.

The saloon was decorated with dusty streamers that were produced every year, like the dinner menu, irrespective of the latitude in which the *Lotus* found herself. The English are the greatest colonizing race in the world, but they show a reluctance to part with their native habits in climates that render them highly unsuitable or even unhealthy. Wherever two Englishmen are together at Christmas the accustomed dinner must be eaten, in its full carbohydrate glory. The weather demanded a little salad and an ice-cream, but we sat down and dutifully faced the full gastronomic trappings of the season—roast turkey, sausages, cold pork, roast beef, boiled cabbage, roast potatoes, mince pies, and Christmas pudding.

'We've got a nice veal and ham pie on as well, if you want any,' Whimble whispered in my ear as we went in.

All the officers off watch were crammed round the saloon table. Captain Hogg sat at the head, with McDougall opposite him. The *Lotus* shivered and started again, and they glared at each other over the tomato soup. Free whisky was given to all hands, and Whimble handed each officer a paper hat, with a plea not to crush it as they would have to make do for the following year.

I was cutting my first slice of turkey when Hornbeam, who was next to me, gave a nudge.

'Your man seems to want you,' he said.

Easter was standing sheepishly in the doorway.

I excused myself to Captain Hogg and went over to him.

'What is it?' I asked.

'Having a nice dinner, Doctor?'

'Well, if that's all you came to say . . .'

'There's been trouble in the poop.'

'Trouble? What sort of trouble?'

'Couple of the lads has been fighting.'

'Oh, all right. Who are they?'

'Two of the stewards. Myrtle and Mavis.'

'Who did you say?'

Easter grinned. 'You'll find out,' he said.

Two tall, silky-haired young men who cleaned the cabins were sitting in the hospital. They were both covered in blood, and one was in tears.

'What the devil's been going on?' I asked the other.

His lip quivered and he, too, began to weep.

'Another little problem of the sea,' Easter remarked tolerantly. 'Them blokes as is a bit late making up their minds whether they're men or women.'

'Oh Lord!' I said. 'What were they fighting about?'

'I didn't do it!' the first one cried. 'I swear on my honour I didn't!'

'Oh yes you did!' the other shouted. 'You give it back at once, you mean thing!'

'How can I give it back if I haven't got it?'

'Yes you have! You've been trying to sneak it all the voyage!'

'I haven't got that beastly lipstick! It isn't my colour, anyway.'

They started pulling each other's hair.

'They're a bit queer,' Easter explained helpfully.

'Well, do something about them, man! Pour water on them! Get the Mate, and I'll have them logged.'

Easter hit one over the head with an arm-splint.

'Turn it up,' he said genially. 'It's Christmas.'

I put dressings on the unfortunate couple and went back to dinner. By that time everything had been eaten and Captain Hogg was on his feet again, making another speech.

'. . . I have said before,' he told the company, leaning on the table, 'and I say it again—I am proud of my crew. The crew of *my* ship. I shall put in my report to the Company that you are the best crew——'

His face clouded over. He snarled. The *Lotus* had stopped again.

CHAPTER XIII

THE rest of the day passed unalarmingly. We were nearing the busy coast of Uruguay, where the River Plate shipping first turns north to Europe and the States. That night I stood on the hot deck in my pyjamas and watched the quiet sea swishing unhurriedly past the *Lotus's* side. Another ship approached us, two broken rows of lights in the darkness, her green starboard light shining into ours. An Aldis light flashed from her bridge, calling us up. I watched the Third Mate reply. I supposed we only wished each other a Merry Christmas and exchanged the usual courtesy queries about name and destination, but it made me realize for the first time that the *Lotus* was not the only ship on the sea : all over the world there were tiny floating communities, with the same sort of people doing the same sort of things as we did—keeping parallel watches, eating similar meals, listening to the identical strokes of another ship's bell. There were other doctors, other mates, other captains, each ship struggling with its own apparently paramount problems. I yawned, as Captain Hogg shrank into comforting perspective.

When I went to turn in I found Hornbeam in my cabin.

'Hello, Doc. Just dropped in for a final peg, seeing it's Christmas night. Do you mind?'

'Not a bit. Help yourself to the Scotch.'

'Thanks.'

He put his feet up on the desk.

'Father made a fine showing to-day,' he said.

'Where is he now?'

'Sleeping it off. I just went up to see if the Third Mate's sober. You've never seen any of us go on watch sloshed, have you?'

'No, never.'

'It doesn't matter about the Old Man. Some of 'em kill a bottle a day and still keep their jobs.' He stretched. 'I wish this one would drop dead,' he said amiably.

'You'd get promotion, you mean?'

He nodded.

'I'm next on the list. Trouble is, all the other skippers in the Company are as healthy as apprentices. They'll have to give me a command soon,' he added sadly. 'I'm getting too old and fat to go running up and down hatch ladders.'

'You'll get one soon enough.'

'I don't know. All I want is a command—it doesn't matter if the ship sinks as soon as we get out of port. As long as I can call myself Captain. That's what I've been at sea for all these years—all the way up, apprentice, third, second, mate. That's what keeps us sane, most of us. Waiting for a ship of our own. Then I'm going to chuck the sea and raise chickens.'

'I bet you won't.'

'It's a mug's game. When you've been at it a couple of years they've got you where they want you. There's nothing for you ashore—what good's a master's ticket in the Labour Exchange? The sea's a positive bitch. You can't run away from her if you want to.'

'I suppose you're right there.'

'You staying at sea, Doc?'

'Me? Oh, no. I'm going back to general practice in the provinces, I suppose.' I saw the grey streets, the grey skies, the grey complexions of the patients; wet winter mornings and acrid summer ones; frightened faces on the doorstep at three in the morning; four o'clock parties with conversation like the weak over-sweetened tea; hedging respectability, the eternal narrowness of the persistent provincial.

'Perhaps,' I added.

'Well,' Hornbeam said. 'The only thing to do with life is to live it, you know. Shall we have a last one?' I passed him the bottle. 'We'll be in B.A. to-morrow,' he added more cheerfully. 'You can have some fun there.'

*   *   *   *   *

'Everything's on the top line here since they had the purity campaign,' the Third said. 'Now it's as clean as Blackpool. Pity.'

We were lying off the big, white, flat city of Buenos Aires, lines of tall, angular buildings running down to the clean water-front.

'It's pretty nice here in the New Port,' the Third went on.

'Where do we go?' I asked.

'Down by the meat works.'

Two hours later the *Lotus* was coaxed through the narrow entrance of the South Dock, and tied up not far from the big grey refrigerating plant.

'Smells like a farm, don't it?' Easter remarked, as we were drawing alongside. 'Don't 'arf get a lot of flies down here. Thick as coppers on a racecourse, they are.'

'So this is where the beef comes from?'

'That's it. They walk in one end and half an hour later they slides out in a tin. Smart, these boys are.'

Our reception was the same as in Santos, except that everyone spoke Spanish. The same functionaries hurried aboard, made for the Mate's cabin, and drank the Mate's gin, from which the business of the ship seemed inseparable. But Hornbeam was determined, for once, to go ashore.

'I've only had a couple all day,' he said proudly to me. 'Look at the bottle for yourself. I'm going to take you lads on a treat to-night. See you about ten.'

'I'll hold you to that.'

'Word of honour, Doc.'

Hornbeam kept his promise. When Trail, Archer, and myself met him in his cabin he was glowing but not extinguished.

'Just a quick one before we leave,' he said, unclipping the cap of another gin bottle. 'It's all on me to-night, boys. I've got plenty of pesos.'

'Where did you land them from?' Archer asked.

Hornbeam winked.

'The Mate's got to have a few perks,' he explained. 'Small present from the stevedores for giving them the pleasure of our custom. Also a token from the chandlers for the honour of pro-viding us with deck stores. Strictly against Company regs., of course. Oh, I've got about'—he pulled some notes from his pocket—'about a thousand pesos.'

'That's forty quid,' Trail said reverently.

'Nothing but the best to-night!' Hornbeam continued. 'Drink up, and we'll hit the town.'

'This is the Boca,' Hornbeam explained, as we walked over the railway tracks towards the gawky German gantry bridge. 'One of the toughest spots in South America. A bos'n I sailed with once got beaten up about here. Left him only his shoes. He was a big chap, too.'

'I wish they wouldn't put ships in such insalubrious districts,' I said. 'It's like living in the slums.'

'They reckon the slums are good enough for sailors, I suppose.'

To reach the town we climbed into a small boat and were rowed across the slimy river towards the Boca's main street.

'Hard work finding a taxi in B.A. these days,' Trail said. 'We'd better climb in a colectivo.'

'A quick one in old Mother Whitehead's first,' Archer insisted. 'After all, it's known to every Liverpool fireman since steam came in.'

We had a couple of drinks described guardedly as Special Cocktails, and ate bits of chopped meat, nuts, mussels, cheese, and olives from the small plates the citizens of Buenos Aires expect to be handed with their drinks.

'On me,' Hornbeam said firmly, pulling out a fifty-peso note. 'Now let's go down town and have a steak.'

We went to the broad, bright Avenida Corrientes, the Broadway of B.A. In one of the grill rooms we sat down and ate steaks three inches thick.

'Nothing like nourishment,' Hornbeam observed. 'I'm going to have another of these. How about you, Doc?'

I shook my head, as my mouth was too full to speak.

'You'll want it in a few weeks' time when you're treating yourself to a nice spaghetti on toast. How about a bottle of Argentine wine? It's not bad. All on me, you blokes.'

We rose uneasily from the table when Hornbeam paid the bill. By now his already generous feelings towards the evening were accentuated by heavy feeding.

'I'm going to show you boys the town,' he said handsomely. 'Everything's my treat. Where shall we go to?'

'How about El Nidito?' Archer suggested. 'Or L'Atelier?'

'There's a joint I used to know round the corner,' Hornbeam said, scratching his forehead. 'Little redhead in there plays the guitar.'

He was delighted to find the bar was still there, though, reasonably enough, the redhead wasn't. It was a small, dim place with a band playing sambas in the corner and a tall girl caressing a microphone not much thinner than herself.

'Lovely grub!' Hornbeam said with relish. 'What's it to be? Scotch?'

There was no Scotch but they gave us the locally distilled whisky, which tasted like an old-fashioned carminative mixture. Trail got into earnest conversation with the girl behind the bar, who came from Lytham St. Anne's, and I sat wondering what the whisky was doing to my gastric lining.

'I've had this place,' Hornbeam said impatiently after a few minutes. 'Let's move on.'

'But we've only just arrived.'

'It's too quiet. Come on, blokes. It's my party, so I can take it anywhere.'

We went to a good many bars. They all offered the same—darkness, sambas, local whisky, and a girl behind the bar who came from some spot comparable to Lytham.

'It's half-past one,' I said to Archer later. 'Doesn't anyone go to sleep in B.A.?'

'Things are only beginning. They go on like this all night.'

'They must be a tougher race than we are. Apart from the hours, they seem to put up with their own whisky.'

Hornbeam was seized with a final inspiration.

'Let's go to the Saratoga, boys,' he announced.

'That's a posh do,' Trail told him dubiously. 'It's an expensive joint, particularly at this hour of the night.'

'Only the best is good enough for us,' Hornbeam insisted. 'Saratoga next stop. I want to see the dancing girls.'

We found a cab and drove down the street to the Saratoga. It was a class above the bars and night clubs we had been to—a small silk-lined place with two bands, a tiny dance floor, and a stage. Hornbeam strode in and demanded a table at the front.

'This is more like it!' he said contentedly. 'I'm fed up with slumming.'

He ordered some champagne.

I looked around me and saw it was certainly more fortunate in its clientele than the other places we had visited. The tone was marred only by our party, in which Hornbeam was now leaning back in his chair, clapping his hands, and demanding 'Bring on the fat women!'

'There aren't any here, are there?' I asked Archer.

'You wait, Doc,' he said. 'Three blokes can't sit down alone anywhere south of Panama without something turning up.'

He was right. A good-looking blonde in a white evening gown sat on the chair beside me.

'You buy me a t'rink, no?' she said.

The waiter had already appeared and brought her a thimbleful of red liquid in a liqueur glass. He also brought a green counter, which he handed to her. This she placed in her handbag.

'I'd better put you wise,' Archer said across the table. 'Out here you buy the coloured water and she gets the commission. If you can last out till four you go home with her buckshee.'

'I don't think I can last out the next ten minutes.'

The girl swallowed her glassful swiftly, like a bad medicine.

'You buy me another t'rink, no?'

The waiter gave her a second glass, and another counter.

'This is going to work out expensive,' I said.

'All on me, Doc,' Hornbeam said grandly. 'Tell her to send her friends over.'

Two more girls appeared and started drinking with the frightening rapidity of their companion. However, we all became very friendly, and Hornbeam ordered some more champagne.

When Trail fell asleep on the table I said, 'Hadn't we better get the bill, Chief? I could do with some sleep myself.'

'Mozo!' Hornbeam demanded. 'Bill, pronto!'

It was given to him immediately, neatly folded on a plate. He scowled at the figures, and began counting notes from his pocket.

'You buy me anot'er t'rink, no?' said the blonde.

'No. The bar's down.'

She got up and walked away.

'Say, Doc,' Hornbeam called. 'Can you lend me five hundred pesos?'

'What!'

'I seem to be a bit short.' Hornbeam spread his notes on the table. He had been carried away by his generosity into a ditch of insolvency.

We searched in our pockets, waking Trail up to join in.

'Ninety-eight pesos,' Archer said. 'That's all we can muster.'

Hornbeam looked shiftily over his shoulder. The waiter, with that second sight which waiters have, was aware that some hitch had arisen and threw dark glances at us. Visions of Argentine prisons shimmered before my eyes: I was sure the Buenos Aires police would arrest with the alacrity of their comrades in Santos.

'This is serious,' I said. 'Hasn't anyone got any money at all?'

We searched our pockets again.

'Not a centavo,' Trail said. 'I've got a couple of bob though.'

'Someone will have to go back to the ship and raise the wind,' Archer said. 'That's all there is for it. The others will sit here and pretend they're enjoying themselves. We'll toss for who goes.'

We tossed a twenty-centavo piece. I lost.

'Better take the ninety-eight pesos and see if you can get a cab,' Hornbeam said. 'Make it snappy. Ten pound notes will cover it at black-market rates.'

I stood outside in the hot dry air, already feeling the apprehending hand on my shoulder. I saw an empty cab on the other side of the street and leapt towards it.

'Dock Sul,' I said.

But the driver could take me only as far as the rowing-boat. I had to cross the river and walk alone across the railway tracks to the ship. I strode breathlessly along the middle of the road, looking behind me more than in front. A cat leapt across my path from shadow to shadow and I yelped. I ran through the dock gates and up the gangway.

The *Lotus* was dead. The quartermaster was in a chair by the gangway, asleep. Everyone not ashore was in their bunks, wallowing in the deep, unhindered unconsciousness of watch-keepers in port.

I thought my best chance was represented by the Chief Engineer. He was lying with his mouth open on top of his bunk.

'Chief!' I called softly. I shook him. 'Chief!'

He stopped snoring and grunted.

'Chief! Wake up!'

He opened his eyes.

'Stop the feed pumps and stand-by all engineers,' he said.

'No, Chief! It's the Doc. Can you lend me some money?'

'Money? What for, man? At this hour of night.'

'I'll explain later. But I must have it now. In a hurry.'

'Wait till I put my teeth in, lad.'

He gave me five pound notes. The rest I collected by rousing Whimble, the Second Steward, three or four of the engineers, and Easter.

I ran back to the ferry, crumpling the notes in my hands. I had to walk half a mile up the long road to the city before I found a taxi. When I jumped out I found my expedition had taken the best part of an hour, and the Saratoga was rising to a final burst of activity before closing for the night. I looked in nervously, wondering if my companions had already been extracted by the police, or had generously been allowed to wash dishes in the basement.

Neither of these misfortunes had occurred to them. In my absence they had all drawn a second wind and were enjoying themselves hugely. They had three new girls and another bottle of champagne.

'I've got the money,' I said breathlessly, falling into a chair.

'Ah, there's the old Doc!' Hornbeam said with surprise. 'Where did you come from?'

'I went to get some money to pay the bill,' I said angrily. 'Don't you remember?'

'That's right,' Archer agreed. 'Good old Doc. Mozo! Bill!'

Another bill was presented. Before they read the figures I knew what was coming.

'That ten quid means five hundred pesos,' Hornbeam said solemnly. 'Then there's this here—have you got any left, Doc?'

I threw him a few peso notes.

'Umm,' he said. 'Looks as if we need about five hundred pesos.'

269

'Well,' Trail said brightly. 'The Doc had better go back for some more.'

I banged the table.

'No!' I said. 'No, I damn well won't! I don't care if we all go to jail, but I'm not going back to the ship!'

The manager, who had been hovering in the distance like a well-preened vulture, put his head into our group.

'Anything wrong, gentlemen?' he asked.

'Yes,' I said. 'We can't pay the bill.'

I folded my arms and prepared to be arrested with the dignity of an Englishman.

'Unfortunate,' said the manager.

'Bloody unfortunate,' Hornbeam said.

'How much are you gentlemen short? Five hundred pesos, I see. You are seafaring gentlemen, are you not?'

'Don't we look like it?' I said.

'A not uncommon predicament. Always seafaring gentlemen. A nice watch you have,' he said to Trail. 'Must be worth at least a hundred pesos.'

'It cost me twenty quid in Durban,' Trail said hotly. I stopped him.

'Hand it over,' I said.

He sulkily unstrapped his watch.

'You other gentlemen have equally valuable time-pieces,' the manager continued.

'Your turn,' Trail said, brightening a little.

Hornbeam, Archer, and I surrendered ours.

'I think,' the manager continued, 'a Parker 51 would settle it.'

I gave him the pen from my pocket.

'Now get the hell out of here, you bums,' he said, 'or I'll get the cops on you.'

We stood, a forlorn quartet, on the pavement.

'Oh well,' said Hornbeam. 'You know what I told you the other night. The only thing to do with life is to live it. Now let's start walking back to the ship.'

CHAPTER XIV

IF you must be broke, there are many conveniences in being broke as a seafarer on ship's articles. The necessities of life, such as food, shelter, cigarettes, and gin, continue to be supplied regularly, either free or on account until the end of the voyage; and the state arouses among one's companions a lively sympathy expressed on land only on occasions of severe illness or other bitter natural misfortune. When the story of our visit to the Saratoga spread round the ship the next morning we were chivvied with offers of help from all hands.

'Had a bit of a night of it, I hear, Doctor,' Easter said jovially.

'I'm afraid so.'

'I don't hold with that there Saratoga,' he continued reflectively. 'Mind you, they has some very posh tarts there, very posh. But they don't 'arf burn up the rhino. Is it worth it? I ask you. Now, me and Chippy goes ashore quiet like, and has a few beers in old Ma Whitehead's. If we feels like indulging, as you might say, we goes round the back to a little place what Chippy reckons he was first taken to by his father when he was sailing as a deckboy. Mind, they ain't no great beauties in there. In fact, Chippy reckons they're the same ones what his father knew. But they come economic like, and that's something these days, ain't it, Doctor?'

'Thank you, Easter. I appreciate your little lecture on thrift.'

'We lives and learns, Doctor. How about a small contribution, if you've run yourself short?' He pulled a bundle of peso notes from his jacket pocket.

'Definitely no!' I held up my hand. 'I insist on suffering justly for my indiscretions. Besides, I am already in debt to you. If you lent me any more you might not have enough left for your own modest pleasures, such as you have just described.'

'That's all right, Doctor. I just flogged some of that there penicillin what was expired. Dr. Flowerday and I used to split it fifty-fifty, but I don't mind taking forty-sixty to oblige. Barmy on penicillin, these Argentinos. I got rid of them there pills we didn't know what they was—them green ones in the back of the locker. Told 'em they was good for virility and charged a peso each. They go in for that sort of stuff a lot down here.'

'It is very kind of you, Easter, but—for reasons which I should be ashamed to confess—I much prefer you to keep the proceeds to yourself.'

'As you say, Doctor. Tip me the wink if you wants anything flogging. Wouldn't like a few tins of beef, would you? I scrounged some when a case bust going into number one hold.'

'No, thank you. But I appreciate your generosity. Just get me another pitcher of iced water from the galley.'

I put on my cap and went on deck. It was almost noon. The sun, as coarse and uninhibited as everything else in the region, shone savagely on the white planks and brown steel of the decks; but the river, the ships, and the quay were as peaceful as an English village on a high summer afternoon. The purring electric cranes were still and stood at untidy angles along the wharf with crates of merchandise at their feet, abandoned by the dockers for the midday break. Some of the stevedores lay asleep in the shade that was sharply cut out here and there by corners and eaves; others languidly masticated their lunch inside the doors of the airless sheds. From somewhere downstream came the subdued hoot of a small ship's whistle, and the regular soft thumping of some essential pump. The steers mooed spasmodically in the unseen corrals behind the meat works, and the flies, unaffected by the general languor, buzzed in thick, irritating squadrons everywhere.

I leaned on the hot rail and looked at the grey walls of the Frigorifico Anglo, which was temporarily inactive for lunch. I began to understand the disadvantages of my abrupt poverty: we should be in Buenos Aires for at least a fortnight, and the Frigorifico, though of superb interest as a commercial and technical undertaking and with appreciable merit as an example of functional design, would soon become oppressive as the largest segment of my daily horizon. I hadn't even the bus fare to the city.

While I was examining these bleak thoughts Trail came and leaned next to me. We discussed our condition in a few words.

'There's not much to be done here if you're broke,' he observed. 'We could rustle up enough to go to the pictures, I suppose.'

'I can do that in London.'

'That's true. They've got some nice parks, so they tell me.'

We had adjusted ourselves to a dull stay in one of the world's gayest capitals when a bright ray of entertainment abruptly shone into our lives from an unexpected source. I was lying on my bunk after dinner, reading the first paragraph of *War and Peace* with the drowsy inattentive righteousness of a good churchgoer sitting through a summer sermon, when Easter pulled aside the curtain across the doorway.

'Father's compliments,' he said. 'And will you come to his cabin, pronto.'

'Oh, Lord! What's eating the old boy now?'

'Search me, Doctor. He's getting the Mate up there, and the Hunk.'

'Hunk?'

'Chief Steward, Mr. Whimble.'

'Very well.' I rolled off the bunk and took my cap from the hook over the desk. 'I hope it isn't his stomach again.'

Hornbeam and Whimble were already sitting on the settee in the Captain's cabin. McDougall was in one of the arm-chairs. On either side of the desk sat Captain Hogg and Mr. Montmorency, the Fathom Line's manager in Buenos Aires. All of them were smoking cigars and drinking liqueurs.

'Ah, Doctor, come in!' Mr. Montmorency called, as I pushed the door curtain away. He got up and seized me by the hand. 'Have a seat. Move over there, Mr. Whimble. Cigar? Real Havana. Won't find them in England, eh? Benedictine, Curaçao, or brandy? Some Kummel, perhaps? Or a flash of the old starboard light?'

'Benedictine will do nicely,' I said. I sat down between Whimble and Hornbeam, while Mr. Montmorency lit my cigar. He was a lean, brown man with a brisk black moustache, dressed in a crisp linen suit. He was an office-wallah, and therefore formally despised; but he was secretly respected as an important and dangerous man in the lives of everyone who depended on the Fathom Line for their pay. Beneath the sunburnt hearty crust was a sharp brain eager to send damning cables to St. Mary Axe, where a few words of code could hold up a man's promotion for ten years or tip him back into the uncertain currents of the shipping pool. Even Captain Hogg was affable to Mr. Montmorency.

'Right, gentlemen,' Mr. Montmorency went on forcefully. 'I have asked you up here to-day for a particular reason, apart from having the pleasure of meeting you. Captain Hogg assures me, I am glad to say, that he thinks highly of your services under his command.'

'A very happy ship,' Captain Hogg declared. He swallowed half a tumbler of Benedictine and glared at the rest of us in defiance of contradiction.

'I am sure it is, Captain. Now, gentlemen, I am going to talk to you on a most serious topic. It is British Prestige.' He took on his smartest Chamber of Commerce manner. 'It is hardly necessary for me to trace the course of events in this bustling subcontinent since the cessation of hostilities—hostilities, gentlemen, in which the Company we represent suffered as grievously as any —but you will, I am sure, all appreciate that the interest of our Motherland in its affairs has increased rather than diminished, though in the face of severe, and sometimes to us inexplicable, opposition. Some more Benedictine, Captain?'

'Thank you, Mr. Montmorency.'

'Pass the bottle round, gentlemen. As I was saying. The tail of the British lion has been severely put out of joint . . .'

He went on about the Old Red Duster, Free Trade, the Socialists, Nationalization, Hard Times, the necessity to pull together, put our shoulders to the wheel, steer a straight course, and not rock the boat. All of us were hazily wondering where the speech was leading him and uneasily contemplating our own guilty consciences. I nervously calculated the turnover in Easter's dockside pharmaceutical dealings, Hornbeam thought anxiously about his stevedores' presents, and Whimble was wondering how to account for the ham and two cases of tinned pears that had somehow vanished between Santos and the River Plate. But, if these skeletons were visible to the penetrating eye of Mr. Montmorency, he was not going to mention it. I suddenly realized he was saying '. . . there will, of course, be a running buffet and the best we can do in the way of drinks. It will give the British colony here a bit of an outing, reassure the local business men, send up the prestige of the Line, and, in a small way, that of the Old Country. Besides, gentlemen, it will fittingly usher in the New Year. Any comments?'

McDougall, who had fallen asleep, woke up at the words 'New Year' and blew his nose loudly.

'A very generous offer,' Captain Hogg growled. 'On behalf of my officers and crew, I should like to express my gratitude to the management.'

'Thank you, Captain. Now, gentlemen, you are the senior officers. You know my plans, and I expect you to make it a success. This dance on shipboard must be remembered in Buenos Aires as one of the events of the season.'

A dance on shipboard. . . . I saw at once Tissot's painting— matchwood decks, fragile rails, graceful bright brasswork; summery officers with downy whiskers, in gold and blue and white; clean sailors, contented bandsmen, delicate ladies in sprays of frills; frail parasols pirouetting beneath a canopy of the majestic ensigns of half a dozen now forgotten empires. . . . Into this they were going to turn the *Lotus*, tied up by a meat works.

The news of the New Year's Eve dance fell upon the ship's company like a heavy breaker on the beach, overwhelming the minor ripples already set up by our misfortunes in the Saratoga the previous night. Reactions to the party differed sharply. Easter was frankly disgusted.

'I ask you!' he said, coming into my cabin and tossing an armful of my clean laundry peevishly on the bunk. 'What a lash-up! Flags, fairy-lights, and ladies' lavatories! Cor! I dunno what they think this hooker is. The *Queen Mary* isn't in it.'

'Surely, Easter, after your experience on the transatlantic boats you would welcome a touch of the atmosphere of a large liner?'

'What, on this old tramp? First-class smoke-room now, that's different. All the nobs in there getting stinko, not noticing you rook 'em on the measure. And slipping you a quid or two to show 'em the way to some young bit's cabin—discreet like. What are we going to get on this old tub? Crowd of shore-wallahs looking for free booze, that's what. Fat lot of good that is!'

'You may be able to interest some of them in the three-card trick.'

He brightened a little. 'I might, that, Doctor. But there ain't no flies on them round these parts.'

Trail was ecstatic. 'Have you seen this, Doc?' he called to me the next day, waving a sheet of typewritten paper. 'Lists of guests. Take a dekko. Don't bother with this lot, Ambassador, Bishop, and so on, asked but not able to come. . . . Look here—Mister and Missus *and daughter*. Here again—*and daughters*. All the way down—*Miss, Miss, Miss*. Lovely grub! The ship'll be like a bloody harem by eight bells!'

'I don't think you ought to get over-excited, Three-o. The Misses are probably elderly ladies, pillars of the Mission, and the daughters will most likely be still in short frocks. In any event, you can be sure they'll be kept under strict supervision by their watchful parents on a ship like this.'

'Steady on, Doc! There's bound to be some nice bits of crumpet among them. I think I know this one down here, anyway. Used to work in the Company's offices on Corrientes.' He rubbed his hands. 'It's going to be a Happy New Year, and no mistake.'

Hornbeam was less enthusiastic. 'More work for the bloody Mate,' he said. 'Half the bunting's gone mouldy and the Bos'n flogged the canvas awnings in the Canaries last trip. How the hell can I get the boatdeck holystoned and painted in three days? I bet we're short of Scotch homeward bound on the strength of it, too.'

A state of despair settled on Whimble. The greater part of the preparations fell to him, and he was expected to account for everything issued from his stores from a crate of Scotch to a jar of Maraschino cherries. Tablecloths, fruit bowls, glasses, and silver came from half-forgotten straw nests in dusty crates stowed under hundredweights of flour, rice, tinned vegetables, and a case of Gordon's gin he had lost three voyages ago and had been anxiously cooking the bar books to replace ever since.

'Oh dear, oh dear,' he said, coming out of the storeroom with his shirt stuck to his chest with sweat. 'Balloons they want now! Did you ever hear of it? I don't know what the office will say when we get home!'

The balloons were a whim of Captain Hogg's; he had taken an enthusiastic and forceful interest in the dance, and spent most of the day pacing up and down the boatdeck rearranging the deck furnishings and decorations.

'Mr. Whimble!' he shouted frequently. 'Mr. Whimble! Where the devil are you? I think the buffet would be better on the port side. Not so many flies. Get it changed over. What's happened to Mr. Hornbeam? Bos'n, take down number three awning and rig it abaft the funnel so the holes won't show. Mr. Trail, are you supposed to be in charge of lifeboats?'

'Yes, sir.'

'You aren't fit to sail a toy boat on a paddling pool. Get those ropes stowed properly.'

'Aye aye, sir.'

'Doctor!'

'Sir?'

'Flies, Doctor. The bluebottles from the meat works. They are a sanitary problem, are they not?'

'Yes, sir. Included in the syllabus for the examination in Public Health.'

'You are responsible for them. I don't want a damn fly on my ship by to-morrow night. Understand?'

'It's rather a tall order, sir.'

'That's your lookout. Get some insect killer from Mr. Hornbeam. I don't care how you go about it, but there aren't to be any flies.'

'Very good, sir.'

I could find only enough insecticide for one spray-gun, and this I gave to Easter with instructions to pump it vigorously round the Captain every time he stepped on to the deck. This seemed to satisfy him. He left me alone until the evening before the party, when he called a conference of officers in his cabin.

'This is going to be a damn good party,' he began sternly. 'The office expects everyone to enjoy themselves, and it's bloody well up to you to see they do. Get me? Now listen to this.' He picked up a sheet of paper from the desk. 'These are the Master's orders for to-morrow night. One: uniform. Clean number tens, with correct epaulettes and white shoes. Collars to be correctly buttoned up.' He glared at McDougall, who came to supper comfortably in carpet slippers, with the high collar of his jacket wide enough apart to allow the dragon tattooed on his chest to peep coyly over his second brass button. 'Doctor, you will wear white ducks, white shirt, black tie.'

'And Company regulation cap, sir?'

'If necessary. Two: guests are to be met at the head of the gangway by Master and senior officers. See the quartermaster's in uniform and sober, Mr. Hornbeam.'

'Aye aye, sir.'

'Three: no ladies are on any account to be entertained in officers' cabins, or elsewhere than on the portions of the boatdeck assigned for that purpose.'

'There goes Trail's evening,' I whispered to Hornbeam.

'Four: all alcoholic liquors on board to be placed under seal at noon to-morrow and no such liquors to be served to any member of the ship's company before the arrival of guests at ten o'clock to-morrow night. Five: all shore leave stopped from noon to-morrow. Six: all members of ship's company to remain decent and sober throughout to-morrow night. My ship is on show, gentlemen. Understand?'

We murmured acceptance of the terms.

'The music will be provided by a band from one of the English clubs,' Captain Hogg continued. 'Get the Sparks to jack up the amplifying system in case we have to play records, Mr. Hornbeam. Have you been through the ship's record library, Mr. Whimble?'

'They seem to be short of operas and stuff, sir.'

'Capital! I like a bit of opera. Right, gentlemen. Oh, Doctor, I've put that man of yours in charge of the bar.'

'Who? Easter?'

'Yes. Strikes me as a reliable honest sort of fellow.'

I swallowed. I felt any opinion of mine would spoil the contentment of both of them.

'Very well. Conference dismissed.'

As we went down the companionway together I said to McDougall, 'The prohibition order's going to delay you chaps getting Hogmanay away to a good start.'

He dropped a red eyelid over a crafty eye.

'It'ud take more than yon pipsqueak to stand in a Scot's way on Hogmanay, lad. Come along to my cabin when you've finished yer tea to-morrow. We'll find you a dram or two from somewhere.'

CHAPTER XV

I WAS called from my shower at eight the next evening to put half a dozen stitches in the forehead of a fireman who had fallen down the stokehold ladder. For this reason I was the only officer who arrived on deck to greet the guests sober. Captain Hogg's orders had been punctiliously obeyed, except for the one impounding the ship's supply of liquor: since tea-time Whimble had been poking his head in his locker like a nervous ostrich in a perilous desert, in the Chief Engineer's cabin Scots accents rawed under the sting of neat whisky, Hornbeam and the Mates poured gin from the water-bottles above their basins, and Captain Hogg himself had been entertaining Mr. Montmorency and his sleek Argentine wife.

The boatdeck of the *Lotus* looked surprisingly attractive. Fairy-lights shone on the fresh white chalk spread over the scrubbed deck, ensigns and signal flags lined the rails and obliterated the stark Frigorifico, and on the long tables garnished with blazing Argentine flowers, glass and linen fell pleasingly and promisingly on the eye. The band—three Argentines with piano, guitar, and drums—was seriously tuning up behind the ensign of the Commonwealth of Australia. At the head of the gangway, which was enlivened with bunting and a string of bulbs, a quartermaster stood nervously in white matelot's rig; stewards in shining jackets stood with silver trays and serviettes between the fresh-painted ventilators; behind the bar was Easter, with an expression of disarming honesty on his face that suggested a bishop going through the Dover Customs with two bottles of brandy in his gyp.

Beside the quartermaster the ship's officers—in clean white number tens, white shoes, correct epaulettes, collar fully buttoned up—stood greeting the guests with great charm and affability. To me it seemed that the decorum of my shipmates had a certain brittleness about it, a nervous over-emphasis. This was noticeable in the way the Chief Engineer tenaciously kissed the hands of the ladies; the hesitation with which Whimble brought a match to a guest's cigarette; Hornbeam's roar of laughter; Trail, open-mouthed, mentally stripping every woman under forty stepping off the gangway; and the abandon with which Captain Hogg was pinching Mrs. Montmorency's bottom.

I felt a tug at my elbow. It was Easter leaning across the bar, holding out a long glass of brownish fluid.

'Best respects, Doctor,' he said hoarsely. 'This is the stuff I'm making up for me and my mates.'

'What is it?'

'Little cocktail I invented on the Western run. I calls it "Fire Alarm."'

'Thank you, Easter. I fancy I have some leeway to make up.'

The guests seemed to be shippers and senior Fathom Line employees who knew each other and Mr. Montmorency well, and were therefore relieved of the cumbrance of social chatter while getting down to the free drinks and lobster patties. As I was not in uniform no one bothered to talk to me, and I was content to stay in the shade of a ventilator by the bar, smoke the ship's cigarettes, drink Fire Alarms, and leave the entertaining to my companions.

'Ché, un cigarillo por favour.'

A slim brunette with incandescent eyes and teeth stood in front of me.

'I beg your pardon?'

'Oh, don't you speak Spanish? I only want a cigarette.'

I handed her one from my own tin.

'Thanks. You work in the meat works too, do you?'

I was hurt. The *Lotus* may have been a rusting old-fashioned tramp, but that night I was proud of her.

'Not a bit. I'm one of the officers.'

'What? Of this old tub? You look too respectable. Why aren't you dressed up?'

'I am the Doctor,' I explained stiffly.

Her eyes instantly shone brighter. 'Well, what do you know? I get the most crippling pain in my back.'

I saw at once that I had committed a social error. During my spell as a general practitioner I had learned that members of the public meeting a doctor socially believe they can entertain him only by briskly trotting out an account of their illnesses. When introduced to the bank manager they do not immediately start talking about their overdrafts, and on shaking hands with the local J.P. they are not compelled to discuss the number of times they have been summonsed. But they firmly hold the idea that the doctor can be diverted for half-hours at a time by details of their symptoms, or even those of faraway relatives and dead acquaintances.

'It sort of catches me round here,' she continued, twining her arm behind her and pushing her sharp bosom forward. 'Whenever I twist round suddenly—Ouch! See what I mean? I've been to doctors all over the world—London, Paris, New York, here in B.A. They never did me a bit of good, though. I still had my pain. Sometimes I woke up in the night and screamed.'

'Very distressing for you, I'm sure.'

'Oh, I began to lose faith in doctors. You don't mind my saying so, do you?'

'Not a bit. Have a Fire Alarm.'

'What is it?'

'It's a drink. Very good for backache.'

She giggled. 'Well, then I went to an osteopath in Wimpole Street—he was sweet. He told me I had a displaced spine. What do you think? He slipped it back again, like shutting a door. There!'

'I think that . . .'

'I only used to get it after that when it rained. Why do you think that was? And then I was playing tennis out at the Hurlingham Club last month, when Bingo! I . . .'

'May I introduce you to our Third Officer?' I interrupted. 'You will find him very charming.'

For the past few seconds Trail had been staring at my companion with his mouth open. He jumped at my remark so much he spilt his drink on the deck; then he stepped forward with the expression of a hungry deckhand going in for his Sunday dinner.

'Mr. Trail,' I said, 'Miss . . .?'

'Ella Robinson.'

'Mr. Trail is our most popular officer,' I whispered to her. 'The Captain thinks highly of him. But if I may speak as a shipmate, he is a little shy and needs encouragement. Enjoying the dance, Three-o?'

'Have another drink,' Trail said thickly.

'I think he's cute,' Miss Robinson decided, flashing him a swift glance of appraisal. I had been treating his spots since we left Santos, and in his clean white jacket and painstakingly Brylcreemed hair he looked as presentable as an Ian Hay subby.

'Har!' Trail said. 'How about a dance?'

'Mmm! I've never danced with a sailor before! Be a sweetie and hold my glass, Doctor.'

Grinning weakly, Trail drew her on to the chalked square of deck and began dancing with the spirit that nightly won him hearts in Reese's dance hall in Liverpool. I contentedly took another Fire Alarm from Easter and leant back on my ventilator. After the night at the Saratoga anyone so pressingly feminine as Miss Robinson was too much for me.

When the music stopped the couple came back to my corner of the deck. Both of them were flushed and breathless.

'You're a swell dancer,' Miss Robinson said to Trail, giving him a hot glance of admiration.

'Am I really?' he asked eagerly. 'Go on!'

'Yes, I mean it. Not like most Englishmen out here. When I dance with you I sure know I'm dancing.'

'Have another Fire Alarm,' I said, signalling to Easter.

'Do you dance, Doctor?' she asked.

'Definitely no. I come from a family with very strong views on the subject.'

'How amusing! Do you know, my pain's coming back. Look!' She turned round. 'Run your hand down my spine. That's right—just there! Ooo! Exquisitely painful! What do you think I ought to do about it?'

'I should go and see a doctor.'

She laughed playfully. 'Gee, you're funny! You're the nicest doctor I've ever met.'

'Thank you. Down the hatch, now.'

We drank our Fire Alarms, and the band began to play again.

'Let's dance,' she said to Trail.

'Not for a minute,' he said. 'Let me show you the steering gear.'

283

'What on earth should I want to see the steering gear for?'

'It looks most attractive in the moonlight,' I added encouragingly. 'Not many people are privileged to see it. Only Mr. Trail and the Captain have the key.'

'C'mon,' Trail said. He gave her a look that would have terrified the heart out of any girl in England and strode off purposefully with her, hand in hand, towards the steel nooks and shadows of the stern. I moved to the rail, leant over the strip of dirty, oil-coated water between the *Lotus* and the quay, and exchanged glances with the two sour Argentine policemen standing at the foot of the gangway. The night was hot, and the awnings prevented ventilation. Shortly the ship's officers unhooked their high collars and wiped their foreheads with coloured handkerchiefs, and sweat began to run down the faces of the guests.

No one bothered me, so I sipped my way through my drink and thought guiltily about England. I was interrupted by 'A hundred pipers an' a' ' from the corner where the band had been playing. It was almost eleven-thirty and the engine-room had by then taken over the party for themselves. The engineers were lolling round the piano with an air of genial possessiveness towards everything they could see, and McDougall was stripped to the waist, his dragon, hearts, and sailing-ship glistening among the grey tufts of hair that sprouted from his thorax and shoulders like bracken on a Highland hillside. Singing with them was Captain Hogg, drunk to the point of harmlessness, and the Montmorencys. The music was provided by Easter, who was playing the piano in the style of Chico Marx.

With a flourish Easter finished his piece, rose to his feet, and announced solemnly, 'Ladies and gentlemen, for my next number to-night I shall give you my rendering of the famous old English ballad "The Lily of Laguna." Jolly good luck to you, gentlemen, jolly good luck!' He sat down heavily and began the tune, to which most of the audience sang the words of 'Annie Laurie.' McDougall then shouted it was midnight by ship's time as the clocks were to be advanced half an hour, and broke into 'Auld Lang Syne'. This was taken up by the company, and I was swept into a chain of crossed hands. McDougall sang with his eyes tightly shut, swaying between a pair of other Scots; suddenly he stopped, shouted 'Kiss all the lasses!' and dived towards Mrs. Montmorency. He grasped her in his moist naked arms and kissed her hotly until he was elbowed out of the way by Macpherson, MacPhail, and Macintosh. These were followed by Captain Hogg, Easter, Whimble, one of the Argentine policemen from the dock, the quartermaster, Hornbeam, and myself. Then everyone sang 'Auld Lang Syne' all over again.

At the end of the verse Captain Hogg shouted 'Eight bells! Quartermaster, ring eight bells! Midnight, ship's time!' Mrs. Montmorency instantly threw her arms open, and was kissed by McDougall, Macpherson, Captain Hogg, McDougall again, myself, Easter, Hornbeam, McDougall once again, Macpherson, MacPhail, and McDougall. She appeared to enjoy these unstinted tributes thoroughly, though Mr. Montmorency, who stood fidgeting beside her, was moved during her fourth embrace with McDougall, to murmur nervously, 'Steady on, Maria! I say, steady on, old girl!' We sang 'Auld Lang Syne' and kissed Maria Montmorency several times, as a member of the circle recalled that it was midnight in Greenwich, Glasgow, Greenock, or some other point of overwhelming importance to himself. Finally her husband grabbed her by the arm and led her to the gangway while everyone cheered and Easter played 'Sons of the Brave.'

The engineers and Hornbeam then decided to visit the taxidance on the other side of the dock.

'Come on, Doc,' Hornbeam urged. 'It's only over the ferry. We can get there in ten minutes.'

'I thought you hadn't any money?'

'I flogged some whisky to the policeman. It's a cheap joint—the girls will darn your socks as well for twenty pesos.'

I shook my head. 'No, thanks. I've got into enough trouble in B.A. already. Besides, I'm tired. I'm turning in.'

I left my shipmates, who were already on the gangway with bottles sticking out of the pockets of their white ducks. I was tired and muzzy. Easter's Fire Alarms had an effect like anæsthetic ether, producing a disturbing numbness and incoordination of the extremities; all I wanted was to lie on my bunk, turn on the forced draught, and sink on to the soft foam that overlies the dark cool liquor of unconsciousness. Yawning, I unhooked my cabin jalousie, pushed the curtain aside, and turned on the light. On the deck was Trail, asleep; two half-empty whisky bottles and some broken glasses were on the desk; lying on my bunk, her skirt round her waist and snoring heavily, was Ella.

I began with an attempt to resuscitate Trail by throwing the remains of my drinking water over him. From this it was apparent that he was in a state of deep surgical anæsthesia, and I could have cut a leg off without his noticing it. While I was shaking him and slapping his face I heard a deep groan from the bunk, and noticed that Ella was wearily moving her arm. I dropped Trail and began flicking her face with the end of a towel. She shook her head and muttered something.

'Ella! Ella!' I called. 'Wake up! Come on—for God's sake, woman! What's that?'

I bent my ear close to her.

'Wanna be sick,' she said.

'Oh, Lord!' I lay the towel over her, poised my empty hot-water can on her bosom, and hurried down to the hospital to find some sal volatile.

When I came back she was sitting on the edge of the bunk, her head held heavily in her hands, her long black hair scattered uncaringly over her shoulders and forehead, her eyes closed, and her face white. She looked like a patient at the end of a long operation.

'Here! Ella! Drink this,' I said cheerfully.

She pushed me away clumsily.

'Don't wan' another drink.'

'This isn't drink—it's medicine. Make you feel better, see? Jolly good stuff. Look! I'm having some myself.'

'Wanna go home.'

'Yes, I know. But drink this first. It's something special.'

'For Chrissake take me home. For Chrissake.'

'Oh, all right then. Where do you live?'

There was a pause. She slowly shook her head.

'Dunno.'

I looked hopefully at Trail, but he seemed unlikely to take part in any conversation before noon the following day.

'Ella,' I said gently. 'Think, please. Where do you live? Haven't you got a phone number?'

'Wanna go to bed.' She started to roll back on my bunk, but I caught her.

'No, you can't go to sleep,' I told her firmly. 'There'll be hell to pay if I don't get you out of my cabin and off this ship. Now try and remember where you live. The street will do.'

I spotted her handbag wedged down the side of the bunk, opened it, and found one of her visiting cards. It bore an address in the Palermo district, which I thought was somewhere on the other side of Buenos Aires.

'All right,' I said, slipping my arm under her shoulders. 'We're going for a walk.'

The gangway quartermaster gave me a grin.

'Lovely grub, eh, Doctor?' he said. He winked and smacked his lips, in case I had missed the point of his remark.

'Benson,' I said sternly. 'I need about two hundred pesos. I should be obliged if you would lend it to me, if you have it. I see no prospect of repaying you until we return home, but if you refuse I shall give you hell should you happen to fall sick on the voyage back. Thank you.'

We stumbled down the gangway together, Ella grasping my collar and groaning. After picking our way over the railway lines and bollards on the quay we reached the little office of the dock police by the gate. I gave the policeman ten pesos and asked him to call a taxi; twenty minutes later we were bumping along the dirty road beside the Frigorifico, Ella already asleep and snoring on my shoulder.

The cab stopped outside a tall block of flats several miles from the ship. I gave Ella a shake, and she woke up with a start.

'You're home,' I said. 'End of the line.'

'Oh God, I feel horrible.'

'So do I.'

'Take me in . . . Please!'

'Can't you make it yourself?'

She shook her head.

'Oh, all right then.'

I helped her out of the cab, making signs to the driver to wait.

We went into a small hall, which contained a staircase and an automatic lift. As I opened the lift doors Ella lent heavily on my shoulder and burst into tears.

She told me, through sobs, she lived in number seventeen, on the third floor; the key was in her handbag. I took her up to her own door and opened it. At that moment her knees gave way. She began to slide slowly down the doorpost.

'The room opposite,' she muttered. 'For God's sake help me in.'

I supported her across the hallway and into the room opposite the flat door. I turned on the light with my free hand, and found I was in her bedroom.

'Put your arm round my neck,' I commanded. She obeyed, and I lifted her up, laying her on the bed heavily.

'All right,' I said. 'You can unclasp my neck now.'

I heard a noise behind me and turned. Standing in the doorway was a tall, stern, greying gentleman with a stiff moustache and a military eye, dressed in a yellow silk dressing-gown. Behind him was a timid, sandy, becrackered woman in a faded housecoat.

'I've a damn good mind to horsewhip you,' the grey gentleman said decisively.

'Now look here, I say . . .' I began.

'I might tell you I consider you an unmitigated cad. I've no idea what your upbringing is, but I don't imagine it's very savoury. If I were a few years younger I'd give you a good hiding with my bare fists. A young puppy like you needs teaching a good lesson.'

'Be careful, Charles,' the woman said nervously. 'You know what you did to the Rolleston boy.'

Charles twitched his muscles under his dressing-gown. Ella seemed to have Bulldog Drummond for a father.

'I should never have let her go on that damn ship,' he said bitterly. 'I believed at least the officers would be gentlemen. I was mistaken.'

'Mind your temper, Charles,' the woman added timidly, covering her eyes with her hands.

'Now, look here,' I said angrily. 'I assure you I have had nothing to do with your daughter . . .'

288

Charles snorted. 'Pray, how do you explain that lipstick all over your shirt? A disgusting exhibition! By God, I'm not at all certain I shan't horsewhip you after all . . .'

'Charles, Charles!'

'You have got quite the wrong end of the stick . . .'

Charles by now had time to look at me carefully and find I was much smaller than he was. He advanced, going red in the face.

'Put them up, you young hound!' he growled.

There was nothing for it. I threw one of Ella's pillows at him, sidestepped quickly, and dashed for the door. I shot into the lift, leaped for the taxi like a survivor grasping for a lifeboat, and drove back to the ship, looking nervously through the back window at every turn for cars bearing greying gentlemen in silk dressing-gowns, who were anxious to relieve the strangling monotony of Buenos Aires' social life by avenging the honour of their daughters. And when I got back I found Trail had recovered sufficiently to climb into my bunk.

CHAPTER XVI

I SPENT the rest of our time in Buenos Aires walking the broad, criss-crossed, sun-drenched streets looking for a cheap watch. I kept out of the bars, and if I thought a woman looked at me I jumped.

The momentum that had carried us headlong into the pleasures of South America had expended itself by the end of the dance; afterwards our lives settled into the unexciting routine of a ship in port. Every morning I read carefully through the English *Buenos Aires Standard*, had a cup of tea with Hornbeam, and strolled round the active decks; in the afternoon I filled my cabin with the last squirts of our D.D.T. spray and slept soundly until tea, in defiance of the rattling winch just beyond my head. Now and then I picked up *War and Peace*, but the freezing plains of Russia seemed so fantastic I killed a few cockroaches with it and finally put the books away for the voyage home.

In the evening, when the sun had gone down and a breeze sometimes blew off the River Plate to refresh our decks, we sat in Hornbeam's cabin with a case of tinned beer playing sober games of bridge or liar-dice. I felt that I had been living alongside the wharf in Buenos Aires for a lifetime, and I sometimes stared at the familiar angles of my cabin in disbelief that they had ever been softened with the shadows of an English winter's day. When I told the others this one evening Hornbeam said: 'You'd get used to living in Hell, Doc, if we sailed there. All these places are the same, anyway.' He lay on his bunk half-naked, fanning himself with a copy of the *Shipping World*. 'They're hot and sweaty, and full of blokes ready to cut your throat for tuppence. It's the same out East and on the African coast. There's no more romance at sea than there is round Aldgate tube station.'

'When are we leaving for home?' I asked.

He shrugged his shoulders. 'I couldn't say. Maybe a week, maybe two. It depends how the cargo goes in. Once you're in port the wharfies have got you, whether it's in Cardiff or Calcutta.

I heard from the agent to-day the boys might be cooking up a strike. That would fix us, right enough.'

'I wouldn't mind a pint of old English wallop out of the barrel just now,' Archer said seriously. 'Or a bit of backchat with a Liverpool barmaid. You can have too much of these high-pressure floozies out here.'

We sat looking miserably into our beer glasses, all suddenly homesick.

'I reckon I ought to have married and settled down,' Hornbeam continued. 'I nearly did once. I'm still engaged to her, if it comes to that. She's in Sydney. Sends me letters and sweets and things. I see her about once every two years.'

'I should have stuck to selling refrigerators,' Archer said to me. 'I did it for a bit after the war, but I had to give it up. Your money doesn't go anywhere ashore these days.'

'You fellows don't know how well off you are in the Merchant Navy,' I told him.

'The Merchant Navy!' Hornbeam said, folding his hands on his bare stomach reflectively. 'It's a queer institution. A cross between Fred Karno's army and a crowd of blokes trying to do a job of work.'

'There's no security at sea,' Archer added gloomily.

'Maybe it's better than sitting on your fanny in an office till you drop dead,' Hornbeam said. 'Pictures every Saturday night and Margate for a fortnight in summer. Drive me up the pole, that would.'

'Margate's all right,' Trail remarked, joining the conversation. 'I knew a girl who lived there once. Her father ran a shooting-alley in Dreamland.'

CHAPTER XVII

IT was a fortnight before we sailed. A quiver of excitement ran through the ship with the fresh vibrations of the engines. The deckhands ambled about their work singing—not sea-shanties, because they heard those only occasionally, on the pictures, but anything they knew, from 'She'll Be Coming Round the Mountain' to 'Rock of Ages.'

'All hands seem to be pretty happy,' I observed to Easter as a man sauntered past chanting 'Every turn of the screw brings me nearer to you.'

'Well, we're going home, Doctor!'

'But we've only been away a couple of months.'

'Still, it's always like this, whether you've been away two years or a fortnight. You gets a bit slap-happy when you leaves your final port.'

'I think I can understand it. For most of them I suppose it's only an attic in Liverpool or a dirty old house in the East End.'

'Still, it's home, sir.'

'You're right. Where do you live, Easter?'

'Down in Cheltenham.'

'Do you indeed?'

'I lives with the old lady,' he continued. 'She keeps a sweet shop down there. Getting a bit past it now, though. Well over seventy.'

The idea of Easter having a mother was disturbing. I had thought of him vaguely as climbing out of the sea on the heels of Venus.

'Are you coming back next trip, Easter?'

'I suppose so,' he replied. 'I've tried it ashore. Done all sorts of jobs. Apart from the halls and the races, I've worked in pubs, laundries, hotels, fish-and-chip shops. Even done a bit of navvying. Sometimes I gets settled into something steady, but . . . well, you know how it is. I goes round to the public library and has a look at Lloyd's List on a Saturday afternoon, and I'm finished. I think how nice it would be getting away somewhere instead of standing in a queue in the rain.'

'I'm afraid I see your point, Easter. But perhaps you'll get married?'

'What, at my time of life? And after what I've seen of women? Cor! I've had 'em all, I have—black, white, brown, and yellow. They're all the same underneath.'

'Do you read Kipling, Easter?' I asked with interest.

'Kipling? He's dead now, ain't he?'

'He doesn't seem to be dead at sea.'

'No, I don't read much, Doctor. No time for books. Takes you all your life to keep going these days, don't it?'

We detached ourselves from the meat works and steamed slowly down the long buoyed channel along the shallow River Plate towards Montevideo and the Atlantic. From here we had a straight run home, broken only at the Canary Islands for oil. The sea was calm and the sky unbroken. Off Montevideo we left the last persevering seagull behind us and were again alone, ourselves and the sea.

'About another three weeks,' Hornbeam said, 'and you'll be having a pint at the Carradoc.'

'I hope it turns out cheaper than the last drink I had with you.'

He laughed.

'Remind me to get you a new pen, Doc. Anyhow, we ought to have a pretty quiet voyage till we reach the Bay.'

And so we did. Two days out Captain Hogg became more morose than usual, then took to keeping to himself. For a few days he came down to meals, which he consumed without passing a word or giving any indication that he sensed our presence at the table at all. As no one else dared to speak this meant that lunch and supper were eaten in a silence that amplified such noises as chewing a stick of celery to the volume of a tropical thunderstorm. After that he took his meals in his cabin, and appeared only occasionally on the deck. He would stand outside his door for a few minutes, scratch his head, blow his nose, and disappear for the day. Everyone was delighted.

'The Old Man's got a proper cob on about something,' Hornbeam said. 'Never pokes his nose on the bridge. When I go to his cabin he just grunts and says he's left the running of the ship to me. Suits me fine. Life's nice and quiet, isn't it?'

'Yes, it's wonderful. I wonder how long it'll last?'

It lasted until the night of the shipwreck.

When we were two days away from the Canaries the weather broke suddenly, within a few hours. The sun was intercepted by heavy English-looking clouds, and a cold wind came down from the north and threw handfuls of rain across our decks. I lay in my bunk, rocking contentedly and confidently in the swing of the ocean. It was shortly after midnight, and I was suspended in the pleasant arcade between sleep and wakefulness, enjoying the best of both. Then the alarm bells rang.

I sat up and switched on the light. Seven short rings, meaning 'Boat Stations.' Someone on the bridge had obviously leant on the alarm button. I was wondering what to do when the whistle blew 'Abandon Ship.'

'Christ!' I said. I jumped from my bunk like a sprinter off the mark. I fell over the hot-water can, picked myself up, and threw open the cabin door. Trail lived opposite me, and had just come off watch. He was looking disturbed.

'What's up?' I asked anxiously.

'It's abandon ship.'

'I know! But why?'

'Search me, Doc. She was all right when I came off the bridge. We'd better get up top.'

I hitched up my pyjama trousers and started for the companionway.

'Your life-jacket, you fool!' Trail shouted at me.

'Oh Lord! I forgot.'

I ran back to my cabin, pulled on my life-jacket, and started tying it. It occurred to me I should make an attempt to save some of my possessions, so I picked up my empty sponge-bag and stuffed one or two handy articles into it. I later discovered I had preserved from the deep a shoehorn, two empty cigarette tins, a roll of film, and a copy of *Teach Yourself Spanish*. Grabbing a tin of morphine from the locker, I hurried towards the boatdeck.

The crew of the *Lotus* had boat drill at four-thirty every Friday afternoon, as prescribed by the Ministry of Transport, and this was always carried out efficiently, with calmness, and in an atmosphere of polite co-operation. There are, however, certain factors that complicate boat drill in earnest which are not operative during its harmless rehearsals. In the first place, it is usually night-time, there is a cold wind blowing, and it is raining. A strong sea is running, which makes it difficult to swing the boats out without smashing them. Everyone has been woken up from a deep sleep and is bad-tempered. The Bos'n has forgotten where he put the handle to one of the davits. The Third has lost the roll-call. All hands are perplexed and naturally worried about saving themselves as well as giving whole-hearted enthusiasm to preserving their shipmates. Also, all the lights are out.

I slipped over the wet deck, now alive with hurrying sailors, and found my way to the huddle of men round my own boat. They were cutting away the strings holding the canvas cover, under the directions of the Third.

'My God, what a lash-up!' the Third said. 'All right, Bos'n. Stand-by to swing.'

'Swing out all boats!' Captain Hogg's voice came through the loud hailer.

'Swing out!' the Third repeated.

Three men swung on each davit handle with an energy usually shown at sea only when arriving in port ten minutes before the pubs shut.

'Swing out, there!' Captain Hogg repeated. 'The ship is going down!'

A rocket flew into the air and exploded into gently falling coloured stars.

'Get a move on, you men!' he shouted.

'Come on, come on!' Trail ordered impatiently. 'Stand-by the falls, there!'

'Excuse my interrupting,' I said. 'But if we're sinking we don't seem to have much of a list on.'

'Cut it out, Doc! Right, lower away there! Steady, forrard!'

Hornbeam, in his life-jacket and underpants, came breathlessly over to us.

'What's up?' I asked.

'Search me. The Old Man started it. I went up to the bridge and he kicked me off.'

Suddenly the deck lights snapped on. We all paused and looked at one another.

'Right!' came from the loud hailer. 'That was the poorest exhibition I've seen in all my years at sea. That was boat drill, see? As it should be done. None of this Friday afternoon tea-party stuff. You're the most inefficient crew I've ever had the misfortune to sail with. Swing 'em in again and dismiss.'

To a chorus of groans and ingenious profanity the boats were swung in and made fast.

I went below to change my clothes and pour myself a drink. I was still towelling myself when Trail came in.

'What the hell does Father think he's up to?' he demanded, throwing his wet life-jacket on my bunk.

'I suppose he's allowed to hold boat drill at night if he wants to.'

'He's allowed to, all right. He's allowed to do anything. He can marry you, bury you, put you in irons, or hang you from the yardarm. That doesn't mean to say he can do it every night.'

'What do the crew think of it?'

'They're complaining to their Union.'

'I wish I could complain to mine.'

Trail pulled his wet jacket off and sat down. 'I wonder what made the Old Man do it?' he asked more calmly. 'It's the first time we've seen him for a week.'

'Probably didn't want us to forget him.'

'That's likely. It's finished with now, anyway. It was bloody cold up there on deck. You're going to have about twenty pneumonia cases to-morrow.'

'Care for a peg before we turn in?'

'Thanks, I'll have a quick one.'

I was handing him the whisky bottle when the whistle blew for the second time.

The scene on the boatdeck was repeated, but it was played at a much more leisurely pace. The crew showed no enthusiasm at all for the exercise.

'Come on!' Trail ordered. 'It's got to be done, so you'd better get it over with.'

'Put your backs in it!' the loud hailer roared. 'Call yourselves sailors? Get a move on with number four, Mr. Trail!'

'For God's sake, lads,' Trail said. 'Keep the Old Man happy.'

Slowly our boat swung out, rocking in the wind, tugging at the arms of the swearing crew.

After twenty minutes on the cold, wet deck, Captain Hogg gave the order to swing in again. The boats were brought back to their blocks, lashed down, and covered with their canvas sheets.

Hornbeam, who had found time to put on his uniform, came back to us.

'All squared up, Third?' he asked anxiously.

'Aye aye, Mr. Hornbeam.'

'All right. You lot can dismiss.'

The voice came from the loud hailer.

'Right! Now repeat the exercise!'

Hornbeam spun round.

'No!' he shouted towards the bridge. 'We won't!'

The wind and sea were making a fair noise, but these were obliterated by the silence that fell upon everyone on deck. I held my breath. The bridge was in darkness, but I imagined clearly the explosive figure standing there.

The loud hailer was still for a few seconds.

'This is mutiny!' it roared.

Hornbeam shrugged his shoulders.

'Dismiss, all hands,' he said. 'Disregard all further alarm signals.'

'Mr. Hornbeam, I'll put you in irons!'

Hornbeam took no notice.

'You'll pay for this, by God!'

'You see everything's lashed down, Third,' Hornbeam continued calmly. 'I'm going on the bridge.'

He made towards the ladder.

'You come up here and I'll kick your teeth in!'

He reached the end of the ladder. A heavy fire-bucket fell on the deck, just missing his head. I got hold of him and pulled him away.

297

'Look here,' I said. 'Don't be a fool. Let me go up and see him. After all, I'm more or less out of this. I can explain it's bad for the crew on medical grounds, or something. He's got nothing against me. I can be an intermediary.'

'Nothing doing, Doc. This is my pidgin.'

'No, it isn't. I don't want to spend the rest of the night putting stitches in your scalp. I'm sure he won't chuck anything at me.'

'All right, Doc,' he said. 'But watch your step.'

Setting my teeth, I climbed up the ladder to the bridge. At first I thought the wheelhouse was empty. Then I caught sight of the Captain, standing by the terrified quartermaster who was steering. He looked like a fat malignant ape.

'Who's that?' he growled.

'Doctor, sir,' I began. 'I came on behalf of the Mate . . .'

'Get off my bridge!'

'I wondered if I might explain that on purely medical grounds . . .'

'Get out!'

'In my professional opinion,' I continued resolutely.

'Get out!' he screamed. 'Or I'll bash your bloody brains in!'

He seized from the bulkhead some heavy instrument. It was, I suppose, a marlin spike or some similar appliance that skippers are traditionally expected to take to beat in the brains of their crew. I did not wait to find out. I scrambled down the ladder and fell hard on to the deck. I hurt my arm and ripped my pyjamas; but already I had forgotten the incident. A new and more terrifying thought took possession of me: Captain Hogg was undoubtedly clinically insane.

CHAPTER XVIII

'DELUSIONS of grandeur,' I read aloud, 'occur frequently in this condition.'

It was the next morning. Hornbeam and Trail were sitting in my cabin while I read aloud from a text-book of medicine. The weather had calmed down and the storm that blew through the ship the night before had abated with it. Immediately after turning me off the bridge Captain Hogg had abruptly gone to his cabin, locked the door, and turned in. He appeared in the morning without making any reference to the night's excitement, and was even faintly friendly towards everyone on board. He gave the impression that he imagined the activity on the boatdeck was part of a particularly enjoyable dream.

'You see,' I explained to the others, 'delusions of grandeur. I ought to have spotted it before. Still, it's difficult in a ship's captain. No one notices if they have them.'

'What's wrong with him, Doc?' Hornbeam asked with interest.

'G.P.I.—general paralysis of the insane, undoubtedly. It's a late stage of syphilis. Listen to this: "The patient is usually a man in his middle fifties who suddenly becomes subject to attacks of bad temper, fits of sulking, and lack of judgment. These may alternate with periods of violent excitement. The condition is usually first noticed by members of the sufferer's family circle rather than the physician." Doesn't that fit in? The old boy picked it up thirty years ago on the Brazilian coast and now we're getting the benefit of it.'

Hornbeam rolled a cigarette thoughtfully.

'It's a serious business, Doc, if you're right.'

'I'm pretty certain I am.'

'Is there any sort of test you can do to make sure?' Trail asked.

'I couldn't give you a definite opinion without examining him.' I ran my eye down the page of the book. ' "The patient has the sensation of walking on cotton-wool," ' I read out. 'Stabbing pains in the legs at night . . . loss of knee-jerks . . . loss of pain sensation in the tendo Achilles . . . pupils do not react to light . . . There's a good many signs, you see.'

'Yes, but do you suppose he's going to let you barge into his cabin and examine him?' Hornbeam asked. 'Have you thought about that?'

'You raise a difficulty in diagnosis, certainly,' I admitted. 'I don't feel he would be a highly co-operative patient. Particularly after last night.'

'Well, we'll have to let him go on being barmy, then.'

I shut the book and took my spectacles off.

'I have an idea,' I announced. 'I remember the way I was once told to examine children.'

'Children! This one's some baby!'

'It's the principle of the thing that matters. They taught us in hospital to deal with unwilling children by distracting their attention and examining what you wanted while they weren't looking. See what I'm getting at? The knee-jerks, for instance. I shall engage him in conversation and drop a book or a bottle of something on his patella, pretending it's an accident. Oh yes, I think that's the answer,' I said, warming to the idea. 'I'll build up a diagnosis in a couple of days and send in a report to the Company.'

'Mind he doesn't bite you,' Trail said.

I had a chance to try my new technique of fragmented diagnosis at dinner. Captain Hogg appeared for the first time since his retirement, and seemed in capital spirits. He sat down next to me at the head of the table, tucked his serviette in with a flourish, and fell upon the roast mutton.

'Good mutton, this, Mr. Whimble,' he said through a mouthful of potatoes. 'Don't get much like it these days. Where did you buy it?'

'London, sir.'

'It's kept well. By the way, Mr. Hornbeam. Get the hatch covers off number three by to-night, if the weather holds. We may be filling that twenty feet in Teneriffe.'

'Very good, sir.'

'I'm pleased to find the weather's cleared, sir,' I said brightly. 'This fresh breeze makes you feel you're walking on cotton-wool.'

He said nothing.

'Do *you* ever feel you are walking on cotton-wool, sir?' I asked.

'No,' he said. 'I don't.'

He swallowed another mouthful of greens and mutton. I was keenly disappointed.

'The weather ought to hold,' he said. 'The glass is going up.'

'I had an aunt,' I remarked. 'Every time the glass went up she had stabbing pains in her legs.'

'Did she?'

'Do *you* get stabbing pains in your legs, sir?'

'What the devil are you talking about, Doctor?'

'Oh, nothing of importance, sir.'

I miserably fiddled with a piece of roast potato. It seemed that my means of eliciting the patient's symptoms was not going to meet with clinical success. I decided I would go ahead and examine for the physical signs. I dropped my serviette on the deck. As I bent down to pick it up I pinched Captain Hogg hard behind the ankle.

'Ouch!' he said.

'I'm dreadfully sorry, sir . . .'

'What the hell are you playing at?'

'I thought . . . I thought it was the Mate's foot.'

'Well, what difference does that make?'

'We were having a little game.'

'I don't like games,' Captain Hogg said. 'Not in *my* ship.'

'Very good, sir.'

I jabbed moodily at my treacle sponge for the rest of the meal, despair freezing my heart.

'Find anything out?' Hornbeam said in my cabin afterwards.

'Not much. Couldn't you see?'

'Yes, you were making a bit of a mess of it. Supposing he's not potty at all, but just acting his own sweet self?'

'I'm *sure* he's insane,' I said heatedly. 'Certain of it. If they put him in the final examinations every student would get through. He's a classical case. The only trouble is I can't get near enough to prove it.'

'We'll have to be pretty certain before we say anything to the Company, Doc. I always believe in clearing my own yardarm.'

301

I banged the desk with my fist.

'Damn it! Here's this man—certifiably insane—with every one of us at his mercy. Why, any time he might break out again like last night! Supposing he goes and puts us aground at the Canaries? Or rams the *Queen Mary* or something off Bishop Rock? He's capable of absolutely anything. What would we do then?'

Hornbeam scratched his cheek with the lip of his pipe.

'It's a teaser, Doc. We'll have to think out some other scheme.' He looked at his watch. 'I must go and tell the Bos'n to take the covers off number three. If I think of anything, I'll let you know. Meantime, I'll keep a sharp watch on Father myself.'

'Thanks. I'll try and work something out. See you for a peg before supper.'

I passed the rest of the day sorting ingenious schemes for diagnosis in my mind. Nothing seemed workable. I thought of confessing frankly to the port doctor in Teneriffe that we had a madman loose on board and asking him to send for a couple of assistants and a straitjacket; but I felt that the port doctor, who was used to ship's captains, might find Captain Hogg not in the least abnormal. I wished sincerely that he would foam at the mouth or do something equally spectacular when we got in.

When Easter brought my tea I admitted my difficulties to him.

'I think the Captain is insane,' I told him.

'Ho, yes,' he said. 'He's as mad as a fiddler's bitch.'

'You've noticed it too, have you?'

'Dr. Flowerday always reckoned he was.'

'Did he do anything about it?'

'Used to slip the Cook half a dollar to lace his tea with a Mickey when he was real bad.'

'I hadn't thought of that. It might do in an emergency.'

'Wasn't much cop, as it happened. He chucked the tea at the steward usually.'

'We must think of some way, Easter, to settle this once and for all,' I said firmly. 'I am prepared to give you ten bob—a quid— if you can think of some legal means of getting the Captain off this ship at the first possible moment.'

Easter scratched his head.

'Very kind of you, Doctor, I'm sure. Can't think of anything offhand, like.'

'Well try, man, try. If I can't think of . . .'

I was cut short by a crash outside my cabin, a loud scream, confused shouting, the clatter of running feet.

'What the hell's happened now?' I exclaimed.

My door flew open. Hornbeam was outside. He was grinning like a tooth-paste advertisement.

'Quick, Doc!' he said. 'Father's fallen twenty feet down number three hatch!'

I ran on to the deck. There was a crowd round the edge of the hatch, hurriedly letting down a rope-ladder. I pushed my way through and climbed over the coaming. In a few seconds I found Captain Hogg had solved all our problems for us by fracturing his right femur in three places.

*   *   *   *   *

Easter and I strung up Captain Hogg in splints on his bunk. He was a heavy man, and still not a remarkably co-operative patient. It took us a couple of hours, and we were sweating when we had finished.

'I'll have that Bos'n logged,' he muttered, as we arranged the pillows under his head. 'Leaving the covers loose like that . . . I'll have the Mate logged, too.'

'Now keep quiet,' I commanded. 'I forbid you to talk or move.'

'I will talk as much as I damn well like.'

'I give the orders now. I'm the Doctor.'

'Well, I'm the Captain.'

'Easter,' I said. 'Just tighten up that splint a bit more, will you?'

'Ouch!' said Captain Hogg.

'Now,' I continued. 'If you will just stay quiet for a moment I can complete my examination. If you don't I shall have to consider putting you on a milk diet. Tinned milk, naturally.'

I pulled out my torch and shone it in his eyes.

'Ah, yes,' I said, in my most menacing professional tone. 'As I thought. Just take this down, Easter. Pupils do not react to light . . . loss of sensation to pinprick over the nose . . . abdominal

303

reflexes absent . . . A classical picture! We will have to put you ashore to-morrow in the Canaries, of course.'

'You will not. I am not leaving my own ship for you or anybody.'

'Damn it, man! Use your sense. This leg has to be set properly. I can't do it here. It needs X-rays and so forth. You will have to go into hospital with it. I hear they have some excellent surgeons in Teneriffe.'

'I will not go, Doctor.'

'If we cable the Company and they say so, you'll have to go.'

'There is no reason why you should cable them. I am still fit to keep my command.'

'It's a bit late to think of that now. The message has already gone.'

'Gone!' He jerked his head from the pillow. 'No messages are allowed to leave the ship without my permission.'

'Really, you are a most difficult patient,' I said gently. 'I will leave Easter to read to you. You will find plenty of literature in the corner, Easter.'

'What, these here?' Easter asked, picking up one of the Captain's library. 'Cor! Looks like a bit of all right, eh?' He settled himself comfortably by the sick-bed. 'Right, sir,' he began. 'I will start with "I was a White Slave. True Confessions of a French Girl Kidnapped from a Convent and Sent to the Infamous Kasbah of Algiers." Cor,' he added to the Captain, 'I know Algiers all right. Funny thing happened to me last time I was there. I'd gone ashore with the Cook, see, and we was looking for a bit of fun, as you might say . . .'

I left them, feeling I had inflicted on Captain Hogg sufficient misfortune for the evening.

Hornbeam was sitting in his cabin writing up the log-book.

'Hello, Doc,' he said cheerfully. 'How's the patient, God rot his soul?'

'As well as can be expected, I'm afraid.'

'I'm just putting it in the log. You'll have to sign down here.'

'When will we get to Teneriffe?' I asked.

'About midday. We should be tied up alongside by one.'

'We've got to put Father ashore, you know. I can't treat a

304

fracture properly at sea. The trouble is he won't shift. He says he won't go without instructions from the Company.'

Hornbeam tossed a cable across to me.

'Sparky just brought that down,' he said. 'Take a look at it.'

I unfolded the paper. It was from the Fathom Line head office.

TO CHIEF OFFICER SS. LOTUS, it said. PLACE CAPTAIN ASHORE TENERIFFE IF DOCTOR SO ADVISES AND BRING VESSEL HOME UNDER YOUR COMMAND STOP PREPARE TAKE COMMAND IMMEDIATELY ON ARRIVAL UK SS. PRIMROSE OWING RESIGNATION CAPTAIN BARSETT.

'Well, Doc,' he said smiling. 'Do you advise?'

'Do I advise! Yes, sir! Yes, indeed!' I grabbed his hand. 'Yes, Captain Hornbeam!'

305

CHAPTER XIX

THE next day we arrived off the rocky, volcanic Canaries, sailed under the lee of the islands, and shortly after noon slipped into the tidy, clean harbour of Teneriffe. Archer and Trail took the bow and stern, tugs flying smoky red-and-yellow Spanish flags turned us round to face the sea, and we tied to the jetty between a smart Blue Star boat outward bound for Rio and a disconnected-looking craft flying the flag of Panama which had cows on the deck.

At first Captain Hogg refused to be moved. We showed him the cablegram but he accused us of forgery. So I filled him up with morphine and sent him to sleep.

He was carried out on the shoulders of the sailors, like Nelson's bier, arranged in a derrick sling, and unloaded by the steam winches between two bales of cowhide.

'You'll find the full history in the letter,' I said, handing the case report to the smiling, handsome Spanish doctor with the ambulance. 'The British Consul's fixed everything else up.'

The doctor shook hands, the ambulance doors swung shut, and Captain Vincent Hogg drove out of my life.

'Get rid of him all right?' Easter asked, as I reached the top of the gangway.

'It seems so. I don't think he'll have much chance to throw his weight about in a Spanish hospital. Especially after that letter I sent with him.'

'Wouldn't mind going ashore here for a spell myself,' Easter said meditatively. 'I've had some fun here, I have. I remember when I was on the South Africa run, the barber and me went . . .'

'All right, Easter. Later will do.'

'They got some lovely girls here,' Easter continued. 'Prettiest in the world, I reckon. Look at that one down there. See? They got the same as our girls at home, but they carry it around better.' He pointed to a slim, dark girl, stepping along the quay with a grace that is unhappily forgotten on cold English parks and pavements.

'Ho, they got some smashing bits here!' Easter said enthusiastically. 'Mind you, you've got to be careful. Do you want a tablecloth?'

'A tablecloth? What should I want a tablecloth for?'

'This is the place to buy them.' He pointed over the side, where the wide pipes ran towards the ship in a pool of black fuel oil. An informal market had been set up on the quay, offering thick brocaded tablecloths, scarves with vivid bullfights on them, canaries in cages, metal ornaments, and dolls four feet high.

'Them dolls is all right,' Easter advised me. 'I used to buy a lot of them at one time.'

'I'm pleased to hear you think of the children, Easter.'

'Ho, crikey no! I used to buy 'em here and flog 'em in Pernambuco. Good business, that was. Canaries, too. Make a good few bob on canaries, you could. Unless the little bastards went and died on you. Or you got gypped. Some of 'em's sparrows fed on quinine.'

'Well, I ought to buy a few presents, I suppose. But I haven't got much in the way of money.'

'They takes all kinds of junk here. Old clothes—a pair o' boots, worn out, if you've got 'em. Fags mostly. Get anything for a few hundred Woods.'

I exchanged five hundred ship's Woodbines for two scarves, a small bracelet, and a decorated picture of General Franco. I supposed I had better make a return with some of the assets of a seafarer.

We stayed eight hours in Teneriffe; then we set off under Hornbeam's command, our next stop England.

The removal of Captain Hogg from the ship had the effect of dissolving a chronic state of anxiety. All hands walked about cheerfully, did their work amiably, and set to it with twice the effort.

'Got to have her looking nice for home now,' the Bos'n said, looking critically at the gang he had set painting the upper works. 'We can't let Mr. Hornbeam down, can we?'

Hornbeam slipped easily into his new rank. He took over the

Captain's cabin and his seat at table. Our mealtimes now were lively with conversation, with the result that everyone ate more contentedly and the cases of dyspepsia among the officers dropped sharply. Even Archer began reluctantly to feel better, and admitted he hadn't taken any stomach powder for a week.

Our only excitement was a message to Hornbeam changing our destination from Liverpool to London because of a threatening dock strike. The order caused disapproval among the Liverpudlians in the crew, but this was charmed away quickly by Easter's account of the fun he had had at various times in London.

'Smashing place, London,' he claimed. 'You wait till you see West Ham.'

The sea became rougher, the weather became colder; spray came once again over the *Lotus's* bows. The broken water took on the green-grey tint of European coasts, and the ship began to groan and stagger in the January waves. But now I was unaffected by the sea, and stood on deck innocuously watching the foc's'le head rise and dip with the swell and the tops of the masts trace wide irregular circles against the sky. All round us were signs that we were coming nearer to our own country. Boxes and cartons were lying in everyone's cabins, the ship's time became synonymous with that of Greenwich, three pounds Channel money was advanced to all hands, the Light Programme assailed us undiminished, and the weather remained persistently foul.

One evening Easter put his head round my door and said cheerfully, 'Want to see the Ushant light, Doctor? Just coming up on the starboard bow.'

Together we stood in the shelter of the storm door leading on to the deck. I followed his finger towards the flashes.

'Well, there's old Europe again,' Easter said. 'Ain't a bad old continent, all things considered. We turns the corner here. The next mark's the Casquettes, then for Beachy. Blimey, I've seen folks in tears looking at that there light! When they've been gone for a long time, that is.'

'Yes, I expect everyone will start being excited from now on.'

'Ho, they'll have the channels to-morrow, you mark my word.'

'The channels?'

'Ah, there's a complaint what even you don't know, Doctor.

All hands goes a bit barmy, like. You wait till to-morrow.'

Easter was right. The channels is a clinical entity that has not found its way into the medical text-books, but is as noticeable as scarlet fever. The next morning the crew were prancing round the decks like highly-strung lambs in springtime. Everyone had a bright word for their mates, a salute for the Captain, and even a few sirs left over for me. Work was done with a lighthearted air that drew scowls of disapproval from the Bos'n, who had been up the Channel so many times that he had developed an immunity to the complaint. Easter repeated his most successful card tricks and thought it a great joke to tell me falsely the hospital was three feet in water. I forgave him readily, for I too was walking the deck murmuring to myself, 'Every turn of the screw brings me nearer to you.' To whom? I wondered. It didn't matter. I could settle that when we arrived.

Beachy Head—white, shining in a brief ray of sunshine turned on like an effective spotlight on a darkened stage. I looked at it with mixed feelings of affection and disapproval that the voyager's first sight of England should be Eastbourne.

We came closer to the land, making for the pilot boat off Dungeness. The Atlantic rollers had flattened themselves in the narrow waters, but the sea was high enough to throw the pilot's launch about unenviably. He came round to the lee side and had two shots at grasping the Jacob's ladder Trail and the Bos'n dangled from the foredeck; the third time he caught a rung as the launch dropped away from his feet. He climbed aboard, his black oilskins running with water, shook himself like a dog, gave me a cheerful 'Nice morning!' and climbed up to the bridge. The red and white pilot's flag broke over the wheelhouse, and the *Lotus* proceeded under the arrangement invariably stated in the log-book as 'Master's orders, Pilot's advice.'

The Channel was busy that day. We passed, or were passed by, a representation of Lloyd's List. There were tankers making for Thameshaven, so low in the water they disappeared to the bridge between the waves; rickety tramps setting out fearlessly for voyages longer than ours; little coasters bound for a rough passage round Land's End; sodden fishing boats; cargo ships of all sizes and states of repair, British, Norwegian, Swedish, and Dutch;

one of the ubiquitous City boats with a black and salmon funnel, homeward bound fully loaded from the Australian wool sales; even a couple of warships. They were a pair of corvettes steaming jauntily down Channel in line astern. The meeting led to a burst of activity at the foot of the mainmast as the deckboy afforded the King's vessels their salute by dipping our ensign. The correct form was for us to dip, watch for the white ensign fluttering down in reply, and follow its return to the masthead. Unfortunately, the wind caught our rain-soaked flag and twisted it in the rigging, so that we passed the fleet apparently in mourning. But the intention was there, and the Navy would be the first to understand.

A big white P. & O. passed us, outward bound for India and Australia and the sunshine that appeared to me to have vanished for ever.

'Be away for the best part of four months, that lot,' Easter remarked. 'All be taking their last look at old England.'

'As long as that?'

'They gets them dock strikes something horrid out Aussie way. It's a lovely life being a wharfie in Sydney or Melbourne—you draws your money and puts your feet up most of the day. Like being a lord. Or—if I may be so bold—ship's doctor.'

'Yes, I suppose you're right,' I admitted sadly. 'Except the dockers get paid more. I suppose they're all pretty excited on board—first night at sea, and so on.'

'Ho, yes. I've seen it often enough on the big passenger boats. All the blokes giving the girls the once-over in the dining saloon. Cor, I've seen them sweet little things with their eyes still wet with tears from saying good-bye to their husbands and sweethearts carrying on something shocking. Hardly out of the River we wasn't, neither.'

The red lamps were shining on the tops of the high radar masts when we crept close to Dover inside the Goodwins. The lights of Ramsgate and Margate passed off our port side, then we cut across to the Nore, where we were to anchor and await the tide. Someone gave me the morning paper that the pilot had brought aboard. I opened it and read the front page with the careless, baffled interest of a holidaymaker inspecting the social column in the village weekly. We had been more or less newsless for three months, but the happenings that used to shake my breakfast table no longer aroused my concern. A paragraph near the foot of the page caught my eye; it was headed 'MAYOR REBUKES DANCERS,' and went on: 'The Mayor of ——, Alderman ——, yesterday refused an application for an extension to midnight at a cycling club dance. He said he was highly disturbed at complaints of immoral behaviour that had followed the dance last year. "The place for young men and women at midnight," he told the secretary, "is in their own homes asleep." '

I knew I was back in England.

CHAPTER XX

THE next morning we steamed into the Thames. The country raised a faint glow of sunshine to welcome us, but the effort was too taxing and the atmosphere soon relapsed into its habitual rain.

We passed the long finger of Southend Pier, which appears a far more dignified structure when seen in reverse, signalled our name, and passed down the channel towards Tilbury. The wet, orderly fields of England on the narrowing banks, with a demure English train jogging through them towards London, had the appearance of a winter's garden after the turbulent unfenced vegetation of the South American coast. Off Tilbury landing-stage we anchored for the Port of London doctor to board us. He was a large, friendly man in a naval battledress and a duffle-coat.

'Have a good voyage, old man?' he asked, running his finger down the pages of my log-book.

'Pretty good, thanks.'

'Going again?'

'Oh, no. I don't think so, anyway.'

'Back to the N.H.S., eh?'

'That's it. If I can remember any of my medicine.'

He laughed. 'You can still sign your name, can't you? All right, free pratique granted.'

We continued down the River, and I was seized with a spasm of nostalgia by catching sight of an L.P.T.B. bus.

In Gallions Reach the tugs set about us and turned us towards the locks of the Royal Albert Dock.

'Is that all the room we've got?' I asked Easter, as we headed for the narrow entrance. As I always had difficulty parking a car in a busy street I filled with admiration for the mates and tug-masters every time the *Lotus* came into port.

'There's bags of room,' Easter said. 'They gets them big New Zealand boats through here easy enough. Look at all them bright lads we've got to help us.'

I saw a chilly knot of longshoremen waiting to receive our ropes as we came into the lock: sad, damp Englishmen, their coat collars up to their sodden caps.

'That one there's been on the job for years,' Easter said. 'We calls him Knuckle 'Arry.'

He pointed to a depressed-looking man with a long moustache standing still and holding a rope fender over the end of the jetty.

'That's an odd name. What's his knuckles got to do with it?'

'The knuckle's what he's standing on. Now you wait.'

As the *Lotus* drew near the stonework the pilot shouted from the bridge: 'Keep her off the knuckle, 'Arry!' The man touched his cap, and solemnly manipulated his fender to save our paint. He then resumed his immobility in the thick rain.

We passed the knuckle, the locks, the entrance to the dock; the tugs dragged us slowly down to our waiting berth; more men in caps and old overcoats secured our ropes to the quay; the ensign came down from the gaff and was rehoisted, in compliance with custom, on the stern jack-staff.

'Lower away gangway!' Hornbeam shouted from the bridge.

The *Lotus* leant contentedly against the dock and, after three months all but five days, we were home.

*　　　*　　　*　　　*　　　*

There was a wonderful end-of-term spirit abroad. Everyone was packing up and behaving with the recklessness of men for whom there are no longer any consequences.

We were paying-off, the morning after our arrival. Mr. Cozens and his colleagues came aboard and treated us with cordial superiority, and we looked on them with good-humoured contempt. Cozens himself questioned me closely about the exit of Captain Hogg.

'Very good, Doctor,' he said. 'I think you did entirely the correct thing. Our *Sunflower* is due at Teneriffe in three weeks' time and she will bring him home. We have your successor for next trip—a Dr. Gallyman. Do you know him?'

'I'm sorry, I don't.'

Cozens sighed. 'I'm afraid he is a little on the old side,' he said. 'Retired from practice some years ago. I believe there was some trouble with the medical authorities, too. . . . Still we must hope for the best. It's so difficult getting doctors for these ships just now.'

Apart from the office staff, the ship filled with taxi-drivers, luggage carters, laundrymen, dry cleaners, marine tailors, and haircutters, all of them pressing their services on the ship's company before it dispersed. I shut the door of my cabin, looked despairingly at the empty cases and my curiously augmented possessions, and wondered how I was going to pack. I started with the volumes of *War and Peace*. I hadn't got beyond the first page, but I had killed one hundred and thirty-two cockroaches with them. I was hesitantly fitting them into a case when Easter came in.

'Letter for you, Doctor.'

It was only the second one I had received since leaving Liverpool. It too was from the laundry.

'*Dear Sir* (it said), *Further to ours of November 28th, I have to inform you that your laundry has been sold to defray expenses of the wash. The sum received was 6s. 3d., which is 1s. 9d. less than your account. We would appreciate your settling this deficit at your earliest convenience.*'

Sadly I put the letter into my pocket.

'Getting the loot packed, Doctor?' Easter asked.

'I only wish I could.'

'The Customs is pretty hot down here,' he went on. 'Not like some ports I could mention. Get away with murder, you used to. So long as you bought your tickets for the police ball.'

'What police ball?'

'I remember once the old arm of the law putting his head round our cabin door and saying, "I'm sure as you gentlemen would like to come to the police ball." Well, I knew the ropes, see, so I says, "Not 'arf we wouldn't. We've been thinking about it all voyage." So he hands over tickets at a dollar a time—but you mustn't take 'em, like. I looks at mine and says, "Ho, constable, I regrets but what I have a previous engagement." So he collects all the tickets

314

back and flogs 'em again in the next cabin. Mind you, he keeps the five bob.'

'Well, I hardly think it worth while my making the investment. Apart from the junk I got at Teneriffe I've only some corned beef and a pair of nylons.'

'That's the ticket, Doctor! Girls round our way will do anything for a tin of corned beef. Show 'em the nylons as well, and cor! they're all over you.'

'I assure you these are destined for middle-aged relatives.'

'Used to do pretty well out of nylons during the war. Some of the blokes on the Western Ocean made a fortune flogging 'em in Southampton. The places they thinks of to hide 'em! Down the chain locker in the foc's'le's usual. One of the lads put a dummy pipe across the deckhead and filled it with nylons and fags. Lovely job he made of it. Painted it up just like it was real. But the Customs boys copped him. Oh, they're very fly, they are. I'll get you an empty beer-case from the Chief Steward.'

'Thank you, Easter.'

I sat wearily among the disheartening jumble. Well, this was the end of the trip. What had I got from it? Some corned beef, some nylons, a cure for headaches, two stones in weight, and a deep sunburn. But much more than that, surely I had found for the first time that the world isn't divided simply into two classes—doctors and patients. Three months at sea had taught me more than six years in a medical school. I had learned to give and take toleration, to grapple with grotesque predicaments, to appreciate there is some goodness behind everybody, that life isn't really so serious, and that doctors aren't such bloody important people after all.

The Customs man—young and keen—came in and rummaged my cabin. He did so like an old-fashioned physician searching for a diagnosis with an irritating air of professional detachment.

'Where did you get these from?' he asked, holding up my best pair of pyjamas.

'Swan and Edgars.'

'Umm. Have you any spirits?'

'Bottle of whisky.'

'Opened?'

'Certainly.'

'Umm. Have you a watch?'

'No.'

'What, not one at all?'

'I lost it one night in B.A.'

He looked at me narrowly.

'Watch your step, Doctor,' he said, leaving me alone.

I managed to throw my packing together before paying-off started in the saloon. It was more a ceremony than a business transaction. We were theoretically not entitled to any pay until the end of the voyage, though we could draw foreign currency at the pleasure of the Captain. Our wages were set out in a long narrow sheet, with additions for leave and Sundays at sea and deductions for advances, Channel money, bar bill, stores account, and anything else the Chief Steward thought he could add without protest.

The pay was distributed by the Fathom Line officials, under the eye of the Shipping Master. They sat at the big table behind exciting piles of five-pound notes, looking like the tote about to pay off on the favourite. Also on the table were the ship's articles and a pile of discharge books—the sailor's personal record—signed by the Captain with a comment on conduct like a school report.

The crew lined up eagerly, all in their best clothes. I had difficulty in placing the clean, modest-looking men in smart blue and grey suits as the half-naked roughs who strode round the decks with paint pots in the Tropics. The Carpenter was particularly baffling: he wore a dark herringbone tweed, a hard white two-inch collar, and an artificial rosebud in his buttonhole, giving the appearance of a moderately liberal-minded clergyman on holiday at Sandown.

Nothing gives such a pleasant feeling of false prosperity as paying-off a ship. By the time my wages had been reduced by deductions I had less than a month's salary in general practice, but I stuffed the notes into my pocket and felt like Lord Nuffield. Then I signed off the book of ship's articles opposite the space where I had signed on them three months ago. My contract with the Commander of the *Lotus* was broken: I was quit of my obligations to him to obey his lawful commands, to work the ship in emergency, to abstain from bringing my own liquor on board, and to check myself from using foul language in his presence. For his part, he had no longer to trouble about feeding me at the required standards, avoiding carrying me into Arctic or Antarctic latitudes, and returning me to my own country within a period of eighteen months. I was free—out of work, but free.

I said good-bye to as many of the crew as I could find; sailors' farewells are brief and shallow, for they make up half their lives. Easter shook hands heartily and impressed on me solemnly the importance of speed whenever I should come to do the three-card trick. Almost everyone left the ship—to go on leave, to quit her for good, or to be in Canning Town by the time the pubs opened. The rain prevented cargo being worked, and the *Lotus* was not only empty of people but silent, as miserable as a school when the children have gone home.

My taxi was coming later, so I went up to the deck to look round the docks. The sheds and the cranes did something odd to the *Lotus's* proportions: at sea, when she was alone and stood unhindered from the water, she achieved a touch of dignity. Now that she lay in relation to other pieces of wood and steel she shrank and became ridiculous. The long boatdeck I used to walk was hardly the size of four railway wagons, and the enchanted spot where I sunbathed and watched the flying fish in the afternoon was nothing but a sooty piece of wet planking. Standing in the rain I saw clearly, but with regret, that the land is ever master of the sea.

I saw Hornbeam, in his blue raincoat, striding alone up and down the few feet of shelter below the bridge.

'Hello, Doc,' he said as I went up to him. 'You off now?'

'In a few minutes. I'm only waiting for my taxi.'

'Oh well, I'm sorry to see you go. We haven't had a bad voyage on the whole. We've made a bit of fun for ourselves.'

'We certainly have.'

We walked for a minute or two in silence.

'What are you going to do now, Doc?' he asked.

'I've no idea. Find a practice somewhere, I suppose.'

'Do you reckon you'll go back to sea again?'

'Some day I will. I'm making sure of that.'

'You might, at that.'

'How about you?' I said. 'Going on leave?'

'No leave for me, Doc. I'm off to Liverpool to-night to join the *Primrose*. She's sailing to-morrow for New Zealand.'

'Of course, I was forgetting. You know, to me our arrival is the end of an isolated adventure. But I suppose to you and everyone else it's just another stop in port.'

'That's it, Doc. Always on the move. It's a mug's life, isn't it? Still, someone's got to do it.'

My taxi came then. I waved to him from the dock, and watched him as I drove away. He was walking up and down the deck again in the rain, an incongruous and lonely figure.

* * * * *

The first person I went to see in London was the psychiatrist. 'Hello!' he said. 'When are you going away?'